The Custom of the Trad
historical saga about the
heartache of World War I

To Jim,

with best wishes.

Shaun

Shaun Lewis

First published by Endeavour Press Ltd in 2017.

Table of Contents

"The Trade"
Rudyard Kipling

They bear, in place of classic names,
Letters and numbers on their skin.
They play their grisly blindfold games
In little boxes made of tin.
Sometimes they stalk the Zeppelin,
Sometimes they learn where mines are laid,
Or where the Baltic ice is thin.
That is the custom of "The Trade."

Chapter 1

March 1912

Just eleven years ago, the current First Sea Lord, Sir Arthur Wilson VC, had described the submarine as, 'Underhand, unfair and damned un-English'. The commanding officer of HM Submarine *D2*, Lieutenant Harold Johnson, thought the admiral was wrong. As the captain raised his binoculars to sweep the horizon, the gold rings on his reefer jacket faintly reflected the light of the lookout's cigarette. In fact, after so many years on the open bridges of submarines, the gold had turned a dull green, save for the newer, thin half-ring in the middle that showed him to be a lieutenant of over eight years' seniority and thus senior in rank to his second-in-command, also a lieutenant. Johnson had every reason to be pleased with himself. He was sad to be leaving his command, of course, but it had been a successful one and he was looking forward to his staff appointment ashore. Over the past twenty-one months he had welded the ship's company into a highly effective team that would be a great credit to the Service in the event of war with Germany. They had acquitted themselves well during their first operational patrol the previous year and had recently shown their worth in a series of exercises with the Home Fleet off Scotland. He had been pleased that during these exercises it had finally no longer been mandatory for *D2* to be accompanied by a ship flying a red flag to mark the submarine's position. This rather stupid requirement had been abolished by the new Inspecting Captain of Submarines, Roger Keyes. Although Keyes was not a submariner, Johnson thought him blessed with tremendous energy and attacking spirit. Keyes seemed determined that the new submarine service should be an integrated offensive arm of the Royal Navy.

That hadn't been trouble-free, though. It was Keyes who had approved his plan to take the submarine secrctly through the Firth of Forth, escaping detection by the Navy patrols and overcoming the navigational difficulties of the strong tides and narrow waters. With some élan, he thought, he had then surfaced *D2* off Rosyth Dockyard and announced that, had he been a German U-boat captain, he could have successfully torpedoed the two cruisers lying at anchor off the dockyard. The Commander-in-Chief had had a sense of humour failure and ordered him to appear in 'full sword and medals' for an ill-tempered dressing-down. However, Keyes had commended him. He thought it a valuable lesson to be laid before the Admiralty and the CO didn't think it would harm his promotion prospects.

Johnson's feeling of well-being on the passage home had been enhanced by the signal *D2* had received on surfacing. The W/T office had informed him that his wife had given birth to their first child, a healthy boy at eight pounds and six ounces. He could not wait to return to the submarine's base at Harwich and take a few days' leave with his wife and new child in his home in Hampshire. The change in appointment could not have come at a better time. He now had a fair chance of spending prolonged periods in harbour as an instructor in HMS *Dolphin*, an old sailing brig based at Fort Blockhouse, the *alma mater* of the submarine force. Nevertheless, fate was taking a hand in delaying *D2*'s return to harbour at present.

He had surfaced the submarine off Aldeburgh and had imagined an easy and uneventful surface passage of just a few hours down the east coast to the Channel. Instead, not only had they encountered thick fog, but one of the diesel engines had developed a defect and had to be shut down. He had consequently been forced to reduce speed to balance the battery output across the two propellers and to signal his motor launch escort that he would be late in his return to Harwich. It was already dark and visibility very poor, so much so that he had lost sight of the escort's lights. He judged that, if anything, the visibility was deteriorating and had closed up extra lookouts, one of whom had excellent hearing. The lookout had just reported the noise of a steam-driven engine, fine on the port bow. Johnson checked his watch. It was 19.45, almost time for the lookouts to be relieved and for the First Lieutenant to take the watch on the bridge. He felt uneasy. He hailed the control room through the voice pipe.

'Control room, Captain. Tell the First Lieutenant to delay the watch change. There's a ship out ahead and I want to keep these lookouts until the danger has passed. As a precaution, shut and clip all collision bulkheads and the lower lid until further notice.'

Like all submariners he always used the word 'shut' in place of 'close' or 'closed' as it was less likely to be misunderstood through a muffled voice pipe. The First Lieutenant himself, Lieutenant Richard Miller, acknowledged the order from the control room. 'Aye aye, sir. Delay the watch change and shut and clip the collision bulkheads and lower lid until further notice. First Lieutenant here, sir. Would you like me to come to the bridge before we shut the lower lid, sir?'

Johnson thought it typical of his First Lieutenant to be in the control room at the right time. He was off watch and should have been relaxing in the wardroom. It was a comfort. His second-in-command must have sensed his anxiety. By shutting the lower hatch between the conning tower and control room, he was preventing the passage of personnel to and from the bridge. The order to clip the collision bulkheads was also restricting free movement throughout the submarine and would delay the watch changes of all the crew.

'No, thanks, Number One. I would welcome your presence down below, just in case. Check the chart for me and tell me how much room you judge I have to starboard and still remain in the southbound channel.'

Johnson was in a quandary about Miller. He had been particularly pleased with Miller's performance in action and as his second-in-command. Professionally, Miller seemed exemplary, but he also had his faults. He was rather an aloof character who seemed ill at ease with the men. As such, he struggled to build a rapport with them and establish the right sort of team spirit. Whilst the ship's company was starting to respect him for his competence, it was clear they did not like him much. That mattered little. It was not necessary for an officer to be liked by his men, but the men had his sympathy, nonetheless. He regretted that Miller rode them too hard. He seemed completely intolerant of any failure. It was true that Miller was equally uncompromising concerning his own standards, but was Miller capable of humanity and understanding towards those mere mortals blessed with less talent? This was odd, as Miller's other failing was his unbending Christian convictions.

Like most naval officers, Johnson was himself a Christian and rarely failed to hold Divine Service on a Sunday, but he did not impose his faith on others. Miller was too evangelical for his own good. He neither smoked nor drank alcohol, and would not tolerate swearing in his presence. This hardly endeared him to the bunch of semi-piratical heathens that formed the typical submarine ship's company.

Johnson used his binoculars to sweep the invisible horizon once more. Miller's character defects and idiosyncrasies would have to wait. Before taking up his leave, he would be calling on the Inspecting Captain of Submarines and fully intended discussing his second-in-command's performance with Captain Keyes. Once his successor had settled in to his new command, it would be Miller's turn for a new appointment and he hoped he could persuade Keyes that, despite Miller's weaknesses, he should now be groomed for a command of his own.

'Captain, sir, First Lieutenant. Our position is just inside the channel, by dead reckoning. You could come to starboard a mile and still have sufficient water to dive if you had to, notwithstanding the pool of errors. All collision bulkhead doors and the lower lid shut and clipped, sir.'

'Very good. Starboard ten. Steer one-nine-five.'

'Starboard ten. Steer one-nine-five. Ten of starboard wheel on, sir.' The helmsman followed the submarine service practice of repeating back the order word for word to demonstrate that he had understood it.

'Course one-nine-five, sir.'

The captain glanced over his shoulder. He could just make out the phosphorescence of the submarine's turning wake and estimated that visibility was no more than fifty to eighty yards. He felt increasingly uneasy and the hairs on the back of his neck started to rise. If his sixth sense was correct, he might soon need maximum battery power for an emergency dive.

'Control room, Captain. Stop the starboard diesel engine. Group up.'

As soon as the din of the diesel engine ceased, he heard the hammering sound of a steam engine, still to starboard. How could that be? The vessel had been on his port bow and, by making a decisive turn to starboard, he should have opened his distance off track and avoided the risk of a collision. Then the noise stopped suddenly, but was replaced by the deep throb of a diesel engine about fifteen degrees on the starboard bow. Suddenly, he realised his error.

'Hard-a-starboard. Full astern together,' he screamed urgently.

There were two vessels out there, one to port and another to starboard, and probably a pair of trawlers. The steam engine they had heard was undoubtedly the noise of a steam winch as the trawlers set or raised their nets. If he was right, he couldn't dive for fear of being caught in the net.

As the submarine began to turn and its forward movement slowed, the dark shape of an unlit trawler appeared fine on the starboard bow. At a range of just fifty yards the two vessels were close enough for the submarine's bridge team to hear the sound of shouting from the deck of the trawler. The trawler was steering north-west and the crew must have just spotted the lights of *D2* or even her low, dark shape. Instinctively, the trawler skipper obeyed the international rule of the sea in such circumstances and spun the wheel to starboard.

'You bastard!' Johnson shouted. The skipper's instinctive action to turn to starboard rather than to port had unintentionally made it inevitable that there would be a collision.

Seconds later, the trawler struck *D2* on the starboard bow, ten feet aft of the starboard hydroplane. The submarine rocked to port and, for perhaps thirty seconds, the two vessels remained locked together. The submarine's bridge crew were knocked off their feet by the violence of the shock and their captain struck his head against the bridge rail, falling dead instantly.

With an agonising screech of grinding metal, the trawler's bow fell away and water immediately gushed into the gaping hole left behind in the pressure hull. Within seconds, *D2* plunged under the sea towards the bottom, leaving the four bridge lookouts and their dead commanding officer floating in the water.

*

Eva Keyes was woken by the ringing of the telephone in the hall of the Fareham home she shared with her husband. Who on earth could be ringing at this time of night? It could only be for Roger and she nudged him in an effort to wake him. As usual, he merely grunted and went back to sleep. Throughout their five years of happily married life, this habit had always irritated Eva. Only two years earlier, Keyes had been in command of HMS *Venus*. He claimed that the experience had taught him to be a light sleeper and instantly awake when called from the bridge at night. Eva didn't believe a word of it. It was one of his many inconsistencies. During the day, she knew few people with as much energy and swiftness of action, but once he hit the pillow, he was dead to the world. Perhaps it was the sign of a guilt-free conscience. No, this really would not do. If she didn't do something, the telephone would ring all night. Mustering all her energy, she rolled Keyes out of the bed and let him fall to the floor with a hefty thump. Keyes woke instantly.

'What the hell?' he cried.

'Roger, the telephone is ringing downstairs. Go and answer it.'

Awake at last, Keyes was immediately a man of action again. Without even pausing to put on his dressing gown and slippers, he leapt down the stairs to the hall.

*

Keyes bounded from the carpeted stairs to the tiled floor of the hall and instantly regretted the absence of his slippers. After crossing the moonlit hall, he picked up the receiver to end the shrill ringing.

'Keyes,' he answered curtly.

'Hello, sir. It's Commander Woodall, the duty commander at the Admiralty. I'm sorry to disturb you at this time of night, but it is rather urgent.'

'Go on.' He was not in the mood for small talk at this hour and he noted from the moonlight's reflection on the grandfather clock that it was barely half past three.

'We've had a report from Harwich coastguard that a trawler suffered a collision with a submarine last night. At about 20.00 and four miles south of Orford Ness. It was thick fog and they didn't see her until too late. The submarine went down, but they fished two seamen and a corpse out of the sea. According to the survivors, the submarine was *D2* and the corpse was their captain, Lieutenant Johnson. There are still two men missing, but the skipper dropped a Dan buoy to mark the position and his partner is searching for the missing men.'

'My God,' Keyes said quietly. It was only yesterday that he had sent the signal to inform Johnson of the birth of his son. 'Where the bloody hell was her escort?'

'Lost her in the fog, it seems, sir. The launch is mounting a search for the missing men, but it won't be easy at night and in thick fog. I doubt they'll have much to report before daylight, sir.'

'What action have you taken?'

'I've alerted C-in-C Nore and he's despatching *Indomitable*, three RNR trawlers and a tug to the scene. They should be on task within the next four hours, soon after first light. He's also sending the Chatham diving team and their tender as soon as it's light.'

'Why is Poore sending Reserve trawlers? He surely doesn't expect to fish *D2* from the deep?'

'No, sir. It was actually one of Admiral Poore's staff that suggested it. They've been experimenting with grappling hooks, fitted to wires, to sweep for moored mines and somebody thought they could do the same to try to locate your submarine.'

'I like it. I could do with that officer on my staff. I'm sorry. Do carry on.'

'Vice Admiral Colville will be the on-scene commander, sir, and he already has a couple of passing destroyers in the area. We've also contacted the Liverpool Salvage Company and they are sending a salvage ship, the *Ranger*, to the area with immediate despatch, but its ETA is not for thirty-six hours.'

'That's too late. The men will have asphyxiated by then. Is there nothing else?'

'Not with large enough cranes to lift a vessel of this size, sir. We estimate the depth of water to be about eighteen fathoms. We're talking to a company in Tilbury with a floating crane platform and hope to get it towed to the site fairly quickly. It might be useful for lowering equipment or something, but it's not up to the job of lifting a submarine. They are also sending a diving bell to the scene. We have requested the Foreign Office to contact the Germans, to check whether they might have a suitable vessel available, but it will be a few hours before we hear anything back. In the meantime, the salvage company are sending one of their top men to the scene, a Captain Young, to help co-ordinate the rescue. We've arranged for the Flying Corps to fly him down from Liverpool at first light. There will also be another team of divers leaving Portsmouth Dockyard by road first thing in the morning, sir. They're just assembling now and getting together their equipment. I assume you will be attending the scene, sir?'

'You're damned right I'll be there. I'm leaving in thirty minutes. Tell them to expect me at Harwich. I shall want a full briefing on my arrival.'

'Fine, sir. Is there anything else you think we should do?'

'It sounds like you have the situation in hand. Actually, there is something else you can do. Contact Fort Blockhouse for me. Tell them to arrange for any of the D-boat COs and Chief ERAs in harbour to get their backsides up to Harwich, PDQ. We'll benefit from some specialist expertise. You might also warn my staff to dig out the next of kin details in case this all goes badly wrong.'

Keyes replaced the earpiece of the telephone receiver and sat down, stunned. This was every submariner's nightmare. Nobody had ever yet survived such an accident. Although not a submariner himself, Keyes knew only too well the slow and dreadful death the crew of the submarine would face as the oxygen levels diminished and the carbon dioxide levels from their exhaled breath concentrated. He half hoped that seawater had already flooded the hull and mixed with the battery to create chlorine gas. Although chlorine gas poisoning would still be an agonising death, it at least had the merit of being relatively quick. Either way, it would be a tragic way to die for such promising young men. As he thought of their icy, watery grave, his brain reminded him of the coldness of his feet and he was brought to action.

'Eva, my darling,' he called. 'Pack my bags. I'm leaving in twenty minutes.' He mounted the stairs at twice the speed he had descended them.

Chapter 2

'God bless ye, ladies.'

The beggar outside one of the elegant shops at the east end of Oxford Street tipped his cap to the three ladies who had just given him some loose change. In many respects they were like hundreds of others that Saturday afternoon of the second of March 1912. Two were well-dressed and, from their dress and deportment, clearly from middle to upper class backgrounds. He spotted that the clothes of the third, although fashionable, were factory manufactured, perhaps suggesting she was from a working class background. The beggar had served as an intelligence scout in a mounted yeomanry troop during the Boer war and had learned to take notice of small details. His curiosity was aroused when he noted that, despite their class differences, what the ladies had in common was that not one of them was wearing a scrap of jewellery. He wondered who they were.

The three women were very different in looks, although they were all tall for their sex. Indeed, it was as if each had been chosen to form the group as a representative of different hair colouring. One of them had the air of being in charge. She was a brunette and slim in build. Her social equal was also slim, but had auburn hair. The odd one out, in terms of her apparent class, was blonde and different, too, in that she was quite stout in her build.

He watched them in their turn scan the busy street, up towards Oxford Circus and then down towards Tottenham Court Road. They seemed satisfied that the coast was clear for their purposes, as they all looked at each other and nodded significantly. The beggar considered whether he should look for a constable, but he had already had his unfair share of interaction with the police, and in any case, none seemed to be present. What did it matter? What harm was he thinking three women could cause? However, after the briefest of pauses, they burst into action, to the obvious shock of the passing shoppers. The brunette reached into her large handbag and started to hurl stones at the windows of the shop facing her on the north side of Oxford Street. Meanwhile, her two colleagues crossed the street and, using hammers previously concealed on their person, began to smash the windows of the shops opposite. As they hurried about their work they shouted in high-pitched voices, *'Votes for Women. Votes for Women.'*

Once the women with the hammers had smashed two shopfronts, they reached once more into their copious handbags and removed several pamphlets, which they began to hand out to the surprised onlookers. The pamphlets were the work of the Women's Social and Political Union, or WSPU.

By now the shock and bemusement of the passers-by had turned to outrage and, spurred on by the generally male shopkeepers in the vicinity, three of whom had just seen their shop windows destroyed, the crowd surrounded the suffragette campaigners to prevent their escape. 'Call a peeler!' one of them shouted and the cry was repeated by several until one of them was actually galvanised to take the action demanded. The three women were herded together and completely surrounded by a large crowd of shoppers and other onlookers. The beggar could no longer see them and moved closer to gain a better view of the altercation.

'What you done that for, you vandals?' one of the male shopkeepers remonstrated loudly. ''oos gonna pay for it? It's my liveli'ood you're playin' with 'ere, make no mistake.'

The crowd seemed to agree with the sentiments expressed and started to hiss at and jostle the three women campaigners. Four of the male onlookers surrounding the blonde and auburn-haired women decided to make sport of the occasion.

'What we got 'ere, ducks? You sure you're women? It's only men that get the vote, ye know. You sure you're not men in disguise? Let's check it aht'. The thugs then began to poke the women and squeeze various parts of their flesh.

'Hey, look! They seem to have the right bumps in the right places, but there's not much flesh on this one, is there, lads?' one of them cried. 'Tho' mebbe we'd be better to take a closer look to make sure, hey?'

'Whatch ye think?' another cackled.

In response, some of the female members of the crowd started to look decidedly uneasy and pulled away a little, but the mood of the crowd was still unsympathetic. The beggar was relieved to hear, in the distance, several police whistles. The peelers could look after the women. They should be safe now. He began to edge away from the crowd, but first heard the plump suffragette whisper to her colleagues, ‘Look, girls. I’m going to create a diversion. As soon as I start, you get out of here, all right?’

The beggar assumed neither of her two partners in the deed had any idea what she had in mind, or, perhaps, they were simply too shocked to debate the issue. Instead, they just nodded and looked for a possible escape route from the current indignities. He made way for them and pointed with his stick to a gap in the crowd.

‘All right, you brave men,’ the blonde suffragette cried out. ‘You want to see what a real woman looks like in the flesh, then stand back and I’ll bloomin’ well show yer.’ At this, she started to remove her coat.

‘Ain’t no one got no music to accompany my turn?’ she called. The crowd stepped back as one in amazement and the thugs were as shocked as anyone.

‘Whoo-hay, this is a bit of awright,’ one of them shouted.

Perhaps still dazed by their recent treatment, the brunette and auburn-haired women hesitated momentarily and then took their cue to pass through the crowd as unobtrusively as possible. As they made their escape, the blonde cried out, ‘Now whose gonna unzip my skirt and let me show yer my bloomers?’

The beggar saw both women shudder at the steps their colleague was taking on their behalf, before they hurried away from the scene. Their escape seemed to have gone unnoticed and they quickly came across the entrance to Tottenham Court Road underground station. Without hesitation this time, they entered the ticket hall and disappeared from the beggar’s view.

*

‘My God, Christabel,’ the auburn-haired beauty exclaimed, ‘I can’t believe Ellie would pull a stunt like that. What will become of her?’

Christabel, the brunette, replied, ‘I wouldn’t worry about her, Lizzy. She knows how to handle herself and I suspect she is timing matters so that the peelers arrive in the nick of time to protect her modesty. I have to grant it was quick thinking, though, and certainly got us out of an awkward spot. The actions of those yobs made my flesh crawl.’

Lizzy shuddered at the memory. ‘So what are we to do now, Christabel?’

'Stay calm. I don't fancy prison any more than you. Go home as if nothing had happened and come up with a story if necessary to explain your movements this afternoon. I think it's time I put into action my plan to relocate to Paris. Are you still up for meeting me there and helping me continue the fight, Lizzy?'

'Of course I am. But is it absolutely necessary to escape to Paris? After all, Ellie's not going to preach and there's nothing to tie us to this demonstration.'

'I know that, but London is becoming too hot. It's only a matter of time before the police catch up with us and I'll confess to you alone, Lizzy, I've not got it in me to put up with what my mother has. The thought of being force-fed revolts me. Now, stop shilly-shallying. Go. I'll follow in two minutes and catch another train. We can talk more next weekend in Paris, right?'

With that, the two women embraced and exchanged a kiss so long and tender that it aroused the disapproval of more than a few fellow passengers of the underground station.

*

The Hôtel Citi Bergère was situated down an alley off the main street. It was, thus, quiet and unobtrusive. Qualities that suited its fugitive guest very well. Miss Amy Richards had fled London the previous weekend on the boat train from Victoria to Folkestone. Having spent a few days in a hamlet near Boulogne, she had decided it was safe to continue her journey to Paris. Even so, she had decided not to use her real name. She had no wish for the Metropolitan Police in London to discover her whereabouts. All day, she had anxiously awaited the arrival of her two friends. Having left London with only £100 on her person, she was keen to receive further funds to enable her to settle permanently in Paris and, perhaps, in due course, in more luxurious surroundings. More importantly, she wanted to hear the latest news from London. Miss Richards had been worried. Her friends should have been here yesterday, but she had received no further news from them, other than to confirm their arrival this weekend. It was, therefore, with much relief when she answered the door to be met with the beaming grins of her two friends, Annie Kenney and Elizabeth Miller.

'Where have you been? I've been so worried about you. You should have been here yesterday.'

'I say, that's a fine welcome after a long journey, Christabel. Aren't you going to invite us in?' Annie replied.

'I'm sorry. Come in. How rude of me. I've just been beside myself with worry.'

The two visitors entered the hotel room and after several hugs and kisses were invited to sit in the small sitting room. Before they settled down to conversation, Christabel Pankhurst, alias Amy Richards, rang for tea.

Annie explained the delay. 'I'm sorry, Christabel. We had a change of plan. We came over on the overnight ferry from Southampton to Le Havre.'

'Why ever did you do that? No wonder it took you so long.'

'It's my fault,' Elizabeth replied. 'Just as we reached the platform at Victoria, I swear I saw my Uncle William catching the same train. It put the wind up me, I can tell you. We thought about taking a later train, but then thought, if the police really were looking for us, then we might be better taking a more devious route.'

'And is there any reason why the police should be looking for you, Lizzy?'

Elizabeth and Annie shared a meaningful look before the latter took up the story.

'Well, yes, actually. I'm afraid, the day after you left London, the police raided the offices in Clement's Inn. They seized several documents and I cannot be sure they didn't find a list of members. Your mother is back in prison and there's a warrant out for your arrest. The good news is that your disappearance is bringing the movement some good publicity. See here, I've brought you a paper.'

Christabel would ordinarily have read the headline, '*Where is Christabel?*' with some amusement, but the news that her mother was back in gaol prompted tears of sadness. Emmeline had already suffered so much at the hands of the establishment and her health was starting to deteriorate after the effects of prison and force-feeding. The two friends remained silent whilst Christabel recovered her composure.

'Oh, dear. We cannot just give up and allow the Government to think they have deprived the Union of all leadership. Annie, I want you to take full charge of the policy and I will continue to write the editorial for *Votes for Women*.'

'But why not get Sylvia to run the policy, Christabel?' Annie interjected.

'No. My sister is not fit for it, Annie. Now, Lizzy. You speak French and are less well-known than Annie. Do you think you could come over every weekend to collect the editorial and update me on the latest news?'

'I'd be delighted, Christabel, but I do have to be back in Liverpool at the end of the month. Perhaps Annie and I could take it in turns if I could find another French speaker to accompany her. What do you think, Annie?'

Annie responded with a rumble from her stomach. 'Ooh, I am sorry,' she said, before putting her hand over her mouth and blushing. 'That's fine by me, Lizzy, but I refuse to discuss anything further until I've had a bath and eaten. After twenty-four hours of travelling, I'm dirty and starving. Christabel, where are you taking us for dinner?'

Chapter 3

After all the confusion and commotion of the past few minutes, Richard Miller thought the submarine strangely quiet. He could hear a few groans forward and made a mental note to check for casualties, but for now his priority was to assess the situation. Most of the lights had gone out after some form of electrical explosion forward, but some were still on and this made his life easier. Clearly the submarine was lying on the seabed. The inclinometer showed a twenty degree bow-down attitude and he could feel the hull was heeled over a little to starboard. The depth gauge showed eighty-four feet.

He first spoke with Chief Engine Room Artificer Waterfield to check on the situation down aft. The CERA reported that the motor room staff had had the sense to stop both engines, without orders, when the submarine had started sinking and, other than a few bruises, were all in good shape. There were no signs of leaks. Forward, the situation was less good. Richard could not establish any communication with the fore-ends and he suspected the compartment was flooded. Otherwise, the hull seemed intact and *D2* was free from flooding. The Coxswain, Petty Officer Goddard, confirmed the flooding of the torpedo compartment and also reported one serious casualty. Leading Seaman Smith had been badly scalded by boiling water from the galley stove and was suffering burns to his face, neck and left shoulder.

Richard retired to the wardroom and drew the curtain behind him, separating the space from the control room and giving himself some relative privacy. Johnson was gone, whether alive or dead, and he was now the senior survivor and in command. It was a moment for which he had been trained, but dreaded. From now on, the lives of the men in *D2* would depend on his judgement and cool thinking. He wondered if he was ready for the responsibility. But, ready or not, the responsibility was his and his alone. He had to succeed. He retrieved his Bible from his bunk and prayed silently to the Lord for courage, inspiration and, above all, luck.

Ten minutes later, Richard summoned Waterfield and Goddard to the wardroom for a council of war.

'Coxswain, how many men are not accounted for?'

'Twelve, sir. That includes the captain and four lookouts. There were seven men in the fore-ends, including the TI and ERA Watts. With those present, sir, that makes an unlucky thirteen survivors.'

'Thank you, Coxswain. As it happens, thirteen is my lucky number. I was born on the thirteenth, so I'd say that's a good omen.'

Richard knew it wasn't a good joke. He recognised that he was not known to have a sense of humour, but the senior rates smiled nonetheless.

'Now, here is the situation as I see it. We're lying in eighty-odd feet of water, not far off the coast. We've clearly collided with something up top and are holed forward, so there's no prospect of surfacing on our own. However, we're lucky that, thanks to the captain's good judgement, the only flooding we've suffered is in the fore-ends. So we're watertight otherwise. I'll be straight with you. I can't be sure if whatever hit us even knows they suffered a collision. It's thick fog and going dark up there. If they didn't notice us going down, then we have to hope one or more of the bridge crew are picked up to report the accident. Otherwise, we'll have to sit tight until we're posted missing by our escort. That might take a couple of hours.'

Richard allowed the two senior rates a moment to absorb the information.

'Could we swim to the surface when it gets light, sir?' Waterfield asked. 'If enough of us get out, then we're bound to be spotted floating on the surface.'

'We could, but I wouldn't recommend it. I'm no diver, but I do know that at this depth we've a chance of contracting the Grecian Bends. Moreover, atmospheric pressure doubles about every thirty to thirty-five feet so, in our position, the air we're breathing will be about six or seven times the pressure of that of the surface. For that reason, we would have to exhale all the way to the surface and avoid our lungs expanding as the external pressure decreases. The odds are that somebody is going to ignore instructions, hold their breath under water and need immediate medical attention on the surface. For that, we need to await the arrival of a salvage force with a decompression chamber. In any case, we're better making sure there's somebody on the surface ready to pick us up before we bob up like corks. It might still be foggy and who knows how long we would float around before somebody found us? No, far better to wait until the boat can be lifted to the surface by crane or we escape when the surface forces are ready. So here's my plan.

'We need to conserve both the battery and air supply. That means we need to reduce the lighting to a minimum and avoid heating the galley stove. We'll leave some lighting on for morale, but I'll leave you to turn off what we don't need, Chief.'

Waterfield nodded in assent.

'Coxswain, I'd like you to arrange for the men to be fed a cold meal and issued with plenty of water. We need to avoid dehydration but, as we can't use the heads, put out buckets. We can empty them in the bilges. Sorry, Chief.

'To conserve our air I want everyone who is not essential, and I would have thought that's everyone but a single watchkeeper, to turn in. For the sake of morale and maintaining bodily warmth, I suggest everyone slings a hammock in the control room area. It'll save on lighting, too. Any questions?'

Both Waterfield and Goddard looked glum. They both started to ask questions, but it was Goddard who held sway.

'How do you rate our chances, sir, and what do we tell the men?'

Richard thought a moment before replying.

'Frankly, if nobody saw us go down, our chances are not good. I'd say our air will last not much more than twenty-four hours. Being morbid, there are fewer of us to use up the air, but we've lost the fore-ends reserve. Nevertheless, however long we've got, there's nothing we can do for the present. That means we have no choice but to tough it out. A sincere prayer might help things along.' Richard spotted the suppressed grins of the two senior rates.

'In the meantime, it's important we keep the men's morale high and give them hope. Tell them that we're in salvageable waters and, if we're careful and with God's help, we can hold out for forty-eight hours before we have to escape. For now, everyone is to get their head down and we'll assess the situation again in the morning. I look to you both to take the lead and look a bit more cheerful. Any other questions?'

Richard made it clear from his demeanour that he was not expecting any more questions and the two senior rates excused themselves and set about their duties.

*

Richard was woken by a gentle shake of his shoulder.

'It's 07.45, sir. You asked to be called.'

It was the watchkeeper, Signalman 'Knocker' White. Richard's brain was slow to focus. He had not slept well. Something was nagging him, but he could not work it out. He could only take shallow breaths and his head hurt. He recalled the events of the past twelve hours and remembered why. This was the effect of low levels of oxygen and correspondingly high levels of carbon dioxide. He was familiar with the symptoms as Johnson had twice before exercised the crew in staying deep for prolonged periods. Johnson's reasoning had been that on a wartime patrol it might be necessary to bottom during the day to avoid the attention of enemy patrols, and then not to surface again until darkness had fallen, to replenish the air and charge the battery cells. However, the longest trial they had conducted to date was twelve and a half hours, so they would soon be in unknown territory.

Out of habit, he reached for the Bible lying next to his bunk. It was his custom to read it for five minutes before facing the rigours of the day. He selected a page at random and read a passage in the available dim light. By chance, it was from the book of Jonah and made for uncomfortable reading.

> *'In my distress I called to the Lord, and he answered me. From deep in the realm of the dead I called for help, and you listened to my cry. You hurled me into the depths, into the very heart of the seas, and the currents swirled about me; all your waves and breakers swept over me. I said, "I have been banished from your sight; yet I will look again toward your holy temple." The engulfing waters threatened me, the deep surrounded me; ...'*

Richard snapped the book shut. The text was too close to the bone and there was much to do. He gently eased himself out of his bunk and pulled back the wardroom curtain. He noted that most of the men were awake, but still in their hammocks. It took too much energy and oxygen to move about. The air stank of oil, the sour smell of the batteries, the unemptied buckets of urine and worse. Every man's clothes were sodden with sweat. The moisture was condensing on the inside of the hull, too, and covering the electric bulbs with fine droplets of moisture. Added to the mixture of oil and water in the bilges, the condensation gave the interior of the boat a look of London in a smog.

Notwithstanding the unpleasant atmosphere, Richard was pleased to note that although nobody, including himself probably, looked a picture of health, everyone seemed free of sickness so far. His attention was drawn to some cursing to his left. One of the stokers was trying to light a cigarette, but the match wouldn't strike and he swore. There was too little oxygen to ignite it. Richard felt exasperated. He wasn't a smoker and didn't like others smoking when the submarine was dived. The air was foul enough as it was and it was a waste of good oxygen. Ill-temperedly he scolded the stoker.

'Surely, Blake, the language of Shakespeare and Chaucer is rich enough in vocabulary to negate the need for profanity to express your frustrations.'

He detailed one of the seamen to serve up some breakfast. It would be a meagre affair of cold tinned sausages and tomatoes, but it was important to keep up the men's strength and stick to as normal a routine as possible.

*

Once he was sure that the officer was out of earshot, Blake whispered to his 'oppo', 'Here, Ginge. You know what's eating our ever so pious, high and mighty First Lieutenant?'

'Not especially. He's always playin' the 'ard bastard.'

'Constipation, that's what.'

'What you on about now, Blakey?'

'It's true. Honest to God. He hasn't had a shit since we sailed. He never does at sea.'

'Is this one of your jokes, Blakey?'

'No, listen out. It was when we were on our first patrol after work-up. He went down to the heads to have a crap, but he couldn't manage the valves properly. He was kneeling over the pan, like you does for the evolution, when he got his own back. Filth all over his face and down his neck. It was right funny, like. I was on watch nearby and saw 'im as he came out. He slipped me a couple of bob and asked me if I'd do the honours and clear up afterwards. Ever since then he's been taking opium pills so he doesn't have to go at sea. Ain't that a lark?'

'Well, I'm blowed. No wonder he's a grumpy old sod. He must be right bunged up.'

'Yeah. He's full of shit, as one might say.'

The two sailors chuckled quietly before they were interrupted by Goddard who had overheard the latter part of the exchange.

'So, we've a pair of comedians here, haven't we? Haven't you two enough to worry about? Get off your arses and empty the slop buckets. Maybe then you'll pipe down and conserve your breath.'

*

Richard inspected the pilot cells of the battery. The battery would last a few more hours at this rate of consumption. He wondered grimly if he and the men or the battery would expire first. It was then that he remembered one of the things that had been worrying him in his sleep and he returned to the control room as quickly as his fatigued, oxygen-starved body would allow.

Realising he was physically less able than normal, he called for the Coxswain. Goddard was a tall and burly man.

''Swain, I've had an idea. I'm only sorry I didn't think of it before. Can you help me crack open the lower lid of the conning tower? I remember the Captain ordering the hatch to be shut and clipped just before the collision. I bet he did the same with the upper lid. If we're lucky, the tower will be dry and it will have a reserve of fresh air. Can you help me unclip the hatch?'

With their combined strength, the two weakened men were able to unclip the hatch and, to their joy, no water seeped in as they broke the seal. Gingerly, Richard opened the hatch and, as he did so, it leapt open and he felt himself sucked upwards and through it. Fortunately, Goddard was on hand to grab both his legs or else he might have been badly injured. The tower was dry and, as Richard gasped at the fresh air, the control room filled with a mist. He realised his stupidity. The lack of oxygen was affecting his judgement. It was a fact that after several hours dived, the pressure in the boat increased due to leaking air from the high pressure air systems. On surfacing, therefore, Johnson had always taken the precaution of having somebody hang onto his legs to prevent being shot through the upper lid. Despite his stupidity, Richard was relieved to see the instant effect his action had on the men as they sucked in the new air greedily. It would at least give them a few extra hours.

The silence of the boat was broken by the sound of diesel engines up top. To Richard's experienced ears it sounded like a pair of trawlers. He ruefully wondered if one of them had been responsible for his crew's present predicament. It was possible that the fishing vessel was blissfully unaware of last night's collision and was happily going about its normal fishing run. He checked the control room clock. It was 08.30, so it should have been light up top for two to three hours by now. That would enable the surface forces to commence their search for them, but had the fog lifted? He checked the weather forecast at the chart table but, to his dismay, realised they only had yesterday's forecast for the east coast. Today's was for the approaches to Portsmouth.

Then he heard the fast throbbing noises of diesel engines passing overhead. The other men had heard it, too, and like him, seemed to be holding their breath and to be united in the same thought. Was this from passing merchant traffic or a search party? Slowly, the noises dissipated and, just as he started to give up hope, he heard a clang and then a metallic rasping on the starboard side of the hull towards the stern. As it reached the height of the casing above, it stopped and changed into a knocking noise for a few moments, and then it was gone. Under other circumstances it would have been a ghostly and unnerving sound, but to Richard and his trapped crew, it was contact again with the outside world.

His brain refreshed from the additional supply of oxygen, Richard was again able to think clearly. The men were by now looking at him quizzically.

'I think that was a trawl net passing overhead. The clanking noise was probably the metal weights and the net snagged on the hull.' He was moved by the instant look of disappointment on the men's faces.

A few minutes later he heard again the approach of diesel engines on the surface. Nobody was surprised this time when soon afterwards they heard further metallic sounds on the port side of the hull, only this time they occurred astern and alongside the control room. The clanking and scraping noises seemed to linger and in Richard's imagination some giant octopus was readying itself to pluck them from the sea like a tiny fish. It was a terrible sound. Suddenly, the submarine was jolted by the stern. The trawl net had clearly stuck fast on something. It was an unsettling feeling.

Almost as quickly, the trawl freed itself and peace reigned once more. That didn't last for long. Alarmingly, Richard heard the loud bang of an underwater explosion on the port side. Ten seconds later it was repeated and then there was another. It could only mean one thing: rescue was at hand. They had been found. Gradually the men worked it out for themselves and started cheering, but Richard cut them short. They still had to conserve oxygen as there was no telling by what means and how long it would take for them to be rescued.

He returned to his bunk to think in private. There was still something he had forgotten, but for the life of him he could not recall it. It was good that they had been found. It removed one uncertainty. But how were they to get to the surface? The safest option would be for the boat to be lifted by giant cranes, but did such machines exist afloat and would it take too long? Despite the influx of air from the conning tower, the men were already suffering physically and he had spotted many with the tell-tale blue lips of oxygen starvation. Perhaps now they should consider swimming for the surface before the men became too weak, but how was that to be done? They could go through the engine room hatch or the conning tower, but that would mean flooding the compartments first. It would then be dark and the men would have to find their way through the hatch by touch. Some were bound to become disorientated and would they get out in time? Moreover, as soon as the inrush of salt water came into contact with the battery, it would create deadly chlorine gas. He was at least comforted by the thought that, only the year before, all the latest submarines of the Service had been fitted with a form of breathing apparatus for escape purposes. Captain Hall had been the Inspecting Captain of Submarines then. He and Fleet Surgeon Rees had worked with Siebe Gorman to invent a 'rebreather'.

Richard couldn't remember all the details of the new apparatus, but he recalled that it included a canister of a newly discovered chemical, Oxylithe, which, when breathed, both gave off oxygen and absorbed carbon dioxide. This would enable the wearer to breathe underwater for thirty or forty minutes, enough time to escape the submarine and ascend to the surface. However, he had heard rumours that, despite the benefits to submariners, the Admiralty was now considering the withdrawal of the sets as they were too bulky for storage in the tight confines of an already crowded submarine. Fortunately, although there was still no formal training of submariners in escape procedures, Johnson had insisted each member of the crew practise donning the apparatus. Nonetheless, Richard decided it would be expedient to organise a further training session.

Then came the chilling thought. Did the surface forces know they were alive? Would they recognise the urgency of rescue? Of course they would, he reassured himself. Why else drop the charges, but to let them know help was at hand. Even so, there was no doubt it would help if he could communicate with those in charge on the surface. How could he get a message to the surface without breaching their watertight integrity? He racked his brains frantically. It was no good. His brain just wasn't working properly. Perhaps Waterfield or Goddard might have the answer. He called them to the wardroom for another meeting and briefed them on what was troubling him.

He was surprised to observe that Goddard seemed to be suffering more than Waterfield. Goddard was a tall, fit man who, when submarine routine permitted, often turned out for the Fort Blockhouse rugby team, where his height was a major advantage in a line out. Waterfield, by comparison, was a short, round-looking man who to Richard's certain knowledge never took any form of exercise. He did recall that, prior to joining the Navy, Waterfield had been a professional opera singer, the only one Richard had come across. Perhaps the discipline of singing had developed his lungs to recycle the air more efficiently than most men. It was Waterfield who seemed to have all the ideas.

'Sir, I've been thinking. Maybe we should vacate the control room and shift the men back aft. We all know that carbon dioxide is heavier than oxygen and, given the steep, bow-down angle, it will collect more readily forward. Indeed, I've noticed on my rounds that the air seems better quality the further aft one goes. In the past I've always put that down to the more rarefied conversations we have back there.'

Richard smacked his forehead in frustration. 'Of course you're right, Chief. I should have thought of that. Hang on a minute, though. You've just given me another thought. I need to do some calculations.'

He pulled out a sheet of paper and a pencil, and started drawing a triangular diagram on it.

'I've got it,' he exclaimed. 'My brain was trying to tell me this all night. The boat is 163 feet long. The control room depth gauge reads eighty-four feet beneath us and we're, say, seventy-five feet from the bows. That means the stern of the boat is about ninety feet from the depth gauge. The boat's at an angle of twenty degrees, so take the sine of twenty degrees, multiply it by ninety and that gives us about thirty feet. Yes! The stern is just over thirty feet shallower in the water. In other words, if we could get out by the stern, then we'd only have to travel fifty-odd feet to the surface. That probably doubles our chances of survival.'

He looked at the two men much as a magician sought approval for a successful conjuring trick, but the two senior rates only looked confused.

'We'll take your word for it, sir. Maths was never my strong point,' Goddard replied. 'So is that the plan then, sir? We escape from the after-ends hatch and swim for it?'

'Well, not quite, Coxswain. I was getting carried away. We need to think of a way of informing the Senior Officer there's somebody alive down here and to prepare for our reception. We don't want to be floating off who knows where with the tidal stream. The after-ends hatch is still some feet forward of the stern and thirteen of us are going to have to get through that hatch once the whole compartment floods. We'll have to consider the risks of disorientation and panic amongst the men.'

Here Waterfield interjected. 'I might be able to help, sir. Maybe if we pumped out the bilges, there would be enough oil to float to the surface to mark our position and tell them up top that somebody's alive down here, and to get a fucking move on. Pardon my French, sir,' he added embarrassedly. 'Am I also right in thinking that the port after tube is empty, sir?'

'Yes. What are you driving at, Chief?'

'Well, it was just what you were saying about the stern being higher. Could not a couple of men escape by crawling through the tube? They could brief the officers in charge up there and it would mean two fewer left to escape through the after-ends hatch.'

'Chief, I like the idea of pumping the bilges, but your other idea seems impractical. You forget that we would have to flood the tube to open the bow cap and the men would drown in the meantime. The rebreather apparatus is too bulky for crawling through a torpedo tube. No, that won't do. On the other hand, we could put three men through the conning tower hatch.'

'Begging your pardon, sir, but I have actually been thinking about that. You remember that visit from the boffins at Siebe Gorman earlier late last year?'

Richard tried hard to mask his exasperation and responded patiently. 'Yes, I do. Mr Davis was trying to interest the Admiralty in a more compact breathing apparatus for use in submarine escape, to replace the Hall-Rees kit. Sadly, the discussions are still going on and, whilst such equipment would be jolly handy right now, we don't yet have the gear. Do you have any more practical suggestions?' He looked to Goddard expectantly.

Waterfield ignored the snub and stuck to his guns. 'Actually, we do, sir.'

'Sorry, Chief. We do what?' Richard was tiring of the discussion.

'We do have some of the gear, sir.' Waterfield was now adopting the patient tone.

Richard was stunned for a moment, but then his heart started to beat faster. 'What do you mean, Chief?'

'It so happens I had a chat with one of the technicians and mentioned that even if the kit wasn't yet approved for submarine escape, it might be just the ticket for an engine room fire. That got us on to the subject of mine rescue and he sent me two sets of rebreathers that have already been approved for use in the mines. He wanted my opinion on their use in submarines but, with everything going on these past few months, I've never got around to unpacking them. But I checked them this morning and they still seem to be in their original condition. I reckon if they work underground, then they should be fine underwater.'

Richard checked his rate of breathing. The excitement was hurting his chest. This news gave him more options, but he would have to decide on a plan to use it. First he needed to see the sets. He adopted a more respectful tone towards Waterfield.

'Chief, you might just be a genius. Could you take me to inspect the sets and, perhaps, you could explain to me how they work?'

Chapter 4

To a casual observer walking along the coast overlooking Ollesley Bay, it looked as if the Royal Navy had taken a luncheon break from its peacetime manoeuvres and stopped for a picnic. A wide variety of vessels were scattered, apparently haphazardly, in the bay. Some were at anchor, some tethered alongside the larger ships, and others criss-crossing the bay aimlessly or on their way to or from Harwich. Largest of them all was a grey battlecruiser, flying from its masthead a flag of St George on which a single red ball was printed in the top left quadrant. This was the flag of the senior officer in charge of this ragtag assortment of vessels, Vice Admiral Stanley Colville. Since the flag of a Rear Admiral included two red balls and that of a full Admiral none, irreverent sailors mused that the higher an admiral rose, the fewer balls he had.

It was a bright sunny day with a slight wind from the north, but barely enough to ruffle the sea surface and to keep the white ensigns of the warships flying. The fog of the previous day had completely disappeared, but the sun had yet to penetrate fully the thin haze above. In the centre of the activity, several red and yellow buoys rocked gently with the ripple of the sea, from the midst of which emanated the steady throb of the Siebe twin-cylinder diving pump on board the Chatham Dockyard buff-coloured diving tender. Just above the waterline twinkled the reflection of the wan spring sunshine off the gleaming brass twelve-bolt helmets of the two divers entering the water.

The two divers checked that the various lines connecting them with the tender were not tangled, including the precious airline connected to the Siebe pump, before giving the signal to their colleagues to continue lowering them into the depths of the waters. The men had been specially selected for the task by the officer in charge of the team, Lieutenant Davies. There was no shortage of volunteers for this hazardous task, but it required a certain type of person to dive at depths greater than thirty-three feet and the senior of the two divers, Petty Officer Brown, was the only member of the team previously to have dived to 100 feet. ‘Buster’

Brown was from nearby Lowestoft and hoped that when his day's work was complete he would be able to pay a visit to his family. He was not very happy about the selection of his partner for the dive, Leading Seaman Davies, no relation to the officer-in-charge, but also a Welshman, as he lacked deep diving experience and this was a tricky dive. Davies had been selected more for his experience as a telegraphist prior to transferring to the diving branch. Brown nevertheless recognised that so far Davies had proved himself competent, with steady nerves, and he was certainly physically strong.

As the divers descended ever deeper, Brown looked up to the surface. Visibility was still good in the turquoise world in which he was now immersed and he could see clearly the shimmering hull of the tender. He could also see Davies quite clearly five feet away, dressed similarly to Brown in his canvas and rubber watertight suit, lead boots and brass helmet with corselet whose twelve projecting bolts gave the helmet its name. By contrast, looking down, he could see nothing but inky blackness. Their descent was gently arrested at the prearranged depth of thirty feet. From now on, the deeper they descended, the higher the risk of them suffering from 'the bends'.

Brown had heard that this condition had originally been known as 'Caisson' disease since it afflicted the construction workers of the Brooklyn Bridge in New York, who worked at great depths below ground to fix the bridge's foundations. It was caused by a concentration of nitrogen in the body's tissues when operating at the increased atmospheric pressure of great depths. If he ascended too quickly, then the nitrogen was released as bubbles of gas, causing anything from a rash to pain in the joints and even to death. However, as an experienced diver, he had consulted Professor Haldane's new tables for 'staged decompression' by divers. When the divers commenced their ascent back to the surface, they would 'stop' at prescribed depths for defined periods in order to allow the nitrogen to dissipate harmlessly. Even so, there was no way of predicting the physiological impact on individuals and it was still a dangerous business. He was glad the Navy had purchased a number of special chambers in which a diver could be re-pressurised rapidly and then slowly de-pressurised, to simulate a slow and controlled ascent from the depths. So far, he had never had to experience life in one of these chambers and had no plans to do so.

Using sign language, he checked with Davies that he was satisfied his equipment was operating properly and in good shape, before signalling to the surface to continue lowering them deeper. Both divers were able to communicate to each other by tugging on their signal rope, but were also equipped with the newly-invented, electrically-powered telephone system connecting each diver's helmet to an operator on the tender above. Neither diver could speak directly to each other, but the communications system was still under development. Brown knew that some of his fellow divers resented the possibility of interference from above. *Divers were independent buggers, but that's what makes us better than the fish heads.* He could see the benefits, both for efficiency and for the divers' safety, and had established a *modus operandi* with the diver above that neither would pass any messages that were not vital.

Earlier that morning the rescue force had established the position of the submarine fairly accurately by the use of wire sweeps beneath the surface. The submarine had confirmed its position and that at least some of the crew were alive by releasing bilge oil to the surface. Brown and Davies now needed to fix the exact position of the sunken vessel and assess its state for salvaging.

Brown had thought it highly unlikely that they would be lowered directly onto the submarine, as the oil slick would have drifted south with the wind, so he planned to sweep the seabed in a northerly direction by walking along the bottom with a rope between them. They both had powerful tungsten-filament flashlights to assist with the task. A pair of civilian dockyard divers was on hand to continue the search should they fail on this first sweep. Even so, Brown was keen that it should be a naval diver that discovered the submarine first and was eager to set about the search, but he had to contain his impatience. The descent was out of his control and could not be hurried. He took the time instead to appreciate his surroundings.

It was an odd feeling to be suspended in the relative darkness. There was no sense of gravity or resistance of the water. Unless he communicated above to stop the descent, his body was out of control and he recalled that on his first deep ascent he had experienced a feeling of panic. It wasn't so bad when one could not see the bottom, but in clear and relatively shallow waters, where the bottom was visible, he had experienced a sense of vertigo and he had almost abandoned the dive. He wondered how the less-experienced Davies was faring. Although he could not yet see the seabed, there was still enough light to see Davies clearly. He offered Davies a thumbs-up signal and it was returned with a nod. It was at times like this that Brown wished he could communicate with his colleague by telephone, to reassure him, but both men were locked in their own silent world, independent of each other.

All too suddenly, the seabed of sand and shale rose up before them. Brown was pleased to be able to see the bottom as it meant their task in locating the submarine would be much easier. Looking to the surface, he could see nothing but the dim light of the sky. They hit the seabed in a flurry of mud and sand and he signalled to his invisible colleagues above to stop lowering and to give them sufficient slack for horizontal movement. Checking that all was well with Davies, he signalled to him the direction the compass indicated they should go.

As the divers separated, Brown paid out the light manila line connecting them at their waists. Every five feet of the line was marked with white cloth and, when Brown had only paid out fifteen feet of the line, he lost sight of Davies. He tugged it three times to alert Davies and secured it to avoid them being parted any further. Together, but out of sight of each other, the two men started their slow march northwards, as if in slow motion. It was hard work and their movements were laboured on account of their heavy boots and the resistance of the water. Neither man could hear any sound other than that of his own breathing. Brown knew that he and the out-of-sight Davies were the only human beings on this section of the sea bed. Their temporary footprints were probably the first ever trodden there by man. It must be like this, Brown thought, for the Antarctic exploration party as each man pulled his share of the sledge behind him, each part of a team, but lost in his own thoughts. One of Brown's 'oppos' had sailed two years earlier on the *Terra Nova*, as a member of Captain Scott's expedition team, but Brown had not heard from him for over a year.

His reverie was interrupted by two hard tugs and two flashes from Davies to his right. It meant he had seen something and Brown crabbed across to join him. At first he could not see what had attracted Davies' attention, even with the assistance of both their flashlights, but after another ten yards he could at last see a dark shape appear before them to their right. As they approached the shape, it grew in height and then it was clear that they had found their quarry at last.

The submarine was lying at an angle, buried in the soft bottom of the seabed from the bows to the hydroplanes. Abaft the hydroplane the starboard side of the hull was rent open, as if by a giant tin opener. Brown estimated the huge gash to be perhaps ten feet long and two feet wide at its broadest point. He had never seen a submarine from beneath the waterline before and he marvelled at its size. It was like an iceberg with most of its hull hidden beneath the water. It seemed rather pathetic now, lying there motionless, a once powerful machine now rendered useless by the natural elements. Brown had visited many wrecks and always found them sad places. They were inevitably associated with tragedy. What had once been home to sailors of his ilk had been transformed into a rusting, lifeless hulk, and very often he had also come across the bodies of the men who had once proudly sailed the vessel. This time it was different and it was strange to think that within the hull of the whale-like submarine there was life, or so he hoped.

He alerted the telephone operator at the end of the line and then he and Davies walked right up to the hull. Both divers were under strict instructions not to enter the submarine for fear their lines might become snagged. In any case, neither had any wish to do so. It was easy to imagine the floating corpses they might come across. Now it was time for Davies to use his previous expertise to justify his selection for the dive. Brown watched him withdraw a large spanner from the bag slung over his shoulder. Taking care to avoid dropping the spanner, Davies struck the hull three times. Brown was disappointed that there was no response. The two divers walked a further ten yards down the submarine's side towards the stern and Davies repeated the signal. Perhaps twenty seconds later they heard three bangs against the hull further aft. This was welcome proof of life on board.

*

The sound of knocking on the hull was not at first recognised by the oxygen-starved and carbon dioxide-poisoned men on board *D2*. Fortunately, the watchkeeper had the presence of mind to rouse the First Lieutenant from his hammock. Richard descended to the deck gingerly. He knew he was exhausted and that any sudden movement could be dangerous. Looking around the other members of the resting crew, he noted the trails of vomit starting to trickle forward from beneath the hammocks of many of them. It was an hour since he had last checked on the health of the men and at least three were seriously ill. If they were to attempt escape, then they had little time left before their strength deserted them. He heard for himself the second set of strikes on the hull from outside and immediately recognised its import. Picking up a nearby hammer, he repeated back the signal and called for Signalman White to join him. The commotion drew the attention of most of the men, but some seemed past caring. Almost immediately, Richard's banging was answered by further regular tapping on the hull, clearly a message in Morse code. White listened to the tapping intently and then translated it for all to hear.

'"*H-O-W-M-A-N-Y-S-O-U-L-S*". It's not easy to work it out, sir. Whoever's signalling seems a bit out of practice.'

Richard wasn't quite sure how to take the remark. Surely it was not professional pedantry in these circumstances, or maybe it was an attempt at a joke. He couldn't be bothered working it out.

'So would you be, wearing great gauntlets underwater, White. So let's keep our replies simple, shall we? Send, "Thirteen all together aft".'

The message was quickly answered.

'Message understood, sir, and we are told to standby,' White translated.

Richard used the delay to check the health of his men. Even in the gloom of the reduced lighting, it was obvious that all were breathing with difficulty. They also had flushed skin and some were twitching uncontrollably. It was now nearly eighteen hours since the collision and, although he guessed they might hold out another six or so hours, there were other factors to consider. Undoubtedly, the best hope for them all would be if the whole submarine could be lifted to the surface, but he had no idea how long that could take or even if it was possible. The only other option was to escape through the after-hatch or through the conning tower. This presented several risks, but their chances would be increased if they escaped immediately, since their health was already deteriorating. Moreover, they needed it to be light on the surface if they were to be pulled out of the water. He decided it was time he briefed those above on their current situation.

*

Similar thoughts were being aired in the Admiral's cabin of HMS *Indomitable* above. Admiral Colville was chairing a meeting that included Captains Keyes and Young, two senior medical officers and the officer-in-charge of the diving team. The Honourable Stanley Colville, aged just fifty, was young to be a Vice Admiral, but he was an experienced and competent seagoing officer. Nevertheless, the technical aspects of submarine salvage were beyond his knowledge. More than ever he wondered why men would exchange the relative comfort and safety of life in surface ships for the squalor, hardships and physical dangers of life in submarines. Submariners tended to keep themselves to themselves, but the few he had encountered looked unhealthy and continually grubby, suffered from poor teeth and had a tendency to discuss 'shop' in the mess. Apart from some brief service in a corvette and a gunboat, his seagoing career had been in battleships and cruisers, and he enjoyed their magnificent firepower and the formality and efficiency of life on board. He had just been briefed on the news that the stricken submarine had been located by divers, but had news of his own for the officers attending the meeting in his cabin.

'Gentlemen, I have just received a signal from the Admiralty to inform me that there is no prospect of a salvage vessel arriving on scene before tomorrow forenoon. The Foreign Office has reported that the German salvage vessel *Vulkan* is in Kiel and cannot be here before the arrival of the *Ranger*. It rather limits our options.'

The news was received with a low groan from those present, but Captains Keyes and Young were not surprised, it seemed. Colville eyed each of the men present in turn before continuing.

'Although I am conscious of your advice that it would be better to lift the submarine, I assume we are in agreement that time is against us and we have no option but to instruct the submarine survivors to manage their own escape?'

Colville's fellow officers received the news glumly and it was one of the medical officers, Fleet Surgeon Macneish from the Royal Naval Hospital at Haslar, who first responded, in his soft Highland accent.

'I agree, sir. The air in the submarine must be nigh on eighteen hours old and the men will be suffering from *hypercapnia* by now. That's carbon dioxide poisoning. They'll be feeling sick, if not actually vomiting, and very lethargic. Not only will the sickness affect their judgement, and particularly that of those making decisions, but it will be sapping their strength to the extent any physical exertion could even cause cardiac arrest.'

'Captain Young, you are the salvage expert. How long do you think it would take to raise the submarine once your ship is on scene?' Colville asked.

'Given fair weather, sir, perhaps nine hours. Now we have located the wreck, the divers can start rigging the steel lifting hawsers, but none of the floating cranes here at present has the capacity to lift something of five to six hundred tons deadweight. We do have another option, but it may still not work.'

'Well, let's hear it anyway, Captain.'

'We could use the divers to plug the hole in the submarine's hull and then try to pump out the flooded compartment. If we were successful, then the crew could blow their ballast tanks and rise to the surface of their own accord. It would, however, take several hours and unless we obtained a good seal it may fail.'

'What do you think, Keyes? You're the submarine expert here.' Colville gestured to Keyes to take the floor.

'I'm sorry, gentlemen, but I think it too late for that. A submarine needs power to drive itself to the surface, as well as negative buoyancy. We obviously don't know the state of the battery, but it must be pretty low by now. Moreover, there is the crew to consider. It needs some skill and expertise to surface a submarine, even under normal conditions. We don't know who is alive, anything of their mental state, nor what other damage the boat might have suffered. Our medical expert just said it. The men will be seriously ill by now and the longer we leave them down there, the less chance they have to help themselves. I say, tell them to make their own escape as best they can whilst it's still daylight, and we will then make further decisions based on who gets out and who doesn't.' Keyes sat down, deflated.

'And how would they go about escaping the submarine, Keyes?'

'Not without difficulty, sir. It's never been done. As the latest class of submarine in service, this type has been fitted with an "after conning tower" specifically for the purpose of escape, but it has never been proved. In their favour, though, I know they carry the Hall-Rees escape apparatus, designed by my predecessor jointly with Fleet Surgeon Rees.

Some commanding officers elect to land them, but Lieutenant Johnson thought them good for morale.'

'And why in heaven's name would anyone land these sets, Captain?' Macneish asked.

'As I said, nobody has carried out a successful escape so there is no proof the apparatus works. The sets are as bulky as a man so they take up valuable storage space, and it's just another piece of kit that has to be accounted for.' Keyes folded his arms emphatically. Colville wondered if Keyes thought that he had made the point so convincingly that there was no further need for debate. Certainly, nobody seemed keen to follow him in airing his thoughts.

Colville could see that all eyes were on him to make the next move, but felt under no pressure to say anything immediately. Only when he had made up his mind did he break the silence that seemed so awkward to his advisers.

'Thank you, Keyes. At least we know the men have the means to attempt an escape. Dr Macneish, earlier you explained that there is a high probability that the survivors who make it to the surface will suffer from the "bends". Do we have adequate facilities on hand for everyone?'

'I regret not, sir. Of course, I have a good medical team on hand, but we need recompression chambers to be available to re-pressurise the afflicted. We have a couple on hand here, but otherwise we're going to have to send casualties to London and Portsmouth. But it's not just the risk of the 'bends' that worries me. At that depth, the air in the men's lungs will be four times that on the surface. Unless they expel that air, it will expand as they ascend, to the point where their lungs burst. They're unlikely to be aware of this. Our only experience of success in submarine escape so far has been in the shallow waters of a harbour. We would minimise the risks to the men if we could educate them to breathe out all the way to the surface, but it will go against their instinct. They'll think they need to hold their breath. Perhaps Lieutenant Davies's divers could pass a message to warn the men of this.'

Davies did not have the opportunity to respond as the meeting was interrupted by Colville's Flag Lieutenant with a message. Colville read the message, grunted in a meaningless manner and addressed the expectant faces.

‘Gentlemen, it appears that whoever is in charge down there is taking matters into his own hands. I have just been informed that we are to expect three messengers from the deep within the next thirty minutes.’

Chapter 5

'All set then?' Richard asked of the three men assembled in the control room of *D2*.

Under less tragic circumstances Richard might have thought they looked comical. Each man was wearing a dome-shaped helmet from which he peered through a single pane of glass, like a modern-day Cyclops. Beneath the helmet the men were dressed in a watertight smock, tightened at the waist by a canvas belt, and sea boots. This was the Hall-Rees submarine escape breathing apparatus. Inside the helmet the men breathed oxygen through one of the double canisters secured within the smock. As they exhaled, the other canister absorbed their carbon dioxide and released the oxygen for further use. After just a few minutes of wearing the apparatus, the men had started to feel fitter and better prepared for their next ordeal.

Richard had selected Waterfield, Goddard and Leading Stoker Lucas to be the first to make the escape attempt. Lucas was in a bad way and Richard feared for his chances. Both Waterfield and Goddard would do their best to set him up for the ascent, but once through the conning tower hatch it would have to be each man for himself. He had chosen Waterfield because he would be the most capable of giving a technical report on the state of the submarine and Goddard for his strength. Richard was concerned that the external seawater pressure on the upper hatch of the conning tower might cause difficulties in opening it. As well as briefing Waterfield and Goddard on the messages to be given to the commander above, he had written three sets of detailed notes and these were contained in oilskin bags within each man's smock. He had taken into account that neither man might survive the ascent and, gruesomely, their corpses might have to serve as messengers.

Two of the strange figures before him answered his question with a thumbs-up sign as it was not possible to speak with the rebreather mouthpiece in place at the same time. The third figure seemed oblivious to anything. It was time to issue his final instructions.

‘Remember to tap on the lower lid if you cannot open the upper hatch and I’ll let you back in. Otherwise, breathe out all the way. Good luck.’

He patted each man on the shoulder and watched them climb into the conning tower. First to go was Goddard, carrying a crowbar in his belt and half dragging the second figure up with his free hand. The last to go up was Waterfield, shoving the pitiable Lucas up as he climbed. Richard stood at the bottom of the tower, watching their progress up the ladder. He watched Goddard slowly unclip the upper lid and give it a shove. Nothing happened. Goddard then pushed the whole weight of his body against the hatch and it gave slightly. As the seal was broken, a steady trickle of seawater started to flow down the tower.

Richard called up, ‘You might need to flood the tower completely to equalise the pressure before opening the hatch. Don’t forget to breathe out. God be with you.’

He shut and clipped the lower hatch and waited. The wait seemed interminable. The air in the control room was even worse than that of the motor room and each breath took a huge effort. He could feel his heart pounding and the joints of his elbows, shoulders and knees screamed with pain. Notwithstanding the extreme discomfort, he willed himself to wait. If Goddard could not open the upper lid, then without his help, they would be entombed in a cylindrical coffin. Whenever his patience wore out he turned on his flashlight to cast a light over the control room clock. The longer I delay, he told himself, then the more likely it is that the men have escaped. After eight minutes his heart and lungs could take no more. He recognised that if he did not move soon, he would pass out. He now regretted not wearing a rebreather himself, but he had not wanted to waste a set. Slowly and painfully he crawled on his hands and knees up the twenty-degree slope back to the motor room.

*

Stoker Petty Officer Collins and five of the remaining hands on board *D2* were aware of the First Lieutenant’s plans to escape and waited anxiously for news of their colleagues. Collins thought that the other three no longer cared and, in their fleetingly conscious moments, probably merely wished death would take them more quickly. The healthier had been drilled in the use of the rebreather and had rigged guide ropes around the motor room and two flashlights at head height by the after-ends hatch to enable them to find it in darkness. Sadly, the First

Lieutenant had collapsed unconscious immediately after his return from the control room, so Collins had no idea how their three colleagues had fared. Signalman Davies and Collins were tending to him. Altogether the crew had been able to scrape together fourteen Hall-Rees rebreather sets, one more than required. However, Collins knew that three were not working correctly and so the two Siebe Gorman Salvus sets CERA Waterfield had purloined would be lifesavers.

Collins was not just the oldest man in HMS *D2*'s ship's company, but now the senior rate onboard and he was concerned. If the First Lieutenant did not regain consciousness, then his would be the responsibility to organise the escape attempt. Although an experienced submarine senior rating, Collins knew he was not a natural leader. He was an extremely skilled mechanic and had earned the respect of the stokers through his hard work and technical competence. In appearance, he was tall, but thin and gangly with a slight stoop. Almost completely bald and very short-sighted, Collins's benign and diffident nature resembled more that of a school teacher or vicar than a mechanic. Collins's concern was not just for his First Lieutenant; he was also worried about the three unconscious men. He had an idea, but decided to share the decision with the next most senior rating onboard, Leading Telegraphist Clarke.

'Nobby, I've had an idea, but would appreciate your opinion. How long would you reckon it will take us to escape once we get going?'

'What d'you mean, how long?' Clarke replied confusedly.

'I mean, once we open that hatch, how long do you think it will take for us all to get out and to the surface? Ten minutes? Twenty minutes?'

'Oh, right, I get your drift. Well, it depends on where you are in the queue, dunnit? Perhaps five minutes for the lucky ones and mebbe twenty minutes for the poor bastards left to the end. What of it, PO? Are you worried about being left behind?'

'Just hear me out. These rebreather sets should last about thirty to forty minutes, right?'

'Yeah. I believe so.'

'Right, so if we used each of our ten rebreather sets for, say, ten minutes on each unconscious man, including the First Lieutenant here, then that's a hundred minutes' worth between four men. That gives each twenty-five minutes' worth and still leaves a reserve of twenty to thirty minutes left on each set. It might not be enough if there's a delay in us leaving, but it might just save their lives. What do you think?'

Clarke took his time in replying. Collins wondered if it was because he could not understand the logic or was contemplating how far he was prepared to risk his life for the sake of his shipmates.

'Alright, PO, I can see the sense in your idea. But the plan is to wait an hour before we make our escape. Twenty-five minutes isn't going to be enough, is it?'

'I know that, Nobby, but it might be enough to stabilise the sick men's condition and keep them alive. If we need to give them more time on a rebreather, we can limit it to just a few sets that we allocate to the first ones to go through the hatch. If we don't do something, then I'm sure somebody's going to die. Are you up for it? Will you help me rotate the sets?'

Clarke hesitated before nodding, perhaps a little reluctantly, and then going to fetch the first four rebreathers.

*

To the relief of both men, after only five or so minutes of breathing unpoisoned air, Richard recovered consciousness. He congratulated Collins on his marvellous idea. However, he shared Clarke's misgivings that the early use of the emergency breathing apparatus was reducing their margins of safety. Nevertheless, he had little time to dwell on the decision and what actions he might have to take before there was further knocking on the hull. This time it was Clarke who translated the coded message.

'2-S-A-F-E-L-Y-R-E-C-O-V-E-R-E-D-STOP-I-N-S-T-R-U-C-T-I-O-N-S-U-N-D-E-R-S-T-O-O-D-STOP-A-L-L-W-I-L-L-B-E-R-E-A-D-Y-A-T-1-6-0-0-END.'

The relief amongst the men was obvious. Richard checked his watch. They had another forty minutes to wait. He briefly wondered who had not survived the ascent to the surface. He assumed it must have been Lucas but, no matter, two had arrived safely and that showed it could be done. It was now time for him to decide on the running order for the mass escape. He first checked the condition of the three unconscious men. There was no question that they had to be in the first group to go. He pondered leaving them until last, on the grounds that they were least likely to survive, but they would need to be helped out of the submarine, and for that he needed others to help. He selected Stoker Scott, a huge Irishman, to help him evacuate these men. That left just five men and he arranged for them to draw lots for the first places. To his satisfaction, Collins and Clarke had decided to leave last in view of their relative seniority.

With ten minutes to go, the men prepared to don their escape gear, the first three men due to go receiving the rebreathers with the shortest remaining life. Richard and Scott dressed two of the unconscious men in the experimental Siebe Gorman Salvus sets. Waterfield had explained that these sets provided fresh oxygen continuously, whereas the Hall-Rees apparatus relied on the wearer to draw the fresh oxygen with his own lungs. With five minutes to go, Richard flooded the empty stern torpedo tube and the men took up their positions ready for the escape. He addressed them for the final time.

'Remember that once we start flooding the compartment it will be more difficult to move around and more than likely it will be dark. Use the guide ropes to avoid getting lost and don't panic. You all have more than enough reserves of oxygen, so take your time in making your escape. There is no need to rush. Once you are through the hatch, you will find divers on hand to direct you to the guide ropes. Take your time to head for the surface and breathe out all the way. The calmer you do this, the better shape you will be in when you arrive. Once you reach the surface, there will be plenty of help on hand to retrieve you from the water, so just enjoy the ride. And think of your fourteen days' survivors' leave.' The men chuckled at the thought.

At precisely four o'clock they all heard two successive loud underwater explosions, the signal Richard had requested in his message to the surface commander to be the indication that all was ready and Richard's instructions implemented. He took one last look around the anxious faces in the motor room.

'Right then. Everybody ready to go? Helmets on. God speed to you all. Chief, start flooding the compartment.'

Richard left them to make their final preparations and headed for the after torpedo compartment with Scott. He operated the lever to open the bow cap of the stern torpedo tube and waited for the indicator to show that it had opened correctly. He and Scott then cracked open the rear door of the flooded tube. Cold seawater immediately started to seep into the after torpedo compartment, too. Within a few seconds the two men had the door completely open and the green water gushed into the compartment in an angry torrent. We've crossed the Rubicon now, Richard thought. We're beyond the point of no return. We'll never be able to shut the door to the tube against the pressure of this gushing waterfall.

Richard and Scott returned to the motor room and Richard indicated to the two men standing by the hatch to unclip it. A series of steady drips of water started to leak into the compartment but, as Richard had suspected, the external sea pressure bearing down on the hatch was too great to allow the men to lift it. They would have to wait for the flooding seawater to raise the pressure within the compartment sufficiently to equalise it with that outside.

Very soon Richard detected the peculiar smell of chlorine gas being given off by the batteries and he realised it was time he donned his own escape gear. It was a relief to be breathing clean air again, but the helmet limited his visibility and he could no longer speak to his men. The earlier eerie silence on board was now totally shattered by the steady roar of the incoming water. The water level was already above the men's knees and, on his signal, a pair of the survivors helped him and Scott drag two of the unconscious men back to the after torpedo compartment.

They had just completed the task when the lights failed, plunging them into almost complete darkness. Looking forward, Richard could see the distant glow of the two flashlights secured beneath the after-ends hatch and he switched on his own, before wedging it between two pipes so that it illuminated the open torpedo tube. He had left Collins to supervise the escape from the motor room and there was no more he could do for his men right now. His priority was to rescue the unconscious.

By now the water had already risen to above waist height so he and Scott tethered their charges to avoid them floating away. A shaft of bright light shone through the torpedo tube and Richard peered as best he could back up the tube. Scott steadied him against the inflow of water and then Richard saw that which he was seeking. What appeared to be a dark underwater snake was sinewing down the tube. He reached up and grabbed it. Pulling it down into the compartment, he nodded to Scott to prepare the first escapee. The line was thick manila cord that the divers had sent down as a rescue line for the unconscious, and Richard was grateful that some proactive soul had had the sense to prepare a loop in the line, to spare him having to tie a bowline knot. His hands were already starting to become numb through the cold. Gently, he and Scott untethered the first of the unconscious men and fitted the loop of the rope beneath his armpits. The water level had risen to chest height so they had little difficulty in floating him towards the tube opening. Richard yanked the line with three sharp tugs and slowly the slack was taken up before the patient was hauled up through the tube by unseen hands.

After a few long minutes, another line was sent down the tube and somebody rapped on the hull to indicate they were ready to take the next man. By now both Richard and Scott were completely underwater and Richard's flashlight had shorted. Except for the loom of the light outside, the compartment was in darkness. It reminded Richard of one of those cloudy days at his home in Lancashire, when the sun briefly broke through the clouds to cast a wide beam of light over the Irish Sea.

The absence of proper illumination made it very difficult for him to secure the lifeline to the second unconscious man. He started to fear that he and Scott may have left it too late to save themselves. It was too dark to see his watch, but he estimated that it perhaps took a further three vital minutes before he had his second charge ready to be hauled through the tube to safety. As soon as he had positioned the man inside the tube, he pushed Scott towards the motor room and signalled to the divers to start hauling away. As the unfortunate sailor was dragged upwards, Richard pondered making his own escape through the torpedo tube, too, but he quickly dismissed the temptation. The bulkiness of his Hall-Rees smock made it impossible to pass through the eighteen-inch, narrow bore of the tube, and in any case he had a duty to ensure all the men had made their escape through the after-ends hatch. It was only then that he realised his mistake. He had not thought to rig a guide rope between the torpedo tube and motor room. He and Scott now had to find their way forward in complete darkness.

Richard was suddenly grateful for his submarine experience. As part of the training to qualify as a submariner, every member of the crew, no matter how junior or senior, was required to learn every system on board and literally know his way round each compartment blindfolded. Scott should be able to find his way, he thought. He felt with his left hand for the port torpedo rack and, keeping contact with it, he carefully paced his way down the slope forward. As his hand came into contact with the propeller blades of a torpedo, he knew he was only about six feet from the bulkhead separating the after torpedo compartment from the motor room. Two paces later he stumbled upon Scott who, notwithstanding his training, must have become disorientated in the corner of the compartment. Guiding Scott with a none-too-gentle shove, Richard continued his passage by feel alone and soon found the open bulkhead door. The two men ducked through the doorway and spotted with relief one of the flashlights still shining by the entrance to the now-open after-ends hatch. It was too dark to signal to Scott, so Richard just grabbed him by the shoulder and steered him towards the hatch. Scott needed no second invitation and clambered upwards and through the hatch on his way to safety.

Richard delayed his own escape for a minute whilst he tried to see if the compartment was clear. Despite his best efforts, even with the faint glimmer of the flashlight, it was too dark to see anything but the hatch. He could only assume that everyone had made it out, and if they had not, then there was little he could do. He felt sadness at abandoning *D2*. She had been a good boat and, under Johnson's excellent leadership, she had had a first class ship's company. Richard just hoped that she could be salvaged.

It was now his turn to escape, but he first appealed to the Almighty to guide him to the surface safely. He regretted that he had left his Bible forward. It had been given to him by his mother and the flyleaf included a personal inscription by Cardinal Bourne, but this was no time for regrets. He climbed through the hatch and was met by the bright beams of two underwater flashlights carried by divers. The nearest grabbed him and pointed at the knotted rope leading to the surface. The diver shouted something at him, but Richard could not distinguish the words. He just responded by giving a thumbs-up signal and, using the rope as his guide, started swimming for the surface using his legs only. Rising through the water, he remembered to breathe out and disciplined himself to slow his upward movement to the speed of the bubbles he was exhaling. It was such an unnatural thing to do, to continue to blow out as he floated upwards, and he wondered how long he could keep doing so before the overwhelming urge to breathe in again overtook him.

After an eternity he broke through the surface. He merely had time to spot the domes of two other people in the sea before he found himself face down in the water. Try as he might, he could not right himself, either to float on his back or to tread water upright. The buoyancy of the dome had a will of its own. Knowing help was at hand, he gave in and resigned himself to the view of the nothingness below. Sure enough, within a few minutes, he felt rough, but nonetheless welcome, hands grabbing him and hauling him into a whaler. Somebody removed the dome from his head and pulled out the rubber mouthpiece to allow him his first taste of the cold, but sweet, early evening air. Richard tried to help, but his body would not respond. He was completely helpless, like a newborn baby. Suddenly, and in his eyes unaccountably, he started sobbing uncontrollably. He saw the seamen in the boat exchange significant looks, but he couldn't control his emotions. What he did not realise then was that the men understood. They were no longer embarrassed by such a reaction. Of the nine men they and their colleagues had rescued alive, most had expressed a similar reaction.

Gradually, Richard regained his composure, but he now faced another problem. The adrenalin in his body had started to subside and he felt a very urgent need to void his bowels.

Chapter 6

April 1912

'Lizzy, that was Father on the telephone. He says he's not coming up to Liverpool tonight, after all. Apparently he's had a short notice invitation to go to Halifax, Nova Scotia.'

'Why on earth would he go there, Charles?' Elizabeth Miller enquired of her elder brother.

'He was quite excited about it. He's had a telegram from Admiral Kingsmill inviting him to address the midshipmen at their new naval college. Father is then to meet up with some of the new Canadian Navy officers and thinks it might lead to a few contracts for our yard.'

'And isn't the yard busy enough with the Admiralty contracts for the C-class cruisers?'

'Possibly, but that won't last for ever. I think Father has the right idea. We should spread our wings a little. After all, we did build the *Melbourne* for the Australians. If Father can make the right contacts early on, who knows where it might end, as far as the Dominions are concerned?'

'I see. So when is he leaving?'

'Thursday. From Southampton. Thomas Andrews was able to fix him a berth on the White Star's new liner, the *Titanic*.'

'That was fortunate. He and Andrews will no doubt have a most agreeable time. I just hope he has enough laundry and suits. It might be a long trip. And Andrews had better not give Father any wild ideas about converting the yard to build liners next. If there's going to be a war with Germany, then we ought to stick with warships.'

'You're always going on about a coming war, Lizzy. You pay too much regard to Uncle William.'

'You would do well to listen to him, too, dear brother. Having been our naval attaché in Berlin for many years, Uncle William should know more of Germany's intentions than anyonc. And I can tell you that his time at the Admiralty has done nothing to assuage his fears. You ask Dick. He'll back me up.'

Charles drew a watch from the pocket of his tweed waistcoat before stoking the fire of the drawing room. Although it was a fine spring day in April, the weather in Crosby, near Liverpool, was still cool. When he removed his round, thick-lensed spectacles, he was a handsome man, with an open and cheerful disposition. His fair hair and blue eyes were inherited from his late mother. His sister Elizabeth shared both his blue eyes and good looks, but she had long, auburn hair.

'Talking of Dick, sis, he and Peter should be here anytime. Is he still using a stick?'

'I believe so. He's still suffering some paralysis down one side after his dreadful accident, but don't mention it. He's very sensitive about it.'

'Don't worry. I'll be tactful. Who's this girl he's bringing?'

'Charles, you never listen. I told you before. It is Peter that is bringing a guest. Her name is Alice Robson. She's a school teacher on the Marton estate.' Marton Hall was the Lancashire home of the Miller cousins.

'So you did. Sorry, forgot. Hark, I think I hear them now.' The sound of wheels crunching the gravel drive could be heard from without.

A few minutes later the butler showed Elizabeth and Charles's three guests for lunch into the drawing room. It was a comfortable room, but a little cluttered, with models of ships and a confusion of maritime prints and seascapes on the walls. Peter and Richard kissed and embraced their cousin Elizabeth before shaking hands with Charles. Peter introduced his companion.

'Lizzy, Charles, may I introduce Miss Alice Robson?'

Elizabeth was surprised by Alice's height of five feet ten inches, but noted critically the slim build, short blonde hair and blue eyes. Alice's unusual height seemed a little ungainly, but Elizabeth had to admit to herself that men would find her attractive.

*

After lunch Elizabeth and Alice drank coffee in the drawing room whilst the men took their port in the dining room. Over lunch Elizabeth had confessed to herself that she found Alice more interesting than she had expected. The large drawing room was furnished with three sofas and the two women sat together on one, but separated by a mahogany tea table.

'You mentioned earlier that you speak German and have a taste for the literature, Alice. Did I hear correctly that you went to university?'

'That's right. I took a Classical Tripos at Girton College, Cambridge.'

'I'm impressed. I have no doubt you graduated with honours. Do you speak any other languages?'

'Yes. I suppose I speak French fairly well. Do you have a facility for languages, Elizabeth?'

'No, not really, although my French is tolerable and I have a smattering of Persian.'

'Persian? Now that is unusual. How so?'

'My Grandmama is Persian. Grandpapa ran a shipping business in India and met her there. I only know enough to say a few polite phrases to Grandmama, but Peter speaks it well and I believe his younger brother, Paul, is progressing well with it, too, at Grandmama's knee.'

'So that explains it,' Alice exclaimed. 'Now I understand why Peter is to be sent to Tehran. He never mentioned his exotic heritage, other than that his mother is Swiss.'

'My cousins can be a taciturn lot. They're not so bad, I suppose, but I would have liked one female cousin. I wish I could have gone to university, too. I'm sure you enjoyed the experience?'

'Very much so, but as a woman one had to learn to hide one's intellect under a bushel. It wasn't all plain sailing. What would you have studied, Elizabeth? Had you had the chance?'

'Engineering, like a shot, but alas, it is considered a subject for which only men are deemed to have the mental capacity.'

Alice raised both her hands with pleasure. 'Elizabeth, you are a woman of my way of thinking. My God, you wouldn't have believed the frustration we felt in listening to the platitudes and patronising of male lecturers who thought we should have remained at home to tend the hearth. But I suppose women must be patient and learn to accept their lot for now.'

'Now there we must disagree, Alice. I do not see why we should. Have you not heard of the activities of the Women's Social and Political Union? I am proud to be a member.'

'Why, naturally! Indeed, I have attended their rallies and even met with Mrs Pankhurst and her daughter, Christabel.'

'You have met Christabel?'

‘Indeed. It was one summer when I was down in London. I helped with some leafleting and was even offered a permanent role, but I had to return to my studies.’

‘And are you still in contact with Christabel or the WSPU?’ Elizabeth suddenly felt a pang of potential jealousy.

‘No. I read that Christabel has disappeared and her poor mother is back in prison. It makes me so angry. Oh, I’m sorry. That was clumsy of me.’ Alice began to mop up the coffee she had spilt on the table-cloth.

‘Don’t worry. The servants will fix it. I’m more interested in your leanings towards the WSPU. Have you not thought of becoming a member?’

‘I have. I did some more leafleting for them in Manchester last year and am tempted to start attending some meetings in Preston. But I have to be careful. I mustn’t lose my place at the school.’

‘You shouldn’t have to worry about that. But, of course, you probably do. How silly of me. I do so hate this oppression the men seem to relish in exerting. And, talking of the men, I fear they are about to rejoin us. Listen. I might have an idea for a way you could help our cause. Would it surprise you to know that I was with Christabel only a couple of weeks ago? May I call you to discuss it?’

‘Good Lord. You know where Christabel is hiding? I’m not sure how I could help, but I would be pleased to do what I can.’

Charles and his two male cousins entered. Charles, it seemed to Elizabeth, had imbibed too much wine and port.

‘You two seem to be cosy,’ he remarked. ‘I hope, Lizzy, you’ve not been boring Miss Robson with your suffragette nonsense. I do apologise, Miss Robson. Our Lizzy’s a bit of a socialist.’

‘Charles, that is unfair and quite obtuse. Socialism and women’s suffrage are completely different issues. We only support the Labour candidates who speak out for votes for women. Now, come away from the fire. You’re hogging all the heat.’

‘I detect a sudden chill in the air, dear cousins.’ Charles turned to Peter and Richard. ‘That’s the trouble with the suffragettes. They want to boss their men-folk about in their own home. We need some more coal. Bend your elbow, Peter, and ring for a servant, old boy.’

‘Charles, come sit down. You know very well that there’s very little coal left. It’s over a month since the miners went on strike. There are plenty of logs.’ Elizabeth turned to Richard and smiled sweetly at him.

‘Dick, dear. Would you mind topping up the fire? Oh. Is that a carriage I hear?’

The doorbell rang in the distance and a few minutes later the butler entered.

‘Excuse me, Mr Charles. There are two inspectors in the hall from the Lancashire Constabulary and desiring to speak with Miss Elizabeth.’

‘Hawkins,’ Elizabeth cut in. ‘If the two policemen wish to speak to me, then kindly address me and not my brother. Show them in.’

Hawkins coloured and bowed deferentially. ‘Very well, miss.’ After he retired from the room Peter spoke.

‘What on earth do the police want with you, Lizzy?’

‘Patience, Peter. Wait a couple of minutes and we will find out.’ Elizabeth fought hard to control her panic. It was a good question. What did they want?

The butler returned with the two policemen. One wore a uniform, but the other was in plain clothes. The uniformed officer nodded to Charles.

‘Good afternoon, Mr Charles. Is your father in?’

Lizzy cut off her brother. ‘I understood, Inspector, that it was with me that you wished to converse. To whom am I speaking?’

‘Right enough, miss, if you’re Miss Elizabeth Miller. I’m Inspector Rimmer and this ’ere is Inspector Mason.’ The plain-clothes officer nodded. ‘Is your father not in?’

‘He is in London. How may I assist you?’

‘Well, it’s a bit delicate, like.’ He looked at the other luncheon guests meaningfully. ‘We were wonderin’ if you might accompany us down the station. We’ve a carriage outside, miss.’

‘Certainly not, Inspector,’ Richard interrupted. ‘If you wish to speak with my cousin privately, then we can adjourn to the orangery. Come, Lizzy.’

Elizabeth was taken aback at Richard’s masterful approach. Rimmer looked to Mason for affirmation before both officers stepped aside to allow Elizabeth and Richard to lead them to the orangery. Richard limped over to a rattan table and, after guiding his cousin to a cushioned bench, he pulled up two chairs for the policemen.

'I presume you have no objection to me staying, Inspectors?' The policemen shook their heads. 'Very well. I shall stand over here and leave you to your discourse.'

For the first time Mason spoke. Unlike his colleague, he did not have a local accent and appeared to hail from London. Elizabeth took an instant dislike to him and wondered why. Perhaps it was his dress, she thought. He looked rather ridiculous, more like a fairground showman than how she perceived a detective should look. He was only just taller than her, with a pot belly. He wore a brown hounds-tooth suit, yellow waistcoat and matching bow tie. Rimmer opened his notebook and readied his pen to take notes.

'For the record, miss, you are Miss Elizabeth Frances Roxanna Miller? And your age, miss?'

'Goodness, Inspector. You should know better than to ask that of a lady. You may say that I am over the age of twenty-one, but have not yet reached my majority.'

'That'll do,' Mason growled. 'And I understand you to be a member of the suffragist movement, the WSPU. Is that right?'

'My word! How do you come to understand that?'

'It's our duty to keep an eye on certain political groups and we found your name on a subscription list in the offices in Clement's Inn. I take it that you do not deny the fact, miss?'

'I see. And do you make it your duty to break into the offices of the Reform Club to ascertain its membership, too?'

'Steady, miss,' Rimmer intervened. 'We're only doin' our duty.'

'Indeed, Inspector. In the same way that your Metropolitan Police see it as their duty to punch and kick defenceless women protesting about inequality in our political system.' Elizabeth's neck began to flush as her temper rose.

'No. I will not deny being a member of the WSPU, but tell me, gentlemen, just when was the Act passed banning the WSPU and its members?' Elizabeth glared at the two policemen and noted with satisfaction the evident embarrassment of Rimmer. His colleague, however, seemed unperturbed and continued his questioning calmly.

'Tell me, Miss Miller, for the record, just where were you over the weekend of the second of March this year?'

Elizabeth noted Richard's interest quicken, but she concentrated on remaining calm and not betraying any reaction. She fought for time.

'Oh, dear. Am I to find that I am suspected of being a master criminal and you are questioning my alibi? As far as I recall, I was not involved in some infamous jewel heist over that weekend. Nor do I remember assassinating any great statesman. But let me consult my diary.'

She took her time in rummaging through her commodious handbag. *I must remain calm. There is surely nothing to connect me with the events of that weekend.*

'Ah, here it is,' she announced triumphantly. 'Now let me see.' She made great play of skimming the pages of her diary. At the same time she thought frantically. How could she account for her movements? She had stayed with Uncle William and Aunt Johanna that night, but they clearly could not vouch for her movements that day.

'Wait a minute, Lizzy,' Richard interjected. 'Do you not remember? We were sailing on the Solent that day. It was Horace Braithwaite's birthday and we took him over to Cowes for lunch. We were a bit late in getting back and you nearly missed your train back to London. You stayed overnight with *Mutti* and Papa. You must remember.'

Elizabeth listened with incredulity. Dick had just lied for her. Prim Dick, who thought it a mortal sin to tell even the tiniest of white lies. Fighting hard to control her relief, her mind raced to think of something to give effect to the lie.

'Of course. Here it is. I was visiting my Aunt Kate at Hindhead and went on down to Portsmouth the following day. Horace was a little tight as I recall, but we had a fabulous day. There, Inspector. I am sorry to disappoint you, or was the great jewel heist on the south coast that weekend?'

'You will forgive me if I check the diary entry myself, miss?'

'Enough,' Richard said, loudly and indignantly. 'This is intolerable. I have just told you that my cousin was with me that Saturday. Do you doubt the word of a lady or even my own? Am I suspected of being an accessory to whatever monstrous crime you believe Miss Miller has committed? Put your cards on the table, man. Of what is my cousin accused?'

Mason looked intently at Richard for several seconds before replying. 'I make no accusations, sir. I am merely enquiring into the truth. You will own that your cousin has quite distinctive hair colouring. A woman with hair of that description, in the company of two others, was reported as taking part in criminal damage in Oxford Street that day, namely the breaking of shop windows. One of them was arrested and we believe another was Miss Christabel Pankhurst. We have witnesses.'

'And no doubt the Metropolitan Police have nothing better to do than to interrogate every good-looking red-head in the country. It's preposterous. I only wish your father was here right now, Lizzy. As a sitting magistrate he would be very interested in this improper use of police time. Gentlemen, you have overstayed your welcome. Either charge my cousin with whatever nefarious act of which you suspect her or withdraw. If you do intend to press charges, then I shall insist on the family solicitor being present.'

Rimmer nudged Mason, but Mason continued to stare at Richard coldly. At the second nudge he dropped his eyes and turned to Elizabeth. 'Very well, miss. I do not wish to impugn your cousin's honour. If he states you were with him in Portsmouth that day, then there is no more to be done. Thank you for your time. Good day. We'll see ourselves out.'

After the policemen had left the orangery, both Richard and Elizabeth stood in silence listening out for sounds of the carriage departing. On hearing the wheels begin to churn up the gravel, they both exhaled loudly. Elizabeth rushed up to Richard and hugged him tightly.

'Dick, you were magnificent. You are truly my hero.'

She took hold of both sides of his head and kissed him several times. 'Thank you. Thank you,' she said.

Richard did not move or respond to her affection. He seemed stunned. Elizabeth paid no attention. Hugging him once more, she thought what a real man he had proved to be.

Chapter 7

October 1912

The sea was not particularly rough today, but Elizabeth Miller could tell that her travelling companions were already beginning to feel a little queasy. As the daughter of a shipyard owner, Elizabeth had often accompanied her late father on trials of the vessels the yard had built. Moreover, she had frequently made this crossing from Folkestone to Boulogne on her visits to Christabel Pankhurst in Paris. This was the first time she had made the crossing in such distinguished company.

The steam-driven packet steamer *Onward* suddenly lurched as she met a wave on her starboard bow and Elizabeth almost lost the contents of her teacup. It was the last straw for George Lansbury, Labour Member of Parliament for Bow and Bromley. He excused himself from the ladies and headed swiftly for the nearby gentlemen's bathroom. Elizabeth regarded her female travelling companion surreptitiously over her tea and with silent awe, tinged with concern. She noted the sallow skin, the beginnings of crow's feet around the eyes and the grey hair peeping from beneath her hat. It was only natural after so much time in prison and invariably on hunger strike, but the lady looked older than her years. Indeed, her companion had only a few months ago been released from yet another spell in Holloway, but without completing the nine-month sentence, and all for throwing a rock at the Prime Minister's house.

'Is the crossing always quite so uncomfortable, Lizzy?'

'I hesitate to state that it is often much worse. It is the vessel's speed that is causing the disturbance and not the weather. We must be travelling at twenty knots, if not a little more.'

'Then I am grateful we are not enduring a winter gale. You, of course, are an *habituée* of this route, Lizzy, and a seasoned sailor after all your visits to my daughter this past eighteen months.'

'I suppose I have been fortunate to have become accustomed to the motion. Even poor Lord Nelson suffered continually through the *mal de mer.*'

‘And let us not forget, Lizzy, you come from seafaring stock. Did you ever accompany your father at sea?’

‘Often.’ Elizabeth reflected on happier days, but still the memories were rather raw.

‘I was sorry to hear of the loss of your father, Lizzy. It was such a tragic waste of life. I don’t know how God could have let such a thing happen to all those innocent people. But forgive me for my insensitivity in raising it.’

‘Ever since the *Titanic* went down I’ve not been sure there is a God.’ After a brief pause, Elizabeth went on. ‘Let us not dwell on such morbid topics. I have the Cause to sustain me. Is there anything I can fetch for you, Mrs Pankhurst?’

Emmeline Pankhurst reached across and laid a hand on Elizabeth’s arm. ‘Bless you, child. I confess to feeling a little peaky, but no, thank you.’ After a quick survey of the other guests in the saloon, she went on. ‘Perhaps, however, we might take a turn around the promenade deck. I rather think that some fresh air might be advantageous.’

‘But what of Mr Lansbury?’

‘I have no doubt that he will have no difficulty in finding us. Come, dear.’

The two ladies linked arms and commenced a slow tour of the *Outward*’s covered promenade deck. Elizabeth was pleased to see Emmeline’s cheeks recover some of their colour.

‘Do you know much of Mr Lansbury?’ Emmeline asked.

‘But, of course. He is a great supporter of our cause. Indeed, I know he, too, has been imprisoned many times, and similarly endured the barbarism of force-feeding.’

‘It is indeed a barbaric practice, Lizzy. I trust you will never experience it. You are pinned down by four brutes whilst a so-called doctor forces a four-foot length of tube down your throat. You vomit, of course, all over your face, hair and body, but they carry on regardless, until every last drop of the bottle is in your stomach. But do you know the worst of it, Lizzy?’

‘No, I certainly do not. I cannot imagine the horror.’

‘Horror is the right word, child. At night I am haunted by the memory of the screams as the doctor passes from one cell to the other.’ Emmeline turned away and looked out to sea vacantly. Elizabeth decided it best not to interrupt whatever dreadful scenes her mind was re-enacting.

Emmeline gripped one of Elizabeth's hands tightly. 'It's the contempt, Lizzy. At the end of the dreadful process the doctor slaps one on the face. How can a man who has taken the Hippocratic Oath do that?'

'Because all men are pigs.' Elizabeth spat out the words with venom.

'No, Lizzy. Don't think that way. There are many men who support our cause. Let's not forget that. I am hoping that Mr Lansbury is going to put that to the test. Tell me, Lizzy, what do you think of the NUWSS's pact with the Labour Party?'

Elizabeth was unsure how to answer and pondered the question for a moment. Following the defeat of the Conciliation Bill earlier in the year, the National Union of Women Suffrage Societies, had formed a pact with the Labour Party to support their candidates when standing against anti-suffrage Liberal candidates. Elizabeth knew their objective was to unseat these Liberals by splitting the anti-Conservative vote and thereby let in the Conservative candidates. She and Christabel had disagreed with the strategy and had tried to disrupt the alliance. The NUWSS was committed to suffrage for women in the long term by peaceful and democratic means, but Elizabeth could not wait that long. It was one of the reasons she had joined the WSPU after it had split from the group in 1903 to promote more militant activity. She knew that Christabel and Emmeline did not always see eye to eye on strategy so she decided to be guarded in her response.

'That is a deep question, Mrs Pankhurst. I suppose that, on the face of it, I consider it a good strategy. However, I am no socialist and I doubt the sincerity of the Labour Party towards giving us the vote. If it was really serious, then it could refuse to support some of the Liberal government's bills. Such Members of Parliament as Mr Lansbury and Mr Hardie are too thin on the ground.'

'Lizzy, you confirm my good opinion of your intelligence. You are quite right. The Labour Party is far too timid. The Party is too weak and their members sit alongside the Liberals like tame pussy cats. MacDonald regards all acts of militancy as "tomfoolery". We need to puncture that complacency and show both the Labour and Liberal parties that women's suffrage has the support of the working man. If all goes well on this trip, Mr Lansbury is going to help us do just that.'

Chapter 8

November 1912

As usual, after leaving harbour and supervising the trim dive these days, the captain was asleep in the bunk below. Richard no longer minded, but did regret the fact had been noticed by the ship's company of HMS *B3*. He was finding it increasingly difficult to be loyal to his commanding officer, but was not sure what to do about it. As Mullan's second-in-command it was Richard's duty to back his captain to the hilt, but it was becoming increasingly clear that morale on board was quickly approaching a dangerously low ebb.

After the loss of *D2*, Richard had been pleased to enjoy nearly six weeks of leave. Two weeks of this had been the normal survivors' leave following any shipwreck, but Richard had suffered a 'bend' during the ascent to the surface and this had partially paralysed his left side. Even today, eight months later, he still walked with a slight limp and sometimes struggled with the grip of his left hand, but he had been passed fit for a return to duty at sea. He had half hoped to be appointed to a command of his own, but Keyes had put him right on that score. He remembered every word of the conversation.

'You did a fine job, Miller, in bringing the majority of your men to the surface safely. It was a nightmarish scenario and you demonstrated considerable coolness under pressure and outstanding leadership. The survivors have much for which to thank you. Such qualities will stand you well in command.'

These last words had caused Richard to dare to hope. Was he to be given a command after all? It was perhaps a little early to have such ambitions but, whilst he could not pretend to a command of a modern boat such as another of the D-class, might he be appointed to one of the C-class? After all, when they had last discussed Richard's performance, Johnson had informed him that, after some initial reservations, he now thought Richard to be shaping up well for a command. Johnson had stated that he fully intended informing Keyes of this before being relieved of his command.

However, Keyes had continued, 'I'll be frank with you, Miller. After what you have been through, it is the least I can offer. When I last spoke to Johnson, in the spring, he spoke well of you, but he did express a doubt about your potential to command your own submarine. He wasn't satisfied you could get your men on your side. I'm struggling to reconcile that opinion of you with those I have heard from the men we rescued from *D2*. Obviously, had Johnson lived, I could have discussed it with him.'

Richard had felt it incumbent on him to say something. 'I very much respected Lieutenant Johnson's opinion, sir.'

'Yes, he was a damned fine officer and will be a great lost to the Service.' Keyes looked away and drummed the fingers of his right hand on his knee. 'Anyway, what are we going to do with you now, Miller? I had thought of offering you an appointment on my staff. I won't deny that your experience of an escape from the deep would come in very handy for developing our new submarine designs. But, in the circumstances, we need to get you back to sea. Back on the horse, as it were. The First Lieutenant of *B3* has requested a return to surface ships so I can kill two birds with one stone. I want you to take his place. I know it might appear as a step backwards after a D-boat, but give it six months and if you impress your new captain, then I will be only too pleased to offer you a command. We sure as hell need some new talent.'

So it was that Richard now found himself heading down the Dover Straits on the bridge of *B3*, a ten-year-old, petrol-driven coastal submarine, commanded by one Lieutenant Thomas Mullan, CGM.

Richard noted that the wind was freshening and the sea state increasing. He knew he ought to tell the captain, but he also recognised from experience that it would not be easy to rouse Mullan for another hour or so. Instead, he sent word below to ditch all gash over the side now. Before long it would not be safe to do so, or maybe Mullan would choose to dive the submarine. The weather at fifty feet would be much calmer.

Fifteen minutes later, the Coxswain, Petty Officer Goddard, reported all gash ditched and requested permission to come to the bridge. That was one comfort, Richard thought. Goddard and Stoker Scott had both been transferred to *B3*, too.

Goddard appeared on the bridge and looked back at the receding view of the white cliffs of Dover astern and to starboard. 'I don't think I will ever tire of that view, sir. There's nowhere like it in the world.'

'Not quite true, Coxswain. It has its mirror on the Alabaster Coast. They are part of the same geological formation.'

'I'm sorry, sir. I don't catch your drift.'

'The French have something similar that they call the Alabaster Coast, over between Dieppe and Le Havre.'

'Well, I never knew that. I can't say the same about this rusty bucket, though. I mean tiring of it, sir.'

'Now it's my turn to fail to catch your drift, Coxswain.'

'Here, Mac. Pass me the glasses and I'll do your trick on the bridge for a bit. You go down below and get yourself a mug of *char*. Mind you don't forget to send two up here.' The bridge lookout seemed enthusiastic about the suggestion. After he had descended the ladder of the conning tower, Goddard expanded on his thoughts.

'I thought the CO's number was up this morning, sir.'

'Really, Coxswain, you are quite enigmatic this afternoon. Perhaps you had better explain.'

'I think Captain Brandt could smell the drink on the CO's breath before we sailed. I was sure the CO would cop it.'

Captain Brandt, until the month before, one of Commodore Keyes's assistants and responsible for the Third Submarine Flotilla, of which *B3* was a member, had bid farewell to *B3* as she set sail for exercises off Portsmouth and Portland before returning to her home port in Gosport.

'Don't be impertinent, Goddard. Many officers and men of the submarine service like to take a drink when ashore. We even issue them with rum daily at sea. Provided a man is fit to do his duty, it is not our concern to investigate his morals.'

'I don't mean to be impertinent, sir, but you seem to have changed your tune since our days together in *D2*. You were well known as a God-fearing teetotaller.'

'It is of no concern to you, Coxswain, but I still love my God and I remain teetotal. I have just learned to keep it to myself and to afford others the same privacy.'

'It's still not right, though, sir.'

'And what do you mean now, 'swain?'

'The captain's drinking. He's down in the wardroom now, snoring like a pig. And the ship's company have noticed that it's become a habit.'

'Really, Goddard. You are pushing your …'

'And that's not all, sir. It's my duty to tell you that if you're not careful, you're going to land yourself with a full-blown mutiny.'

Suddenly, Richard was all ears. 'What do you mean by that?'

'There's resentment down below, sir, and soon enough it's going to explode. ERA Thompson has taken to storing his tot and drinking it at sea. The pressure of keeping this boat going is telling on him. Stoker Scott tells me that he's hardly coherent at times. And the other senior rates resent the captain's relationship with the TI. Evans returned on board barely five minutes before the captain this morning, drunk as a lord.'

Petty Officer Evans was the senior torpedoman on board. Mullan had once been a Torpedo Instructor, too, and it was as coxswain of a torpedo boat during the Boer War in 1902, he had displayed an act of conspicuous gallantry that had led to his immediate promotion to Lieutenant.

'You know very well that I saw Evans come on board myself this morning and I intend raising it with the CO.'

'But with respect, sir, we've been here before. You know I've tried to have Evans disciplined for drunkenness many times, but the captain always waives the proceedings. His precious torpedomen can do no wrong.'

'Petty Officer Goddard, you, of all people, given your responsibility for maintaining discipline on board, have no business saying such things. It's insubordination. I will hear no more of it. Please go below and send McIntyre back up to complete his watch as lookout.'

Before Goddard could comply, the control room called the bridge. 'Bridge, control room. Captain coming to the bridge.' It was not necessary for the captain to ask permission to visit his own bridge, but the message both warned the Officer of thc Watch that the captain was on his way up and ensured that lookouts, when relieved of their watch, did not attempt to leave the bridge at the same time.

‘Here we go then. Now the fun starts,’ Goddard muttered, but loud enough for Richard to hear.

Despite his age of forty-two and a heavy drinking bout the night before, Mullan reached the bridge in remarkably good time. With his long, greying beard, closely-cropped grey hair and piercing blue eyes he might have been mistaken as of Nordic extraction. Instead he had been born and bred in Belfast of a staunchly Protestant, pro-Ulster family. Within seconds of his arrival on the bridge his experienced eye took in the submarine’s position and course, the sea state and the coming weather.

He then turned to Goddard, broke wind loudly and asked scathingly, ‘What the fuck are youse doing up here, Goddard? Where’s the proper lookout? Or is this some *D2* survivors’ reunion? No doubt you’ve been bleating about how fucking hard done by you are, not to be in a modern submarine with all the comforts you *carlin’* demand. Fuck off down below where you belong, ye *hallion.*’

Long ago Richard had stopped being shocked at the way Mullan spoke to the most senior rate on board. He stiffened himself for the onslaught he knew was coming his way. Goddard went below without uttering a word, or tellingly, the traditional response of, *‘Aye aye, sir.’*

‘The wind’s up and the weather’s deteriorating. Why didn’t you report it, you papist bastard?’

‘You were asleep, sir, and I didn’t like to disturb you,’ Richard lied and silently prayed. *Hail Mary, full of grace. Pray for us sinners. Amen.*

‘You thought I was asleep? Is that some kind of dig at me, Miller? It’s no fucking excuse. What do my standing orders say about changes in the weather, you *Taig*?’

‘To report the fact to you immediately, sir.’

‘So, knowing this, you still failed to obey my orders. That’s fucking wilful disobedience, sonny. You’re not fit to be my second-in command, let alone to receive my recommendation for a command of your own. I ought to land you. Now, skitter to windward. I need to have a dump.’

Like Richard, Mullan chose not to use the ‘head’ or WC onboard to void his bowels. It was a complicated apparatus to flush and often resulted in the embarrassment of, ‘receiving one’s own back’. The endurance of the B-class was only three days in winter so Richard deliberately constipated himself at sea with the assistance of opium tablets. Mullan had his own solution. He would surface the boat every day and perch on the edge of the bridge like a seagull whilst voiding over the side.

As Mullan dropped his trousers, he spotted the look of distaste on Richard's face. 'What's your problem, oh pious one? Haven't you seen a proper cock before?'

One of Mullan's many less-endearing traits was his willingness to flaunt his member. Richard had heard a rumour that Mullan and the TI had once held a competition in the fore-ends to see who could store most pennies up their foreskin. Richard had no idea who had won.

*

A submarine is designed to sink. There is a law of physics that the greater the metacentric height of a ship, the difference between its centre of gravity and its metacentre, then the more stable the ship. A submarine's design is such that on the surface or at periscope depth, the metacentric height is virtually nothing. In the words of the sailor, 'They would roll on wet grass' and Richard, never a good sailor, was beginning to feel queasy.

The wind had risen to about thirty knots with a sea state of about five, meaning that life was very uncomfortable on board *B3*. It was not quite blowing a gale outside, but it was enough to generate waves between fifteen and twenty feet in height. In such seas many a hardened sailor feels sick, or at least green about the gills. For the submariner the conditions were especially bad and most of *B3*'s ship's company had already begun vomiting. Some had made it to a bucket, others had not made it, or had missed the target as the boat was lifted high into the air by a wave and then slammed down into the trough. The B-class submarines were not fitted with accommodation for the men, so those not on watch lay on the deck-plates or spare torpedoes or crammed into any available nook or cranny. Only the officers had been afforded the relative luxury of a single bunk at the forward end of the control room. Naturally, at sea one officer was always on watch so the bunk was shared. In harbour the men, except for the duty watch, were accommodated in the relative comfort of hammocks on board the depot ship or ashore.

Richard had served with some sympathetic captains who would dive the boat to avoid much of the poor weather, but Mullan was not one of them. He delighted in rough weather to show off his cast iron stomach and constitution. Moreover, *B3* was not only faster on the surface, but could run her engines to charge the batteries. Dived, the batteries would only last about four hours at about six knots before the submarine would have to surface again anyway. Mullan had told Richard that he had an evening lined up with one of his 'aunties' in Portsmouth that night and did not want to waste time by diving. As it was, they were running late anyway, since even Mullan had seen the sense in reducing speed to eight knots in a head sea.

Richard had wedged himself into the wardroom camp-chair rather than lying in the bunk. It was more comfortable, but sleep was impossible. Outside, the sounds of the slamming of the waves against the hull and the smashing of the hull into the sea competed with the noisy chugging of the 600 horsepower Vickers petrol engine running flat-out to turn the single screw and keep the batteries charged. Facing aft, he watched with fascinated horror a large pool of vomit creeping from the engine room towards a recumbent sailor stretched out on the urine-soaked deck at the back of the control room. Every time the bows pitched into a trough, the trickle of vomit advanced another foot or so, but as the bows rose again to meet the next wave, it only receded a few inches.

Besides the cacophony of noise, Richard found the stench almost unbearable. The rough weather had upended several buckets of urine as well as vomit, but this was not the principal problem. Unlike his old submarine *D2*, *B3* had no bulkheads dividing the engine room from the control room. The submarine interior was one open space. It meant that the fumes from the engine permeated the whole submarine. He was due to relieve Mullan on the bridge in half an hour but, for the sake of something to do in the meantime, he decided to check on the health of the white mice the boat carried to give warning of any dangerous build-up of carbon monoxide. *B3* carried two cages of mice, one hanging from the deckhead of the engine room in accordance with normal custom and practice, and an unofficial one in the torpedo compartment. As was the wont of sailors, all the mice were not only overfed but named, and there was intense rivalry between the seamen and stokers as to who had the healthiest, fattest and cleverest mice. As it was nearer, Richard started with Fratton Park, the cage of the stokers' mice. Leading Stoker Benthall rose from his squatting position to make way for him. Richard spoke directly into the stoker's left ear. It was impossible to have a normal conversation with the noise of the engine running. The stokers tended to communicate with each other by tapping the deck with a spanner or by sign language.

'Hello, Benthall. I've just come to check on your mice. Is all well?'

Benthall shouted back, 'Why thank you, sir. They're grand as 'owt. Mind, I think little Harry Taylor there is looking a bit peaky.' The stokers had named their mice after Portsmouth's football team members, before learning that their star centre forward was female.

'I see what you mean. She does look a bit dopey, but the others seem all right. Maybe she's pregnant again.' Richard put his finger through the bars of the cage and one of the mice gave it a bit of a sniff before retiring in disgust.

'I'm sorry, sir. I didna' catch your meaning. Dopey?'

'Sorry, Benthall, it's an Americanism. I meant drowsy and under the weather.'

'Ah, that's very good, sir. Under the weather. I wish we bloody were. I'm right sick of this pitching and rolling.'

'Don't worry. We should still make Pompey before the pubs shut tonight.'

'I hope you're right there, sir. I'm duty watch tomorrow so tonight's my only chance of a run ashore.'

'There'll be a chance between exercises off Portland, and we're due a port visit to Torquay at the end of the month besides.'

'Aye, sir. True enough, but there's a certain barmaid in Pompey whose acquaintance I'm keen to renew, if you know what I mean, sir?' Benthall winked conspiratorially at Richard.

'Oh, I think I understand you perfectly. Just remember that the last liberty boat leaves from the Portsmouth side at 03.00.'

Chapter 9

It was not just the rain that had dampened Elizabeth's spirits. All day she had tramped the streets of Bow, handing out leaflets espousing the cause of women's suffrage. A blister on the heel of her left foot was causing her pain, the two smallest toes of her right foot were pinched and she was wet through. She looked down at the filth that had collected at the base of her skirts; a mixture of mud, horse dung and the general ordure of the East End. Despite her hat, her hair was wet and bedraggled, but she counted herself fortunate in her decision to reject make-up. She might have looked a worse sight in front of the crowd of costermongers, whose vote she was attempting to entice. One of them had taken on the role of spokesman for his fellows.

'Ye still ain't explained, madam, why our MP had to resign 'is seat. He only won it for Labour two years ago.'

'Sir, I was about to explain that,' Elizabeth replied patiently, trying hard to avoid sounding vexed. 'The Labour Party is only paying lip service to the issue of votes for women. Mr Lansbury is a man of conscience and recognised this. By resigning his seat and forcing this by-election ...'

'Walkin' away from his responsibilities, more like,' the costermonger cut in.

'Not at all, sir. Mr Lansbury is now standing as an independent member of the Labour Party in the cause of enfranchisement ... Is now standing directly for the cause of giving women the vote. If you re-elect him, it will show the country that the working man is also in favour of women's rights.'

'I'm not 'avin' none of those rights for women in my 'ouse,' somebody called out. 'My missis is bossy enough without 'avin' the right to tell me what to do.' The crowd cheered in support.

'That's right,' the spokesman continued. 'I'm more interested in our MP fighting for improved 'ousin' and better wages for the workin' man than women's votes. Whaddya toff women know about life in the East End? Tonight yer chauffeur'll take ye back to yer cosy 'ouse in the West

End an' we'll still be 'ere.' The costermongers all burst into applause and shouted, ''ear, 'ear.'

Ever since Lansbury had triggered the by-election in his constituency of Bow and Bromley nearly two weeks earlier, Elizabeth and her WSPU colleagues had met similar resistance. The voters wanted bread, not votes for women. It did not help that they regarded the WSPU activists as well-to-do. Even though the local Labour Party was not fielding an official Labour candidate against Lansbury, the members were being uncooperative. They seemed to resent the burden of the election. Elizabeth had discovered that the majority of working-class wives were sympathetic to the campaign, but their husbands, who wielded the votes, wanted to use the election as an opportunity to cut the Pankhursts down to size. Elizabeth feared that Emmeline and Christabel's strategy was going to lead to the avowedly anti-suffragette Conservative candidate, Reginald Blair, winning the seat in two days' time.

*

Richard finished checking the pilot cells of the battery and satisfied himself both that the battery was fully charged, ready for sailing in the morning, and that it was properly ventilated. 'Battery gassing' was a problem in charging the batteries. They gave off hydrogen and, without proper ventilation, one spark, many of which were encountered in a submarine, could ignite the gas and cause a serious explosion. On completion of his rounds he did not neglect to check the draught marks.

It was a cold evening with a strong south-westerly wind blowing across Haslar Creek where *B3* was berthed on one side of the depot ship, between *B4* and a C-class submarine. It was not easy to see the draught marks in the dark, even with the aid of a flashlight and the powerful gantry lamps over the side of the depot ship. However, it was important to take the readings carefully. *B3* had taken on fuel and fresh water that day and this would have affected the displacement of the submarine. Unlike the new D-boats, the B-class only had a ten per cent reserve of buoyancy. With their very low freeboard it would not take much for water to flood an open hatch and sink the boat alongside. It was Richard's job to ensure not only that the submarine was not dangerously low in the water, but he had to calculate the diving trim for the exercises off Portland over the next few days.

Having satisfied himself that all was well, he considered joining the other officers in the wardroom of the depot ship 'inboard'. Then he remembered that over dinner he had witnessed Mullan becoming increasingly inebriated with the COs of two other boats alongside. Richard reflected that Mullan would no doubt take advantage of his presence to humiliate him further in front of his fellow officers. It called to mind Goddard's comment about ERA Thompson's drinking. He was intrigued. Thompson was the senior ERA, in charge of the engineering department. Without a doubt, he had a difficult task in keeping the relatively elderly *B3* fit for sea, but he had always struck Richard as a quietly competent technician. Ever since their arrival in Gosport the week before, Richard had discreetly observed Thompson carefully, but had neither seen nor smelled any indication of excessive drinking. Richard shrugged his shoulders and decided that, instead of returning inboard, he would retire to the part of the control room defined as the wardroom. He pulled the curtain across to give himself relative privacy from the duty watch and settled himself into the chair with his Bible.

As a consequence of Johnson's guidance on the subject, Richard had since been careful to maintain his religious beliefs more privately and he was careful not to read the Bible in Mullan's presence. However, it still pricked his conscience that he had lied to his captain about the weather on leaving Dover. He chose to read Psalms fifteen to twenty-three, but found he could not keep his attention on the text. His mind wandered to the subject of Mullan and what to do about the situation.

It was open to him to state a complaint against Mullan. Complaints were treated very seriously by the Admiralty hierarchy and it was said that a sailor had the right to take his case even as far as the House of Lords, if he did not receive redress. However, King's Regulations stated that any complaint should be made in writing and passed through the commanding officer. Richard could well imagine Mullan's reaction. In any case, were Mullan even to forward a complaint, the interests of naval discipline would ensure that the senior officers backed the commanding officer and it would make Richard look weak and a sneak. Similarly, he could not ask his father to place a few words in the right quarters. Richard knew that Keyes had once fought with Papa in China. But if he failed to act, then it was obvious that his submarine career would soon be brought to an end. Mullan had made it very clear that he would not recommend him for command and, if he could not obtain a command, then he would be returned to the surface fleet. Richard shuddered at the thought. It wasn't that he could not bear the idea of being a mere watchkeeping officer in a capital ship. Like all submarine officers he had spent a compulsory year in a surface ship and had been well received. The captain and the Gunnery Officer had been pleased to make use of his technical acumen. He might even enjoy a spell in destroyers. No, the problem was that there would be the stigma of failure with him forever.

Perhaps I should resign my commission, he thought. He would at least be spared the remaining few months under Mullan's command. *Should I kill myself? Should I kill Mullan?* He realised that these were fanciful ideas without merit. He had no real choice but to stick it out, come what may. This wasn't war or a life-or-death situation. Papa had seen action in the Sudan, China and South Africa, and been awarded the Conspicuous Service and Victoria Crosses. What would Papa think if he quit? Jesus had suffered far worse tribulations prior to his crucifixion. Somehow, with God's help, he would persevere.

Something else troubled him, though. Perhaps it was a life-or-death situation, after all. Mullan's heavy drinking was now affecting his competence and Richard suspected that some of the ship's company had noticed. Several instances came to mind. Whilst exercising dived off Dover three weeks before, Mullan had taken his turn on watch in the control room. When adjusting the trim he had forgotten to shut the suction valve on the forward trim tank before opening the trim tank aft. As a result, water had rushed back and forth, making the 'bubble' uncontrollable. Had it not been for the swift action of one of the stokers in shutting the valve, *B3* might have hit the sea bed at an unhealthy angle and speed. Mullan had thrown a tantrum and publicly screamed at Richard that he must have handed over a bad trim. Just two days earlier, when bringing *B3* to periscope depth prior to surfacing at the end of an exercise with two destroyers in the Solent, he had failed to carry out an 'all round look', a 360 degree sweep of the horizon, and instead focused on the destroyer ahead. But for the swift action on the bridge of the other destroyer, it might have rammed the submarine from astern. Both incidents had occurred on the first day at sea after a night in harbour. It was a pity as, despite his foul temper, when Mullan was not afflicted by alcohol, he was a first class seaman and a very competent submariner.

Richard's musings were interrupted by a rumpus on the casing above. As he approached the main access hatch to investigate, a body fell on him, almost knocking him to the deck. It was Mullan, clearly the worse for wear.

'I thought you might be skulking down here. Why aren't ye in the mess with the others? Oh, I see. You've been reading yer precious Bible again. You really are a fucking prig.'

Richard regretted that he was still holding his Bible in his hand.

'I was just walking round the boat, to ensure we're ready for sea tomorrow, sir.' Richard felt comfortable that this was not actually untrue.

'Really? Tell you what then, my conscientious Number One. Why don't we have a wee drink down here then?' Mullan produced a bottle of whiskey from inside his reefer jacket. 'It's good stuff. Proper Irish.'

'Er…- no, thank you, sir. I don't drink.'

'Oh yeah, I almost forgot. Well I think you should change your mind. Come on.'

Mullan shuffled over to the wardroom, perched on the bunk and poured two glasses of whiskey. He gestured to Richard to resume his seat in the wardroom chair.

'You know what I discovered tonight, Miller?' He didn't wait for a response, but gulped his drink and poured himself another. 'I heard that your Da is a Captain at the Admiralty and some sort of fucking hero. Fancy that.'

Richard could not think of a suitable response.

'So what have yer to say to that, then?' Mullan slammed his glass down onto the chart table.

'It's true, sir. But I don't see what difference it makes.'

'Too fucking right, Mister. My last First Lieutenant was the son of an admiral and I still broke him. It's time you pampered gentlemen realised that you're better off in cruisers or battleships than in a real man's world. Are ye no' drinking?'

'No, sir. I don't.'

'Then give it to me you lick-spittle. I'll not waste it.' Mullan downed the contents of the glass in one. 'You don't like me much, do you, Miller?'

'I respect you, sir, as is only proper for one's commanding officer.'

'Hah. That's a mess-deck lawyer's answer. I'd have expected better from you, Miller. Do ye know what I think of yous?'

'I think you have made that very plain already, sir.'

'You're a sensitive bugger then. I know ye don't like me, ye snooty bastard. Ye think I'm coarse because I drink and swear. Hang on a minute.' Mullan raised his right leg and broke wind loudly, several times. 'Aye and I fart, too. Yer soft and spoiled, Miller. I'm no Johnson.'

'That's very true, sir.'

'Fuck yous, smarty-pants. I'll tell ye why yer last boat sank. We all know why. Johnson was soft and he let ye run a slack boat. If you'd been doin' yer job properly, you'd never have let him make such a monumental fuck-up.'

Richard rose to his feet. 'I resent that remark, sir. Lieutenant Johnson was a fine officer and is not here to defend himself. He ran a very happy boat and was hugely respected by his men.'

'Aye and many of whom are now dead thanks to his or yer incompetence. Listen to me ye arrogant bastard. I was serving in this man's navy when you were still sucking yer ma's tits. I don't give a fuck that ye don't like me. In fact it suits me jes fine. But I'll no' let ye take me down. You won't catch me out. Do we understand each other, sonny?'

'Perfectly, sir.'

Mullan nodded and closed his eyes. After a minute or two's absence of the usual abuse, Richard began to wonder whether Mullan might have fallen asleep. He was still standing and wondered about retiring to the depot ship. He took a step backwards, but Mullan stirred.

'Are we ready for sea?'

'We are, sir.'

'Then fuck off inboard and leave me in peace.' Mullan poured himself another glass of whiskey.

Richard needed no second invitation.

Chapter 10

The ship's company of *B3* were in good spirits. It was exactly four weeks to Christmas and they and the boat were destined to be back in Gosport before then for maintenance and Christmas leave. The exercises in the Solent and off Portland were now complete and *B3* was alongside in Torquay for some deserved rest and recreation. Strangely, Richard, too, was feeling cheerful. Since their conversation on the eve of their departure from Gosport, Mullan had been much less mendacious and had handled *B3* well during the last exercise. He had even given Richard leave to go ashore briefly in response to the message that had awaited *B3*'s arrival in Torquay that morning.

Richard had no difficulty in finding the Torbay Hotel, just a few minutes away from the quayside. Similarly, it had been easy to spot the writer of the surprise note that he had been given on arrival in Torquay. Looking across the *salon de thé*, Richard noted his quarry seated by a window. Despite it being the end of November, weak sunshine filtered through the window panes and lit up his cousin Elizabeth's face. He stood there for a moment admiring the view. It reminded him of something Millais might have painted. Her golden hair shone in the sunbeam and perfectly illuminated the pale skin of her face. It was a vision of loveliness that was immediately broken by Elizabeth noticing his arrival and waving to him.

Walking between the tables of the other hotel guests, Richard suddenly became quite self-conscious. Several of those he passed wrinkled their noses or put hands over them, expressing looks of disgust. Richard realised that he was the object of their disgust. He was still dressed in his seagoing clothes, although he had taken the time to shave and wear a proper uniform.

'Dearest Dick.' Elizabeth rose to meet him and extended her arms to embrace him. As he bent forward to kiss and hug her, she immediately recoiled six inches before accepting a kiss on the cheek.

'I'm sorry about the smell, Lizzy, but I came as soon as I received your note.' Richard looked round at the nearby guests apologetically. He noticed a waiter heading for him.

'Oh, no, Lizzy. I think I'm about to be ejected from the premises.'

'Over my dead body, Dick. You're my guest.'

Richard noted Elizabeth's cheeks colour and her eyes sparkle. He recognised the signs. She was steeling herself for a fight.

The waiter approached them and spoke quietly, almost confidentially. 'Excuse me, sir. Madam, I wonder whether you might prefer to entertain your guest in the library. The fire is lit and it would be most comfortable. I'm afraid, sir, that not all our residents understand the privations of life within His Majesty's submarines.'

Richard was relieved to see Elizabeth shrink by about two inches and moved aside to allow her to pass. He smiled apologetically at the other guests, who seemed equally relieved to see his departure.

Richard enjoyed both the tea and the warmth of the fire on such a chilly day, but he could tell that Elizabeth was nervous. After some social chat about family, he decided to bring the conversation to its crux.

'Lizzy, this is a most pleasant surprise, but I have to be back onboard soon. We're hosting a cocktail party this evening for the Mayor and a few other guests and I must oversee the preparations. What brings you here at such short notice?'

'Short notice, fiddlesticks, Dick. You told me last month you were making this visit to Torquay and you said I would be welcome onboard at any time. Are you not pleased to see me?'

'Of course I am, but I'll be seeing you at Christmas anyway, and Torquay is a long way from London.'

'Yes, well, I needed to be out of London for a little while and I needed a rest. What better place to come than Devon?'

'Not coming up to December, old girl. Come on. What's up? Have you fallen out with someone or is it something to do with your suffrage project?'

'Darling Dick. You are so direct. I fear you spend too much time in male company. All right then, since you asked. Have you read the by-election result?'

'Which by-election result, Lizzy?'

‘Dick, where have you been these past few weeks? The Moon? The Bow and Bromley by-election, of course.’

‘As your nose has already borne testimony, old girl, I have been at sea most of the month. Now you mention it, I do recall that a by-election was held a couple of days ago. What of it? It’s a solid Labour seat as far as I recall.’

‘Not any more it isn’t. Your blessed Conservatives won it.’

‘They are not my Conservatives. I just vote for their candidates, along with the rest of our family. But now I remember. There was a Labour candidate standing on a platform of woman’s suffrage. That explains your need for a break. No doubt you have been hard at work on the campaign these past few weeks. But why leave London?’

‘Yes, I was campaigning and the result was a huge disappointment, but …- Dick, something terrible is about to happen. Swear to me that you’ll not breathe a word of it, but I have to tell someone.’

‘Steady on, Lizzy. I don’t like the sound of this. What have you been up to?’

‘Nothing. Well, nothing serious. But first swear to keep my secret.’

‘All right then, I swear it.’

‘Swear by Almighty God to say nothing of what I am about to tell you, Dick.’

‘Really, Lizzy. You do try a man’s patience sometimes. Very well. I swear by the Father Almighty, the Lord Jesus Christ and the Virgin Mary that I will not reveal to another soul any detail of the information that Miss Elizabeth Francis Roxanna Miller is about to impart to me. Is that good enough?’

‘Now who’s being perverse?’

‘Look, Lizzy. I really have to get back to my boat. The CO’s been unusually lenient with me as it is and I don’t want to push my luck. If there’s something you want to tell me, then that’s fine, but do get on with it.’

‘Dick, I’m going to have to ask Aunt Johanna to give you some guidance on small talk with the opposite sex. Wait -,’ Richard had started to stand up to leave, ‘- I’m worried that the WSPU is becoming too militant and I’m too deeply involved.’

‘Go on.’

'Up to now I've only been involved with smashing windows and splashing paint on politicians' property.'

'Only? For goodness' sake, Lizzy, that's criminal damage.'

'Not really. We're careful to ensure that we frequent the shops we damage, to give them our trade, and occasionally I've gone back and paid the damage out of my own pocket. As for the politicians, they deserve it. Anyway, a few months ago I was in Paris with Christabel Pankhurst -…'

'So she's in Paris. That's why the police can't find her.'

'Dick, stop interrupting. You are so behind the times. Don't you ever read the newspapers? Actually, she's now in Boulogne and her whereabouts have not been a secret since September, when she invited reporters from the *Daily Sketch* to run a piece on her. Anyhow, she has since moved to Boulogne. Don't you dare interrupt!' Richard raised his hands in submission.

'In the summer she asked me to burn down Nottingham Castle, but I refused.'

'Oh my Lord, Lizzy. I've heard it all. You make it sound as if it were a mere favour. Are you all mad? What on earth gave her that idea?'

'I'm not too sure. Something that pig, Sir Charles Hobhouse, had said. The point is that now Lansbury's lost his seat, she and her mother have embarked upon a plan to set fire to pillar boxes.'

'Compared with Nottingham Castle, it sounds rather tame. What was your objection, apart from the fact that it's illegal, dangerous and a hare-brained idea, dear cousin?'

'It's going too far. Attacks on politicians are fair game, but this is an attack on the public. As well as dropping incendiaries into pillar boxes to set light to the mail inside, they've recruited a London University scientist to devise parcels that will burst into flames when opened. I'm worried that innocent people may get hurt.'

'Lizzy, this is outrageous. You have to go to the police.'

'No, Dick, I can't. I've already had one scrape with the Law and they won't believe I'm not involved. They'll arrest me for conspiracy. In any case it's too late. The campaign will have started by now. That's why I had to leave London. By visiting you I will be clear of suspicion.'

Richard was silent for a short while. He was shocked by the news of the means the suffragettes were considering to achieve their end, but he understood their frustration, too, and considered that the Establishment was overreacting to their antics. Secretly he admired his cousin for her commitment and pluck. Lizzy was not like any other girl he had ever known. He thought himself fortunate to have met many intelligent women, several of them good-looking and witty, too, but Lizzy was special. She was independent, passionate about the things in which she believed and fiercely determined to get her way. At twenty-four, she wasn't many years younger than him and, as they had grown up together, they had become very close friends. Indeed, their friendship was stronger than that. He regarded her as the sister he would have liked to have had and loved her in the same way. In fact, some members of the family had considered their friendship as rather unhealthy. His cheeks burned with embarrassment at the memory of the scolding they had both received as infants, when they had been discovered skinny-dipping together one summer's day. It had taken him years to discover the reason behind the upset.

'Don't flash up at me, Dick. I can see you're getting angry with me.' Elizabeth must have misunderstood his emotions.

'No, I'm not angry, Lizzy,' he replied gently. 'Just disappointed. I thought you had come to see me. I now feel as if I'm just another part of your suffragette cause. I'm just your alibi.'

Tears started rolling down Elizabeth's cheeks and she gripped both his hands with her own.

'Don't think that, Dick. I promise you that I would never use you. It is I who feels used, by Christabel. I feel as if the scales have been lifted from my eyes. I could have gone home, but I came here, to see you. I needed a friend. Somebody I could talk to. I needed you, Dick.' Elizabeth was by now sobbing without restraint.

Richard's heart melted. He had never seen Elizabeth cry before. She was too strong for that. He rose and, pulling her up to him, embraced her tightly.

'I'm so sorry, Lizzy. I didn't mean it. I beg you to forgive me. It's just … I was so pleased to see you. You will forgive me, won't you?'

He kissed her gently on the cheek and she turned to look up at him. He looked into her bright-blue eyes, reddened and dulled by tears, but still sparkling.

Elizabeth laid a finger on his lips. 'Hush. There's nothing to forgive.'

Richard's emotions overcame him. Without thinking, he kissed her passionately on her lips. Elizabeth gripped him tightly by the shoulders and responded equally passionately. Richard's only thought was that a dam had burst and he felt a hitherto latent love surge through him. After what he thought one joyful eternity, it was Elizabeth who broke off the kiss. Holding him gently by both ears she said, 'Dick darling. I do love you. Dearly. I've probably loved you all my life, but really! You do stink like nothing I have ever known.'

Chapter 11

The news of continuing problems in the Balkans and the likely declaration of independence by Albania from the Ottoman Empire seemed of little concern to the officers at breakfast in the wardroom of HMS *Venus* today. HMS *Venus*, formerly an *Eclipse*-class protected cruiser, was more usually the depot ship for destroyers, but today, the twenty-ninth of November, she was lying in Torquay harbour with the submarines *B3* and *A7* tied abaft her starboard beam. Devoid of sleeping accommodation, cooking and sanitation facilities, fresh water and the means to generate their own power in harbour when deployed from their home bases, the submarines were dependent on these 'mother ships'. The depot ship's officers and their submarine guests were intently interested in the domestic news today. The morning newspapers were full of reports of GPO pillar boxes being set alight by incendiary devices. It was rumoured that the suffragette women were to blame.

Richard sat eating his meal in silence as many of his comrades berated these dastardly acts of violence by the so-called fairer sex, whilst a minority sympathised with their cause. He squirmed inwardly with guilt for his cousin Elizabeth's involvement in the movement, but felt relieved that she was not to blame for these attacks. Careful study of his Bible had done nothing to assuage his feelings of guilt about the demonstration of his passion for Elizabeth, though. *Leviticus* had eased his conscience a little in that relations between first cousins was not explicitly mentioned as being forbidden. Even so, he still wondered if he and Elizabeth were committing a sin. As soon as he could get ashore again he would have to visit a church to make his confession.

However, until this afternoon, his duty to God would have to take second place to that of the First Lieutenant in *B3*. At the cocktail party on board *Venus* the night before, he had rashly agreed to offer the Mayor and his lady a tour of *B3* after their lunch with the Captain of *Venus*. First he would have to lend a hand in ensuring the boat was scrubbed thoroughly from stem to stern. At least Mullan would be out of his hair, since he had announced his intention to spend the day ashore.

He thought again about Lizzy. She had come to the cocktail party, looking radiant. His duties as a host officer had given him little opportunity to spend time in her company, but he had been immensely proud of her. She had completely enthralled his brother officers with her dazzling beauty, poise, wit and charm. Even Mullan had spoken well of her, although not without some lewd remarks, of course. Richard could not wait to see her again. She was due at 14.00, in time to join the mayoral party's tour of *B3*, and they would afterwards spend the afternoon together.

He wondered again at her choice of words in the hotel. She had said that she loved him. Until that moment he had not realised that he loved her, too, more than cousins or even siblings could feel for each other, and he could not live happily without her. He could no longer bear her absence. It was perhaps as well that he had several hours of cleaning and scrubbing ahead of him to keep his mind free of such thoughts.

*

It was unfortunate that Mullan decided it was his place to host the mayoral visit. Richard could tell from experience that he had been drinking, but to the casual observer it would not have been as obvious. He displayed no unsteadiness on his feet or slurring of his words, but one could smell alcohol on his breath and his eyes had a far-away look. It was equally unfortunate that the Lady Mayoress was extremely corpulent. It had required some effort on her part to fit through the forward hatch. At one point Richard had thought that she might have to remain behind on the casing, but some coaxing from her husband and the effects of gravity had been enough to guide her down the narrow entrance to *B3*'s interior.

The touring party was kept small, owing to the confined nature of the boat, and comprised only the Mayor, his Lady, two councillors and Elizabeth. However, Elizabeth had engaged in a technical conversation with ERA Thompson in the engine room and separated herself from the others. *B3*'s visitors seemed more interested in the torpedo compartment. The Lady Mayoress and councillors seemed aghast by the conditions on board, despite the crew's best endeavours to clean the boat, but the Mayor was genuinely interested in his tour.

'So you only carry two torpedo tubes then, Captain?' the Mayor asked.

‘That’s right, sir, but the more modern submarines are being built with a stern tube as well.’

‘And how many men do you have onboard at sea?’

‘Thirteen in all, sir. Plus myself and the Second Captain.’

‘A quaint title.’ Turning to Richard, the Mayor asked, ‘But is it not now the fashion to address you as the First Lieutenant?’

‘It is, sir,’ Richard replied. ‘The Submarine Service has caught up with the surface fleet. Although I am certain I am called many other things behind my back. To my face I am sometimes addressed as, “Number One”, “Jimmy the One” or, plainly, “The Jimmy”.’

‘And why is that, Lieutenant?’ the Lady Mayoress asked.

‘I’m not too sure myself, madam. It might be a corruption of James the First. I’ve never thought it a good idea to enquire into the origins of naval slang in case it should turn out to be quite rude.’

‘And do tell me, Captain, do your men sleep in the depot ship at sea?’

Mullan seemed taken aback by the Lady Mayoress’s question. ‘I’m sorry, madam?’

‘I mean, do you come to the surface at the end of the day and spend the night in the depot ship, before returning the next day to continue your patrols?’

Richard tensed. He could see that Mullan’s unusually calm temper might be under strain.

‘No, madam. The depot ship stays in harbour and we go out to sea for three to four days on our own. We wouldn’t want the presence of a depot ship to alert the enemy to our presence, would we?’

‘Oh, silly me. But where do you sleep and eat? I haven’t seen any cabins or the galley yet. Is there another deck below?’

‘No, madam. Beneath us lie the battery cells only. We sleep wherever we can find a space and generally eat cold, tinned food at sea.’

‘But how dreadful. I mean, what about- ..?’

‘I think it time we were going, Marjorie,’ the Mayor interrupted his wife and gently took her arm. ‘We’ve already taken up enough of the crew’s time. They’re only here for a short while.’

The two councillors climbed the ladder through the hatch to the casing and waited for the Mayor and his Lady, but a delay ensued. The Lady Mayoress was struggling to squeeze her bulk back through the hatch. After much huffing and puffing it became clear that she was stuck. The councillors took her arms and tried pulling her. The Mayor tried encouraging her. Some of the duty watch below started to smirk with amusement. Richard suggested to the Mayor that he should rearrange the folds of her dress to ease her passage but, after three minutes of pulling and cajoling, the lady remained stuck fast. It was left to Mullan to solve the problem. Impatiently he pushed the Mayor to one side and, despite the impropriety of looking up a ladder into a woman's skirts, climbed up part way and balanced on the rungs with his hands free. Simultaneously, he grasped the lady's buttocks with both hands and shouted, 'Madam.. – shift.. – yer.. – great.. – fat.. – arse…' and, with a last heave the unfortunate Lady Mayoress passed through the hatch like a cork from a wine bottle.

*

To spare embarrassment, Richard decided it would be imprudent for him and Elizabeth to join the Mayor's party on the boat ashore. Instead, he opted to wait for the next liberty boat. He half wondered if news of Mullan's action might make its way to the Commodore (S) and if this might serve as a means for him to be rid of Mullan. Although cold and grey, it was a dry day and he waited with Elizabeth on the quarterdeck of HMS *Venus*, watching the comings and goings in the harbour. *A7*, a boat eight months older than *B3*, was berthed outboard of *B3* and preparing to slip. The duty Petty Officer in the depot ship was overseeing the arrangements. In the distance Richard noted the imminent arrival of a destroyer, one of *Venus*'s more usual charges.

'So, Lizzy, now you've met him, what did you think of my CO?'

'Not at all the ogre you painted him to be, dear Dick. He had obviously had a drink and was a little rough, but he behaved towards me in a most charming manner.'

'He probably fancied you.'

'Well, a lady enjoys a little attention from men once in a while. You're going to have to remember that in future.' Elizabeth drew closer to Richard and pecked him on the cheek. 'I certainly admired his style in ejecting that silly woman. I cannot imagine more gallant officers taking such spirited action. No, he's not the one that worries me. That ERA needs watching.'

'Who? Thompson? The one with whom you were so engrossed in the engine room?'

'If that's his name, yes. You must have noticed that he's cracking up.'

'Actually, I hadn't. He seems perfectly competent to me. Although I've had a report that he might drink too much at sea. But I haven't seen it for myself.'

Richard leaned over the guardrail to wave goodbye to the CO of *A7* as the little black boat increased speed and headed out to sea in the direction of the destroyer.

'You've clearly not worked in a shipyard. The really serious drinker is a master at disguising it, and by serious I am talking of a scale well past that of your captain. It's the eyes that give it away. Smells can be disguised and, quite frankly I'm surprised you smell anything in those foul boats. And another thing, Dick. Are you sure he's totally competent?'

'Absolutely. These B-boats aren't as reliable as the new D-boats and he's worked marvels in keeping her fit for sea.'

'Really?' Elizabeth responded suspiciously. Across the harbour they both heard the shrill pipe of a boatswain's call as *A7* paid her respects to the more senior captain of the destroyer. 'I see you are taking on fuel.'

She gestured to the fifty-gallon drums being hoisted onto the after casing of *B3*. A crowd of on-lookers were collecting. Fuelling with petrol always presented an opportunity for some hilarious inebriation at the king's expense. For this reason the change to diesel was not being universally welcomed in the submarine service.

'Yes. We need a top-up for the return to Portsmouth. What of it?' Richard asked archly.

'Only that, as we were leaving, I noticed one of the electricians lifting the plates to the batteries.'

'Yes, he will be checking the pilot cells before we recharge the batteries tomorrow.'

'I am well aware of the reason, Dick. My point is that you in turn will be aware the batteries emit hydrogen.'

'Naturally, Lizzy. We aren't imbeciles. The last thing we want in a petrol-driven boat is a spark igniting either gas or fuel. That's why we keep the batteries well ventilated with fans and having both the forward and after hatches open will assist.'

'Alright, but I don't think it good practice to lift the deck plates when fuelling. You know as well as I that hydrogen and petrol fumes are an explosive combination. Why increase the risk?'

'I dare say you're right, Lizzy. I'll bear it in mind next time. In any case, Mullan doesn't seem to be bothered about it. Look, he's just coming onto the casing.'

Mullan had indeed come up through the forward hatch and started to ascend the accommodation ladder up the side of *Venus*.

'Hark, look at her,' Richard suddenly exclaimed. 'That CO's keen to arrive in style.'

Richard and Elizabeth's attention was diverted to the approaching destroyer. Instead of cutting his speed to slow, the CO was approaching at half speed, as evinced by the impressive bow wave and stern wash. The ship passed down the starboard side of *Venus* and *B3* in a mighty curve, smoke flaring from her twin funnels like that from a dragon's nostrils. As the destroyer passed the stern of *Venus*, the CO saluted Elizabeth. He struck Richard as awfully young to be in command. The CO then immediately ordered the helm full over to starboard and, using the enormous power of the destroyer's engines, took the way off the ship such that it gently glided along the *Venus*'s port side. The shrill of the boatswain's call rang out once again and the ship's company on the upper deck and bridge came to attention as one, to salute the captain of the *Venus*.

Richard was secretly impressed. The manoeuvre had been smartly executed. 'What a shameless piece of swashbuckling seamanship. Hang on. What's going on?'

He swung round to the source of the commotion. It was coming from the casing of *B3*. The party of spectators observing the fuelling were roaring with laughter. The fuelling party had clearly been soaked to the knees by the wash of the destroyer and they were not laughing. They were desperately trying to shut the two hatches to prevent further water flooding into *B3*. Suddenly, Richard recognised the immediate peril facing his submarine. The weight of the petrol drums on the after casing had depressed the boat further into the water. Under normal conditions the freeboard aft was only a couple of feet anyway and the destroyer's wash had flowed over the casing and poured down the after hatch. With so little reserve of buoyancy, the boat had sunk even deeper and any moment the water would cascade down the forward hatch, too. If that happened the boat would surely sink. Richard sprinted forward towards the accommodation ladder leading to the submarine. Ahead he saw Mullan running just as quickly and heard him roaring orders.

'Ditch the fuel overboard, you fuckers. If seawater touches it, that battery might jest explode.'

The idlers on the starboard waist and accommodation ladder stopped seeing the joke and started to scatter. Those on the ladder started to climb upwards but, sadly for them, Mullan was already on his way down.

'Get out o' me fucking way,' he shouted and threw himself on those beneath him, flailing his fists as he went. Some swung out of his way, others decided it prudent to jump overboard. Mullan was like a rogue steam train. Richard noted no apparent hesitation in jettisoning the fuel drums. He silently thanked the Lord that fuelling had not already commenced or else a hose might have fouled the hatch, preventing it being shut. Thankfully, somebody had managed to shut the forward hatch, too, and Richard could only pray that *B3* had not already shipped enough water to sink her. The casing was awash with up to six inches of water. Mullan seemed to have another preoccupation, though. He climbed up the conning tower and descended into the boat through the upper hatch. Richard decided it would be best to follow him but, as he reached the casing, something stopped him dead in his tracks.

It was the smell that first caught his attention. It was a pungent, irritating odour of bleach. He recognised its significance immediately and covered his mouth and nose. Looking up at the bridge of the submarine, he saw the start of a greenish-yellow cloud venting itself. It was obvious to any submariner that the seawater had hit the battery cells and, acting as an electrolyte, caused the lead-acid batteries to produce chlorine gas. Richard changed his mind about following Mullan. He thought he would be better placed on the casing to receive the inevitable casualties.

'Send for the first aid parties and some breathing apparatus. We'll also need stretchers and ropes. Hurry!' he shouted frantically.

The submariners nearby needed no second prompting. They constantly lived in dread of chlorine poisoning. Urgent commands were relayed up to the depot ship. Meanwhile, Richard refolded his handkerchief and tied it over his mouth and nose, in the same manner he had seen in illustrations of cowboys, and climbed up to the bridge. He was just in time to help one of the stokers through the hatch. He tried to remember how many men had been down below when he had left the boat. He thought it might be four, plus the CO now, of course. The unfortunate stoker was struggling to breathe. His eyes were sore and streaming with tears and he was coughing and spluttering. Other, gentle hands took hold of him and guided him down the side of the conning tower, but Richard would not let him go. 'Jones, how many are down there?'

The stoker was reluctant to answer and only seemed interested in getting off the submarine, but one of the men helping him cut in. 'Come on, Jonesy, how many fellows were in there with you? Come on now. You know it's important.' Jones responded by raising three fingers of his right hand and gasping, 'Three more... and the skipper.'

The gas was becoming more pungent and Richard could now barely see. He started coughing himself. He heard, rather than saw, another shape emerging from the hatch and Mullan's command, 'Get the fuck up there, you wimps.' It was the electrician, dragging behind him one of the seamen. Richard was surprised to find he had been joined by Goddard, similarly strangely masked. He couldn't raise the wind to ask Goddard how he came to be here, but he was grateful for his strength. Together they managed to pull the two survivors through the hatch to safety and pass them onto the forming first aid party.

In his peripheral vision Richard noted a medical officer rapidly descending the accommodation ladder. Three down, one to go, he thought. He realised it must be ERA Thompson still down there. Surely he couldn't still be alive. And what of Mullan? He had been down there too long already.

'Sir, let me go down there. I hear the skipper's gone down already.' Goddard gripped Richard by the arm tightly.

'No, Goddard. It's foolhardy. You're better off here.' Secretly, Richard had been wondering the same thing and only Goddard's prompt had dissuaded him from ignoring common sense and sliding down the hatch.

Seconds later, he heard a movement below, but could see nothing through the noxious cloud. Then a weak and rasping, but no less familiar voice cut through the fog, 'Lend a hand, you lazy bastards!'

Before Richard could stop him, Goddard leapt down the hatch, but his feet met an obstruction part way. Reaching down with both hands, he grabbed by its overalls the prone body below and heaved with all his considerable might. Slowly, he managed one rung of the ladder at a time until the last survivor was within reach of Richard. With Richard's help they dragged the unconscious Thompson to safety and Goddard collapsed to one side, gasping for breath.

This time Richard had no hesitation. He leapt down the hatch and hit the deck below with a solid thud. Lying nearby was Mullan, unconscious and breathing only shallowly. Richard knew he didn't have Goddard's strength and could not lift Mullan unaided. He shouted up the hatch for a rope with a bowline knot already tied in it. He didn't trust his judgement in the poisonous air to tie the loop himself. Within seconds some forward thinking hand threw down exactly what he needed and another rope similarly prepared. Richard looped one rope beneath Mullan's armpits and positioned him beneath the hatch, before taking the other loop beneath his own armpits. He called up to his fellow rescuers to begin heaving.

Inch by inch he climbed the tower, supporting Mullan all the way with his shoulder, and anxious hands took up the slack of both ropes. Looking past Mullan, he could see the grey, round window to another world, broken up by the blurred faces of those guiding the rope. The climb was infinitesimally long and he knew he would not make it before he passed out. He shouldn't have worn those lead boots for this task, he thought. The weakness in his left side now prevented him hauling his weary body up another rung. If only he could float to the surface like last time. *Mutti* had been so cross with him for serving in submarines. What would she say now? Up above he could see two dazzling lights. Gradually his addled brain recognised them as belonging to Lizzy. He thought of those dazzling-blue eyes that had sparkled up at him as he had kissed her. She was waiting for him. He had to fight. He had to climb this ladder just a few more feet. His heart was pounding, his lungs were bursting, but he moved his legs painfully and when he next looked up, the dazzling-blue eyes had turned into flashlights and somebody was grabbing him by the shoulders.

Chapter 12

December 1912

Richard made the short crossing from Gun Wharf to Fort Blockhouse with some trepidation. It was a grey, cold December morning and he was one of several passengers on the Admiralty Yard Craft Service boat. He was feeling much refreshed after a month of convalescence at home in London, but his leave had been interspersed with regular visits to the Royal Naval Hospital at Haslar near Gosport. Today, however, the objective of his crossing to Gosport was not to visit Haslar, but HMS *Dolphin*, the *alma mater* of the Submarine Service and the office of Commodore (S). He had been summoned to attend by telegram two days earlier and he felt sure he knew the purpose of the meeting. It would be the end of his career in submarines and that could hardly come as a surprise. It had been made clear to him that he needed Mullan's recommendation for command and that evening in Gosport just two months earlier, Mullan had been emphatic that no such recommendation would be forthcoming. He supposed that since the events in Torquay were no fault of his own, there was a faint chance that he might be reappointed to *B3* with a new CO and thereby have one last chance to prove himself. Then again, was he considered blameless for the accident in Torquay? The Board of Inquiry had exonerated both him and Mullan, but it might not take much for the submarine fraternity to spot the common factor in the sinking of *D2* and the near disaster in *B3*.

It was a flood tide and the Admiralty boat stemmed it as it made its approach to the jetty at Fort Blockhouse, giving Richard and the other officers looking over the stern, a full view of the dockyard on the Portsmouth side. Several ships were in, the biggest of which was HMS *Queen Elizabeth*, the first of the Royal Navy's super *Dreadnought* battleships and due to be commissioned in just a few days. The ship was alive with sailors and dockyard workers cleaning the ship, ready for the big day. Richard wondered if within a few days he might be serving as a junior officer in such a ship, although he still hoped he might have a chance at an appointment to a destroyer.

Fifteen minutes later, he was shown into the office of the Commodore Submarines. Richard noted that Roger Keyes appeared tired and strained, but as was his usual custom, he received Richard affably.

'Please take a seat, Miller. How are you feeling?'

'Much better now, thank you, sir. I still have a bit of a hacking cough that drives my parents up the wall, but as you can see, the blisters have gone.'

'You were lucky to get off so lightly. It's nasty stuff that chlorine gas, or more accurately hydro-chlorine gas. According to the docs, it mixes with the body's natural fluids and forms hydrochloric acid. Thank God we only lost ERA Thompson. But for Mullan, and then you, it would have been far worse.'

'How is Lieutenant Mullan, sir? I haven't seen him since my discharge from Haslar.'

'Not good, I'm afraid. Fleet Surgeon Macneish thinks it might take him a year to recover. The man must have the constitution of an ox. He ought to be dead.'

'What will happen to him, sir? I mean, will he be medically discharged?'

'What? Over my dead body. The man's a bloody hero. It would make a fine display of ingratitude to beach him for risking his life for others. No, we'll find him a billet somewhere, but it won't be back at sea. Macneish and his fellow witch doctors are set on that. It's not public yet, but he's to be awarded the Albert Medal.'

'Really? I am very pleased for him.' Richard realised that he had, perhaps, said this rather stiffly and added, 'He thoroughly deserves it.'

Keyes was too good a judge of character to let this pass by. 'Do I detect a hint of animosity, Miller? I know Mullan wasn't the easiest of COs.'

'Not at all, sir. I'm sorry. Lieutenant Mullan is an extremely courageous man and I don't know of anybody else who would have had the strength and pure willpower to have done what he did. It is one of his many idiosyncrasies.'

'Look, Miller, I wasn't born yesterday. I know Mullan had a reputation for driving his officers hard and he wasn't the easiest CO under which to serve. But you seem to have earned his approval. He did recommend you for command after all.'

Richard wondered if he had misheard. 'I'm sorry, sir. Did you say he ***did*** recommend me for command?'

'You seem surprised, Miller. Why wouldn't he? He told me that you were a most competent officer, who handled pressure well and had gained the full respect of the ship's company. I might add that you have proved you have courage, too.'

Richard's world had begun to spin and he wondered if he was in a dream. 'Forgive me, sir, but I am surprised. Lieutenant Mullan led me to believe the opposite was true. I mean, I don't think he liked me.'

'Respect and likeability are two separate things, Miller, and you should know that. Other than those who have actually exercised command of a submarine, very few understand the pressure it places on a man. A submarine captain operates completely independently and holds the lives of his men in his hands through his actions and decisions. As a service, we are fortunate to have more volunteers that we need and hence, can afford to be an elite. Mullan knows this. He came up through the school of hard knocks and, perhaps, he was a little hard on his subordinates. But as you may find one day, Miller, being tough on your men might save their lives.'

Richard decided it was not politic to take issue with Keyes on any of this. In his view, Mullan's action went well beyond toughening up his subordinates. He was cruel, a bully, divisive and didn't take responsibility for his mistakes. But nonetheless, Mullan had apparently recommended him for a command. It didn't make sense.

'Excuse me, sir, but when did Lieutenant Mullan recommend me for command?'

'For Heaven's sake, man! If you're worried it was in gratitude for saving his life, think again. He wrote me a letter in October, before sailing for the Portland exercises. Why the inquisition? Are you not pleased?'

'Of course, sir. Just a little taken aback. I'm sorry.'

'The question is what to do with you now? Fleet Surgeon Macneish won't countenance you returning to sea for at least three months, and only then if your lungs are better. I think what we'll do is attach you to my staff temporarily. It keeps you near Haslar and I think it would be useful. Would that suit?'

'Whatever you think best, sir. Do you have anything definite in mind?'

'Let's see. Do you know Nasmith?'

'Yes, sir, but not well.'

'He's setting up a school for teaching offensive tactics. I think he plans on calling it the Attack Teacher. You could give him a hand if you like. It might come in handy for your command.'

Richard's ears pricked up at those last magic words.

'I would also like you to work with a few people on how we might devise a proper system for submarine escape. You know, talk to the medical types and engineers. Develop procedures for the surface forces, training of submarine new entrants, that sort of thing. Your experience in *D2* will be invaluable. If you keep your nose clean and convince the quacks you're fully fit to return to sea, well we might fix you up with a command in the second half of next year. I'll expect you here on the second Monday of the New Year. Sound alright?'

Richard struggled to manage a conflicting mix of emotions - pride, happiness, relief, shock. None of it mattered. He was far from finished in submarines. That was all he cared about at this moment. Moreover, play his cards right and he would have his own command this time next year.

'Absolutely fine, sir. And thank you. I'll make sure you don't regret your faith in me. If there's nothing else, sir, I'll pay a call on Lieutenant Mullan before I return to London.'

'Yes, that will be all. Good idea to see Mullan. Apparently he doesn't get many visitors.'

*

Richard paid a visit to the *Dolphin*'s wardroom whilst awaiting transport to the Royal Naval Hospital and the driver kindly took him to a greengrocer's stall on the way. On arrival at the hospital, he quickly located Mullan's ward, but as his visit was outside normal visiting hours he had to see the ward sister first.

'No problem, Lieutenant,' a pleasant and friendly sister told him. 'He's in a single ward on account of his disturbing the other patients anyhow. I'm not surprised he doesn't receive many visitors. He's a cantankerous old devil. And such bad language!'

Richard was shocked by Mullan's appearance. He was propped up in bed, gazing out of the window. His head and hands were completely covered in bandages, leaving only his eyes and mouth visible.

'You have a rare visitor, Lieutenant,' the sister announced before withdrawing.

Mullan turned his head and replied, 'So it's youse. You're the last fucker I expected to see. Come to gloat have ye?'

'Not at all, sir. I've brought you something.' Richard handed over the fruit and the other bag he had recently purchased, but as he unwrapped it, Mullan suddenly became animated.

'God bless you. I take it all back. Mebbe there's a grain of decency in a Papist bastard after all. Are ye sure yer not a proddy?'

'It's proper Irish, sir. The wardroom Chief Steward said it was good stuff and the best they had.'

'I couldn't give a fish's tit if it was Scotch. I've no' had a drop for weeks. Those starched aprons who claim to be angels of mercy out there won't give me anything stronger than tay. Ye'll have to pour it fer me, though.'

Richard duly unscrewed the bottle he had smuggled into the hospital with the fruit and poured Mullan a large measure of the whiskey. He had to hold the tumbler to Mullan's lips.

'God bless ye again. I think it might jes now be worth livin' a while longer.' However, as he finished his sentence, Mullan started spluttering and then gave a long gurgling cough. 'Fucking lungs. Still playing up,' he said apologetically. 'So to what do I owe the very great pleasure of your visit?'

'I came to thank you, sir, for recommending me for a command. I've just heard the news from the Commodore.'

Mullan looked back to the window. 'No need to thank me. 'Twas no more than ye deserved. And don't call me sir. I'm no longer your superior officer.'

'I'm sorry. Force of habit I suppose. But why did you change your mind, sir? The last time we discussed it you seemed emphatic that you wouldn't.'

'I told you. Because you deserved it, that's all. You're still the usual gentleman officer with wealth, privilege and family connections. I've no doubt I'll be calling you sir before long, but you didn't buckle under my pressure and you've got guts. You proved that when you saved my life. Not that I'm sure I thank ye for it.'

Mullan turned back to face Richard and raised his heavily bandaged hands. 'Besides, you're a fucking liability as a First Lieutenant. No CO will ever have you again. Yer a fucking Jonah.'

For the first time ever in Mullan's presence, Richard laughed. 'An odd reason to recommend me for command, but I'll accept it nonetheless. Can I offer you another sip of whiskey?'

Mullan nodded and this time the drink did not bring on a bout of coughing. 'Are ye goin' t' join me? Or are you still a fucking prig?'

'Why not?' Richard was surprised to hear himself say. He poured himself a small measure and sniffed it tentatively. The aroma assaulted his nasal glands, but then the vapour subsided.

'This is my first and perhaps my last drink, so I'll make it a toast. To your swift recovery.' He took a sip of the whiskey and swallowed. It immediately burned his throat and he was reminded of an unpleasant cough mixture.

'Thanks,' Mullan responded. 'I know what that meant to you. Now I think ye'd better go before Miss Starchy Knickers catches ye. You'd better take the bottle, too. It's a pity as it's good stuff right enough, but I can't help myself to it.'

'Fair enough, Mullan, but I'll tell you what I'll do. I'm joining Keyes's staff in January. It means I can come and smuggle the bottle back in. How's that?'

Mullan said nothing for a short while, but then went on to say, 'You'd really do that? You'd come and visit me again?' He spoke unusually quietly for Mullan.

'Yes, I will, but on one condition. You don't make me drink this awful stuff again. I cannot fathom what you see in it.'

'Aye, fair enough. It's a deal. Now fuck off and let me rest.'

Chapter 13

May 1913

Richard had never visited a prison before. He found the experience distasteful and embarrassing. His discomfort had started when he had had to wait outside the main gate to gain entry to the prison. He had felt sure that every passer-by was staring at him and thinking, *'Oh aye. Even fine gentlemen have criminal connections.'* How could Lizzy have done this to him? No wonder she had given a false name. That just made Richard even more uncomfortable. He had had to back up the lie in stating his business as a visit to see Miss Phyllis Westerman. As far as he could recall, it was only the third time he had lied in his life.

After announcing himself and being admitted to the prison, he was led down a seemingly unending maze of corridors. The journey was protracted by the constant unlocking of doors and relocking of them afterwards. Every time a door was shut and locked behind him by the female warders, the slam served to shake him. His mind began to play tricks. Might he ever be released into the light of the summer's day? He had, after all, told a falsehood to gain entry. Stop worrying, his reason told him. Holloway Prison was built to house women prisoners only.

It was not just his aural senses that were being assaulted. The linoleum-lined corridors reeked pungently of a mixture of floor polish, boiled cabbage and carbolic soap. After an eternity, Richard was escorted to the visiting room. The large room was dimly lit by electric lamps and furnished only with a few trestle tables and simple wooden chairs. He was invited to take a chair to his left. Seated on the other side of the room a lawyer inclined his head towards him and resumed reading one of the many pieces of paper strewn on the table before him. Richard's escort left the room and the only other occupant was another warder, dressed forbiddingly in a dark gown and cap, with a long chain suspended from a black leather belt. Richard smiled at her weakly, but the warder's stentorian expression did not alter to acknowledge him.

Five minutes later, he heard a jangling of keys from behind the steel door in the corner opposite. He stood in expectation of seeing his cousin, but the pretty young woman who entered, followed by another warder, was not known to him. The prisoner's dark chemise and white apron was covered with arrows and a large, circular tally hung from her left breast. She crossed the room and sat opposite the lawyer. Richard noted that the circular tally was covered in a few letters and numerals, but no name. As the second warder withdrew with another clang of the door and jingling of keys, he heard an appalling shriek originating from down the corridor, the other side of the door. The lawyer immediately started talking in a low voice and Richard forced himself not to tune into the conversation. He found this hard, as there was not much else to catch his attention. The room was featureless except for a clock to his right. The walls were whitewashed and completely devoid of decoration. As he was forced to wait yet longer, he began to wonder what had caused the shrieking. Lizzy had told him tales of how women were tortured in prison, but he had not believed her. *Might she have been right? Could it have been Lizzy shrieking?* He shuddered at the thought.

Fortunately, before his imagination could conjure up the scenes of horror that might be being enacted, the door opened once more and Elizabeth entered the room. Unlike her fellow prisoner, she was dressed in her normal clothes, since she was on remand. These days she seemed to favour outfits in white, green or purple, the colours of the WSPU. Today she was dressed in purple. He was shocked, but not too surprised, to see she looked pale and haggard. Her beautiful, golden hair had lost its lustre. The normally pink cheeks were slightly sunken. But for the strict instructions he had received that there was to be no physical contact between prisoners and their visitors, he would have flung his arms around her in protection. Lizzy looked so frail and vulnerable. Then she smiled and he saw the same old sparkle in her jewelled eyes was still there. Lizzy wasn't beaten yet and his admiration for her spirit and his love for her overcame his pity.

Elizabeth sat down on the chair on the other side of the table. Neither of them spoke until the second warder had withdrawn from the room. The first warder remained impassive, at a discreet distance, but nevertheless within earshot. Elizabeth made to put her hand on

Richard's, but withdrew it in time, in response to the sudden stiffening of the watching warder. She spoke quietly.

'Oh, Dick, thank you for coming. I really could not think who else to call. I hope ...'

'But, Lizzy, what's this all about? How long have you been in this cursed place?'

'Patience, my love. I'll tell you eventually. We don't have much time now, so don't interrupt, and hear me out.'

Elizabeth's eyes bored into his, daring him to contradict her edict. He knew better than to take up the challenge.

'Oh, very well. Tell me in your own time and I'll just listen.'

'You didn't tell them my real name, did you?' Richard shook his head silently. 'Good. It would make matters even more awkward if Charles or Uncle William were to find out I'm here. You mustn't breathe a word, agreed?' Richard just nodded.

'You have to find me a lawyer. I'm up before the bench the day after tomorrow.'

'But, Lizzy. What's wrong with Sir Robert? He always handles the family affairs.'

'Can't you see? That's just the point. He would be bound to peach on me to Charles.'

'As you wish, but I can't think of one right now. I'll ask a couple of fellows at the Naval Club. Yes, of course, I will be discreet. Look, is there anything I can get you? Pardon me for saying, but you do look a bit peaky. Are they giving you enough to eat?'

'I'm not eating. I've been on hunger strike ever since they pinched me three days ago.'

'You've not eaten for three days! Why ever not, you chump? The food can't be that bad, even in a hell hole like this.'

'We never do. It's our way. It won't be for long. I'll explain everything when I'm out. Now, Dick, there's just one more thing. I'm in here with Alice Robson. You know, the school mistress Peter was seeing before he left for Tehran. The lawyer needs to represent her, too.'

'Oh, my word, Lizzy. How on earth is Miss Robson involved in this?'

'Never mind that now. I can explain everything once I'm out of this beastly place. Just be a perfect poppet and get me that lawyer.'

‘You can’t leave it there. I still don’t know what’s going on? What about Miss Robson’s people?’

‘Yer five minutes is over now, Westerman. Time to be sayin’ yer goodbyes,’ the warder interrupted. She then rapped on the steel door back to the cells. The jingling of keys and turning of the lock was repeated. Elizabeth stood to leave and, leaning forward, she brushed Richard’s cheek with her fingers.

‘Mum’s the word, my darling. And remember, I’m known here as Phyllis Westerman,’ she whispered. ‘Take care and thanks awfully.’

‘But … Er, Miss Westerman. You must eat,’ he called after her as she was led away.

‘No, dearie,’ the watcher replied. ‘Them’s not their ways. Wish I ’ad ’arve their courage, but it’ll do them no good.’

Richard commenced the journey back to the main gate and took his handkerchief to the tears rolling down his cheeks.

*

‘Please help yourself to more sandwiches, Miss Robson.’

Richard passed the plate across the table. He, Alice and Elizabeth were taking afternoon tea in a nondescript hotel in Westminster. He had booked them a room there in order to use the facilities to bathe and change after their release from custody earlier in the day. Richard would have preferred The Ritz, but Elizabeth had insisted on a location not frequented by the family or friends of their fathers. Alice did not take much prompting to take the last two sandwiches.

‘I hope you don’t mind, Mr Miller. I’ve not left you any. I’m absolutely ravenous.’ Alice did not wait for the response before wolfing down the sandwiches in an unladylike manner.

‘Careful, Alice,’ Elizabeth warned. ‘After seven days without food, you’ll be sick if you carry on like that. Drink more tea.’

Richard regarded Alice discreetly over his teacup. He had met her once before, but her appearance had changed in just a year. The hollow cheeks and protruding cheek and collar bones were clear evidence of a recent and rapid weight loss. She was a good looking woman and he could see the physical attraction his brother, Peter, must feel for her. He wondered how on earth she had become mixed up with a firebrand such as Lizzy.

‘I have to say,’ Elizabeth continued. ‘I feel like a new woman after a bath and change of clothing. I’m going to burn those clothes I wore in Holloway.’

‘How nice for you, Elizabeth. When I get back to Lancashire I’m likely to find myself out of a job. My clothes are going to have to last me a long while yet, I’d say.’

Elizabeth winced at Alice’s remark and grabbed her hand. ‘I’m sorry, Alice. That was tactless of me and it’s all my fault you were ever involved.’

‘Lizzy, I cannot restrain my curiosity further,’ Richard intervened. ‘I’ve given up leave to trot up from Portsmouth to answer your call of distress. I’ve gone to the expense of hiring you a lawyer and renting you a room in this establishment. Worst of all, I’ve lied to cover for you and Miss Robson and to protect your true identities. In just what have you been involved? How is it that a few days ago you were facing two months’ imprisonment and now you are here scoffing sandwiches? I reckon you owe me an explanation.’ Richard placed his cup and saucer on the table with such force it attracted the attention of some of the other hotel guests.

‘You’re right, of course, Dick darling. You’ve been such a sweetie. Alice and I were attending to WSPU business last week when the police arrested us. We’ve been attending classes in *jiu-jitsu* these past few weeks to become members of the Bodyguard.’

‘Just a moment. What’s this joojitsoo, and what do you mean by the Bodyguard?’

‘It’s a technique for self-defence from Japan. One of our members, Edith, is training a few of us how to handle violent hecklers.’

‘But is that absolutely necessary, Lizzy? I mean, a few insults from the crowd are hardly likely to lead to broken bones.’

‘Dick, you can be naïve at times. We often get treated like dogs. And the police are no better. Remember how they killed two women on Black Friday?’

‘Elizabeth is right, Mr Miller. And it’s not just violence either. Some men use it as a great opportunity to molest us outrageously, too.’

‘But that’s preposterous. I can’t believe that men would behave so indecently, and surely not the constabulary.’

'Dick, believe me, it's true,' Elizabeth retorted sharply. 'And the prison warders are no better. You would think we were animals, the way the Establishment treats us. You must know about the force-feeding?'

'Of course I do, but I thought that was all over. After all, has the government not just passed legislation to stop all that?'

'What rot, Dick. You're referring to McKenna's Cat and Mouse Act. All that happens is that after we fall ill from hunger, they release us for a few days under licence and then re-arrest us a week or so later. They think we'll be too weak to cause trouble whilst out on licence and they don't get undue publicity for their barbaric tube feeding. The trouble is that it's working. That's why we've formed the Bodyguard and how our altercation with the police came about.'

'But, Lizzy, you've still not explained all that.'

'You tell him, Alice. You're the teacher.'

'You mean, I was until last week, Elizabeth. Quite simply, Mr Miller, the role of the Bodyguard is to prevent our leaders being re-arrested under this new legislation, the Prisoners Temporary Discharge for Ill Health Act. Last month our leader, Emmeline Pankhurst, was scandalously given three years and sent to Holloway. She immediately started a hunger strike and ten days later was released under licence, even before this new act had received Royal Assent. Her licence required her to return to prison to complete her sentence on the twenty-eighth, but she was too ill to do so. Since then she has been under siege by the police in the home of one of our number in Norfolk Square. Oh, Mr Miller, might I have just a little more to eat? I'm still ravenous.'

'No, Dick. It would only make her ill. Alice, you must be careful. Finish the tea instead.' Elizabeth poured the last of the tea from the pot.

'Oh well, Elizabeth. I suppose you're right. Anyway, to continue our story, last week two detectives tried to force entry into the house with a warrant for poor Emmeline's arrest. Naturally, as members of the Bodyguard, we took action to prevent this and, in the ensuing scuffle, we were arrested and charged with assaulting a police officer. The truth is that it was more the other way round. Elizabeth can tell you the rest. I'm feeling a little tired.'

'There's not much else to add, anyhow. We went on hunger strike, too, and, as you already know, were due to appear in court a few days ago. Then, thanks to that darling little lawyer you sent us, the police seemed to have had a change of heart. The case was deferred and the next thing we knew was that we were bound over to keep the peace and released.'

'And will you keep the peace, Lizzy?'

'Fat chance. Thanks to our little ruse and your connivance, they don't know our real names, so we are free to continue the fight.'

'And what of your plans now, Lizzy, and you, Miss Robson?'

'I'm going to Boulogne to see Christabel, lay low and recover for a short while. As soon as I'm feeling stronger, I'll re-join the Bodyguard and help keep Emmeline free. You're going back to your aunt's are you not, Alice?'

'I suppose so, but I'm not sure what I'm to tell my Aunt Emmy. If she finds I've been in prison, she'll skin me alive and my mother would die of the shame. And I'm not sure that there'll be a job for me at the school. I've missed the best part of a week.'

'You may not have too much of a problem there, Miss Robson. I took the liberty of telephoning Miss Brockles and telling her you had been taken ill with a gastric problem whilst on a visit to my cousin in London. It was not too far from the truth and your present emaciated appearance will give credence to the deception. But, Lizzy, whilst I support your cause, please don't ever ask me to lie for you again. Now, if there is nothing more you require of me, my love, I shall catch the next train back to Portsmouth. I have been neglecting my duties a little this past week, but fortunately Commodore Keyes is too polite to pry into my personal affairs.'

Chapter 14

November 1913

Most women would have thought it unusual to be standing over a dry dock watching riveters at work. Elizabeth Miller, however, was not like most women of 1913. She was fascinated by the skill of the men working in teams of four. The heater boy would insert the rivet into a coke brazier using long tongs to heat it until it was red hot. He would then toss the red-hot piece of metal to the catch boy, who would catch the rivet in a wooden bowl, before using another pair of tongs to place the rivet into a pre-drilled hole of two overlapping steel sheets. However, she knew that these 'boys' could in fact be of any age these days, and were generally strong, tough and wiry, due to the physical nature of the work. Each red-hot rivet could weigh a pound and if the heater and catch boys were clumsy, it could easily fall on a worker below and cause serious injury or death. The third man, and she was acutely aware riveters were always men, was called the holder up. It was his job to place a hammer over the head of the rivet. Finally, the fourth member of the team, the basher, would work from inside the ship or submarine to hammer the end of the rivet flat and in this way, bind the two steel plates tightly together. The team had to work quickly, not just to insert each rivet whilst it was still molten, but because they were on piece work. In her brother's shipyard one team of riveters was known to have driven over 2,000 rivets in a single shift of twelve hours. It was extremely hard and often dangerous work, and it was no wonder the shipyard workers were a close-knit bunch. Like her brother and late father, Elizabeth had enormous respect for these men and, unlike some employers, paid much attention to their safety and welfare.

On this unusually lovely November day it was not the riveters of the family yard she was observing, but those of the Naval Construction Yard in Barrow, belonging to recently renamed Vickers Limited. Richard had persuaded her to make the visit. He was now proudly sporting an additional thin ring between the two thick gold stripes on his sleeves.

'Come on, Lizzy, that's not her. She's in the next dock.'

Elizabeth could see that Richard was clearly impatient to show off his new command, HMS *E9*, laid down just five months earlier and now being fitted out for commissioning the following year. Even so, she thought he seemed to appreciate the genuine interest she was showing in the build of this other E-boat, recently laid down for the Royal Australian Navy.

'You should be glad I'm interested. Visiting a shipyard isn't exactly most girls' idea of a birthday treat after all.' She had obtained her majority just a few days earlier.

'Forgive me, Lizzy, but just look this way. Isn't she beautiful?' Richard's eyes gleamed with pride. 'She's the first of a new improved design, with more powerful engines and an extra bow tube. I'm even working on the builders to fit her with a gun, but their Lordships are frustrating me on that at present.'

'I wouldn't describe £100,000 of metal as beautiful, but I can see you are bursting with pride over her, Dick. I am so pleased for you, although you wouldn't catch me going to sea in her, especially after your experience in *D2* last year.'

Richard visibly shuddered at the mention of the experience. Elizabeth immediately regretted bringing up the painful subject and mentally kicked herself. He had once told her that it was the closest he had ever come to death and she knew he had lost several of his shipmates. Most regrettable of all, he had lost his mentor, Johnson. The shock of his death had completely overshadowed the joy his widow had felt on the birth of their child. Richard assumed a far-off look and seemed completely unconscious of his surroundings and his cousin's presence.

Elizabeth laid a tender gloved hand on his forehead, softly touching the scar he had sustained during his escape from the sunken submarine, and gently brought him back to the present.

'Dearest Dick, I'm sorry. Let's look forwards not backwards. Now we'll have a look at my rival for your affection.'

There had not been much to see of Richard's submarine. The builders had been unwilling to allow a woman down into the dock, whether through prejudice or a genuine concern about safety, Elizabeth was unable to judge. But on reflection, she could see their point. The boat was still only partially built and a hive of activity with several different trades represented, fitting cabling, pipework, machinery and all the other essential materiel of a modern warship. It would have been the same in Birkenhead. Visitors of any form were an unwelcome nuisance.

As they took afternoon tea in the nearby Majestic Hotel, she quizzed her cousin on the principles of battery propulsion and the benefits of twin propellers. She also asked some very searching questions on the changes of metacentric height on diving beneath the surface.

'Gosh, Lizzy, you seem very well up on technical matters.'

'And just why should that surprise you, Dick? Father and I often discussed the work in the yard. He always treated me as Charles's equal. We both recognised that he had to groom Charles to take over the running of the yard. There was no way the men would accept a woman in charge and I am the younger sibling, in any case. But Charles has always been more interested in commerce than engineering. Now, with dear Father gone, Charles quite often relies on me to oversee the drawing office. Maybe within twenty years we will have women naval architects. It doesn't take brawn to design a triple-expansion engine.'

'I take your point, Lizzy, but wonder whether twenty years might be a little optimistic.'

'Who can say, but first we have to obtain the vote.'

'I wish you well with that, too, dear Lizzy, but let's not discuss that now. I want to talk about our future.'

Elizabeth affected not to notice, but a surge of emotion passed through her bloodstream. 'Golly, this is more like a birthday treat, Dick. These cakes are lovely. Thank you for inviting me up here.' She squeezed his hand fondly.

'I'm just glad you were able to drag yourself away from your suffragette friends for a day, Lizzy. I hope you had nothing to do with the burning down of Lloyd-George's house. I rather fear the public are tiring of Mrs Pankhurst's attacks.'

'As it happens, I wasn't involved, but I don't condemn the act. Lloyd-George had it coming to him.'

'But I rather thought he is considered in favour of your cause. He has certainly given enough speeches supporting votes for women. Why turn against him now?'

'Hah! Words not deeds. That was when he was in opposition. Now he's in government he's turned Asquith against the idea. He and

Churchill are a devious pair. They have both promised our cause every assistance possible, short of actual help. But for them, Asquith would have given sufficient parliamentary time for the Second Conciliation Bill to have been passed two years ago. As it is, the latest bill has been voted down by the Irish and there are no further plans to offer us the vote.' She banged the table in frustration.

'Hush, old girl. I can understand your vexation. You know I support your cause. I don't understand why the Irish thought votes for women would be used to prevent Irish home rule, but then I don't understand politics. I also don't understand why your WSPU would bomb the Chancellor's second home when he is seen as a prominent supporter of votes for women.'

'But that's just my point, Dick. He says one thing and does another,' Elizabeth replied in a hushed tone and with gritted teeth. 'He and the wobbler, Churchill, worked out that if middle class women were to be given the vote, then it could potentially add hundreds of thousands of votes to the strength of the Tory Party. So they persuaded Asquith to introduce a bill to extend the franchise to the four million working men not entitled to vote and their widows. Of course, the beauty of this measure is that it not only appears more democratic, but attracts the working class vote to the Liberal Party. As a politician you can't argue against it, but in the meantime we are left nowhere.'

'I sympathise, but let's leave the subject of politics alone for a while. I'm sorry I raised it. More happily, I received a rare letter from my brother, Peter, last week. He seems happier in Tehran than in Paris.'

'He may not be the most constant of correspondents, but he has found time to pen a few epistles to a certain young lady in Marton, I hear. Alice seems quite smitten with him, but like all of us, complains about the length of time between each of his letters.'

'I had not forgotten you and Alice had become such chums. She's a pretty lass, but I had hoped that after your brief stay earlier in the year at His Majesty's pleasure, she at least might have cooled her support for the suffragette cause.'

Elizabeth blushed at the memory and shame. At least Dick had been as good as his word and not mentioned the incident either to his father or her brother.

‘You need have no worries there, Dick. We both learned our lessons and Alice is still grateful to you for covering for her so that she could keep her job at the school.’

‘Don’t mention it. I was pleased to help and cannot help but worry for you both, that’s all. I regard it as my Christian duty. Do you think there may be a future in this relationship with my brother?’

‘I think it too early to say. They seem close enough, but absence doesn’t always make the heart grow fonder. Moreover, I sense that Peter has still to find himself in some way or other. Latterly, before this latest posting, I thought him dissatisfied within himself. He appears to be seeking something. He may yet return from Tehran a changed man. And, of course, one hears so many tales of the harems of Arabia.’

‘You know very well he’s in Persia, not Arabia, you goose. I cannot say that I have your perception. I just miss him and long for his safe return. I know *Mutti* is worried about him, but then she frets about all her sons, including me for some reason.’

‘Perhaps last year demonstrated just cause for her concern for you, Dick. It came as a shock to us all. I couldn’t have borne it if you had died.’ Elizabeth’s eyes watered up and a tear escaped down her cheek. She looked away and reached into her handbag for a handkerchief. Richard took hold of her hand tenderly.

‘Don’t worry about me, old girl. I don’t think God’s quite ready for my company yet.’

‘Oh, Dick, you really can be an idiot sometimes.’ She did not elaborate, but dabbed her eyes with the handkerchief and composed herself once more.

‘But tell me more of your beloved E-boats. Note my use of the word “boat”, mind, and not “ship”, dear cousin. I know that in the RN, submarines are referred to as boats by the *cognoscenti*, in that ships carry boats and submarines do not. You see, I’m picking up the naval slang. How does the speed and endurance compare with the D-Class, or even your old rust bucket, *B3*?’

Richard appeared frustrated by the change of subject. ‘Lizzy, you know I cannot give away the technical details. Who knows what use your suffragette friends might put to the knowledge? And don’t remind me of *B3*. Suffice to say, they are faster and have a longer range, as the boats have been designed to operate overseas rather than confined to the waters off our own coastline. I will have a bigger crew and even a Third Hand to act as Navigating Officer. However, neither of my officers, nor many of the crew will join much before the Commissioning next summer. But I didn't invite you up here to talk about them. I want to talk about us. You know I love you and you say you love me.'

'Don't talk rot, my darling. Of course I love you. I have long held men as a sex in pretty low esteem, but not you, Dick darling. You are kind, decent and gentle. I love you with all my heart and always have.' Elizabeth held up her hand to Richard's lips to kiss.

'Dearest Lizzy. I must speak with you and beg you will not interrupt. To be parted from you is like ripping my heart in two. It hurts. I have never been a passionate man as a rule, but in your presence my ardour for you becomes all consuming. I have never cared for anyone else so much in all my life and I just know that I could not live without you.'

Richard paused to stretch his starched collar and Elizabeth noted beads of sweat forming on his temples. Her heart began to beat in anticipation of what he might be about to say. It was indeed not like him to be sentimental. He took hold of both her hands tightly.

'Lizzy, I have to ask you this. Will you do me the honour of becoming my wife?'

Elizabeth felt confused. She had contented herself with her love for Dick and it had never crossed her mind that they might marry. They were cousins, after all. Tears began to fill her eyes.

'My dearest love. I am quite taken aback at your proposal and need a few minutes to compose myself before I reply. Will you excuse me a short while?'

She rose from the table and headed to the ladies' powder room. There she sat at the dressing table to dry her eyes and adjust her make-up. For several minutes she examined her innermost feelings. She had a brother, so was not unused to male company, but in Dick she felt she had a soul mate. He seemed to understand her and had never seriously mocked her for her views on women's suffrage. She felt she could share any of her inner thoughts with him, without fear of judgement or disclosure. The only other person she had felt this close to was Christabel, but since the start of the arson attacks the year before, Elizabeth had felt betrayed and not seen Christabel again. She admitted to herself that she had been fascinated by Christabel. They had even kissed and often shared a room, but Elizabeth knew that she was not really a lesbian. She had just wanted to explore her sexuality before meeting a real man. In her eyes men were pigs who together conspired to put down women, but she knew Dick didn't fall into that category.

She liked all her cousins, but Dick stood head and shoulders over them. Hitherto, she had regarded him as solid and reliable, but not the sort of man a woman could marry. He had changed, though, since that dreadful accident last year. For a start he didn't go on about religion quite so much. As far as she knew, he still attended church regularly, but she wondered if he had left something of his faith behind at the bottom of the sea. She had once thought him far better suited to a life in the clergy rather than the Navy. It was only natural that a near certain prospect of death might change one, and many of Dick's shipmates hadn't survived. He'd confided that the death of his captain had cut him deeply. But there was something else, too. He seemed to have lost some of his supreme assuredness and confidence. She quite liked that. It made him more human and even a little vulnerable. Dear Dick. He deserved this command and she was pleased to see him so happy. She suddenly felt a strange feeling well up in her bosom and recognised that she wanted him, too.

She looked into the mirror again and regarded carefully the reflection that looked back at her. Are you worthy of such a man, she asked her reflection silently. Could you truly make him happy? Her reflection smiled back at her reassuringly and she knew her answer.

When she returned to the table, Richard rose to greet her again. He seemed to have lost the colour in his cheeks. Really, she thought, how could this noble and brave man seem so under-confident of her reply? Instead of resuming the seat offered her, she brushed Dick's dark fringe with the back of her hand.

'Dick dear, you asked me a straight question and I feel a straight question deserves a straight reply. Of course I will marry you.'

Chapter 15

June 1914

In all her thirty-two years of married life, Johanna Miller had never attended a commissioning ceremony before. Today, on the ninety-ninth anniversary of the Battle of Waterloo, she only half listened to the naval chaplain conducting the service of dedication at the commissioning of the Royal Navy's latest addition to the Fleet, HMS *E9*. She knew it was a proud day for her eldest son, but even so, she could not find joy in the occasion. Next to her sat her husband, Rear Admiral Miller VC, CSC and several other decorations besides, and he was the cause of just one of her irritations that day. As a flag officer, he should have been wearing the traditional frock coat for such a formal occasion. Despite the advancing years, he was still, in her opinion, a handsome man and would have looked most distinguished in the naval finery, but instead, he had opted to dress similarly to the many civilians attending the ceremony, in his morning coat and matching top hat. William's reasoning was that he was attending in the private capacity of the father of the commanding officer of the new submarine. By not wearing his uniform he had not drawn attention to himself as the senior officer present and left the way clear for Roger Keyes, the Commodore Submarines, to take on the role of the senior naval representative at the service.

It meant that William looked no different from the many functionaries of the shipyard, but her main cause for disgruntlement sat further down the row, next to her son Peter. As usual, Elizabeth was dressed in purple, white and green, the colours of the WSPU. According to her niece, purple stood for the royal blood flowing through the veins of every suffragette, white for purity in private and public life, and green as the colour of hope and the emblem of spring. Before Richard had announced the news of his engagement to Elizabeth, Johanna had always loved her. Ever since the death of Elizabeth's mother, and despite Johanna's attempts to offer her niece the love of a mother, she had, nonetheless, become headstrong. And now she was involved in this suffragette nonsense. Edmond should have taken a firmer line with her, but men were always too indulgent of their daughters, even in her native Switzerland.

Johanna's thoughts were interrupted temporarily by William. The chaplain had just invited the congregation to sing the Naval Hymn.

'I always find this the best part of Divine Service, my dear. It gets the lungs going,' William uttered quietly.

'*Eternal Father, strong to save, whose arm hath bound the restless wave,*' William sang with gusto. He had a fine baritone voice, of which he was proud and not afraid to let ring out for all assembled to hear. Johanna looked across at Richard. He, also, seemed to be giving his all to the hymn.

'*Oh, hear us when we cry to Thee, for those in peril on the sea!*' William's powerful voice had often carried in the teeth of a gale and was now available to the whole of Barrow. Several people turned to see who owned this lusty and mellow tone. Johanna nudged him.

'William, you're too loud as usual,' she hissed.

'Nonsense, my darling. I must do Dick proud. *O Christ! Whose voice the waters heard,*' he continued singing.

Johanna barely heard the rest of the hymn. Her mind was on Elizabeth. Her intuition was that her niece could not make Richard happy. She sensed Elizabeth was still searching for something in her life and might not yet be ready to settle in a serious relationship just now. *Worst of all, what if they were to have children?* Marriages between cousins might not be illegal, but they were only one step removed from incest. Her grandchildren might turn out to be half-wits! But Richard would not listen to reason. He and Elizabeth had gone ahead and issued the invitations to the wedding for the first weekend of August, to tie in with the bank holiday, despite her quite reasonable objections. William had been of no help either. He had announced that nothing but a war would keep him from his son's wedding and, if necessary, he would attend without her. Thank God he had stopped singing.

*

'Hello, Elizabeth. My, you grow more beautiful every day, despite your outfit. Do allow me the pleasure of kissing you.'

Elizabeth silently seethed at Admiral Miller's remark. 'Why, of course, Uncle. You are looking very handsome yourself, although I am disappointed you are not in uniform on such a grand occasion.' She offered up her cheek to be kissed. 'As for my outfit, let's not discuss politics today. I know you quietly agree with our cause.'

'My dear Elizabeth, "quietly" is the operative word, but you are quite right. Now is not the time to debate the merits of militancy. How are the wedding plans coming along?'

'Fine, I suppose,' Elizabeth answered resignedly.

'Come, dear. You don't sound too enthusiastic. What's the issue? Cough up, girl.'

'I'm sorry. It's just that I was rather hoping for a quiet and private ceremony, but now it is to be a grand affair in Westminster Cathedral. I don't mind being married in a Catholic church, but does it have to be on such a big scale?'

'I see. That's your Aunt Johanna's influence, I'm afraid. But is it such a great ordeal? It's meant to be the happiest day of your life. Why not flaunt it?'

'I don't know really. Perhaps it's because neither of my parents will be there. I can't explain it. All I know is that I want to marry Dick and slink away without any great fuss.'

'Elizabeth, my dear, I hope you will come to look on me more as a father than a proud uncle. I could not be happier to see the two of you entwined.'

She forgot the earlier patronising comment and gripped William's left arm for balance, before reaching up on tiptoes to kiss his cheek. 'Dear Uncle, you are such a poppet. But I know Aunt Johanna doesn't approve of me.'

'Oh, don't worry about her. Mothers are always protective of their cubs. No girl could ever be right for one of their sons. I suppose I might have felt the same about a potential son-in-law had I been blessed with a daughter. Your aunt will come round. Especially if you provide her with a grandchild.'

'But is that not just her objection, Uncle? She is convinced that any children of ours will be Mongoloids.'

'You'll prove her wrong. I'm sure of it. There is no scientific basis to such a theory, anyway. Even our great thinker on evolution, Charles Darwin, married his cousin. Just you leave your aunt to me and stop worrying. Oh, stop fussing, lass.' Elizabeth hugged him tightly.

'Let go, girl. Your brother's coming across. Good afternoon, Charles. It must be several months since I've seen you. I'm pleased you could come to support Dick.'

'Good afternoon, Uncle William,' Charles replied affably.

'So how's business then, Charles?'

'Fair to middling. The *Caroline* is on the stocks and I've just signed a contract with the Greeks to build them two cruisers, too. I'm even thinking of building a few of these E-boats. I don't see why Vickers and Chatham should get all the business.'

'Charles, I'll leave you and Uncle William to discuss business. Thank you for the chat, Uncle.' Elizabeth had spotted Peter Miller near the refreshment tables and availed herself of the opportunity to slip away and join him.

'Hello, Peter. You're looking well. I hear you've been taking some leave at Marton Hall.'

'Oh, hello, Lizzy. Yes, I wanted to tell Grandmama about my time in Persia. I met up with one of our cousins, you know?'

'So I've heard. Darius wasn't it?'

'Correct. He was a jolly useful contact actually. He, er, helped me learn the more colloquial and modern features of Persian.'

'I rather fancy you haven't just been calling on Grandmama. You're still looking awfully tanned. I suspect a certain young school mistress finds that rather attractive?'

Peter's blushes at the reference to Alice, confirmed to Elizabeth that he had indeed been seeing her.

'Yes, I have been catching up with Alice. You two seem to have become thick as thieves whilst I was away. She has been telling me the news of your joint activities with the WSPU. The death of that woman at the Derby last year was clearly a tragedy, but surely there was no need for someone to take a meat cleaver to Velázquez's *Toilet of Venus*. It is, after all, a national treasure. Neither you nor Alice had a hand in it, did you?'

'Peter, I despair with you. I've had to get used to being patronised, but I don't have to take it from you. You quote the death of a woman and the damage of a painting in the same sentence, as if they were equally tragic. The Diplomatic Service doesn't seem to have taught you tact. Can you not see how strongly we feel about the cause of votes for women? I and my sisters are prepared to die to obtain that right for each other.' Elizabeth felt she could no longer harbour her frustrations. Something seemed to burst within her.

'That painting was just an excuse for men to feast their eyes on an image of a nude woman in the respectability of the National Gallery. Something had to be done to shock you men into understanding the depth of our feelings.'

Elizabeth's voice gradually began to rise and her speech attracted several stares from other guests.

'Calm down, Lizzy. I've told you before. I'm in favour of the vote for women, but these things take time. I just hope you or Alice aren't involved with such extremism.'

Elizabeth cut off his homily. She snapped and started screaming at him.

'Why don't you understand? You're just like all the men. You think that by patting us on the heads and saying, "Calm down, dears", we'll be satisfied. Well it won't wash. I will not be patronised. We're sick of such sentiments. We want real change and far from being your precious and innocent little cousin, I admire the militants and wish I had the courage to be one. In fact I'll show you.'

She strode off in the direction of *E9* and, just as the Red Sea parted before Moses and the Hebrew people, the crowd of shocked onlookers parted before her fury. She reached the jetty without anyone having the presence of mind to stop her. Hunting amongst the neatly piled stores in the vicinity of the submarine's gangway she found what she wanted. She stooped, grunted with satisfaction, and angrily slung the can in the direction of the submarine. It was a prodigious effort whose results pleased her. The can hit the fin and, bursting open upon impact, deposited its contents of green paint across the fin and onto the casing.

'That's what I think of you boys and your toys,' she shouted with delight.

Later she recalled that the colour of the paint was a symbol of hope.

Chapter 16

July 1914

'Darling very much regret may need to postpone wedding STOP All leave cancelled pending international developments STOP Much love Dick'.

When Richard had commenced his leave in readiness for his wedding, there had been no talk of war. *E9* had just begun a period of maintenance and his First Lieutenant, Lieutenant Reginald Ashridge, had had everything under control. Now, just four days before his wedding, he had received a telegram ordering him to re-join his submarine, in Immingham of all places. Richard was confused as he had previously understood the Eight Submarine Flotilla's war station to be Harwich. Papa had not been able to explain much either. Even before the telegram had arrived, he had hurriedly packed his bags and announced he would be sleeping at the Admiralty until further notice. All Richard had been able to glean was that the Austro-Hungarian Empire had declared war on Serbia and that Germany had rejected Britain's calls for an international conference to settle the differences between the warring nations. He had tried ringing Elizabeth but, not being able to reach her, had with great sadness sent her the telegram suggesting that the wedding might have to be postponed. To his surprise *Mutti* had not seemed too distressed at the thought of cancelling all the arrangements.

On arrival at Immingham a day later, Richard had discovered the depot ship, *Maidstone*, and eight of her submarines had moved there earlier in the week. All leave for the submarine service had been cancelled by Keyes and the submarines ordered to prepare for war. Ashridge had efficiently arranged for the embarkation of the spare torpedoes, warheads, fuel and stores, as well as charging the batteries. There seemed little else that Richard could do except to await developments.

It was not until the following day, the thirtieth of July, when all submarines were ordered to move to Harwich, that Richard had finally reconciled himself to the fact that he would not be getting married on the

Saturday after all. There followed two days of practice attacks on the *Maidstone* and another depot ship, HMS *Adamant*, before berthing in Harwich and further fuelling and storing.

Richard found the weekend frustrating, but he was not alone in that. All his fellow submarine officers in Harwich seemed to feel the same. Keyes had now raised his pennant in *Maidstone* and called his submarine COs together for a conference on the Sunday night.

'Gentlemen, before I brief you on my plans, let me bring you up to date with the latest news. Some of you, no doubt, have been keeping abreast of events through the newspapers, but I have learned not to place my faith in journalists.' Richard did not join in with the polite tittering of some of the other COs.

'Following the declaration of war by Austria-Hungary on Serbia, the Grand Fleet has sailed to its war station at Scapa Flow. The Austrians have started to bombard the Serb capital of Belgrade and this has enticed the Russians to come to the support of their Slav allies. As for the Germans, they have moved their more modern ships through the Kiel Canal to north-coast ports. Closer to home, the German yachts have withdrawn from the Cowes regatta and I view this as ominous.

'Last night Germany declared war on Russia and warned her ally, France, to remain neutral. The view at the Admiralty is that France is unlikely to comply. The French have long memories and are spoiling for a fight to avenge themselves for their defeat in the 1870s. Which, of course, means that at any hour our nearest neighbour may be at war with Germany, too. Is everybody with me so far?'

Most of those present merely nodded, but the CO of *E7*, Feilmann, had a question.

'Sir, if France goes to war, are we then not committed to join her? Is that why we are readying ourselves for war?'

'That is a question our illustrious Cabinet has been debating all weekend. The sea-lawyers are maintaining that the *Entente Cordiale* is not an alliance and does not bind us to come to the aid of France.' This comment provoked a roar of outrage amongst the COs.

'Gentlemen, gentlemen. Settle down. Please.' Keyes managed to restore order within a very short while. 'The Admiralty has no wish to see French ports in the Channel bombarded by the Germans. It has persuaded the Cabinet to warn the Germans that the Royal Navy will intervene should the Imperial German Navy undertake any hostile acts against the French in the North Sea or Channel. My understanding is that, perhaps at this very moment, our ambassador is delivering the message to the Germans. I can assure you, gentlemen, that the First Sea Lord believes if France declares war on Germany, then we will stand by her.'

'But, sir,' one of the COs chimed. 'I've heard that the Foreign Secretary and the Chancellor are dead against a war with Germany.'

'That may be so, but I am not privy to the Cabinet discussions, although I believe the First Lord of the Admiralty is of the belief we must side with France.'

'But what of our honour should we not, sir?' somebody shouted indignantly. 'We can't just stand back. What would happen if Germany took the Belgian and French Channel ports? If the frogs were knocked out, then we'd be next. In any case, were we to remain neutral, then the Navy would never be able to visit a foreign port again. We'd be spat at. We'd lose our trade and the empire would be forever crippled. It's not just honour that's at stake here, sir, but our very future.'

'Would you mind if I said something, sir?' Richard cut in. 'I've lived in Berlin, but only during the school hols, so I cannot pretend to understand the German psyche, but my father can. He was the naval attaché. He's convinced of one thing. If the Germans are to take on the might of the Russian Army, they cannot fight on two fronts simultaneously. France must either remain neutral or be knocked out quickly. According to my father, the Germans have a plan to by-pass the French forts and defences by taking them in the flank in a surprise attack through Belgium and Luxembourg. Should that happen, then we are committed to protecting the neutrality of these countries.'

'What you say is true, Miller, and the Intelligence Division is of the opinion that were Germany to invade Luxembourg and Belgium to attack the French, then only the most lily-livered of our politicians would argue that we should stand aside. But Grey and Lloyd-George aren't the only ones holding out for a non-military solution, and it's not our job to second guess our elected politicians. Events are already moving more swiftly than I could have envisaged and I do not wish the submarine service to be caught napping.' Keyes handed each of the submarines COs a sealed thick envelope.

'Gentlemen, these are your sealed orders in the event of war with Germany. Included are the secret codes for use with the French Fleet. You may open them when you return onboard your boats. For now, please give your attention to this chart.' Keyes's staff officer unfurled a chart of the German coastline along the North Sea and the COs huddled around it.

'You are all aware that there are four main rivers that flow into the North Sea from Germany, at the end of which she has her main naval bases. In all, there are 200 miles of coastline between the Dutch and Danish borders, but I am only interested in the seventy miles that adjoin the Heligo Bight. My plan is to use our submarines to impose a tight blockade of these ports. I regret that owing to a lack of foresight by our lords and masters, much of the submarine flotilla comprises boats designed for coastal work only. They are of little more use than mobile mines. That means that the brunt of the patrols is going to fall on our few overseas submarines, namely, you gentlemen. So return to your boats, examine your orders and study the charts well. In the next forty-eight hours I want you to know the coastline of the Heligo Bight as well as the back of your hands.'

Chapter 17

August 1914

As the First Lieutenant of *E9*, Lieutenant Ashridge was responsible for the trim of the boat. The submarine was at periscope depth and proceeding on the electric motors at three knots. It was a fairly calm summer's day and Ashridge knew that his captain would expect as little of the periscope to be exposed above the surface as possible. Just a one foot variation in depth could make a difference.

'Happy with the trim, sir,' he reported. He knew that his captain, Lieutenant Commander Richard Miller, had last seen the coast line of Heligoland almost exactly three years ago. The circumstances this evening were very different. Three years earlier the island of Heligoland had been barely defended, although construction work to build fortifications had started. Now these works had been completed, the Admiralty would have a much more difficult task in mounting an amphibious operation ashore to take over the island. Furthermore, the great works to build two harbours to the south of the island had been completed, the entrance to which was *E9*'s objective today. More significantly, fewer than twenty-four hours earlier, war between Britain and Germany had been declared.

'Up. Stop.' Richard called to the periscope operator in the control room. 'Come two degrees to starboard. Down. First Lieutenant, there's no immediate sign of any warships in the outer harbour, but I intend making a comprehensive search. The trim seems fine so I think we can afford the risk of entering blind the narrow channel into the harbour.'

'Aye, sir,' Ashridge replied.

A few minutes later, when the captain must have judged he had passed through the harbour entrance, he again ordered the periscope to be raised and the main motors to be stopped. The control room team waited in silent anticipation whilst he surveyed the harbour.

'Ah, well. There's always tomorrow,' Richard muttered to himself and then aloud, 'Down.'

The periscope was lowered and Ashridge waited anxiously for his captain's report.

'Disappointingly, the only craft I could see were small support boats and none was worth attacking. The Imperial High Seas Fleet is clearly not here. First Lieutenant, take her down to the bottom. We'll lie here overnight and see what fish we can fry in the morning. Once we're settled, you can send the hands to dinner. Ask the Chief to give me a report on the state of the batteries. I'll be in the wardroom.'

'Aye aye, sir.' Ashridge replied and started to give the orders to flood the ballast tanks and sink the boat gently on the bottom of the harbour.

'He's a cool one, the skipper, don't you think, sir?' Leading Seaman Barker, the helmsman asked Ashridge. 'What impudence. To sit in the enemy's harbour and wait for them to come back. The Germans 'ave got it comin' I reckon.'

'He's certainly unconventional, but he knows what he's doing,' Ashridge replied.

He had served under Richard's command for nearly a year now and respected him enormously. Although a little shy and remote from his men, the captain also showed compassion and was a decent sort when you got to know him. Yet first impressions were often terrifying. The CO was a hard task master who drove himself hard and expected the same from others. He was intolerant of any form of slackness or lack of effort. He also knew his mind and was confident in his own decisions. In his view, it was acceptable to offer an alternative opinion, and indeed, unlike many senior officers, he welcomed other ideas or challenges to his views. However, once he had heard you out, if he decided otherwise, then you were expected to get on with it. Ashridge had often heard Miller say that it was better to go in the wrong direction in unison, than to take no direction due to disharmony. After all, he had stated, if it was the wrong direction, everyone would soon work it out. As the First Lieutenant, Ashridge had quickly learned that the CO was usually right, but he appreciated him being open minded. He hoped that the boat might see some action in the morning. The men were anxious to strike an early blow against the Germans and prove the capability of their submarine.

Once Ashridge had judged the boat was safely settled on the sea bed, he sent the ship's company to dinner, but before returning to the wardroom, he checked the time of sunset and sunrise. The CO would probably have checked this already and would expect his second-in-command to know, too. Ashridge did not wish to look foolish.

*

'Captain, sir, bridge. Smoke bearing red three-zero, range 10,000 yards.' The Navigator had the watch on the bridge of *E9* as she patrolled her now familiar hunting ground between Heligoland and the German mainland. *E9* had spent the previous night on the bottom to rest the men, but had surfaced an hour earlier at dawn to charge the batteries.

Richard rushed to the periscope to look for himself. It had been a frustrating few weeks since the declaration of war. Along with other submarines of the Eighth Submarine Flotilla at Harwich, they had mounted frequent patrols in the North Sea and Heligo Bight. Whilst the submarines had provided information to the Admiralty on the disposition of the enemy, they had not as yet had the opportunity for action. Richard rued the fact that on the only occasion the German Navy had made a foray into the North Sea, *E9* had not been anywhere near the area. Late in August, a battle had taken place in the Heligo Bight between light cruisers and destroyers of both navies, but it was not a decisive battle. He knew the Royal Navy was keen to bring the whole High Seas Fleet to battle and to destroy it once and for all. It would be the greatest sea battle in history since Trafalgar, but the Germans were not playing their part in the script. The action at the end of August seemed to have made the German Navy even more reluctant to venture out to sea. He and his ship's company were desperate to blood themselves, so the report of smoke was rapidly passed down the boat.

It took him a little while to spot the smoke for himself. The sea was shrouded by sporadic and wispy banks of early morning fog. Looking back towards Heligoland, six miles to the north-west, Richard reflected that the Navigator or his lookout had done well to spot the smoke at the extreme range of the visibility. He considered taking the submarine to periscope depth, but decided that to remain on the surface would give them a better vantage point to identify the smoke's origin.

'Officer of the Watch, Captain. Come left to a course of 110 to close the range. Report when you see the ship hull down.'

He chided himself for the last remark. It had been unnecessary and would have given the impression that he lacked confidence in the new navigator. Sub Lieutenant 'Paddy' O'Connell was a reserve officer, called up from the Merchant Navy for his navigation skills, but still new to submarines. Indeed, he did not have to wait long for a further report.

'Captain, sir, Officer of the Watch. I can see more smoke. It looks like a large warship with a couple of escorts, but it's difficult to see in the mist.'

'Very well. I have the submarine. Come below. I intend diving the submarine.' He could have instructed the Officer of the Watch to make an emergency dive as a means to keep him and the crew practiced, but he wanted a little more time to observe the approaching group.

Within a few minutes of diving *E9*, he was back at the periscope. He first swept the horizon quickly in what was termed an 'all-round look', to determine that the submarine was not in danger of being run down. His practised eye took in the fact that the mist was thinning, but visibility remained poor. He then took more time to search carefully the quadrant of the horizon to the south-east. A dim shape caught his attention and he focused in its direction. A moment later the strands of mist broke up to reveal a glimpse of an elderly light cruiser and then it was gone behind another cloud of mist.

'Bearing that. Range 4,000 yards. Angle on the bow red seven-zero.'

The control room team immediately sprang into action to plot the co-ordinates of the target and calculate its course and speed. The men worked in complete silence lest they disturb their captain's concentration. Knowing the bearing of the submarine relative to the ship's head allowed the attack team to estimate the target's course. Regular updates would enable them to finesse its speed and range.

Meanwhile, Richard altered course to port to close the cruiser's range and to put *E9* in a position a little ahead of his target. Confident that his periscope would not be visible in the mist, he continued to scan the horizon and soon established that the cruiser was being escorted by two destroyers and a flotilla of torpedo boats. He passed their bearings and approximate ranges to be plotted. He was not just concerned with closing the cruiser, but in avoiding detection by its escorts. One of the destroyers was on a course to pass between *E9* and the cruiser, and he judged it prudent to lower the periscope.

'Flood and equalise all tubes. Keep fifty feet,' he ordered. *E9* was fitted with five eighteen-inch torpedo tubes, two in the bows, two on the beam and one in the stern. The torpedo tubes needed to be flooded in order to equalise the pressure inside the tube with the seawater outside. Richard normally left the tubes dry until the submarine went to action stations, since any torpedo not fired would have to be 'drawn back' after the attack, washed down with fresh water to prevent rusting, dried off and re-greased before reloading. The interior fittings of the tubes also had to be re-greased. He recognised that this involved much work for the torpedo team, but whilst he hoped to fire only two torpedoes, he needed all tubes ready in case of counter attack by the destroyers.

He started his stop watch and mentally calculated the time he would need to run in towards the target before returning to periscope depth. He had to judge it carefully as he first wanted to pass under the nearest destroyer in order to give himself a clear shot at the cruiser. At the same time he had to consider that either the cruiser or the destroyer might have altered course since his last look. Ideally he wanted to fire from a range of 1,000 yards, but if he came up too soon, he risked counter detection, and if he delayed, then he might miss his chance for a successful attack. Only he could make that decision.

In his peripheral vision Richard could see members of his ship's company tensed, waiting on his actions with bated breath. Just a week before, HMS *Pathfinder* had been sunk by an enemy submarine and it was time to even the score. Gradually, he heard the throbbing and swishing sound of a destroyer passing above from right to left. The only sounds within *E9* were those of the motors and the control room machinery. Even the quiet whirring and clicking of the hydroplane and steering wheels seemed deafening.

Richard tried to ignore the obvious tension around him. He recalled the many hours he had spent eighteen months earlier in the Submarine Attack School at HMS *Dolphin*, preparing for just this moment. His friend, Martin Nasmith, had used a periscope and small moveable model ships to teach him and his fellow students the principles of attacking. Now all that theory had to be put into action. He checked the stop watch. They had ducked the port destroyer screen and the interval suggested they were now 1,000 yards off the port beam of the cruiser. It was time to commit to the attack, but instead he decided to wait a little longer. He wanted to open the range of the destroyer to his stern.

The seconds ticked by and he could feel the men willing him to return to PD and take the shot. They would have to wait, he thought. That was the power of command. He prayed silently to God to guide his torpedoes home and then broke the silence.

'Stop both motors. Open One and Two tube bow-caps. Ten up. Keep twenty-seven feet.'

The clunk of the bow-cap doors reverberated throughout the hull, but otherwise the tense silence continued. Richard crouched on his knees by the periscope and quietly ordered it to be raised. The mechanism hissed until he ordered, 'Stop' at the point the rubber eye-piece rose to the level of his eyes. To his satisfaction, the cruiser was exactly where he wanted her, fine on the starboard bow at a range of 600 yards and about to cross ahead. He recognised her as the *Hela*.

'Fire One ... Fire Two,' he ordered and reset his stop watch. He heard a quiet cheer from forward of the control room, followed by a hiss and the muffled explosion of the air bubbles as the torpedoes left the submarine. He waited only long enough to see the tell-tale tracks of the torpedoes running true before lowering the periscope. He had no wish to alert the cruiser to his presence before the torpedoes had run their full course.

Thirty seconds later he and all the ship's company heard the noise and felt the shock of two explosions in rapid succession. This time the whole crew responded with a loud cheer. They had hit the enemy hard. Richard ignored them and, cutting the revelry short, ordered the periscope to be raised again.

He surveyed the scene above with satisfaction. The *Hela* had been struck twice amidships and was dead in the water. She was taking on a heavy list, but he could not tell whether the damage he had inflicted was fatal. He was debating the use of one of the beam torpedoes when he saw a salvo of shells fall into the water around the periscope. Swinging the periscope round swiftly, he espied a destroyer bearing down on him at full speed and the flash of another salvo from its forward guns. Without hesitation, he once more took the submarine back down to fifty feet and increased speed. He was annoyed with himself. Any submariner worth his salt would have avoided his basic error in forgetting to conduct an all-round look and looking for the escort he knew to be in the vicinity. He felt no elation about hitting the target. His basic error might have been fatal to all the men under his command. In any case the task was not yet complete.

As Richard manoeuvred the submarine clear of the datum of the attack, he and his men could hear the continuous noise of enemy traffic above. Several of the vessels emitted the distinctive whine of steam-driven turbines, indicating that there were more than the two destroyers about that Richard had sighted through the mist. Slowly he edged *E9* south-west into deeper water, but he still needed to satisfy himself that he had delivered a mortal blow to the *Hela*. Gradually, the noises of the surface traffic abated and he ordered a return to periscope depth.

This time he did not neglect a 360 degree sweep of the horizon and noted a pair of armed trawlers nearby, stopped in the water, before concentrating on the sector where he knew the *Hela* to be. He was relieved to see both no sign of the stricken cruiser and that several ships were picking up survivors from the water, including a destroyer. It presented a tempting target, but he had scruples about attacking a ship engaged on a humanitarian mission. In any case, he had to be wary of the nearby armed trawlers.

Sure enough, on his next sweep he spotted a sailor on the foredeck of one of the trawlers pointing excitedly at his periscope. He ordered *E9* back to fifty feet and resumed the crawl south-westwards. *E9* was capable of a speed of ten knots submerged, but this was no match for the thirty-two knots or more of the enemy destroyers and torpedo boats above. Moreover, Richard faced a dilemma. The faster he pushed the boat on her electric motors, the quicker he would drain the batteries, and he had not been able to charge the batteries fully whilst on the surface prior to the attack.

Within minutes, the whine and thrashing of the turbines and propellers of at least four destroyers could be heard above. Richard briefly wondered why such an elderly cruiser had been so heavily escorted, but he had other problems to consider. Whilst *E9* remained deep she was invisible and could not be attacked, but she had to come up for air sometime to charge her precious batteries. When she did so, she would be vulnerable to shellfire or ramming. The risk would be reduced under the cover of darkness, but sunset was still eight hours off. Should he bottom the submarine in the present shallow depths and hope the enemy would tire of the search, or continue to head for deeper water? He decided to share his decision with the control room team, knowing it would quickly permeate throughout the whole ships' company.

'Firstly, I deem that a successful attack. There was no sign of the target on my last look, but I did see survivors in the water. As you will have gathered, we seem to have stirred up a hornet's nest and there is a veritable armada up there looking for us. For those of you less familiar with Norse mythology, Hela is the goddess of death and the underworld. I have no intention of allowing anyone in *E9* to join her realm, so I plan to evade slowly to the south all day and surface this evening to charge the batteries. With that in mind, I want all but the most essential equipment switched off. It's going to be an uncomfortable ten to twelve hours, but I've known worse. Any questions?'

To his embarrassment, one of the seaman responded by calling, 'Three cheers for the skipper. Hip, hip, hurrah.' Even Ashridge joined in the cheering.

*

Richard's plan to surface after ten to twelve hours proved to be over-optimistic. For the next forty-eight hours they were hunted by the German forces seeking revenge for the loss of the *Hela*. On each occasion that *E9* surfaced to run the diesel engines and recharge the batteries, she was driven down by destroyers attempting to ram her. Trawlers were then brought in to locate the dived submarine, using towed sweeps. Every time one of the metal tendrils from the surface scraped along the hull or jumping wire of the boat, Richard was reminded of his last hours in *D2*. In these circumstances the batteries were run down to dangerous levels and the atmosphere extremely uncomfortable. Even so, he was proud that the men remained cheerful, buoyed by their success. He was embarrassed to hear them say that he had encountered worse and still brought his men to safety. Somehow they managed to coax the batteries to stay alive just long enough to evade the enemy. When *E9* entered Harwich harbour with the triumphant news of the avenging of the *Pathfinder* a wag in the fore-ends persuaded Richard to fly the Jolly Roger. The last but one First Sea Lord, Sir Arthur Wilson VC, had, after all, suggested that all enemy submariners should be hanged as pirates.

Chapter 18

October 1914

'Hello, is that you Ashridge?'

'It is, sir, but it's a bad line, so you'll have to speak up.'

'Well, I can hear you fine just now. Is that any better?' Richard raised his voice.

'Much better, thank you, sir.'

'What's up? Durton, my father's butler, said it was urgent.'

'It is urgent, sir, but I thought I would try to catch you on the telephone, rather than send a telegram. I'm glad I caught you in London.'

'I leave for Lancashire tomorrow. I thought I would have a few days up there before the wedding. My mother has already gone up.'

'That's what I'm ringing you about, sir. We've had fresh orders.'

A tingle of excitement ran through Richard and for a moment he forgot about his wedding that weekend.

'I've just seen Captain (S) and he's told me to cancel all further leave. Everyone is to report back on board within seventy-two hours. We and two other boats are on standby for some sort of special mission. But Captain (S) knows you're getting married, sir, and wondered if you might be able to bring it forward. It's bad luck you being inconvenienced twice this way, sir.'

Richard was silent for a minute. Several things were passing through his head. His first thoughts concerned what needed to be done to make *E9* ready for any form of special mission. The boat was in the middle of a maintenance period and half the ship's company had just returned from a fortnight's leave. The other half, like him, had only just started their leave. There were bound to be more than a few disgruntled by the sudden recall. The maintenance work would have to be halted and the boat put back together again. There was storing to be considered, fuelling, the loading of new torpedoes and a hundred and one other things. It wasn't fair to impose such a burden on Ashridge, competent as he was. Then he remembered his wedding and he imagined Lizzy's disappointment at a second postponement, and after all the aggravation in persuading *Mutti* to attend, too. Might he be able to obtain a special licence and marry in a registry office? No, it was unthinkable. It was just one of those exigencies of the Service. Of course they would still marry, but the arrangements would just have to be put on ice for a little while.

'Can you give me any clue as to the nature of our possible mission, Number One?'

'I can't, sir, because I don't know. All Captain (S) said is that three E-boats would be involved, but he is waiting for Boyle and Cochrane to get back from a preliminary recce, and then it's all dependent on some hush-hush conference for the go-ahead. It might all come to nought.'

'Very well, Ashridge. I need a little time to sort out my affairs, not least in breaking the news to my fiancée, but I'll be back in Harwich by tomorrow evening. In the meantime, I am relying on you to start making the boat ready for sea at short notice. Is there anything you need to ask?'

'No, sir, but that's not my only news.'

'Really? Carry on.'

'Captain (S) also told me that I am to have my own command.'

'Why that's capital news, Ashridge. Congratulations. It's thoroughly well deserved. Any idea which boat and when you're to take over?'

'Yes, sir. I'm to take over *C9* on Tuesday and my relief is joining tomorrow,' Ashridge said apologetically. 'I don't expect it is welcome news, sir. I mean, a new First Lieutenant just at the moment.'

'It is quite short notice, but these things can't be helped, so the sooner we get this war over, the better. I admit the timing is a bit awkward, but I'm still delighted for you. I bet you can't wait to take command. Do you know the new chap's name?'

'Yes, sir. Steele. The cricketer. Do you recall him?'

'Not the chap that played for England and the MCC?'

'That's him, sir. He was on the winter tour in South Africa this year and hasn't been to sea for two years.'

'May the Lord help us then, Ashridge. That settles it. I'll definitely be with you tomorrow evening.'

*

'I was sorry to cut short your leave, Miller. Weren't you supposed to be getting married?'

'Yes, sir. Today in fact.' Richard was seated in the day cabin of Captain Waistell, captain of the depot ship *Maidstone* and Captain (S) Eighth Submarine Flotilla at Harwich. Berthed alongside the depot ship were three submarines of the E-class, including *E9*.

'Ah. Pity about that. Might be a while before you get another chance. The fact is you may be away quite some time.' Waistell rose and walked over to the sideboard on which lay a small selection of decanters. 'Drink?'

'No, thank you, sir. I'll stick with the coffee.'

'Oh, yes. I forgot. You don't, do you, Miller? I'm going to have one. It's been a bloody day. I suppose you've heard that the Germans have taken Antwerp? The Belgians have been completely routed.'

'No, I hadn't heard that, sir, although it was on the cards. I fear my cousin may be involved.'

'Oh, dear. A complete mess. Churchill did his best, of course, with the naval brigades, but where were the French or the BEF? I hope your cousin was one of the lucky ones who escaped to the Netherlands. Means internment, of course, but better than capture.'

Richard listened to Captain (S) calmly, keeping his emotions in check, but his thoughts were with Lizzy. She wouldn't know any of this and when the news broke, she would be fearful for her brother, Charles. He wished he could be with her to offer her comfort.

'Can you be ready to sail within the week?'

'Yes, sir.' Richard replied without hesitation.

'I suppose you know where you're going, Miller. It's meant to be a bloody secret, which means everyone round here knows.'

'My TI tells me the word in the bomb shop is that we're off to give aid to the Russians, sir.'

'Spot on, though I'm sorry you didn't hear it from me. The least I can do is explain why. You didn't hear that from the bomb shop via your TI, perchance?'

'No, sir. I suspect the men attach more importance to this afternoon's fixture between Pompey and Brighton and Hove Albion than to the conduct of the war.'

'Quite. The fact is that the new Kiel Canal is allowing the Germans to use the Baltic both to exercise their navy and to import essential goods. Specifically, iron ore from Sweden. You and the two other E-boats will sail a week today, that is the seventeenth. You penetrate the Skagerrak, proceed up the Baltic and rendezvous in the Russian naval base of Libau. There you will receive further orders according to the situation you encounter. Any defects?'

'None that should pose a problem, sir. My chief's worried about one of the armatures, on the port motor, and we're having a slight problem with the rudder, too. I'm confident we'll fix both very quickly, sir.'

'And how is your new First Lieutenant, the Honourable Algernon Steele settling in?'

'Fair to middling, as we say in Lancashire, sir. I confess to being disappointed to lose the experience of Ashridge, sir. He was a competent officer. I'm a bit worried about Steele's lack of experience, but you cannot fault his keenness. He's never out of his coveralls and is quickly learning every system stem to stern.'

'Yes, I'm sorry about Ashridge, but Steele comes well recommended. You know his grandfather, the eleventh earl of Storrs, was a vice-admiral?'

'I didn't, sir.' So that's it, Richard thought to himself. Steele has been foisted on me after spending the best part of two years playing cricket, just because his grandfather's a Scottish earl who still has friends in the Navy. Patronage will out, despite Fisher's reforms. He started to sympathise with his former CO, Mullan.

'Right, I'd better let you get back to your boat, Miller. Plenty to do, no doubt. Just one more thing before you go. You've been put up for a DSO for sinking the *Hela*. Their Lordships tried to fob you off with one of these new Mentioned-in-Despatches, but Keyes wouldn't have any of it, so congratulations. Now, this mission won't be easy, but it must be better than hanging around the German Bight. You and your fellow COs will have the chance to take the war to the enemy instead of waiting for him to come to us. So more than enough opportunity for a few more medals all round. Knock on my door if you need any help.'

'Very good, sir. Thank you, sir.' Richard returned to his cabin and as he did so, he wondered whether he felt more deflated or elated after his interview with Captain (S).

*

Few people lined the quayside on the afternoon of the seventeenth as the convoy of three submarines and two destroyers set sail for the North Sea.

Richard presumed that after two months of war, the residents of Harwich had tired of the coming and going of the submarines and destroyers based there. His attention was drawn to two little girls vigorously waving coloured handkerchiefs with their free hands whilst their mother held the other. The farewell may have been for one of the destroyers as he saw a petty officer, on the quarterdeck of one, offer a discreet wave back. He hoped that one day he and Lizzy might have children and be on the jetty to wave him farewell. Instantly, he felt a pang of regret that he was not leaving these shores as a married man. Lizzy had taken the postponement well and promised to throw herself into the work of the shipyard. Now that her brother, Charles, had joined the Navy, too, Lizzy was running the yard singlehandedly.

He wondered again whether he should invite Steele to the bridge to dive the submarine. If he was to make any mistakes after two years ashore, it would be better that he made them in the relatively benign home waters, rather than in the face of the enemy. But he had been through this several times, he thought. It's the First Lieutenant's role to supervise the trim on the first dive after being in harbour and for that his place is in the control room. He again resolved to learn to accept that he was no longer a First Lieutenant and he had to trust his officers. If he changed the normal routine, it would only betray to the ship's company that he lacked confidence in his new second-in-command. No, it would be better to exercise Steele along with the rest of the ship's company on the crossing of the North Sea. He intended to work the boat and her crew hard on his way to the Baltic.

He watched the E-boat ahead open her main vents and her captain give him a friendly wave as he took a last leisurely look around the bridge before going below. It was an unusual luxury to see another submarine dive. Soon it would be the turn of *E9* and the signalman was already in the process of clearing all the paraphernalia needed on the bridge for leaving harbour, but completely superfluous once dived.

The plan was that the destroyers would remain in company with the submarines until they had completed their check dives. The three E-boats would then proceed independently across the North Sea and on to Libau. With luck and good judgement, this should take no longer than a week. The passage to the mouth of the Sound between Helsingborg in Sweden and Helsingor in Denmark had been found practicable by two fellow E-boat captains in September. However, they had reported that the narrow channel was swept by swift currents and navigation would be difficult. The lights of the towns of the two neutral countries on either side of the sound masked the navigational lights and depth keeping was likely to be a problem. Not only was the depth of the channel a maximum of thirty five feet, leaving only nine feet below the keel at periscope depth, but the seawater was a mixture of fresh and salt water. The different densities would play havoc with the carefully derived trim. To add yet another degree of difficulty to the task, it had been reported that the Germans were mounting regular destroyer patrols at the southern entrance to the Sound. Richard and his fellow COs had concluded that their best option in light of the shallow depth of water was to trim down as low as possible in the water and then make a dash for it at night. However, Richard had another idea up his sleeve. He wondered whether he might follow a neutral ship through the Sound at night and switch on his own navigation lights in the hope that he might be mistaken for another merchant vessel. He had decided to delay finalising his plans until he had seen the lie of the land.

He watched the other E-boat return to the surface after her trim dive. Her bows broke through the surface at a steep angle and at great speed, creating a huge splash even before the fin became visible. He made a mental note to brief Steele that he wanted a gentler and more level return to the surface. There was no point in advertising their presence before they had to, as in a calm sea at night any disturbance in the water would be visible as a spume of phosphorescence.

*

The check dive off Harwich had not passed off without drama. Firstly, Steele had trimmed the boat light such that it took too long to dive, the so-called married man's trim. After correcting the trim and checking for the absence of leaks, Richard had ordered Steele to surface the submarine. To everyone's consternation, the Outside ERA at the blowing panel had reported that he could not blow one of the after ballast tanks as the valve had come off in his hand. With no buoyancy aft, the only way Richard had managed to prevent the seawater spilling over the conning tower hatch had been by ordering maximum speed, but he had not dared risk returning to Harwich as the reverse course would have given him a following sea. Fortunately, the crew of *E9* had managed to navigate the submarine to nearby Gorleston to carry out the necessary repair.

Four days later, *E9* was at last proceeding on the surface heading north-east. Steele had learned from his mistake and the boat was in perfect trim. Richard had just finished his lunch on the second day out from Gorleston when he was called to the control room. The Navigator, O'Connell, had the watch on the bridge.

'What is it, Pilot?' Richard called from the search periscope.

'Green seven-zero, sir, about 10,000 yards. I've just seen a seaplane land in the water.'

'Did you recognise it as one of ours?'

'I'm not sure, sir. It might have been one of ours or a Frenchie, but I'm pretty sure the markings are not those of a Hun.'

'Very good. We'll take a look at her. Increase speed to fourteen knots and alter course to intercept her. I'll be up when we get a bit closer.'

Ten minutes later, it was clear that the seaplane belonged to the Royal Naval Air Service. The two crewmen were standing on the floats waving to the approaching submarine. The sea state was slight and the waves were gently washing over the tips of the floats to wet the boots of the aviators. Richard had no difficulty in carefully manoeuvring the submarine upwind of the biplane whilst Steele organised for the rubber coracle to be floated towards the seaplane with a line attached to retrieve it. With the minimum of fuss the two airmen stepped into the small boat and assisted the sailors in hauling it alongside *E9*. Richard met them on the casing.

'Good afternoon, Captain. Thank you for picking us up. I am Flight Commander Edward Adams and allow me to introduce my observer, Lieutenant Erskine Childers. We're awfully pleased to see you.'

Adams reminded Richard of his brother Paul, another member of the RNAS. Adams did not appear much older, despite the difference in rank.

'Lieutenant Commander Richard Miller. Pleased to meet you both. You're not by any chance an author are you, Childers?' he asked.

'I am, sir. Have you read my book, *The Riddle of the Sands*?' Childers spoke with an
Irish accent.

'Indeed I have, and I very much enjoyed it. But I had no idea you had joined the Flying Corps. I thought yachting was more your line. In fact I had no idea you had joined the RN.'

'Oh, this is just a temporary assignment and I'm on an RNVR commission. I wonder. You say your name's Miller. I think I work for your father. He has a son in submarines. Is he …'

Adams cut him off quickly. 'Miller, in the same way that it would be wrong of me to pry into your mission, you will understand if we cannot divulge the reasons for our presence here. We were on a reconnaissance mission over the mainland, encountered thick fog, became disorientated and ran out of fuel and oil. It might be a perfectly decent day here, but it's a completely different story over the coast.'

'Frankly, Adams, I don't give a fig for your mission. I might add that coming to your rescue is greatly inconveniencing my own. However, I suggest you both come down to the wardroom for a mug of hot tea and we can decide what we are to do with you.' Richard turned his back on the two aviators and descended into the submarine without a further word.

Over a mug of tea and a cold ham sandwich Adams was a little more conciliatory as he explained that his aircraft had been launched from the seaplane carrier HMS *Engadine* and he hoped to be able to return to his ship. Clearly *E9* carried no aviation spirit, so the best he could hope for was a tow.

'I'm not towing you all the way back to England,' Richard retorted.

'Not at all,' Adams quickly added. 'If you would give me your present position, then we could work out a course for *Engadine* or one of the escort force. They shouldn't be more than thirty miles distant.'

Richard and Steele showed the pilot the position and together they calculated that it was more likely that *Engadine* was forty miles away. After exchanging a few private words with Steele, Richard reached a decision.

'I'm sorry, Adams, but I can't afford the time to offer you a tow. It would take me the best part of a day and who knows where your mother ship might be by then. She would no doubt have given you up for lost and moved on.'

Richard could see the dismay on both Adams's and Childers's faces. 'Instead, I intend sinking your machine and running you pair back to your ship. All told, we could achieve that in four to six hours and I can then proceed in accordance with my orders.'

'But, I beg you. That's a valuable machine. Besides, we would need to recover the photographic plates. Without them, several lives might be lost needlessly.'

'My mind is made up. That's the best I can offer.' Richard turned to Steele. 'Take two seamen with you and place some gun cotton charges on the seaplane. These gentlemen can give you a list of anything valuable that ought to be retrieved from the machine first. Just don't take too long about it. We're late for our rendezvous as it is.'

*

Within the hour, Steele and his assistant, Able Seaman Davies, had removed the seaplane's camera and plates, mission notes and charts, and were preparing to set the gun cotton charges. The seaman in the rubber coracle drew their attention to a smudge in the air to the east. Steele called for the binoculars and recognised the cigar shape of a German Zeppelin approaching at high speed. Looking across to *E9*, he was relieved to see that the lookouts on the bridge had spotted it, too, and Miller quickly appeared.

'I say, Davies, pray pass me that satchel. Quickly, if you please. Thank you. Now I suggest you return with this stuff to the boat PDQ and leave me to set the charges. I have no doubt that our captain may be anxious to make a hurried dive very shortly.' Steele passed over the last of the objects to the seaman in the coracle.

'But what about you, sir? Am I to send the boat back for you?' Davies asked.

'Perhaps not just yet, Davies. Let's see what develops, shall we? We'll leave that decision to the captain. Now cut along. I'm busy.'

Steele commenced setting the charges, but did so unhurriedly. He hadn't handled explosives for some time and was anxious to do the job properly. Even so, as he heard the engines of the airship above, it was tempting to abandon the task and attempt to swim back to the submarine. He felt sure that Miller would be preparing to dive the submarine at any minute. After setting the charges on the aircraft's floats, he decided it would be prudent to place another in the tail and clambered back up to the fuselage. He looked up at the Zeppelin. It was now making a low pass over *E9*. The noise of the propellers was quite deafening and he could clearly make out the airship's tactical number. Looking back to his submarine, he could see that the inflatable boat had been stowed inboard, but to his surprise, there seemed to be no signs of *E9*'s bridge being cleared preparatory to a dive. Indeed, he saw Miller waving his cap in a friendly manner to the crew of the airship above. It was disconcerting to see that the down-draft of the Zeppelin's powerful engines was driving the seaplane further from *E9*, but there was nothing he could do about it for the moment.

He crawled down to the tail of the seaplane and laid his final charge. Behind him he could hear the Zeppelin's engine noise recede as it completed its pass overhead. The charges laid, he was able to observe its movements more carefully. The airship began a lazy turn to port with the apparent intention of making another pass overhead. Surely the Germans must have recognised *E9* as British by now? After all, it was obvious from her markings that the seaplane was British. Miller, too, must have had the same thoughts as Steele suddenly heard the bang and rush of air as the main vents of *E9* were opened and the submarine began to dive. Mercifully, all the main vents opened this time and he saw Miller just had enough time to give him a wave before, seconds later, the fin of the submarine disappeared beneath the waves.

Meanwhile, the Zeppelin had completed its turn and lined up on the wake of the invisible submarine. It quickly caught up with *E9*'s last visible position and dropped two bombs ahead. Steele dived head first into the cockpit and heard the two bombs explode. Tentatively raising his head above the side of the aircraft, he looked for any sign of *E9*, but saw nothing. After fifteen anxious minutes, a feeling of dread gripped his guts. Had the bombs struck home and sent the submarine to the bottom? If not, then it looked as if Miller had rightly put the submarine first and abandoned him. Either way it was clear that he was marooned.

Chapter 19

'Admiral Tate will see you now, Miss Miller, Mr Marshall. Please come this way.'

'Here we go, Mark. It's time to enter the lion's den.' Elizabeth and her chief naval architect, Mark Marshall, followed the young Paymaster Lieutenant from the ante-room into the office of the Controller of the Royal Navy and Third Sea Lord, Rear Admiral Frederick Tate.

'Mr Marshall and Miss Miller, of Miller's Shipyard, sir.' The Paymaster Lieutenant closed the mahogany double doors behind them and left the Christians to meet their fate.

Marshall was not surprised to see that the Admiral was accompanied by his naval assistant, Captain Edwards, but he did not recognise the Commodore to his other side. Elizabeth, however, appeared to know them both. Miller's yard had built the battleship HMS *Audacious*, in which Edwards had served as the Engineer Commander, so he and Marshall had met already. He was amused to see the surprise on Tate's face at meeting Elizabeth. The poor man looked in shock and quickly scanned a piece of foolscap paper on the gleaming mahogany conference table behind which he was standing.

'I'm sorry, madam, but there seems to have been a misunderstanding. When I agreed to this meeting I was led to understand that Miller's Yard would be represented by the managing dDirector, Mr Charles Miller. Who may I ask are you?'

Marshall was pleased to see that Elizabeth appeared calm and serene in the face of such misogyny.

'Good morning, Admiral. May I present Mr Mark Marshall, our chief naval architect? I am the managing director of the yard. Gentlemen, please take a seat and I will explain.'

Elizabeth smiled both at Keyes and Edwards and, as she shook their hands, Marshall noted that the latter was barely containing his amusement at his admiral's discomfort. Without waiting to be invited, Elizabeth sat down at the other side of the table and beckoned to the three men opposite to do the same.

Before they took their seats, Edwards introduced the Commodore. 'Marshall, delighted to see you again. Allow me to introduce Commodore Roger Keyes, the Commodore Submarines. Commodore, I believe you already know Miss Miller.'

'Indeed. Miss Miller and I became acquainted last year at the commissioning of her cousin's submarine. I am delighted to renew the acquaintance, Miss Miller. I am only sorry to have twice been the cause of the postponement of your wedding.' Turning to Tate, Keyes went on, 'This young lady is engaged to be married to one of my officers, but alas, the exigencies of the Service were such that he sailed on patrol before having time to complete the nuptials.'

Elizabeth acknowledged Keyes with a nod and replied, 'I am beginning to wonder, Commodore, whether, perhaps, I should have asked you to lead me down the aisle as a means of ensuring the event went ahead.' She turned to Tate.

'Admiral, my brother Charles handed over the running of the business to me soon after war was declared. He has joined the colours and is presently serving with the Armoured Car Squadron, somewhere in France or Belgium, I presume. He doesn't tell me in his infrequent letters.'

Having followed his visitor's invitation to take a seat in his own office, Tate appeared to have recovered from his surprise. 'Madam, I mean, Miss Miller, I was sorry to hear of the tragic loss of your father. He was well regarded in ship building circles, but I cannot see how this meeting is to serve any purpose. After all…'

'Thank you for your kind sentiments, Admiral, but I hope we can agree that Miller's have continued to construct some fine ships, even after my father's untimely death. Would you not agree, Captain Edwards?'

'Very true, ma'am. The destroyers *Wolverine* and *Lizard* both met, and in the latter case, even exceeded, the contract requirements for twenty-seven knots. My old ship, *Audacious*, is proving a most reliable ship, too,' Edwards replied.

'That may be so, Miss Miller, but that was with your brother at the helm of the company. Let me be candid. I never wanted this meeting. Were I to agree to meet with every prospective yard seeking an Admiralty contract, the day would need to be seventy-two hours long. Indeed, I thought it rather underhand of your uncle to have used his position in the Admiralty to exert undue influence on the First Lord, to insist on me discussing your yard's proposal. Some might call it profiteering. Now I learn that the yard is headed by a young woman, however charming and good looking.'

'Let me stop you there, Admiral, before you slander my family further. My Uncle William did no such thing. It was Lord Fisher who approached Mr Churchill on my behalf.'

Marshall held his breath as he looked sideways at Elizabeth. He saw her neckline begin to redden and recognised the danger signal from painful experience. It meant that Elizabeth's temper was rising. If Miss Elizabeth lost her rag then there would be no way of securing the Admiralty contract. So far, the temper was in check, but he knew that the level of the flush would increase in proportion to her anger. If the reddening reached the ears, then God help all present.

'Miss Miller speaks the truth, sir,' Keyes cut in.

'And how come you by this information, Keyes?' Tate asked acidly.

'Sir, I and various other parties have been holding meetings with Sir John Jellicoe on how we might take a more offensive stance towards the enemy. We have agreed that with more E-class submarines we would have an opportunity to take the fight to the enemy in Germany's own back yard. It was Sir John who asked Lord Fisher to approach the First Lord informally.'

'But we already have yards building these submarines. Vickers have already built eight, including the two Australian boats, and Chatham four. They're both proven yards at building this type of submarine.'

'But, sir,' Keyes replied patiently. 'These yards are taking between twenty and thirty months from laying down the keel to completing the boats. We simply cannot afford to wait that long. Not only do we need more yards turning out more submarines, but if you examine the proposal carefully, sir, you will see that Miller's are proposing to truncate the build time to just eight months. Should the war go on beyond Christmas, as we all know it will, then that time difference might well prove vital. Indeed, I have recently attended a meeting with Admiral Jellicoe and the War Staff to finalise plans for an imminent offensive operation that centres on the deployment of this class of submarine.'

'The shortened build time had not escaped my notice, Keyes. I am quite capable of assimilating a report.' Tate tapped the paper before him.

'Tell me, Miss Miller, how is it that it takes experienced yards up to thirty months to build an E-class submarine, but suddenly a yard led by a woman with no ship building experience, can do the job in a mere eight months?'

'Very well, Admiral.' Elizabeth addressed him in an icy tone. 'I have spent all my life in my late father's shipyard and come to understand it top to toe. As a mere woman, long ago I learned the art of listening to men talk. My cousin happens to command one of these boats and, thanks to him, I and Mr Marshall here have had the opportunity to inspect every frame and system of my cousin's submarine. It is apparent to us that by making just a few modifications to the design, we can streamline the build process and turn out three submarines in the time it takes to produce one today.'

'But your cousin had no right to let civilians wander over one of our submarines willy-nilly. That sort of thing is confidential, if not secret. Nobody so irresponsible should be in command.' Tate retorted. 'Who is this young pup, Keyes?'

'Sir, the irresponsible young pup in question has just sunk a cruiser and been awarded the DSO.' Keyes replied with apparent satisfaction.

'Indeed?' Tate appeared to think that this fact made everything all right. 'Be that as it may be. What are these modifications that you think will make all the difference, then, Miss Miller?'

'They are quite simple, really. I have listed them in my proposal, but the first of two key differences is that we will not manufacture the engines ourselves. I am aware that Vickers have not been meeting their contractual deadlines of late, largely on account of difficulties in the production of the engines for the submarines. Our plan is that this task would not only be sub-contracted to Vickers, but also to FIAT in Italy. We would simply fit the first engines available and the remainder would be made available to you for other submarines in build, or the component parts would act as spares for defective engines.'

'And who would meet the bill of the increased order for engines, Miss Miller?'

'That is covered in our proposal, Admiral, but to answer your question directly, the Admiralty. My engineers estimate that you will need at least one spare engine for every four hulls. That leads me to the second key proposal.'

Marshall could see that Tate was starting to take Elizabeth more seriously now. Elizabeth continued.

'The nation is at war and much of the peacetime paraphernalia of red tape must be brushed to one side. Whilst regular reporting and close scrutiny of the costs of alterations and additions is laudable in peacetime, cost must now be subordinated to speed. We propose that a senior technical officer is appointed to our yard with the authority to approve any increases in expenditure of up to a budget of twenty per cent of the build cost *without any paperwork whatsoever.*'

Tate gasped at the idea, but recovered and turned to his technical aide. 'And what is your view, Edwards. Do you really think this will make the claimed difference?'

'Sir, I am no expert in submarines, but technically the proposal appears to have some sense. I venture that the proposal has legs.'

'And what do you propose to charge for your services, Miss Miller? It is apparent you will not deny yourself the opportunity to profit from the country's urgent need for these submarines.'

The two naval officers winced and Marshall noted Elizabeth's flush deepening in colour and fast approaching the ears. Oh my God, he thought. She's going to blow any minute. However, Elizabeth affected not to have noticed the jibe.

'I am aware, Admiral, that Vickers and Chatham have charged you up to £107,000 for their hulls, but now that war is upon us, they are proposing an increase of ten per cent to cover the increased costs of sourcing raw materials.'

'And how, by Jove, have you come by that information? Is your uncle the source?'

'No, Admiral. All men and even women of business like to keep their ears to the ground and we each have our sources in our competitors' yards. We are offering to build each of the E-class submarines, to the revised specification listed in our proposal, at a cost of £105,000 each. That small reduction in cost is in spite of the improved design and the sub-contracting of the engines to Vickers and FIAT, but … provided we receive a minimum order of six submarines to cover the costs of the investment in a new slipway.'

Marshall started. That wasn't what they had settled before the meeting. The yard only had the capacity to build three boats and they had agreed to bid for four and compromise on the three, or even a contract for two hulls.

'And how might we have confidence in your ability to deliver each vessel to cost, specification and time, Miss Miller?'

'Had the Admiralty any qualms on that score, then I hardly see that it would be continuing to give us orders for the light cruisers we currently have on the stocks, Admiral.'

'Yes, but no offence, dear lady, that was before we learned of the change in management of the company. Indeed, are you not the same Miss Elizabeth Miller that sabotaged *E9* just a few months ago in the name of the suffragette movement?'

'Oh, I am sure you meant no offence, Admiral. Yes, I splashed some paint over one of your precious submarines, but it cannot have done any harm. This very submarine has just sunk a cruiser. Perhaps we should christen every submarine the same way.'

Tate looked as if he was going to choke at the idea. Oh, no, she's gone too far this time, Marshall thought, but was relieved to see that the neck flush had receded below the level of the jaw.

'Have no fear. The suffragettes are old news now and no threat to you and the Establishment. Have you not heard of the cessation of hostilities for the duration of the war?'

Elizabeth smiled sweetly and Marshall noted that she had moderated her tone, as if addressing a child.

'You see, Admiral, we woman are on your side. In any case, rest assured that my chief architect and the fitters remain male. We might have a female managing director, but we still confine our women employees to typing tasks and making the tea. Although, am I right, Mr Marshall, that we have recently engaged some women as delivery drivers to replace men sent to the front?'

Marshall remained silent. His whole attention was fixed on Elizabeth's red neck.

'Mark?' Elizabeth glared at Marshall and he was stirred into speech.

'That's true, ma'am. I believe there are now six women in the driver pool and there's talk of a couple of women being trained to man the gantries, but all the fitters, plumbers, electricians and boiler makers are still men. They're all in reserved occupations.'

‘Well, that’s something at least,’ Tate responded in a relieved tone. ‘What’s your view, Keyes? You’re the one that has to operate the damned things.’

‘Frankly, sir, I don’t care if they’re built by Martians, if we can have them quickly. I say give Miller’s a chance.’

Tate looked at Edwards for his opinion and received a silent nod in response. ‘Very well, Miss Miller. I’m happy to agree to your proposal, but I have some conditions as follows. The order will be for three hulls initially, and only if they are produced to time, specification and budget, will the order for the second tranche of three go ahead. Is that acceptable?’

‘Perfectly.’ Elizabeth betrayed no emotion in her visage as she agreed to the condition, but Marshall had to strangle a howl of glee and covered his astonishment with a fit of coughing.

‘The contingency budget that you propose must be reduced to fifteen per cent of the agreed cost of each hull.’ Tate smiled for the first time in the meeting as if he was master of the situation and dictating terms. Marshall, however, was amazed that the Controller had agreed to any contingency without the usual paperwork. The Admiralty must be desperate, he thought. He and Elizabeth had hoped to agree on a figure of ten per cent.

‘Finally, you will appreciate that the nation must pull together to vanquish the foe and we must all subordinate our individual needs for the common good. I am sure that with a brother and cousin making their own contribution to the war effort you will agree with me, madam.’

Marshall could see that Elizabeth was wondering what was coming next, but she continued to smile sweetly at Tate.

‘To that end, Miss Miller, I must insist that your revised designs are made available to other yards that the Admiralty might engage to build these E-boats. If your design is as good as you make it out to be, then surely it is in the interests of the country that all yards should decrease their build time.’

Marshall thought he detected a slight tremor in Elizabeth, as if her heart had missed a couple of beats, but he couldn’t be sure. She just stared silently at Tate. Marshall could see the sense in the idea, but there was no knowing with Elizabeth. Surely she would accept the condition, he thought. After all, she had at least secured an order for six hulls and that was more than she had hoped to gain from the meeting.

The tension in the room began to mount and after, perhaps, a minute of silence, Elizabeth released Tate from her gaze and looked deeply into the eyes of Edwards and Keyes in turn. Marshall willed her to look at him so that he might silently appeal to her to accept the deal, but she did not offer him a glance before replying coolly.

'Naturally, Miller's Yard stands ready to support the war effort in whichever way it can. I am, therefore, willing to comply with your conditions in exchange for two of my own. Firstly, you increase the order to eight submarines, in two tranches of four. Finally, you pay my yard the same price per hull you agree with any other competing yard. Do we have a deal?'

Marshall did not dare breathe. The only sound in the room was that of his pulse beating in his head. Just as he thought he must faint from the unbearable tension, he saw Elizabeth smile and extend her hand to Tate in anticipation of his assent. He first looked sideways to his naval colleagues for agreement, before taking the proffered hand and shaking it. 'Madam, you strike a hard bargain, but it is one I am willing to accept. I will leave you and the contracts managers to sort out the fine detail of the contract and bid you good day.'

Captain Edwards offered to escort Elizabeth and Marshall to the entrance to the Admiralty. He warmly congratulated her on the negotiation before she and Marshall exited the building to cross the courtyard towards Whitehall. As they passed under Admiralty Arch, Elizabeth turned to Marshall.

'You're not happy, are you, Mark?'

'It's not that I'm unhappy, ma'am. More that I worry how we are to cope. We went into that meeting with the hope of securing an order for three submarines. Now we have a potential order for eight. Why did you do it, ma'am, and just where are we to obtain the manpower?

'I would have thought that was obvious, Mark. That supercilious oaf made me angry, but as my dear father said, "*Don't get angry, get even.*" As far as labour is concerned, think of the great untapped pool of manpower on your doorstep.'

Marshall looked puzzled. 'I'm sorry, ma'am. I don't catch your meaning.'

'Womanpower, Mark. Womanpower.'

Chapter 20

The sound of the two explosions reverberated throughout the submarine, but *E9* was already too deep and far way for them to bother her. Richard settled the submarine on a depth of sixty feet and reduced speed to two knots. He needed time to think before committing the submarine to action.

The natural thing to do would be to wait around until the Zeppelin returned to base. He could then surface and recover Steele. The problem was that this would be exactly what the Zeppelin pilot would be expecting. Richard knew enough about airships to know that they had the endurance to remain on task for several hours. In all probability, the Zeppelin could wait above until dusk. He also knew that from altitude it was not difficult for a vigilant lookout to spot a submarine on the surface, even when trimmed down. On a calm day, even the feather of a periscope would stick out like a sore thumb, so he had to be wary of returning to periscope depth.

He considered his options if he continued his passage to the Baltic without Steele, but dismissed them. Steele's best hope would be for the Zeppelin to alert the German surface forces to capture both him and the seaplane, and this would condemn him to internment as a prisoner of war. Alternatively, Steele would die of thirst or drowning. Moreover, it would give him two other problems. He would be short handed in forcing a passage into the Baltic and what was he to do with two unwanted passengers?

He checked the control room clock and mentally calculated that he had about two hours of full daylight left. With the current sea state, he might be able to risk raising a periscope to observe the Zeppelin's movements. Somehow he also had to maintain contact with the seaplane. Although he could account for the tidal stream, he had no idea how far the wind would push the seaplane on the surface. He resolved to loiter in his current position for an hour before raising the periscope. With any luck the captain of the Zeppelin might think he had sunk *E9*.

Adams interrupted his thoughts.

'Excuse me, Captain, but have you given any thought as to how we might get Childers and his photographic plates back to our ship?'

'I hadn't actually. I'm more concerned with rescuing my second-in-command at present. It's strange that two hours ago your main concern was rescuing your machine and now it's getting home.'

'I say, that's a trifle unfair. I'm not concerned for myself. Machines are precious, but they can be replaced. One could say that of pilots for that matter. But those plates and Childers's knowledge are priceless. It's vital that they make it back to the Admiralty. I promise you that many lives are at stake.'

'Adams, let us understand each other fully. My mission is also vital and the lives of my men precious, too. My first priority is rescuing my First Lieutenant. I cannot then afford the time to return to England.'

'But not long ago, you were all for meeting up with the *Engadine* or one of her escorts. What has changed?'

'Lost time. That has changed things. Have you thought how difficult it is for a submarine to approach surface forces without being shelled, rammed or bombed? You must know how difficult it is to tell friend from foe when it comes to submarines, so again you will know that all naval forces are under orders to sink *any* unidentified submarine on sight. Accordingly, I am under orders to avoid chance meetings with friendly forces at all costs. In fact, there are no forces friendly to submarines. Now, assuming I am able to rescue my First Lieutenant, I would be approaching an escort destroyer at night.'

'Could you not use your wireless set to send them a message?'

'What? And alert the German Navy to our position? They use direction-finding stations, too.'

Adams seemed to have no response to the last statement and it took him a few minutes of reflection before he replied in a low voice. 'Is there somewhere private I could discuss this with you further?'

Richard could see the hydroplanesmen smiling to themselves at this question, but he refrained from laughing. 'I regret, dear Adams, that there is not even six inches square that is private in a submarine. I worry that what I say in my sleep will be known to the entire ship's company before I wake.'

Adams took Richard gently by the forearm and whispered pleadingly, 'It really is important. What I have to say is most secret.'

Richard could see the whole control room crew were now listening even more intently. 'Fine. There is a way. Come with me, but it had better be important.'

Adams followed Richard into the torpedo compartment. Richard spoke quietly to the TI and, although he seemed surprised by the request, the petty officer nonetheless started clearing the compartment of men, including those off watch and asleep on top of the spare torpedoes. The latter quit the space with much murmuring and grumbling, but no argument. Richard shut and clipped the watertight door linking the fore-ends to the rest of the submarine.

'Right, Adams. Let's hear it, quickly. My men need their sleep.'

'Very well, Miller. Those Zeppelins are becoming a menace. There's one based on the island of Borkum that regularly reports on the positions of the mines we have laid to impose the blockade on Germany. Within a day, the German minesweepers are out clearing the minefields as quickly as we lay them. The Zeppelins are also shadowing the Fleet and reporting back its position and manoeuvres.'

'They're none too welcome by submariners either, Adams, but get to the point.'

'I was about to,' Adams replied tersely. 'Intelligence has been received to suggest that the Germans are planning to use their airships to mount bombing raids on the civilian population of London and other English cities. You can imagine the panic that would cause. The RFC is tied down in France so Churchill has volunteered the RNAS to deal with the menace.'

'So just shoot them down. Their size must make them sitting targets.'

'Don't believe we haven't tried. The trouble is that they fly higher and faster than any of our current generation of machines. As soon as our chaps approach anywhere near the height required to make a kill, the crew order another pot of coffee, wave us goodbye and rapidly gain another couple of thousands of feet in altitude.'

'So you have a plan and this reconnaissance of yours is related to it, I suppose.'

'Quite. The RNAS has been ordered to switch its focus from tactical support of the Army in France to strategic bombing. As well as the railways, our targets will now include the sheds where the Zeppelins are manufactured. If we can't get them in the air, we'll stop them being launched. The RNAS is planning a series of raids from our bases in France, but we don't have the range to hit the sheds in Cuxhaven. The Air Department and the Intelligence Division have accordingly come up with a daring plan, but it is most secret.'

'Adams, neither I nor my men are hardly in a position to leak anything from the confines of a submarine at sea.'

'True, but the operation is not planned to take place for six to eight weeks. The plan is that we use ships to launch seaplanes from nearer the Frisian coastline to bomb the Zeppelin sheds at Cuxhaven. Childers knows the coast well and has been seconded to assist with planning the raid.'

'My word. That is a daring plan, Adams. I wish you well with it.'

'Nothing like this has ever been done before. Imagine if it succeeds. It could be the start of a series of raids against Germany from the sea. But we need those photographic plates. And there's something else you should know. The plans for the operation have been signed off jointly by the Directors of the Air Department and Intelligence Division, namely Commodore Sueter and your father.'

*

Feeling cold and cramped, Steele eased himself out of the cockpit of the seaplane and climbed down to one of the floats for the exercise. The sea remained slight and he estimated the wind speed to be no more than ten knots, but it was enough to drive the aircraft before it like a sail. Any hope he had of being rescued by a German destroyer was quickly evaporating. He must be many miles from the position the Zeppelin would have reported.

The airship had loitered within sight of the seaplane for about an hour before heading eastwards for home. Steele suspected that the Zeppelin captain was either low on fuel or wanted his dinner and a warm bed for the night. There had been no sign of *E9* and Steele surmised that she was either sunk or he had been abandoned to his fate alone. Awful as his situation was, he hoped it was the latter. He had started to feel at home in *E9* and liked her captain and men.

He pondered whether he might have worked faster in removing the aircraft's camera and setting the charges? Had he done so, Miller might have dived before the arrival on scene of the Zeppelin. Steele began to wonder if his grandfather had been wrong in using his influence to gain him this appointment after a two year absence from submarines. He was rusty and taking too long to come up to the demanding standards of service in submarines. He was surprised that Miller had been so patient. To his certain knowledge he had made two mistakes so far. Miscalculating the trim on diving after Harwich was, perhaps, forgivable. He knew of many new First Lieutenants guilty of the same crime. But failing to wipe the upper lid before shutting and clipping it on diving was a schoolboy's mistake. As the submarine's fin had passed beneath the water line, a torrent of water had flooded the control room. Steele recalled the captain's patient question in the earshot of the whole ship's company, *'Did you wipe the rim before coming down, Number One? No? Then take her back to the surface and we'll try again.'* After surfacing, Steele had found a tiny flake of paint on the hatch rim and this alone had been responsible for preventing the hatch from sealing properly. Even the most junior of the ship's company must have thought the new Jimmy an idiot.

Steele now wished he smoked. It would give him something to do. Yet again he surveyed the horizon with his glasses. To the west he could make out the reddish glow of the autumn sun setting. It was too cloudy to see the sun itself, but its presence was evident. Once more he looked south-east in the hope of seeing the approach of a ship, but again in vain. He continued his anti-clockwise sweep and something caught his attention to the east. He focused in that direction, but saw nothing. Was it his imagination, he thought, and then he saw it again. It was like the flash of a heliograph and then it was gone. Whatever it was, it had to be man-made. He tried looking again without the binoculars, but for a moment nothing caught his attention. Then suddenly, less than a mile away, he saw the sea starting to boil and from its midst, a dark shape appear. It was no monster from the deep. It was *E9* come back to rescue him.

Within a minute, he saw a figure appear on the bridge and men on the casing. He quickly appreciated that the men on the casing would be assembling the inflatable coracle with the intention of floating it down to him, but time was short. This would take several minutes and the sun was already setting. He had to move quickly. He shouted across to *E9*. It was too far away in this light to identify who was on the bridge, but it had to be Miller. His shout was acknowledged, but he could not make out the words. Steele set the fuse on the float charges. The tail could take care of itself. He had ten minutes, time enough, he thought, and removed his boots and jacket before diving into the sea.

It was a hard swim as he was heading into the sea. The CO had positioned the submarine upwind of the seaplane so that he might drift down onto it. This would cut the distance, Steele thought. Thank God, I'm still fit. It's only eight hundred yards. With powerful, easy strokes he carved his way through the water. He was still half way when he saw the flash around him, quickly followed by the noise of the explosion as the charges on the seaplane went off. In the flash of the explosion he could see that *E9* had drifted a little to his right and he adjusted his course accordingly. The saltwater started to sting his eyes, but he carried on. Stroke, stroke, breathe - stroke, stroke, breathe. Now he began to feel cold, but he still felt fit. He would make it and he would make up for his mistakes. Stroke, breathe - stroke, breathe. Looking up, he could see it was not far to the dark hull of *E9*. She looks awfully large from this angle, he thought. He also noted that a ladder had been slung over the casing for him.

At long last he touched the beautifully-cold, solid metal of *E9*'s hull and crabbed across to the ladder. He had done it. All he had to do now was climb the ladder, but perhaps he wasn't so fit after all. He felt incredibly cold and tired. He thought he might float a little and rest awhile. It seemed such a long way up the side of the casing. Oh, hang on a minute. Somebody was ripping his shirt by the neck. Somebody was in the water beside him and trying to grab him. Unhand me, sir. This is my pool. What is the rude fellow doing? He felt a tug beneath his armpits, and another. Slowly, he realised that he was being hauled up the casing on the end of a line.

He was laid on his front and he felt the welcome solidity of the casing. Somebody pumped his back to expel any water he might have swallowed. He heard a voice he couldn't place in his tiredness pipe, 'Blimey, Coxswain. That swim was all of a thousand yards, an' in this temperature. The new Jimmy's a ruddy super hero.'

He was home.

Chapter 21

April 1915

Steele read the letter from his mother one more time. It had been posted almost six weeks ago, in late February 1915, but had only just caught up with *E9* after their short notice deployment to the Eastern Mediterranean. His mother's letter enclosed another, from his grandfather, the Earl of Storrs. Steele had known something was wrong as soon as he had read the address on the outer envelope, '*Lieutenant The Viscount Algernon Steele, Royal Navy.*' The title had belonged to his father, but now his grandfather was dead and Steele had suddenly become a Viscount. It was typically tactless and careless of Mother to have broken the news this way. How quickly would the news spread round the depot ship *Adamant* and then *E9*, he wondered. Should he inform Miller? He didn't want his new title to make any difference to the way he was treated and certainly did not want potentially to undermine his captain's authority by being addressed as, '*My Lord*'. Over the last few months, since the episode with the seaplane and Zeppelin in fact, Steele had started to feel more comfortable with the men of *E9*. From the moment he had been dragged out of the sea, cold and exhausted after his long swim, he had been treated with kindness and compassion. That had been the moment when he had ceased to feel quite so awkward with the men under his orders.

It was stupid, he now recognised, but ever since joining the Navy he had felt a need to distance himself from the common sailor. It wasn't just a case of discipline, although he clung to that as an excuse. It was more that he could not relate to these men of a different class. They were common, they swore, drank too much and broke wind, but they knew more about their trade than he and he had always feared looking foolish before them. Hence, he had taken leave to join the MCC tour and been reluctant to return to the submarine service afterwards, but grandfather had insisted, citing the opportunities the war would create to distinguish himself and to maintain the family honour. Grandfather had even used his influence to gain him this appointment. He knew Admiral Miller and felt confident that the younger Miller would prove a good commanding officer. The old man had been right on that score.

Steele could not think of one occasion on which Miller had expressed impatience at his new First Lieutenant's lack of preparedness for the role. In all the many tasks and duties he had delegated to his second-in-command, Miller had appeared to express full confidence in him. Looking back, Steele recognised the efficacy of the approach as he had responded by trying ever harder to merit the trust placed in him. Whilst he had shared his captain's frustration in not reaching the Baltic, the four months *E9* had since spent patrolling the Heligo Bight had turned out to be a useful proving ground to her new First Lieutenant and several other new members of the crew.

After landing Flight Commander Adams, his observer, camera and photographic plates back in England, the CO had been keen to have another crack at heading for the Baltic, but Keyes had cancelled the deployment. The other two E-boats had succeeded in meeting up with the Russians, but in penetrating the Sound, had stirred up the Germans to be ready for more incursions and Keyes had decided it prudent to let matters lie for the present.

Since then, the war had continued past Christmas 1914, as everyone in uniform knew it would, and Steele's only excitement had been in December when two German battlecruisers had shelled the towns of Hartlepool and Scarborough. On learning of the raid, Keyes had immediately set sail in his ship, HMS *Lurcher*, leading seven British and one French submarine off the coast of Germany to await the enemy's return home. *E9* had been patrolling at periscope depth off the River Jade estuary in rough weather when Steele had sighted the leading ships of Admiral Hipper's squadron. Ducking under the protective screen of the destroyers, the captain had launched his first torpedo at the leading ship from a range of only 400 yards, but the short, snappy waves close inshore had caused the torpedo to buck like an unbroken horse and it had passed too deep beneath the target. Steele had been amazed by Miller's coolness as he had then attacked the third ship, but the trail of the first torpedo had already given the alarm and the target had altered course sharply, increased speed and attempted to ram *E9*. For several hours Miller had feverishly manoeuvred his command amidst the dashing destroyers, narrowly avoiding several attempts to ram the submarine, but even so, failed to make a successful attack on the retreating battlecruisers. The offensive operation had been one of Keyes's last acts in command of the submarine service as in February he had been reappointed. Steele had not known him long, but even so, regretted his departure.

He glanced once more at the spidery writing filling half a sheet of parchment. To his dying moment grandfather had continued to use a quill and his mother had explained that the unfinished letter was his last act on earth. Grandfather had pushed the parchment away, laid down his quill and fallen asleep, without recovering, before dying thirty-six hours later. Steele wiped away a tear. His grandfather had died only a day after *E9*, in company with another two E-boats and their depot ship, HMS *Adamant*, had left England. The ship's company had received the news of the deployment with real pleasure.

He folded the two letters and put them away in a drawer with his other personal effects. The captain should be back soon, he thought. Miller and the other E-boat COs had been summoned to a conference on board the flagship. Perhaps the captain might bring back news as to their future employment. He made his way up to the waist of the depot ship to look out for signs of the barge returning.

*

Commodore Roger Keyes could not help feeling rather disappointed by his new appointment as Chief of Staff to the Commander of the Combined Fleet at Mudros in the Eastern Mediterranean. In his eyes it was a less prestigious and exciting appointment than flying his own broad pennant in HMS *Lurcher* as the Commander of the Submarine Service. He had relished the thrill of leading his flotilla into action at the Battle of Heligoland the previous year, but now he considered himself a mere understudy of the Commander-in-Chief, Vice Admiral de Roebuck. He knew he had the new First Sea Lord, Admiral Jacky Fisher, to thank for this apparent demotion. It was no secret that the two men did not see eye to eye. However, as he surveyed the assembled officers in his cabin on board the flagship HMS *Queen Elizabeth*, Keyes saw an opportunity to make his mark once more. Indeed, had it not been for his success in deploying his submarines to penetrate the Skagerrak into the Baltic, thus proving to the First Lord of the Admiralty that submarines could go where surface ships could not, then the little flotilla of submarines would not now be based off the entrance to the Dardanelles.

Keyes brought the meeting to order and addressed the four submarine commanding officers present.

'Gentlemen, I have been reviewing the employment to date of our submarines and concluded that we could be making a greater contribution to the war effort. Until recently, their lordships at the Admiralty have regarded our activities here as a mere sideshow. Happily, they have now been persuaded that our little force might succeed where the Fleet has failed and, hence, why you and your E-class boats have been sent here. Unfortunately, it has become painfully clear that the Fleet is not going to be able to clear the forts and minefields barring the Dardanelles Narrows. Instead, it is intended to land an allied army ashore on the Gallipoli Peninsula and the soldiers will capture and destroy the forts. I, therefore, intend that a British submarine should pass through the Narrows and enter the Sea of Marmara.'

Keyes noted that the commanding officers did not appear to receive the news with enthusiasm and merely exchanged knowing glances with each other. This struck him as strange. Normally his COs were extremely keen on demonstrating the utility of the submarine.

He continued, nonetheless. 'As you well know, Turkish rail and road communications between Constantinople and this part of the world are poor. They lack motor transport and must rely on the camel. So their only practical means of reinforcing the peninsular is by sea through the Marmara. I intend that Allied submarines sever this vital supply route. The French are bursting to have a go, but I want the honour of leading the way to fall to the Royal Navy, or at the very least, to a submarine from the empire. So far, Holbrook in *B11* has led the way in showing what can be achieved with pluck and he damned well deserved his VC for the attempt, but the B-boats are not up to the job of going all the way up the Narrows. The E-boats are much more suited to the task, as they showed in penetrating into the Baltic. Charles, what are your thoughts, first?'

Lieutenant Commander Charles Brodie was an experienced submarine commanding officer and was now also serving on Keyes's staff.

'I don't think anyone should under estimate the difficulties of what you are asking, sir. If I might draw everyone's attention to the chart here, you will see that the full distance from the entrance to the Dardanelles at Kum Kale to the relatively open waters of the Marmara is thirty-five miles. The width of the Lower Dardanelles varies from just two to a maximum of four miles. After twelve miles, one enters the Narrows, aptly named as they are only 1400 yards wide. It really calls for some extraordinarily accurate navigation. Just to make matters worse, the current is against one and it varies from two to four knots. As if that's not bad enough, the Turks have laid mines in ten successive lines, from four miles short of the Narrows, right up to them.'

Keyes was pleased to see the avid attention the other three COs were giving to Brodie's brief. He wondered who would be the first to volunteer to make the mad dash through the Narrows. He looked at each one in turn and decided it would probably be Miller. Brodie was continuing his brief.

'Although these mines have been laid near the surface to catch the surface ships, that's just the depth we would need to be at to use the periscope for fixing. Moreover, there are plenty of rivers running into the passage, so there will be a shallow layer of less dense water to play havoc with the trim. The obvious answer might be a surface transit, perhaps at night. But I should warn you, gentlemen, that anyone contemplating such a feat should first consider that there are eleven forts guarding the Narrows and their approaches. There are numerous searchlights and heavy guns just waiting to catch the unwary intruder and even a series of torpedo tubes. I would say that any attempt to breach the passage would be fraught with interest.'

The under-statement, typical of submariners, evoked a chuckle from Brodie's fellow officers, but his pessimistic message had sunk in and Keyes noted that nobody seemed keen to follow him in speaking. He was disappointed by the absence of a positive response and gazed at each officer intensely, trying to judge their thoughts. Richard Miller eventually broke the silence.

'Sir, we've seen from the experience of the French submarine *Saphir* that if one runs aground, then there is no chance of rescue. On the other hand, Norman Holbrook has demonstrated that if one can overcome the hazards of navigation, then the minefields can be breached with skill and care. My concern is what happens if a submarine does make it to the open sea. There is no chance of resupply and we would be out of wireless range. Completely alone in fact. It goes without saying that any form of offensive action will make the return passage that bit more difficult. The Turks will be alerted and waiting for us.'

Keyes sighed with dismay at the response. This was turning into a gloomy meeting. He expected Miller of all people to display a little more élan. Even so, he had come to respect Miller and could see that there was something in what he said. In his ardour to take offensive action, Keyes knew he had not given any thought to the logistics of the operation. However, this was not a fact he cared to admit.

'Gentlemen, these are mere details that can be worked out in very quick time. Where there's a will there's a way. Is not one of you prepared to take the risk for the sake of your country and the Service?' He fixed on Richard expectantly.

All four submarine COs smarted at the potential insult, but it was Richard who responded. 'Sir, were it just myself, I would happily volunteer for such an undertaking, but I am not prepared to speak on behalf of my ship's company until I am satisfied that all necessary preparations have been made to reduce the risk to their lives.'

There was an embarrassing silence for a few moments. Keyes was stung by the response. He's back to his priggish self, he thought. Johnson warned me about that long ago. He started to feel the anger rise within him, but fortunately it was cut short by the commanding officer of *E15*, Lieutenant Commander Theodore Brodie, the brother of Charles, who broke the awkwardness of the occasion.

'I'll do it, sir.'

Keyes promptly responded with obvious relief, 'Well it's got to be tried and you shall do it.'

*

After the meeting had broken up, Richard returned in a sombre mood to the submarine depot ship. He immediately called together his two officers for a discussion in his cabin. The first to arrive was Steele. At six feet six inches in height, the fair-haired and blue-eyed officer was unusually tall for service in submarines. Even in the relative comfort of a cabin of the depot ship he could not stand straight and Richard had noticed that he tended to bend his lithe, athletic frame against the bulkhead whenever standing. It reminded Richard of a new moon. Steele's height was not the only characteristic that seemed out of place in submarines. Richard found his languid manner quite irritating. Initially, he had mistaken this for laziness, but he now readily admitted his error. Steele had the makings of a first class submarine officer and one who might well deserve his own command over time. Richard couldn't explain his irritation. Was it that he detected an air of superiority in Steele's insouciance? Or could it be, he wondered, that knowing his aristocratic background, Richard was looking for such a trait? Steele was quickly joined by the Third Hand. He, by contrast, was a reserve officer, called up from the Merchant Navy for his navigation skills. Sub Lieutenant 'Paddy' O'Connell was a short, stocky red-haired Ulsterman whose earthy sense of humour helped him rub along very easily with the ship's company.

Richard invited both officers to take a seat on his bunk and debriefed them on the meeting he had just left.

'So there you have it. *E15* has been given less than seventy-two hours to prepare for the passage. Frankly, I don't hold out much prospect for success. However, the Commodore is right. At least one of us has to get through to cut the Turks' supply lines. My cousin will be one of those landing ashore and I wouldn't want to be in his shoes if the Turks are well dug in. Whether or not Brodie succeeds, I want *E9* to be the next boat to have a crack at the Narrows, but we have to plan to succeed. So, any ideas?'

O'Connell was the first to reply. 'As far as I can make out, sir, we're scuppered if we haven't a clue where we are. Those waters aren't just narrow, but shallow, and I don't fancy being high and dry under those guns. I had a good chin wag with the Navigator of *B1*, but he couldn't say what lay beyond Chanak.'

'I'm not disagreeing, Paddy, but it has to be done nonetheless,' Richard replied. 'I have had an idea, however. As you may already know, my younger brother is a pilot in the Air Service and I've heard on the grapevine that his former CO, Charles Samson, is over here with that detachment of seaplanes. I thought I might ask if he could take me up for a recce.'

'That sounds a jolly good idea, sir,' Steele responded. 'But may I be so bold as to proffer another suggestion, sir? The last thing we want in confined waters is the bally gyro compass toppling on us again. I propose that young Pilot here takes personal responsibility for cherishing it as if it were an ancient Greek painted vase, and doesn't let any ham-fisted tiff get his oil-soaked hands on it.'

'That's a fair point, First Lieutenant. Navigator, make it so. Now if we do break through into the Marmara, we will operate entirely without support. If we have a mechanical breakdown, it will be up to us to fix it. I might be able to impose on Commander Samson to fly us out some spares in an emergency, but prevention is better than cure. I want you to inspect every inch of the boat with the engine room staff and triple check every pipe, hose and valve for any sign of wear or defect. Then I'm going to do it, too. I'm taking no chances. Is that clear?'

'Aye aye, sir,' Steele replied. 'But how might we communicate with anyone, whether to call for emergency spares or otherwise. The range will be too far for our W/T set.'

'The Commodore's staff has thought of that. They plan on stationing one of our surface friends in the Gulf of Xeros. That will put them in range of any submarine transmitting from the western end of the Sea and the ship can then relay the message on. My bigger concern is resupply of torpedoes. Even if Commander Samson could drop us some engineering spares, he cannot bring us a torpedo. I imagine there will be plenty of targets and so torpedoes will be at a premium.'

'There are plenty of ways to skin a cat, sir.' This time it was O'Connell's turn to make a suggestion. 'Do we need to use a torpedo to sink them, sir?'

'And what troubles your Celtic mind, dear Pontius?' Steele asked.

'Well, sir. If we come across a nice juicy battleship or cruiser, then fair enough. We use a torpedo. But I would imagine we could board some of the smaller craft and simply blow them up or set fire to them the same way our ancestors did last century. Of course what we could really do with is a few bloody fat cannons and we could sink them with a broadside.'

'Bravo, Paddy. That's not a bad idea and it gives me another. I might just go and winkle out one of the technical staff to discuss the feasibility right now. But before I do, just one final thing, First Lieutenant. We're going to need a perfect trim and even so, depth keeping is going to be hard work. Talk to the Coxswain and see if it might be possible to get a couple of hands from the spare crew to lend a hand. We'll need to sort out some messing arrangements for any extra hands, too. Now, gentlemen, if you will excuse me, I'm going to see if I can find a big fat gun.'

*

Despite having a pilot for a younger brother, Richard had never flown before. It was not that he feared flying, but he had never had the opportunity. Accordingly, he did not know what to expect as the twin-seat Farman bi-plane took off from the island of Tenedos with Commander Charles Samson at the controls. At sea level it was an almost windless day, but Richard had been surprised by the draft he now felt. The aircraft was described as a 'pusher' in that the propeller was mounted behind the nacelle. This offered Richard a better view from the front of the aircraft and also a better field of fire. Prior to take off, he had been given a machine gun in case they should meet a German fighter aircraft.

Very soon they were over the Narrows and he was surprised by how easy it was to pick up the detail of the terrain and fortifications. He understood now how the aeroplane was playing such a crucial role on the Western Front and why the enemy went to such lengths to deny the skies to reconnaissance aircraft. Richard wondered what his brother Paul was doing these days and whether he was safe. His thoughts were interrupted by Samson pointing down at the brown puffs of smoke and shrapnel fired from the forts, but bursting harmlessly below them. Due to the reflection of the sun on the water he was disappointed not to be able to spot any of the minefields, but he was able to note some interesting landmarks that would assist his navigation. Before he knew it, they were over the Sea of Marmara itself and Richard asked Samson to take them lower to observe the island of Marmara and its neighbours. He noted with satisfaction that these islands were not occupied and it occurred to him they might afford *E9* a hiding place on the surface from time to time. He would have liked more time for the reconnaissance, but all too soon it was time to return, since the Farman was low on fuel. As the aeroplane headed west towards the setting sun, he observed the fighting on the beaches of Cape Helles and Suvla Bay and the vast armada of vessels afloat in support. Somewhere down there was his cousin, Charles.

The Allies had landed on the beaches just a few days before and already it was apparent that the troops were faring badly. They had encountered stiff resistance from the Turkish defenders and were still stranded on the beaches in full view of the enemy and with little cover. The men were reported to be exhausted and to have suffered heavy casualties, but Richard did not know much more. However, he had heard some positive news. On the same day that their compatriots in the ANZAC Corps were landing on the beaches of the peninsula, the Australian submarine *AE2* had made an attempt through the Narrows and succeeded in sinking a Turkish torpedo boat. Keyes was overjoyed that a submarine from the British Empire had achieved this feat ahead of the French.

Sadly, by contrast, and as Richard and several others had feared, Theodore Brodie and *E15* had failed to penetrate the Narrows a week earlier. For some reason *E15* had run aground in Kephez Bay, just short of the Narrows, and the news had only recently come through that her CO had been killed by shell fire. Several submarines and surface ships had taken great risks to run the gauntlet of Turkish gunfire in order to sink the submarine before she could be captured by the enemy.

Richard had been determined to pick up every scrap of information he could on the hazards he and his men would face in forcing a passage through the Dardanelles and he had spent days quizzing those who had penetrated its outer reaches, including merchantmen and the French, and plagued the intelligence staff for an accurate map of the Turkish defences. He had found his meetings with Holbrook and Charles Brodie particularly valuable. Both officers had entered the Straits in the operation to sink *E15*. Whilst he had been successful in obtaining an accurate chart of the straits and defences, he had been disappointed by the paucity of information on the underwater currents. At least he had managed to persuade *Adamant*'s engineering staff to fit a three-inch twelve-pounder gun to the casing of the submarine and for a volunteer gun layer to be loaned to his crew. The CO of *Adamant*, Commander Frederick Somerville, was himself a former submariner and he had readily placed all the resources under his command at Richard's disposal.

Richard was certain that, following *AE2*'s success, he and *E9* would soon be ordered to make a further attempt at reaching the Sea of Marmara. He felt confident in his preparations, but now the Turks had been alerted that it was possible for submarines to make the passage, he had one more task to complete.

*

Richard cast a final look around the horizon of the Aegean Sea off the island of Mudros. To the east was the vast armada of Allied ships, but the sea was clear to the west, except for the comforting presence of their destroyer escort. Everything was ready and it was time to put the crew of *E9* through their paces. He pressed a button and Klaxons immediately sounded throughout the submarine as the men went to Diving Stations.

The Coxswain reported through the voicepipe, 'Captain, sir, control room. Shut off for diving, sir. Both engine clutches out.'

'Very good. I'm coming below.'

Richard waved his hat to the destroyer to give them the pre-arranged signal to start the fun in thirty minutes and climbed down into the conning tower. Before shutting the hatch above him, he remembered to wipe it with a piece of towelling. He met Steele in the control room and ordered, 'Slow ahead both motors. Flood One, Two, Five, Six, Seven and Eight main ballast tanks.'

Steele repeated the order to acknowledge it and then ordered the stokers to open the Kingston valves and main vents. As the submarine gently sank beneath the waves, Steele monitored the depth gauge and the bubble on the hydroplanes operators' inclinometer to assess the trim of the boat. He made a slight adjustment to the trim and once the boat was level, Richard ordered the flooding of the remaining main ballast tanks.

'Happy with the trim, First Lieutenant?'

'Aye, sir. Submarine horizontal. Depth fifteen feet.'

'Very good. Take her down to thirty feet.'

As the boat settled, level at thirty feet, Richard ordered the periscope to be raised. After carrying out an all-round look and checking the position of the destroyer, he was satisfied.

'Down periscope. Five down, keep fifty feet. Check for leaks.'

For the next ten minutes everything was quiet. The only sounds were the quiet whirr of the electric motors, the clicks of the brass wheels turning to operate the hydroplanes and the voices of the men reporting the absence of leaks throughout the submarine. The boat was completely dry. The engine room staff's preparations and attention to detail was paying off.

'Permission to fall out from Diving Stations, sir?' Steele asked.

Richard checked his watch. The evolution had taken twenty-two minutes since diving.

'Not yet, Number One. Take us down to eighty feet and make another check for leaks.'

Within just a few minutes of settling on the new depth and just over thirty minutes since Richard's signal to the destroyer on the surface, the submarine was rocked by an enormous external explosion.

'Jesus Christ!' somebody was heard to exclaim. 'What the fucking hell was that?'

'First Lieutenant,' Richard called. 'Pass the word that the destroyer is setting off underwater charges at two minute intervals and at a depth of fifty feet. There is no need to panic, but keep a watchful eye out for damage.'

Steele implemented the order and returned to the control room just as the third charge exploded. 'I assume you arranged this little surprise, sir?' He kept his voice low.

'I certainly did. It's time the men gained an inkling of what they might expect. Twenty minutes of this will not only sort the sheep from the goats, but check our watertight capabilities.'

'Twenty minutes?' O'Connell groaned. 'That means we're only thirty per cent of the way through this shenanigan and my head already hurts.'

Still keeping his voice low, Steele added, 'You might have warned me, sir. I am your second-in-command.'

Richard stared at Steele. He felt a mixture of surprise and anger, but replied quietly. 'I am well aware of your position, Steele, but remember mine. I am in command here and I will decide what I confide in you.'

'How can you be sure the charges will not go off deeper than eighty feet, sir?' Steele met Richard's eyes confidently.

'Because I arranged with the destroyer's CO to tow some lines with charges fixed at that depth to simulate Turkish mines. He's paralleling us on the same course and speed I briefed him we would take on diving.'

Richard shifted his gaze and raised his voice. 'Damage reports if you please, First Lieutenant.'

Mercifully, the damage to the boat seemed very minor. The Chief ERA reported a few flexible couplings had been shaken loose and the odd lamp had shattered. One of his stokers had lost his footing after the first explosion and hurt his collar bone, too. Otherwise the boat was taking the hammering remarkably well.

After the seventh explosion, Richard ordered Steele to take *E9* down slowly to 120 feet, the submarine's maximum diving depth. He was pleased to see how quickly the men had adjusted to the explosive shocks after overcoming their initial surprise. Rather than holding onto any fixed piece of equipment and looking upwards warily, as if expecting the sea to start pouring in at any minute, the men were going about their normal working routine. Nevertheless, this changed with the latest order to go even deeper and the tension in the control room was obvious. In fact, although he appeared to be leaning nonchalantly against a bulkhead with his eyes half-closed, as if nodding off, Richard, too, felt tense. Supposing the charges had caused some invisible damage. Was it wise to go down beyond the maximum diving depth without surfacing and checking for external damage? As the eighth charge went off, he sneaked a look at the needle on the depth gauge. They were passing one hundred feet and the boat now barely noticed the shock waves above. There were still no reports of any damage. The gauge needle slowly moved clockwise towards 120 feet and then it could go no further. The Coxswain and Second Coxswain both looked at their captain for permission to reverse the hydroplanes to arrest the slow descent, but Richard ignored them.

Steele declared expectantly, just as the ninth charge exploded, 'Depth 120 feet, sir.'

'We'll keep going another minute or so,' Richard replied. He was annoyed by Steele's challenge to his authority. The man hadn't earned that right yet. Then again, he thought, would he have reacted similarly towards Johnson in his days in *D2*? He could see Steele betraying his concern by continually glancing at the bulkhead. From now on they were in unknown territory. They were beyond the builder's recommended maximum safety depth. However, the average depth of water in the Strait was 150 feet and Richard wanted to see how far he could push not just the boat, but his men, and that included his new First Lieutenant.

Slowly, as the seconds passed and the submarine floated ever deeper, the hull could be heard to creak from the increased pressure of the water outside. Richard knew that now would probably be a good time to return to the surface, but he had to give his men the confidence that their boat could cope.

As the tenth and final charge exploded, far away it seemed, he addressed Steele, 'Reverse the 'planes. Take us back to Periscope Depth.

Prepare for some gunnery practice.' He noticed a slight ripple throughout the boat and imagined that it might have had more to do with the huge sighs of relief being exhaled rather than the shock waves of the charge.

'My God, sir,' exclaimed Steele, 'I would swear the bulkhead was becoming convex then.' Everyone in earshot bellowed with laughter. Richard had to grant that Steele had cleverly deflated the tension. He had redeemed himself a little and Richard felt pleased. Not only had *E9* passed the trial with flying colours, but the men had reacted well and would now have more confidence, not just in the boat, but in themselves when they faced a Turkish counter attack. Even so, despite the recent success, he was still not content that *E9* was ready to go to war with the Turks.

Chapter 22

May 1915

E9 was alone. It was two-thirty in the morning of the nineteenth of May and the escort had just turned for home. To the south, the powerful searchlights of Kum Kale swept the waters of the entrance to the Dardanelles and the beams illuminated the white cliffs of Cape Helles on *E9*'s port side. The submarine was proceeding on the surface, propelled by the diesel engines to save battery power, but trimmed down to present as small a profile as possible to the searchlights. As usual for this time of night in May, it was clear and starlit, but it was far from quiet. To the north could be heard the loud thuds of artillery fire and the occasional crackle of machine gun fire. Somewhere out there the Royal Naval Division was dug in and Richard hoped his cousin Charles was safe and well. Before slipping from *Adamant* he had made enquiries about his cousin, but the situation was so chaotic that nobody could tell him anything one way or the other. All he knew was that his cousin was not yet on the official casualty lists, so that at least was positive.

He was joined by Steele on the bridge.

'Under different circumstances I would venture to say it was a lovely night, sir. I have always dreamed of visiting the Hellespont.'

It was indeed a balmy night, but Richard was in no mood for conversation. He merely grunted in reply, but Steele was not put off.

'You are familiar with the Classics, I presume, sir? Since time immemorial these waters have been the scene of heavy fighting and played a prominent part in the Trojan Wars.'

Richard had indeed studied and enjoyed Classics at naval college, but had other things on his mind at present. Nevertheless, he recognised that it would be impolite to dull Steele's enthusiasm. By rights he should be asleep down below.

'My recollection of the Trojan Wars is scant, Number One, but I do recall some connection with Lord Byron and these waters. Do remind me.'

'Gladly, sir. It was here that the Persian Emperor Xerxes tried to cross the Strait to invade Greece by building a pontoon bridge across it for his troops. I can't recall exactly when. About 400 BC, I think. Anyway, a storm blew away the bridge and Xerxes ordered the waters to be punished with 300 lashes. It's a pity about the connections with war as ordinarily I have heard tell it is a most engaging spot.'

'Quite, but what is the connection with Byron?'

'Oh, yes, sir. It is quite a tale of romance. It was said that in ancient times Leander made the swim nightly from the Asian side to meet his love, Hero, on the opposite shore, but one night he was drowned in a storm. On seeing his dead body, Hero then threw herself off a cliff into the sea to be with her lover. One hundred or so years back Lord Byron swam across the water to commemorate the legend of Leander and Hero. I might try it myself if we return, sir.'

'*"If we return,"* First Lieutenant? Did you not mean, *"when we return"*?'

'Of course, sir. A slip of the tongue, I assure you.'

'No problem, but remember that the men will be looking to you for confidence over the next few days. We all have to believe in ourselves and our ability to succeed.'

'Quite right, sir. I apologise and will not let you down, sir.'

There was an awkward silence for half a minute which was broken by Steele. 'If you will excuse me, sir, I'll go below to take some rest. The day promises to be fraught with interest.'

Richard felt sure he had heard that phrase somewhere recently, but could not place it. He was happy to be left alone to his thoughts. He wondered if Steele had merely visited the bridge to show off his education, and if so, why had he felt the need to do so? Could it be that he felt Richard to be his social and professional inferior? He reflected that he had worked hard to build the man's confidence after such a lengthy period without sea service, but he now wondered if he had been too successful. To be fair, Steele seemed to be more relaxed with the men. The ship's company had even started referring to him good naturedly behind his back as, *'The Duke'*. Richard was not sure how this had come about, but presumed that they were poking fun at his title as an 'Honourable'. It was harmless enough, provided they did not take it too far.

Forgetting Steele, he looked ahead to the sleek bows of the submarine, slightly illuminated by the bio-luminescence of the disturbed plankton, and he felt a tremendous thrill. He now had under his command one of the world's most powerful submarines and a highly effective crew. For the past week he had pushed his men hard, practicing gunnery, crash dives, torpedo attacks and emergency evolutions. He recalled Keyes's last words to him as he set sail. *'Go and run amuck in the Marmara.'* His men were well rested and, if the next twenty-four hours went well, he would be nicely placed to wreak havoc in the Sea of Marmara. By doing so, he might ease the pressure on his cousin and the allied troops.

*

As *E9* was running on her diesels, the deep bass notes of her engines added to the noisescape. Notwithstanding the gunfire, Richard was concerned that the engine noise could be detected from either coast as the land on either side was only a little over a mile away. He would have preferred to have been dived, but it was imperative to conserve the precious batteries for the dangerous transit of the Narrows. As they passed the old fort of Seddul Bahr to port, the gap between Europe and Asia widened so Richard edged closer to the Asian side and felt more confident about remaining on the surface. He judged that they had about another hour before the return of daylight at dawn. He pondered increasing speed to make more headway under cover of darkness, but feared it might increase the visibility from shore of their bow wave and wake. *I'll just have to be patient, but I might as well take advantage of the delay.* He bent over the voice pipe.

'Control room, Captain. Is the First Lieutenant there?'

'First Lieutenant here, sir,' Steele replied.

'I plan on staying on the surface for another fifty minutes or so. If the stove is still hot, it might be worth setting up an early breakfast before we shut down the diesels. The next chance of a hot meal might not be until tomorrow.'

'I already have it in hand, sir. Mustard or tomato sauce on your bacon sandwich, sir?'

Richard was impressed with Steele's initiative. 'You're spoiling me, First Lieutenant. I'll have both with a banger and a big mug of *char*. You'd better send something up for the Third Hand and lookouts too. I don't feel I should dine alone this morning and you know what a gannet the Navigator is.' He smiled in response to the bridge crew's grins of anticipation.

'Aye aye, sir. Chef reckons he'll have it all ready in ten minutes.'

Replete from his middle-watch snack, Richard checked their position again on O'Connell's chart. They were now heading north-east, off the Suan Dere river to the north. For some minutes he and the bridge crew felt they had been illuminated by the searchlights at the approaches to the Narrows some five miles distant. Then, since the regular sweep had not wavered, they had assumed that they had escaped detection so far. Even so, Richard felt he had already stretched his luck too far. Moreover, it was becoming lighter to starboard and he feared being silhouetted against the Asian coast to watchers on the European side. After arranging for the bridge to be cleared, he ordered the engines to be stopped, clutches out and the submarine's ship's company to Diving Stations. The next time they surfaced would be in the Strait.

E9 proceeded under the surface at a depth of ninety feet and speed of three knots. The whole crew knew they were very close to the first of the mine fields, but hoped they would pass under them at this depth. Just as they dared hope they were through safely, everyone heard the clanking and rasping of a wire passing down the port side of the hull.

Alert to the danger, Richard ordered both engines to be stopped. Without even the hum of the electric motors, the silence was eerie as every man held his breath listening to the terrible noise outside the hull. Two of the sailors crossed themselves unconsciously. Richard was very conscious that if they snagged the wire on any protrusion from *E9*, it would drag on top of them one of the sinister, spiny mines tethered above. If just one of the horns of the mine acting as a detonator hit the hull sufficiently hard, then it would be all over.

He held his breath, too. The last time he had heard such a terrible sound, he had been in *D2* on the bottom of the North Sea. Then the noise had led to his salvation. He prayed silently and listened for signs that the wire was moving aft. When he judged the wire to have passed the control room he ordered, 'Hard a-port. Slow ahead starboard.'

He aimed to avoid fouling the port propeller on the mine. For over ten minutes he and *E9* played this dreadful cat and mouse game with numerous mines, but at last the only noise was that of the motors and hydroplanes. They had scraped through safely – this time!

Although the danger of further minefields could not be ignored, his concern now was navigation as it was an hour since they had obtained their last fix. He ordered Diving Stations prior to ordering the submarine back to periscope depth. The evolution did not prove simple.

'I'm sorry, sir, but we seem to be stuck at sixty feet,' Steele reported. 'The 'planes are full to rise, but it makes no difference.'

Richard thought this was odd as on diving *E9* had caught a perfect trim.

'I'll pump out the auxiliary tank, but may I increase speed, sir?' Steele requested.

'Just a minute, Number One. I think I know what's wrong. It's not something I have ever experienced, but other COs have mentioned it. It's the mixture of fresh and salt water that's the root of this.'

'I'm sorry, sir, but I don't follow.'

'Don't worry, Number One. I should have thought of it earlier. Several rivers cascade fresh water into this Strait on its path to the Aegean. The water is heated by day and this makes it even less dense. However, the outgoing fresh water in the Strait is being continually replaced by colder, denser salt water from the Aegean. This colder water runs deeper and the boundary between the different density waters is acting like a physical barrier for us.'

'Gosh, I think you have something there, sir. Indeed, it explains a queer story I read a couple of weeks back, when I was looking into the history of the region.'

'You've been studying the local history, First Lieutenant?'

'Why, of course, sir. I thought it might come in handy somehow.'

'So what's this story then?'

'Apparently, a few hundred years ago, a member of the Sultan's entourage became rather over familiar with one of the harem, if you follow my meaning. So the Sultan had the man bound and tied in a weighted sack. He was duly dumped in the Strait, but to everyone's surprise the body appeared twelve miles upstream and not downstream as would have been expected.'

'I 'eard that story, too, mate,' the periscope assistant muttered to his 'oppo' on the plot. 'His name was Mustapha Fuk.' The two sailors' raucous laughing was cut short by O'Connell. Richard winced, but ignored them.

‘And you deduce that this would be on account of a deep current flowing into the Strait from the Aegean, counter to the flow of the outgoing surface water then, Number One?’

‘Well it is only a legend, sir, but it might fit the facts.’

‘Possibly and it is something we will have to bear in mind. The only charts available don’t give any information on a deeper current, but if you are right, then we might find it aids our passage up the Strait when dived. You’ll have to take that into account, Pilot.’

Richard thought over all that had been said for a few minutes. He concluded that he would have to increase speed, thereby wasting valuable battery power, pump out water from the compensating tanks and increase the angle of ascent. He briefed Steele and the two hydroplane operators on the problem.

‘First Lieutenant, the trick here is to penetrate the layer, but not to bob to the surface like a cork afterwards. Before we make the ascent, I want you to pump out the auxiliary tank. Keep a note of how much you pump out. When I give the order for full ahead, I want full rise on the hydroplanes to achieve a twenty-up angle and, as soon as we gain momentum, flood the auxiliary tank like mad with the same number of gallons you pumped out. I’ll reduce speed and you’ll need to reverse the ’planes to avoid surfacing. I want to settle at thirty feet. I need this to be right first time. If we go up too quickly, we will surface and give away our presence. On the other hand, if we are too cautious, then we’ll be stuck beneath the layer and have wasted valuable amps. Is that clear?’ The three men confirmed they understood what was required.

‘Right then, First Lieutenant. Start pumping.’

Richard certainly found the next few minutes were exciting, and probably for all concerned. Having made the boat deliberately light, increased the speed to seven knots and put the hydroplanes hard a-rise, *E9* took on a very steep angle as she was driven to the surface. At fifty-five feet, the boat started to increase her rate of ascent and Steele, correctly assuming the boat was penetrating the layer, started to flood the auxiliary tank to regain the original trim. Richard ordered slow ahead and a reduction in the angle on the hydroplanes, but even so the submarine started rocketing to the surface. Feeling sure that he had overcooked the speed and dreading the boat would surface, he immediately despatched three members of the crew to run from the after part of the submarine to the bows, in order to take off some of the angle. Even so, the boat did not level out until twenty-five feet, a depth at which the top of the fin just broached the surface. Once back at thirty feet and Steele had satisfied himself that the boat was back in trim, Richard ordered the periscope to be raised very gingerly.

He looked through the periscope and was amazed to discover that they were further up the Strait than they had predicted. It suggested that Steele had been right about an underwater current, or at the very least, the strength of the current at depth was much less than that predicted at the surface. Kephez Point lay behind to starboard and they were only about a mile short of the Narrows between Chanak and Kilid Bahr. He did not take the time to reflect on it as the sea was like glass and he feared the feather of his periscope in the rapidly increasing light would give away their presence. He lowered the periscope and briefed O'Connell on his discovery.

He now considered his dilemma. They were about to enter the narrowest part of the Strait and the only way of fixing the submarine's position was by eye through the periscope. However, he feared raising the periscope in the approaching daylight in view of the mill pond conditions just where the Turkish defences were most concentrated. After a discussion with O'Connell and Steele, he decided to pass through the gap at a depth of fifty feet as close to Kilid Bahr as possible. Naturally, there was a risk of grounding, but they would have plenty of water above them to avoid being stranded. He only hoped that if they did show themselves above the surface, then the gunners' concentration would be at its lowest after a long night watch.

Creeping forward slowly on a north-easterly course *E9* touched bottom on three occasions. At each grounding, Richard altered course to starboard on a more easterly course and soon it became obvious that they had rounded the point. He altered course to north to set up *E9* for the sharp right hand turn to pass Nagara Point. If they could just get past this point, then the navigation would be easier, as the Strait opened out to two miles wide. He ordered a check of the electrolyte in the battery cells and was pleased to hear that they might have sufficient power to avoid a surface charge before clearing the Strait. Notwithstanding, he still had to weather Nagara Point and that meant raising the periscope for a fix before the turn to starboard. It was essential to keep well away from the shoal at the end of the point.

He raised the periscope a few inches above the surface after increasing speed slightly to give the two coxswains on the hydroplanes an easier task of maintaining the depth. The men had now been at Diving Stations for over two hours and he was glad Steele had managed to borrow two extra coxswains to share the toil on the hydroplanes. The work was not only physically demanding to rotate the brass wheels operating the hydroplanes, but required enormous concentration. One mistake could cost the lives of every man on board. It was not easy on the periscope either. The E-class boats were fitted with two periscopes. The search periscope was binocular, affording better vision, but offered too great a profile above the surface. The attack periscope was monocular and much thinner. To avoid raising the mast too far above the surface, Richard was operating it on his haunches in a similar posture adopted by the Cossacks in their famous dances. He found it very uncomfortable and tiring.

Surveying the Strait through his round window on the world, he noted with satisfaction that *E9* was just about where they had estimated she should be by dead reckoning, testament to O'Connell's skill as a navigator. They were almost at the wheel over point to head east. On both the European shores to the north and west, and the Asian coast to the east and south, the great searchlights were making their regular sweeps, but now the sun was beginning to rise. As he was about to order the periscope to be lowered, something caught his eye to the south.

'Smoke, bearing that,' he called. 'Green one-five-zero, 160 degrees,' responded the periscope assistant. 'Down,' Richard ordered and the periscope was gently lowered back into its well.

'All positions, there are at least three warships to the south at a range of about two miles, following us up the Strait,' he announced to everyone in the control room. 'One of them is most certainly something big, at least a cruiser and possibly a battleship. I couldn't see clearly because they were in the shadow of the coast. I'll have a better look once we are settled on our new course to pass Nagara Point. If we're lucky, I can use both the bow and beam tubes to get a shot at her and then run like the blazes to clear Nagara Point before they can counter attack. Tell the TI that I want the settings on the bow torpedoes changed to run deep for the heavy.'

The torpedo compartment suddenly became a hive of activity. Under the supervision of the senior torpedoman, known as the Torpedo Instructor or TI, the fore-ends' crew opened each bow tube, withdrew each torpedo using chain slings to take the massive weight, reset the depth setting and swung the torpedo back into its tube, before shutting the inner door. It was a physically demanding task, but the crew were well practiced after the numerous drills Richard and Steele had put them through. At last the tubes were reloaded and flooded ready for the impending attack. Meanwhile, *E9* was on her new course at thirty feet.

Richard took a second look through the periscope.

'Pilot, there are two battleships moving up the Strait in the company of four destroyers. They're both *Brandenburg*-class. What does that make them?'

O'Connell quickly scanned the details of the potential targets pasted to the control room bulkhead. 'They must be the *Turgut Reiss* and the *Heirreddin Barbarossa*, both bought from the German Navy in 1910, sir.'

Richard took one last bearing of the main body before lowering the periscope. He closed his eyes and conducted some rapid mental arithmetic. *E9* was now ideally placed to fire, but he would have to alter course to starboard to bring the bow tubes into action. Unfortunately, once he made this course alteration he would be head on with the approaching enemy ships. The 'bows-on' aspect of the ships would present only a minimal target for a 'down the throat' shot. He judged that he would have to fire at close range to offer a better chance of a hit.

When he estimated the main body was 2000 yards distant, he ordered a new course of 180. As the submarine settled on its new course, he raised the attack periscope. Within seconds of raising the periscope, he realised that they had been spotted from ashore as the surrounding water was peppered with the splashes of falling shells. Clearly the gunners were alert after all. Perhaps the anticipation of breakfast had improved their concentration. Immediately the leading destroyer, about 1200 yards distant, altered course towards the periscope and the crew could hear the steady throb of the propellers increasing speed. The nearer of the two battleships was now at a range of 1600 yards, within firing range, but far enough away to have time to alter course to avoid oncoming torpedo tracks. He reacted quickly and was about to fire the two bow torpedoes when he spotted the nearest battleship starting to turn to port to open the distance from the submarine. It gave him an idea.

'Down periscope. Come right fifteen degrees. Full ahead. Standby to fire the port beam tube.' He now gambled he could close the distance by 200 yards or so and perhaps get a beam-on target. He also wanted to keep the nearest destroyer occupied. He ordered the bow caps of the port and forward torpedo tubes to be opened and the tanks charged for firing. Ninety seconds later, he ordered the port beam tube to be fired blind. It was clear by the noise of the propellers that the destroyer was close, but he could not tell the bearing without use of the periscope. Thirty seconds later, he reduced speed and raised the periscope.

He couldn't believe his luck. The destroyer was only 600 yards on the port beam and correctly altering towards the torpedo tracks now clearly visible on the flat surface of the sea. The gun's crew were fully alert and had immediately started shooting at the periscope. The destroyer was certainly well handled. Amazingly, the battleship was fine on the port bow, beam-on at only 1000 yards. He couldn't miss. He quickly altered course five degrees to port and ordered both bow tubes to be fired before lowering the periscope. Everything was now down to fate and it was time to clear the area.

'Keep ninety feet. Starboard twenty. Steer three-five-zero.'

As the submarine dived and started its turn, the loud plops of shells, fired from ashore or the destroyer, could be heard entering the water above. Miraculously, not one had hit the exposed periscope or exploded against the hull. Nervously, Richard and the crew awaited the hoped-for explosions to indicate the torpedoes had struck their intended targets. Running at a speed of thirty knots it would take less than a minute for them to reach their destinations. It was very quickly evident that the beam tube torpedo had not struck home, though. Richard recognised that even if he had fired accurately, the torpedo may well not have had time to come to the correct depth to hit the shallow-draught destroyer and had probably passed underneath. The tension in the air was palpable as the ship's company silently joined him in counting down the torpedoes' run times. After fifty seconds, they were rewarded with two loud rumbles as both torpedoes detonated against the hull of the battleship fore and aft. It was nine months since their last successful attack and cheering erupted throughout the boat.

Richard felt nothing but satisfaction his calculations had proved correct. He dismissed a thought to return to periscope depth to take a look. It was too risky and now his main aim was to clear the datum of the attack and round Nagara Point. Grimly, he reflected that their operational patrol had barely started and they still had to reach the open Sea of Marmara.

Chapter 23

Early afternoon, twelve hours after diving off Cape Helles, O'Connell advised Richard that they should be in the Sea of Marmara. Richard had not dared raise the periscope to take a navigational fix since the morning, so the officers were relying completely on dead reckoning. Before ducking beneath the minefields off the town of Gallipoli, Richard had spotted Turkish trawlers dragging wire sweeps to search for the submarine. The air was now monstrously foul and the heat oppressive. Every man was soaked in sweat and ashen-faced. None moved much if they could avoid it. It took too much wind and made them feel even hotter. Steele had been inspecting the batteries frequently to monitor the electrolyte and reported that they were as exhausted as the men. Richard knew that he needed to surface to replenish the air and recharge the precious batteries.

Nervously, he ordered *E9* to fifty feet and a speed of two knots. The whole ship's company listened intently for the throb and swish of propeller blades on the surface. The only sounds were those of the men's laboured breathing. He eased the boat to thirty feet and apprehensively raised the attack periscope. Even before it broke the surface, he could see it was a brilliantly sunny afternoon. When the water cleared the periscope lens, he could see no sign of Turkish surface forces. He ordered a depth of twenty-six feet and conducted a full sweep on the search periscope. He saw that the Strait was well behind and they lay about four miles off both the Asiatic and European shores. The view was beautifully peaceful and he was tempted to surface the submarine to ease his men's discomfort. Instead, he ordered the submarine to fifty feet and altered course south-easterly, towards the European shore. He could see the strained and disappointed looks on his men's faces. Steele looked at him questioningly.

'It's all clear, Number One. We've done it. Well done, Pilot. We're well into the Sea of Marmara, about here.' He pointed to a position on the chart and then marked a cross in the shallows of the southern coast. For the benefit of the listening sailors he addressed Steele again.

'First Lieutenant, I want you to bottom the boat in the position I have marked on the chart. When you have done that, fall out from Diving Stations. I intend staying on the bottom until it gets dark tonight. If we surface before then, we risk being spotted by coastal watchers and I'm not minded to have my precious sleep disturbed by a bunch of excitable destroyer captains. In the meantime, everyone, bar a single watchkeeper in the control room, is to get their head down. I want minimum movement throughout the boat. Carry on.'

'Aye aye, sir,' Steele replied. 'But with your leave, sir, I think I'll take the Coxswain with me to tour the submarine and check for any leaks after the excitement of grounding, mines and shell fire.'

In the two minutes he lay conscious on his bunk before falling into an exhausted stupor, Richard reflected that his First Lieutenant was showing promise.

*

The following morning, a working party was organised under Steele's supervision to mount the gun in position on the casing and bring up its ammunition. The gun had been stowed below during the transit of the Strait for fear that it might snag on a mine. Richard was conscious that the length of their patrol was limited, not by food, but by the number of torpedoes carried. *E9* only carried five reloads, one for each tube, and he had already expended three torpedoes during the attack on the battleship and destroyer off Nagara Point. Food was already rationed, but in the intense heat of the submarine interior, the men's appetites were low. In any case, he reasoned he might be able to obtain food from one of the many small craft known to ply the Sea. Where possible, he hoped to sink his targets by gunfire. The submarine was well stocked with three-inch shells. The Coxswain, Petty Officer Haines, had also managed to borrow a gunlayer, Leading Seaman Dodds, and a seaman gunner, Seaman McIntyre, from the depot ship. Dodds seemed to be competent and had fitted in well with the other sailors, Richard thought, but he had not taken a liking to McIntyre.

Richard and Dodds had agreed to stow the shells, or 'bricks' as they were known by the ship's company, beneath the fore-hatch. Speed would be essential in any form of gun action. The gun had to be brought into action to disable the enemy before the target could retaliate. To this end, they had rehearsed that the layer would exit the submarine though the conning tower immediately as the tower broached the surface and the fore-hatch then opened when full buoyancy was achieved. The gun barrel would be flooded with water and so one round would be stored in the barrel on diving, to be fired immediately as a clearing round. By this time, fresh ammunition would be passed through the hatch by a designated ammunition party. Richard had also instructed the signalman to order dozens of ensigns for the bridge staff. Unusually, *E9* would dive with the staff rigged and the ensign flying. The ensign would become shredded over time, but it would save any delay in showing colours before opening fire.

O'Connell had the watch on the bridge and looking up through the conning tower, Richard could see a clear blue sky above. It seemed a pity to wage war on a day such as this.

'Excuse me, my lord. Where d'ye want this stowing, then?'

Richard swung round, seething. McIntyre was being insolent and he could see Steele blushing. 'Coxswain,' he called, 'I'll see that man at my table.'

'But whit fer, sir?' McIntyre remonstrated.

'You know very well, McIntyre. Insubordination. You will address all officers with respect.'

'But I wisna bein' insubordinate, sir. I wis addressin' the First Lootenant by 'is praper title.'

'Sir, if I might explain,' Steele cut in. 'I need to speak to you privately.'

The two officers retired to the relative privacy of the wardroom and Richard drew the curtain behind them.

'Very well, First Lieutenant. Explain.'

'I'm sorry, sir. I should have told you. I only found out just before this patrol. By virtue of my grandfather passing away recently, I have inherited the title of Viscount. Technically, McIntyre was correct in the way he addressed me.'

Richard felt his blood rise and he replied quietly, but with venom. 'Don't presume to lecture me on etiquette, Steele. We'll discuss this on the bridge.'

He swiftly clambered up the conning tower ladder, followed by Steele.

'I have the submarine, Officer of the Watch,' he addressed O'Connell. 'Go below with the lookouts until I call you back. I want a private word with the First Lieutenant.'

O'Connell stared at him incredulously and then at Steele, but Steele cocked his head sideways and O'Connell quickly cleared the bridge.

Richard swept the horizon once with his glasses and then turned to Steele in a fury.

'And why was I the last to hear of your elevation to the peerage, my lord? Or was it beneath you to confide in me?'

'Heaven forfend, sir. I haven't told anyone. I didn't think it of anybody's business but my own. I am mightily sorry to have embarrassed you, sir.'

'Let's get this straight, Steele, Viscount Storrs or however else you are known. This is my submarine and anything and everything is my business. Do you understand?'

'Indeed, sir.'

'Understand this, too. I've had enough of your condescending ways. Your father may now be an earl. Your late grandfather may well have been an admiral. You may well speak your fancy language and look down your nose at me, but I'm the Captain and just because you've been on board half a dogwatch doesn't mean you will be superseding me anytime soon. You remain my subordinate, even if you are indeed given a dukedom. Is that clear?'

'Indubitably, sir. I heartily apologise for any offence I may have offered, sir. Believe me when I say that it pains me to mortification that you should think so low of me. I only …'

'Spare me your dandy speeches, Steele. Get off my bridge. I'm sick of the sight of you.' He turned his back on Steele and opened the cover to the voice pipe. 'Control room, Captain. The First Lieutenant is coming below. Send up the Navigator and lookouts once he's clear of the conning tower.'

Two minutes later, the control room called, 'Captain, sir. Permission for the Coxswain to come to the bridge? He wants to speak to you.'

'Negative. Tell him I will see him when I come below.'

'He says it's urgent, sir.'

Richard sighed and tried to calm his temper. 'Very well then,' he responded resignedly.

Coxswain Haines was slightly built, short, bearded and hailed originally from Barnstaple. Unusually, in Richard's opinion, he was quietly spoken and mildly mannered for his position. By the usual naval standards, one might have thought he lacked what was known as 'power of command', but Haines seemed to achieve good results quietly and unobtrusively. He was also, unusually experienced. It was compulsory in submarines for ratings to return to the surface fleet after five years and then to re-volunteer for further service in submarines. This was one of the means employed to maintain standards and build an elite body of men for service in the submarine fleet. Haines was on his third stint in submarines.

'Yes, Coxswain. What's up?'

'Begging yer pardon, sir, it's you what's up. It ain't right the way yer treating the First Lieutenant.'

Richard was shocked. 'I beg your pardon, 'swain. This is sheer impudence. Are you looking to lose your rate?'

'Threaten me all ye like, sir. Makes no difference. If I don't speak my mind, then I have no business bein' a cox'n anyway. I 'eard ye ballin' out the Jimmy, tellin' 'im all that goes on this boat be yer business.'

'You listened in to my private conversation, Coxswain?'

'Weren't that private, sir, the way you were ballin' and yellin'. I just stood at the bottom of the hatch and could 'ear ye, even above the roar of the intakes. Nobody else could 'ear, though, sir.'

For a moment Richard was too stunned by the Coxswain's directness to reply.

'As far as I be concerned, sir, what goes on 'tween decks is rightly my business as Cox'n. I be responsible for discipline and morale and the lads are worried yer turnin' into some kind of martinet, sir.'

'Are they now?' Richard was in two minds how to respond next. His natural instinct was to dismiss Haines from the bridge and have a charge of insubordination brought against him, too, on return from patrol. However, Haines was widely respected throughout the submarine service and common sense suggested to him that he should swallow his pride and hear out his coxswain.

'I can tell you plan on speaking your mind, Coxswain. Go on then. Have your say and be on your way.'

'Aye, right enough. Thank 'ee, sir. You've a good 'n' there, sir, in the Jimmy. I've been in boats nigh on twelve years now. Started on the *Holland.* I've seen a few officers in my time. He may be a toff and don't get on with the men as well as Paddy, but the lads have come to like and respect him, sir. Yer running 'im too hard. You leave 'im be and mark my words 'e'll turn out a first class submarine officer. An' if he says he didn't tell nobody he was a Viscount, then you should believe 'im, sir.'

'Oh, really? So just how did McIntyre find out then 'swain?'

'Some letter came addressed to him with the title, sir. You know boats, sir. As soon as one of the plate-lifters inboard saw it in his mail rack, then the whole world gets to know.'

'Except me it seems. So that's why some call him the Duke then.'

'Reckon's yer right there, sir, but the men don't mean no 'arm by it. You could call it affection. It's the same with the Navigator. No man has the right to call him 'Paddy' to his face, but we all does, behind his back.'

'I begin to wonder what they call me behind my back, Coxswain.'

'Arr, not my business to say, sir. But don't you fret about it. Yer respected well enough. Just ye keep killin' those Huns and Turks and the men'll follow you to Hades itself.'

'Thank you,' swain, for your frankness. I will, of course, apologise to the First Lieutenant. Perhaps I should in future consult with my ship's company before submitting the confidential reports on my officers, 'swain.'

'Mebbez ye should. We're the poor buggers as 'ave t' follow yer orders, I reckons. But thanks for the chat, sir. I'm glad we un'erstan' each other better, now. But hang on a minute! Look yonder, to starboard, sir.'

Richard swivelled round in response to Haines's urgent appeal to look in the direction of his coxswain's outstretched hand. He flipped open the lid to the voice pipe and ordered the submarine to Diving Stations. Haines had spotted smoke and the superstructure of a small steamer was already visible.

Chapter 24

June 1915

Eleven days into her patrol and *E9* was on the surface, nestled in the shelter of Marmara Island. During his air reconnaissance Richard had marked the spot as being a relatively safe place to rest the ship's company, as it was off the main shipping routes and the surrounding islands masked them from watchers on the Asian shore. He was now sitting at the chart table updating his diary and writing up his patrol report. So far they had sunk a steamer by torpedo and another by gunfire. They had also sunk a sailing vessel with explosive charges. Unfortunately, they had missed out on sinking a gunboat and destroyer through the torpedoes, or 'mouldies' as the crew named them, failing to run properly. He had, therefore, decided that it would be good for morale to break up the usually tense patrol routine by allowing the hands to bathe with a 'make and mend'.

Today the sea was covered by a light mist, reducing visibility and the prospect of sighting a target, so it seemed a perfect opportunity to rest the crew whilst waiting for the mist to burn off. The normally languid Steele had surprised them all by turning out to be a fitness fanatic and was using the break to exercise the men in Swedish Drill, before allowing them to mess about in the water. He had even built them a raft out of old timbers and oil drums salvaged from a dhow they had destroyed by fire a few days earlier. Richard could hear the splashing and laughter of the men diving from the casing or raft and swimming in the warm water. Rather ingeniously, Steele had constructed a dummy periscope on the raft so that it could act as a decoy if they were surprised by enemy aircraft. Richard was beginning to consider himself very lucky to have such an able officer as his second-in-command and regretted his intemperate words to him a week or so earlier.

He rubbed his smoothly shaven jaw with pleasure. Owing to the shortage of fresh water, it was not usual for submariners to shave on patrol. Now the fresh-water inland sea provided an ample supply, but even so, most of the ship's company were not bothering. Some were competing to see who could grow the best beard before the reassertion of normal discipline at the end of the patrol. Others were experimenting with leaving the upper lip unshaved to experience the novelty, for a sailor, of a moustache. Richard was content to allow the men their fun, but he had insisted on the men bathing whenever the opportunity had arisen, such as today. The atmosphere of a submarine was fetid enough without the added odours of unwashed bodies in close proximity. His thoughts were interrupted by O'Connell, already sporting the makings of a fine red beard.

'Begging your pardon, sir. The First Lieutenant has asked me to tell you that the forward hatch is now shut and clipped and the casing is clear of swimmers. He requests you join him on the bridge as he wants you to see something.'

Richard sprang from his camp chair, grabbed his binoculars and, donning his reefer jacket, headed up the conning tower ladder to the bridge. Reaching the top of the ladder, he noted Steele and the lookout were gazing intently through binoculars towards the north-west.

'What's up, Number One?'

'Sorry to disturb you, sir, but I think there's a sail out there, just to the left of the headland, crossing right to left, perhaps eight or ten thousand yards away. It's difficult to see in the mist.'

Richard had a look for himself. He could appreciate Steele's difficulty. Normally the coast was visible from here, ten miles distant, but today the mist still obscured the coast and moreover played tricks with the eyes. After two frustrated minutes, his patience was rewarded when the dancing vapours on the sea surface opened momentarily for him to see a definite shape emerge. It was a large twin-masted ketch under full sail in the light winds. Just as the curtains of cloud closed on the view once more, he noted smoke rising from the stern of the vessel. He had no doubt that the ketch was large enough to be carrying cargo and, hence, potentially a viable target.

'You're right. Well done. Diving Stations, First Lieutenant. We'll run in dived to avoid alerting her until it's too late.'

Richard skilfully manoeuvred *E9* to within half a mile of the ketch's stern before returning to periscope depth to observe her. She was on a port tack in the light north-easterly wind and he judged her speed to be only about a knot. On his next look he found himself 300 yards on the port quarter. Painted on the transom of her light-blue painted hull was the name *Alondra.* Her superstructure was manufactured from teak or mahogany and Richard admired her handsome lines. Unlike many of the Turkish sailing vessels *E9* had come across so far, this one was plainly well maintained. On the poop deck he observed the source of the smoke. The five crew members were seated around a brazier on which they appeared to be cooking their lunch. He noted that the boat was well down in the water and that meant she was probably carrying cargo. Judging by the course, she was bound for Gallipoli. She was worth boarding.

'Surface,' he ordered and lowered the periscope.

A few minutes later, the feasting Turks were disturbed from their meal by the scene astern. The water appeared to be boiling, a phenomenon caused by air being forced into the main ballast tanks of *E9* to expel fountains of water. As the Turks gazed intently at the disturbance, their interest suddenly turned to alarm as a huge, black sea creature burst through the bubbling waters. Watching them through the ports of the conning tower, Richard chuckled to himself as the look of fear on their faces turned to relief once they recognised the monster as man-made, and then alarm once again as they realised the implications. Within seconds, he unclipped and opened the upper hatch and climbed up to the bridge. He was followed by the two lookouts, both carrying rifles.

By now the Turkish crew were alive with activity, heaving on the sheets to try to coax out a little more speed and the helmsman had altered course to starboard. A little man on the poop deck, wearing a red fez, a short red jacket and white baggy trousers, was gesticulating and shouting wildly. Richard hailed him with the megaphone and called for him to heave to as he positioned the submarine fifty yards off the port beam to steal the ketch's wind. His hail was answered by more shouting, gesticulation and a further sharp alteration of course to starboard. Another change of course of this nature would result in the boat gybing, Richard thought. It was time to bring about some co-operation. He turned to the two lookouts.

'Smith, Cooper. Two rounds each into the after masthead and in your own time. Make sure you don't hit any of the crew.'

The rounds were noisily despatched and Richard observed two pierce one of the sails, but there was no sign of the other two hitting anything.

So much for all that training at Bisley! However, the demonstration of intent had had the desired effect as the master ordered the sheets to be let fly and took hold of the wheel himself to bring the ketch's head into wind. Having taken the way off the boat, he ordered the sails to be lowered, before shouting and waving across to the bridge crew, '*Ne tirez pas Messieurs. S'il vous plait. Ne tirez pas.*'

Richard brought the submarine alongside and sent Steele and the boarding party on board the ketch to search her. The crew were rounded up and grouped on the casing under the watchful eye of the armed bridge crew. Richard sent for the master to meet him on the casing of *E9*. He addressed him in French.

'You don't speak English?'

"No, sir, only French and some Italian. Please, sir, do not harm me or my crew. We will co-operate.'

'What is your cargo and where are you bound?'

'Just wood and some coal for Cardak. I assure you I have no military supplies.'

'Your French is very good, master. Where did you learn it?'

'At school in Smyrna, sir. I am Roman Catholic and attended a *Levantin* school. You too speak good French, sir. But you are English, then?'

'Yes. This is a Royal Navy submarine. Excuse me a moment.' He spied Steele appearing above a hatch coaming of the ketch. 'First Lieutenant, what's the cargo?'

'Mainly wood, sir, with some coal. We haven't found any contraband. Well, not yet anyway. We still haven't finished rummaging the vessel.'

'Fine. We can save on gun cotton and burn her, then. It seems the Navigator can recreate the activities of his forebears after all. It seems a pity, though, as she's a lovely vessel. I'll just inform the master.'

'Master, please gather your men in the skiff. You may take whatever possessions, food and navigational instruments you require, but no weapons. I am going to burn your vessel, but I mean no harm to you or your crew.'

The blood drained from the Turkish master's dark-skinned face. 'No, sir. That cannot be right. I have done you no harm. I have no part in this stupid war. I am just trying to make a living to support my family. See there.'

The Turk pointed to a young man seated in the stern sheets. 'He is my son. I have five children and a wife to support. Please, I beg you. Do not take away my livelihood.' He dropped to his knees in supplication.

Richard was embarrassed, but also affected by the man's plea. He believed in the master's innocence, but then, what was to stop him carrying barbed wire or pit props for the Gallipoli Peninsular on his next run? His heart hardened as he thought of his cousin on the beaches under Turkish fire.

'I am genuinely sorry, but our two countries are at war and I have my duty. Now please gather your men in the skiff.'

'No, sir,' the Turk beseeched him. 'This is not my war. I merely live in Turkey. My family come from Genoa originally and I have many relatives in Toulon. I take no sides. Wait. I might be able to help you.'

The Turk seemed in two minds as to whether to continue or not, but after a glance back at his beautiful ketch he made his decision. Richard waited in silence.

'Sir, I have information that may help you. If I give it to you, will you spare my boat?'

'I cannot give you that undertaking without knowing the value of the information. Tell me what you know and if I think it worth something, then I will consider a deal. You will have to trust me.'

The Turkish master looked once again at his fine sailing vessel and then across to his son before making up his mind irrevocably.

'Last week I was in Constantinople picking up this load. I noticed a huge transport ship, the *Guj Djemal*, being loaded with artillery, equipment and ammunition. The word in the docks was that she was embarking a brigade of troops bound for Gallipoli. Whilst drinking tea in a *kiraathane* near the docks, I overheard one of the ship's officers talking of several submarines in the locality. Your exploits and those of your colleagues are famous, sir. The Turks fear you greatly, sir.'

'Please come to the point, master. My time is short.' Although Richard had responded tersely, he was pleased to hear that the Turks thought more than one submarine had penetrated the Strait.

'I am sorry, sir. Yes, this officer was bragging that their ship would avoid you and the other submarines by crossing the sea via Kalolimno Island and the south coast. She had not finished loading when I left, so you should have time to meet her. But take care, sir, you are no doubt aware that she will be heavily escorted.'

'How do you know she is carrying artillery?'

'I saw the guns, sir. She is carrying a battery of artillery to Gallipoli and I saw their three-inch field guns. It is rumoured that she carries 6,000 troops for the front, too, sir.'

Richard's interest was piqued by the information. Since entering the Sea of Marmara, *E9* had failed to find a high value target. He still had three torpedoes left and this could make a fitting end to the patrol. He did some mental calculations. It was about fifty miles to Kalolimno Island. At fifteen knots on the surface he could be there in fewer than four hours, but even in this mist, he risked being spotted as the diesel exhaust fumes might be observed from a higher platform above the low lying mist. Dived at a maximum speed of nine or so knots he could be there in about six hours, but the battery would be exhausted by then and he could only risk charging at night. Furthermore, what if the Turk's information was wrong and the transport was actually taking the more usual route to the north? He might miss her if he was deep. There again, what was the hurry? He had no way of knowing when the vessel was due to sail and might have to hang around the island for a few days yet. No, it would be better to make his way slowly across the sea, charge the battery overnight on the surface and lie in wait at periscope depth during the day. The mist was a worry, though. Whilst it reduced the risk of *E9* being seen from ashore, even if he stayed on the surface, he was also unlikely to see much either and ran the risk of collision if a ship suddenly loomed out of the mist. If he dived, he would see nothing and waste an opportunity. He looked up to the wind vane on the ketch's masthead to check the wind direction, but it was obscured by the mist, even though Richard could see the faint glow of sunshine above. It suddenly gave him an idea and as a Classics scholar it appealed to him. He turned his attention back to the Turk.

'What is your name, master?'

'Giovanni Koc, sir. Whom do I have the honour of addressing?'

'I'm afraid, Captain Koc, that I cannot tell you that for fear it might compromise the identity of my submarine. Anyway, Captain, I have decided that in exchange for the information you have just given me and one other thing, I will spare your beautiful sailing vessel. Please stand up.'

Koc's relief as he stood was palpable. 'Oh, thank you, thank you, sir. You are an English gentleman. But er - what is the other thing?'

'I wish to borrow your boat for the rest of the day. You and your crew will be at liberty to move freely under supervision, and tonight we will release you and your men to continue your passage. Is that a deal?'

Koc must have recognised that he had no choice because he readily agreed. Richard called across to one of the boarding party, 'Able Seaman Davies, pass the word to the First Lieutenant that I wish to see him in the control room when he has finished searching the ketch. Allow the master to rejoin his crew.'

When Steele joined his captain in the control room he found him peering intently at the chart.

'Did you find anything of interest, Number One?'

'No contraband, sir. We did find some live chickens and oddly enough a couple of piglets too.'

'The crew are Catholics not Muslims. Maybe they might sell us one and a couple of chickens. I'm fed up of tinned bully beef. Did you find out anything else?'

'I checked the papers and manifest and the cargo is bound for Cardak, not Gallipoli. With all that wood and coal on board she'll burn easily enough.'

'I've changed my mind on that. I've had another idea. Did you learn anything about the Trojan Wars at Winchester?'

'Of course, sir. My father shelled out a substantial sum of cash to ensure I could recite the *Aeneid.*' Steele affected a pained expression as if to indicate the quality of his Wykehamist education had been impugned. He went on, 'I do recall that the island of Tenedos, where the RNAS are based, was the main base of the Greeks when they laid Troy under siege.'

'Full marks, Number One. We have in the *Alondra* our very own Trojan Horse. My plan is that we remain tied alongside the ketch, but on the starboard side. If we trim down first, the sails will hide us from any watchers on the European side as we head east. The wind will be behind us, so nobody should be too suspicious if we motor along at three to four knots. At the same time, I want you to place a lookout at the forward masthead. He should be able to see above the mist and warn us of any potential targets. Tonight we will slip the ketch and her crew, and charge the battery ready for tomorrow.'

Richard briefed Steele on what he had learned from the Turkish master.

*

The following day was frustrating. Richard established a twenty mile patrol line north of Kalolimno Island and was pleased to see two steamers. However, he declined to attack them and kept his distance. He wanted both to conserve his final three precious torpedoes for the transport and not scare her away by evidence of his presence in this part of the Sea. Early in the evening, as the sun was beginning to set, his patience was rewarded by the sight of smoke in the direction from which they were expecting the convoy to appear. He immediately dived the submarine and altered course to close the range and to lie in wait for the approaching ships. A quick look through the periscope established that the convoy comprised two large transports and an escort of three destroyers fanned out ahead of the larger ships. Neither destroyer seemed to be actively searching for a potential quarry and both transports remained on a steady south-westerly course, about two miles astern. He concluded they were not expecting allied submarines this far east. He calculated that if he remained on this course at four knots, the more southerly destroyer would pass close ahead, but he could then close the transports and set himself up to fire from a range of between 1,600 and 2,000 yards. He would be like a fox in a chicken run.

After the earlier problems with defective 'mouldies' and with still a week of his patrol to run, he could not afford to waste any of his precious torpedoes on the destroyers. There was still a chance of a juicy target on the homeward run or that he might need to fire a torpedo at a destroyer in self-defence. His normal practice was to fire two torpedoes at a high value target, one just ahead of the bows in case the target was either faster than he guessed or increased speed, and the other at the boiler room. He had a difficult decision as how best to use his torpedoes. It was a decision he opted to defer until he saw how the situation developed.

From its bow wave, he estimated the nearest destroyer was making fifteen knots, meaning it would be upon them within five minutes. He delayed raising the periscope again. The surface was calm, and although the light was fading, the periscope would create an obvious V-shaped feather. Whilst he tried to relax and remain calm, Steele and the ship's company, with the exception of the 'planesmen, were rushing about preparing and flooding the two bow and single stern torpedo tubes for firing. O'Connell, by contrast, was looking bored at the chart table, awaiting fresh bearings of the ships to plot on his chart.

Within a few minutes, nobody had time to be bored. Richard was occupied by the approaching sound of fast-turning propeller blades above. Everyone listened anxiously for any indication of increasing revolutions that might suggest the Turk had seen anything untoward, but the destroyer passed ahead without incident. The propeller noises receded and Richard ordered the control room lights to be turned off or dimmed. The setting sun would silhouette the destroyer, but the descending darkness would make his periscope less visible to any stern lookouts. Dimming the control room lights afforded him an opportunity to gain his night sight before raising the periscope.

'Keep twenty feet,' he ordered. 'Raise periscope. Stop.'

The tip of the periscope had barely broken the surface and the control room was in absolute silence to allow the captain to concentrate. Steele focused intently on the trim and hydroplanes operators. It was vital that the depth was held absolutely steady. If the submarine rose to nineteen feet, then the periscope would be raised a foot further out of the water. If it sank more than a few feet, then the periscope would 'dip' beneath the water, potentially blinding the captain and ruining his concentration at a vital moment. Richard turned the periscope quickly onto the expected bearing of the nearest destroyer.

'Fine. That destroyer's disappearing quickly. Let's look for the transports.' He swivelled the periscope until he caught sight of the transports.

'That's a pity. Revolutions for seven knots. Bearing that. Down.' Both targets were further away than he had estimated.

'Pilot, the nearest target is at a range of 3,000 yards and the other approximately 500 yards off her starboard quarter.'

O'Connell plotted the two targets whilst Richard quickly calculated the angles and his options. He thought it a pity to let both ships go as they looked heavily laden, but he could only fire two torpedoes at a time and the tracks would give away his presence.

Silently, *E9* sliced through the water under the power of her electric motors. Some of the men muttered instructions or conversation, but generally there was silence except for the humming and rattling of the boat's machinery. An air of nervous excitement pervaded the entire boat. A rumour had started that there might be 6,000 troops on each transport and, if true and the attack succeeded, they were about to become very rich. Under an old Prize Law of 1708 re-enacted by the King in March that year, '*if in any action any ship of war or privateer shall be taken from the enemy, five pounds shall be granted to the captors for every man which was living on board such ship or ships so taken at the beginning of the engagement between them'*. Such prize money was normally divided amongst all allied vessels in the vicinity, but in this instance *E9* was entirely alone. The crew might stand to gain as a whole £60,000. Once shared out that could amount to thirty years' pay.

Patiently, Richard waited for the second hand of the stopwatch around his neck to show the elapsing of six minutes before he reduced speed to four knots and raised the periscope for a final look before firing. It was almost 20.00 and he knew the light would fade very soon. If he had miscalculated or the convoy had altered course, then there would be no second opportunity of pursuing the attack.

Once the periscope pierced the sea above, the murmuring of conversations stopped. The only light in the control room was a disc reflected through the periscope off Richard's right eye. He broke the tension within seconds.

'Bearing that, 1,500 yards. Fire One and fire Two.'

He need not have worried. He had judged it perfectly. The nearest transport, a three-masted, two-funnelled, former White Star liner, was fine on the starboard bow and the range was good. Knowing that there was no destroyer in the vicinity, he kept the periscope raised to observe the run of the torpedoes. To his dismay, the port torpedo's gyro malfunctioned and it veered off to port. The starboard torpedo appeared to be running true and provided it did not run under its target, looked certain to hit, but he suspected that one hit would not be enough to guarantee sinking the ship. He slapped the side of the periscope. If only he had not wasted his valuable torpedoes, he rued, but this was no time for crying over spilt milk.

'Down periscope. Port twenty. Standby to fire the stern tube. One of the torpedoes is a miss. I'm going to take another shot at the nearest transport,' he announced to the control room team. The news was received with a groan. Everyone knew that there was only one torpedo left and that now meant only half the potential prize money. Steele immediately tried to silence the muttering, but it was no use. A few seconds later, however, they heard a huge explosion and this time the men began cheering. The second torpedo had run true.

Richard brought the euphoric hands back to reality by cancelling the turn and settling *E9* on a steady course ready to fire the stern torpedo. He raised the periscope and saw darkness was now enveloping the two targets, but the nearer transport was stopped in the water and definitely sinking by the stern. There were several splashes alongside. Some of these might have been caused by falling debris, but he could also see men in the water. He suspected many of the troops on board were panicking and jumping over the side, rather than waiting for the lifeboats to be launched.

Seeing the men in the water brought it home to him that there were real human beings on the ship and several would no doubt die as a result of his actions. The thought sickened him. The war had to be brought to an end and this was the best way he knew of assisting that process. He focussed his attention on the shapes just visible through the periscope. In the fading light he found it difficult to assess the range of the transports and impossible to judge his angle on the bow of the second ship, now a dark shape to the left of her stricken sister. The reflection of the moonlight on her bow wave indicated she was not heaving to in order to retrieve survivors. Rightly so, he thought. He contemplated a second shot, but could not rid himself of the thought of the men in the water. The ship was doomed anyway and was not worth the expenditure of his last torpedo. After ordering *E9* deep and altering course and speed to clear the area he wondered if he had become squeamish.

Chapter 25

August 1915

Most of the men of *E9* lay asleep where they could and barely a sound could be heard apart from snoring and an occasional grunt. The single watchkeeper sat in the control room trying to read in the dim lighting. Given that the submarine was dived at a depth of seventy-three feet in the Sea of Marmara, surrounded by the enemy, and not sitting on the bottom, it was a novel situation. The fact was that she might as well have been sitting on the bottom. Richard had discovered by experiment that instead of there being a gradual change in the density of the water, there was a clearly defined line of demarcation between the fresh water layer and the denser, salt water beneath. This salt water layer was sufficiently dense to allow the submarine to sit on it. It meant that *E9* did not have to leave the shipping lanes for long periods to seek shallow water to allow the ships' company to rest and conserve the battery's precious amps.

Richard lay on his bunk reflecting on his experiences of *E9*'s first patrol in the Sea of Marmara and the news from home. It was one of the few moments he had to himself to relax whilst on patrol and he had much to consider. In his hands he held two letters closely to his chest.

He and the men of *E9* had been surprised to return from their first patrol in the Dardanelles as heroes. The ships of the Allied Fleet had manned the sides and cheered the submarine as it had returned at the end of June. Richard had then discovered that he had been promoted to Commander on the spot and recommended for another decoration. It had come as a huge shock when he learned, just prior to sailing on this second Dardanelles patrol, that he had been awarded the VC. Despite his embarrassment by the attention, he secretly felt enormously proud to have equalled his father's achievement in winning the most prestigious decoration for valour in the face of the enemy. It had given him greater satisfaction, however, to learn, also, that both Steele and O'Connell had been awarded the Distinguished Service Cross and, moreover, every member of the ship's company the Distinguished Service Medal. They all had Commodore Keyes to thank for this. Richard thought it very appropriate that the Admiralty had rewarded his men in this way as they had all shared the same risks on the patrol. It had struck him as unfair that when the previous year, following the sinking of the German light cruiser SMS *Hela,* he had been awarded his DSO, his men had not been similarly commended. The tradition of the Royal Navy was to honour the men through their commanding officer.

He hoped that Papa would now understand his decision not to follow in his father's footsteps, but to become a submariner and make his own mark. He was sure that Papa must be proud of him, but was equally sure that he would never show it. Thinking of Papa, brought him back to the terrible news his father's last letter had brought. The letter had been written in February, but caught up with *Adamant* only after he had sailed on the last patrol through the Strait. His brother Paul had been declared, 'Missing - Presumed Dead' after being shot down in a raid on Ostend. Moreover, it was clear that *Mutti* was in very low spirits and all was not well between her and Papa.

Tears welled up in his eyes as he thought of Paul. Might his aircraft have caught fire, exposing Paul to a slow and agonising death? He had always recognised the risks of aviation accidents, but he had thought Paul safe from the enemy in Dover. He wiped away his tears and as his heart ached with the pain that he knew *Mutti* must be feeling, he had to stifle a potential sob. He couldn't risk being heard to blub. He reached for his Bible to distract him, but didn't open it. He felt helpless sitting here hundreds of miles away. It wasn't fair to blame Papa either. Somebody had to tell their mother that Papa had never openly encouraged either of his sons to join the Navy. She might have now read the publication in the London Gazette of his citation for the VC and be feeling some solace. Moreover, the news of Paul was not definitive. It was not 'Killed in Action', so there was some doubt. Perhaps by now Paul might have surfaced as a Prisoner of War.

He cast his mind back to his farewell with the Commodore before sailing on this patrol. Keyes had informed him that on his return, he would be sent back to England for leave and a new appointment. If he and his men could survive just a few more weeks, then he could offer some support to *Mutti*.

The thought of returning home brought to mind the other letter in his hand. It, too, had been written six months earlier, but this one, by contrast, evoked tears of joy. Lizzy had written several sheets of news about the yard and her success in gaining several contracts for both ships and submarines as part of her war effort. He chuckled at the account of how the men had reacted to several hundred women being employed in the yard alongside the skilled trades. The suffragettes might have temporarily abandoned their push for women's suffrage, but Lizzy had transferred her passion into showing that women were the equal of men in the workplace. Good on her. The letter was not without sentiment, though, and Lizzy expressed her impatience for his return and the chance to hold their delayed wedding ceremony. He made a mental note to write to her to start planning the event and then it occurred to him that he would probably be home before any such letter - provided he survived this patrol.

He assumed that by now she would have had the news of her brother, Charles. He, too, had been decorated, with the DSC, for his courage and actions on the beaches at Gallipoli, but at the expense of terrible wounds. Richard had not been able to visit his cousin prior to his evacuation to Malta on the hospital ship, but he knew that his wounds were serious. It made him all the more determined to survive to return home, but for now it was his duty to contribute to bringing this terrible war to an end quickly.

He again considered a germ of an idea he had had on his earlier patrol. *E9* and her sister submarines were without doubt a thorn in the side of the Turks and making a vital contribution to the war effort. They were now operating in pairs and had delivered on Keyes's objective to run amuck. However, the targets were starting to dry up. The Turks were retaining the larger ships in port and when they did venture out, they were usually heavily escorted. Whilst frustrating to the hunter instinct of the submariners, Richard recognised this for the strategic success it was in cutting the Turks' vital supply line. The land between the main Turkish supply base in Constantinople and its forces on the Gallipoli Peninsula was extremely mountainous. The two railways available to support the defending armies each only went part way. The roads were little more than mule tracks. As a result, nearly all supplies had to be sent by sea. The mere suspicion of the presence of the submarines made them a 'fleet in being'. The sea was now largely denied to the enemy, as he knew it had been to the French by the Navy during the Napoleonic Wars. He derived pleasure from the fact that many of the Turkish reinforcements now faced a long and tiring march before reaching the Front. He did not discount the prospect of continuing the war of attrition by sinking as many transports and cargo vessels as possible, but he felt a fresh responsibility. Back home he was no doubt now a national figure and so he should be setting an example and playing a more strategic part in the War. He resolved to discuss his idea with Steele in the morning. For now he needed his sleep.

*

For once Steele was at the periscope as *E9* lay in wait for her next target. His right eye was glued firmly to the rubber eyepiece. Richard had told him that it would be good for his second-in-command to gain the experience. He was after all the 'Second Captain' and would have to take command should the captain be incapacitated. As always, the control room was in complete silence except for the clicking of the telemotors powering the hydroplanes and rudder, and the hissing of the periscope hydraulics as the periscope was raised and lowered. He observed Leading Seaman Dodds, the gunlayer, checking again that his team was ready at the fore-hatch before returning to his position in the conning tower, crouched beneath O'Connell.

Despite the obvious tension, Steele bided his time patiently. If he surfaced too soon, then it risked scaring the enemy. *E9* was lying off San Stefano Point on Turkey's northern shore, not far from Constantinople. At last he judged the moment as ripe.

'Surface. Standby gun action,' he ordered.

Within seconds, O'Connell opened the conning tower upper hatch whilst Dodd clung to his legs. Both were deluged by seawater, but they ignored it. Dodds rushed to the gun and quickly adjusted his sights to the range and bearing of the target as the fore-hatch was opened. He slammed home the breech block and the gun fired its first shot. Meanwhile, fresh shells were now being passed in a relay to the casing by the ammunition party below. By the time O'Connell reported the shell as falling short, Dodds had fired the second. It still fell short, but by a lesser margin. Dodds adjusted the elevation and swung the gun round further to take into account the target's movement. The third shell was a direct hit. The locomotive of a troop train burst into flames and the train squealed to a halt. Some of the carriages derailed, flinging horses and men onto the trackside. Dodds adjusted the bearing of the gun and commenced a continuous fire on the carriages, wreaking carnage. In less than three minutes the train was completely wrecked.

Steele joined Dodds and tapped him on the shoulder. 'Shift target.' He pointed to a tall, brick-built viaduct ahead of the shambles of the train. The Turks would have to clear the wreckage before they could use the line again, but if the viaduct was destroyed, the delay would be months.

Dodds adjusted the aim of the gun carefully. There was no longer any urgency to the task. No threat to the submarine was visible. He expended the last of the ready-use ammunition, about twenty shells in all, but the viaduct continued to stand tall. The three-inch shells were making insufficient impact to destroy it, despite several gouges in the brickwork. Steele ordered the gun's crew below and retired himself to the control room. He wanted that viaduct destroyed and had another idea.

*

The following day, *E9* continued her patrol for enemy shipping in the north of the Marmara, south of Constantinople, trimmed down on the surface. O'Connell had the watch on the bridge whilst Richard and Steele held a council-of-war in the fore-ends. The Leading Torpedo Operator had opened up one of the spare torpedoes for their inspection.

'I've been thinking, Number One, that we might have a problem with the sinking valve of this mouldie,' Richard muttered quietly to Steele.

'Really, sir? It looks fine to me.' Steele inspected carefully the fourth chamber of the torpedo. This contained the Brotherhood three-cylinder engines that propelled the torpedo and the gear for controlling the depth at which it would run. In addition, it contained a range wheel and a sinking valve. In the event of the torpedo missing its target, at the set range for its 'end-of-run', the sinking valve opened to allow water into the air and buoyancy chambers, and the torpedo would sink harmlessly to the bottom.

'Just suppose we were to blank off the sinking valve or set the range to zero. What do you think?'

'Naturally, the torpedo would float to the surface, sir. But, I say, sir. That would be against the international convention!' The convention stated that unexploded torpedoes should be set to sink at the end of their run, so that they did not become floating mines and a danger to neutral shipping.

'Quite right, Number One, so I am doing this on my own responsibility.' Richard adjusted the range wheel to zero, thereby ensuring the sinking valve would not operate.

'But why, sir?' Steele seemed aghast at this cavalier and illegal act.

'We can't afford to run out of torpedoes again. And don't worry about the convention. We'll be picking them up again if they miss. From now on, I want all the torpedoes set to float at the end of their run. Understood?'

'Aye aye, sir.' Steele nodded to the LTO to implement the captain's intention.

'Now there was something else you wanted to discuss, Number One.'

'Indeed, sir.' Steele pulled out a notebook on which he had made some sketches. 'If you care to peruse this rough map, sir. It shows the Turkish railway system around the Marmara. As you can see, there are several points at which the railway runs along the coast, within range of our gun. We've already agreed that the bridges are the vulnerable points, but as we saw yesterday, we can't do too much damage to them with a bally twelve-pounder. However, if you would permit me to swim ashore with a raft of guncotton, I could destroy the supporting pillars of a viaduct by explosion. As to a likely spot ...'

'Just hang on a minute, First Lieutenant. As far as I am concerned, you are the most important man on board and I'm not going to risk losing you on such a hare-brained venture. The risks are too great. It's out of the question.'

Steele opened his mouth to remonstrate, but clearly thought better of it. Richard fixed him with a determined stare. Satisfied that the discussion was over, he changed the subject.

'I'm sorry to dampen your enthusiasm, Number One, but I think I can offer you plenty of excitement of another sort. I have it in mind to enter the Golden Horn.' He paused to gauge Steele's reaction and was not disappointed.

'Holy smoke! Enter the harbour of Constantinople?'

'Yes. I thought we might have a crack at the *Goeben* in her lair.'

'Capital, sir. It's just the sort of audacity to tickle my fancy. It would be worthy of de Ruyter.'

'Go on, First Lieutenant. Educate me. I know you are dying to demonstrate the superiority of your Wykehamist learning.'

Steele ignored the barbed comment. 'It was during one of the Anglo-Dutch wars, sir. The second, I think. Admiral de Ruyter led his ships up the Thames and Medway, captured the town of Sheerness and burned ships of the Royal Navy in Chatham Dockyard. The raid caused panic in London and brought about an early end to the war on favourable terms to the Dutch. You might achieve a similar effect, sir. It would indubitably create mayhem in the very heart of the Ottoman Empire. The Turks no doubt feel secure from attack and the effect on morale of the people might just influence the government to end their alliance with Germany. At the very least, it would upset the movement of troops and supplies to the front.'

'Thank you, Number One. I had not considered an historical parallel, but you have grasped the sentiment of my plan. As you say, it would do no harm to disrupt the transport of troops and supplies to the front, but my main objective is the psychological impact the sudden appearance of a submarine in their long impregnable capital would have on the Turks. So, if we're agreed, we go in tomorrow morning.'

*

The hands were called at five in the morning for prayers in the control room. The turnout was high. The men knew the challenge before them and the high risks involved, but they knew they were an elite crew, under good officers, and relished this opportunity to strike at the enemy's heart. Some recognised the historic significance that success might bring to the submarine service. Stealthily, hidden beneath the sea, *E9* crept into the jaws of the point where Asia and Europe met at the entrance to the Bosphorous. Above the surface, the sun had already risen above the mountains to the east, casting a corridor of gold on the flat-calm sea between Oxia Island and the occasional reflection off the bobbing periscope lens of the menace beneath the waves.

*

Richard felt like Peeping Tom spying on Lady Godiva as *E9* gently closed the northern shore at two knots. Criss-crossing the outer approaches, a myriad of fishermen and dhows conducted their daily lives, oblivious of the one-eyed creature's observation. He could see the remains of the city walls, within which lay the flat-roofed houses of

Constantinople's inhabitants. Dotted among the buildings were the strange-looking domed buildings, glinting in the reflection of the sun and flanked by the needle-like towers that he understood to be called minarets. One such building dominated the skyline because of its size. Its strange domes and the upper part of the surrounding towers, all appeared to be covered in blue tiles. The minarets reminded him of well sharpened pencils. However, like most of the other conspicuous buildings, it was not marked on the crude chart. Of ships entering or leaving the great harbour, there was no sign, but otherwise it appeared to be a normal, everyday scene. He felt a pang of guilt that he would soon be shattering this calm. Except for the different architecture and lateen sails of the dhows, the scene might well have been that of the port of London on the same day. Every look through the periscope brought more detail to the scene and by lunchtime he could pick out the people on foot, the horses of cavalrymen and the occasional carriage, and the many donkeys hauling carts behind them. It was time for action.

'Flood tubes One and Two,' he ordered. Very soon he hoped to sight his first target since, once he rounded Seraglio Point, he would have a clear view up the Bosphorous.

'We should be approaching wheel-over, sir,' O'Connell called. 'We're far enough off the bank, sir.'

Richard issued the order for the alteration of course to port. O'Connell was calculating the course changes by dead-reckoning to avoid too much exposure of the periscope. This close inshore, the sea was ruffled by a light breeze, but it was nonetheless prudent to remain invisible as long as possible. After another five minutes, Richard raised the periscope. He noted that the colour of the water was now a brownish-green rather than its usual blue-green.

'That's good,' he muttered. 'I can see a steamer heading north.' He had been attracted by the red ensign against the white transom of the steamer.

'That is indeed a relief, sir,' Steele answered. He and Richard had feared that the stretch of water might be mined.

'Still no sign of any warships.' Richard continued his commentary. 'There are still too many buildings in the way. Watch it, First Lieutenant. You're dipping. Down periscope.'

The submarine had sunk too low for him to see above the sea, but he masked his annoyance. Steele did not have to say anything. One of the coxswains automatically made the adjustment to the hydroplanes and called out his apology.

'Depth twenty feet, sir,' Steele reported.

Richard raised the periscope for another quick look. The white lighthouse to port indicated that they were now in the Bosphorous. Less than a mile to starboard lay Asia and he checked the docks of Haidar Pasha for potential targets before lowering the periscope. Very soon he knew he would be entering the main harbour of Constantinople to port.

'Navigator, stand by for a fix,' he called. He was confident he was about a quarter of a mile off the European coast, but a more precise position would do no harm.

'I'll give you the bearings of Old Seraglio Point, Leander Tower and the right hand edge of Haidar Pasha, in that order.'

'Ready,' O'Connell replied.

'Up,' Richard ordered. 'Bearing that. Bearing that. And bearing that. Port five. Steer 350.' The periscope assistant called out the bearings and O'Connell plotted them very quickly. Within seconds of settling on the new course, Richard could see the Galata Bridge and the naval arsenal beyond. He looked for the masts of the *Goeben*, but was interrupted by a sailor in a dhow trying to grab hold of the periscope.

'Down,' he ordered quickly. *E9* was now in the main harbour and there were small craft everywhere. No doubt the surprised sailor would give the alarm, but too late, he thought. He had seen a possible target.

'Open bow caps,' he called. A buzz of excitement immediately spread throughout the boat. Within a minute he ordered the periscope to be raised again.

'Port ten. Steady. Fire One and Two.' He had seen two large transports berthed alongside the Turkish Army barracks, loading stores. He hoped to hit both. He kept the periscope raised to check that both torpedoes ran true. The first, however, curved off to port, jumped into the air like a porpoise and disappeared into the water. The second ran better, displaying its tell-tale ruler-straight wake. Satisfied that it would hit one of the transports, he wondered if he could offer a beam shot, but his train of thought was suddenly interrupted.

'My word,' he gasped. 'Full ahead both! Keep seventy-five feet. Flood the auxiliary. Get her down quickly.' Steele and the two coxswains responded without question and dived the boat.

'Port thirty-five,' Richard shouted. 'We're being torpedoed!'

Instinctively, some of the control room team braced themselves for an explosion and seconds later everyone heard the terrifying sound of a torpedo's propellers as it approached them at forty or more knots. The sailors tensed and then the noise passed overhead.

As the men relaxed, they heard a loud underwater explosion and almost immediately, the sound of shells bursting in the water. They also heard noises against the hull, like gravel being thrown at a window pane. Richard assumed it must be shrapnel, but he suddenly had other matters on his mind. The boat shuddered and heeled sharply to port, knocking several men off their feet. Just as quickly, *E9* began shooting to the surface like a cork and she continued to spin round anti-clockwise.

'She's not responding to the helm or 'planes, sir,' the coxswain called.

'Keep her down, First Lieutenant,' Richard shouted. 'Full ahead!'

Steele started flooding the auxiliary tank again to gain ballast and ordered the hydroplanes hard down, but it made little difference. The swing to port was checked, but *E9* continued to speed to the surface. With a huge shudder the boat broached the surface. Immediately, the boat was rocked by two direct hits from shells on the fin.

'Good gracious,' Steele exclaimed. 'Those gunners are good.'

'Never mind that, First Lieutenant. Get her down,' Richard barked and almost simultaneously *E9* took on a steep bow-down angle and dived beneath the shell pock-ridden surface.

'Stop engines. Hydroplanes hard a-rise. Blow the auxiliary,' Richard ordered. He suspected that the boat was not fatally damaged, but caught in swirling cross currents.

'It's no good, sir,' the Coxswain reported. 'She's heavy and I can't hold her.'

'Full astern,' Richard replied. 'Stop both engines. How's the bubble?'

'Five degrees down, sir. Depth steadying at seventy-five feet, sir. The helm's answering now, sir. Course 180,' Steele replied.

'Very good. Steer that for now. Are you keeping up with this, Pilot?' Before O'Connell could reply, the submarine lurched violently, first to starboard and then to port.

'Now what?' Richard demanded. The ship's head had started to veer wildly to starboard and it became clear that the boat was caught in some form of whirlpool. Again *E9* began to rise sharply and, almost as suddenly, the boat shuddered and everyone heard a scraping sound against the hull. The depth gauge showed forty feet.

'I think we've run aground off Scutari, sir,' O'Connell opined. He had barely finished speaking than with another lurch the boat seemed to have been swept off the bottom and the ship's head spun to port.

'Full ahead,' Richard ordered. He had spotted the rapid ascent towards the surface. The plop-plop sound of shells hitting the water not far away was sufficient reminder to avoid broaching. At a depth of sixty feet the boat hit the bottom again, but was quickly pushed along by the current into deeper water. The compass was swinging wildly and it was difficult to know which way they were facing, but he did not dare return to periscope depth whilst the Turkish gunners were so active. He had no idea whether he was heading out to sea or further into the Bosphorous. It was imperative to ensure that *E9* neither broached, to face the accurate gunfire of the batteries above, nor ran aground under the eyes of the Turks. He made an instant decision.

'Stop both engines. Flood One, Two, Three and Four main ballast tanks.'

Steele repeated the order and regarded his commanding officer quizzically before carrying it out. By flooding the main ballast tanks *E9* was taking on an extra six tons of ballast.

The submarine began to sink. The compass continued to spin. One of the coxswains began to call out the depth.

'Eighty feet, sir. Ninety feet, sir. One hundred feet.' A frisson of tension rippled through the control room. '110 feet ... 120 feet,' the Second Coxswain intoned.

'That's the maximum diving depth, sir,' Steele mentioned casually.

'What's your point, First Lieutenant?' Richard asked acidly.

'It's just that the depth gauge doesn't go beyond 120 feet, so we can't report the depth, sir.'

'Quite. I'm sorry, Number One.' Richard felt stupid. 'Well, we've been here before and know the dear old boat can take it. What's the maximum depth, Navigator?'

'It depends where you mean, sir.' O'Connell met his eyes and turned back to the chart. 'Assuming we are to the south of the strait, sir, perhaps 200 feet.'

The compasses continued to swing and the depth gauge remained obstinately at 120 feet. The hull began to creak. Everyone on board instinctively looked for signs of exploding rivets and leaks. Richard saw some of the men cross themselves and regretted not having his rosary with him. At what depth would the plates buckle? He knew he might be close to God right now. Nobody spoke a word. The plops in the water ceased and the only noise on board was that of the steel plates that formed the hull complaining at the intolerable pressure of the outside seawater. There was nothing more he could do. He had made his decision and it was now in God's hands as to whether he and his men lived or died. They all felt the thump forward as *E9* hit the bottom, followed by the thud of the stern settling, too. The submarine was at the bottom of the harbour of Constantinople, but he could not say where or at what depth.

Chapter 26

September 1915

Steele profited from the enforced inactivity on board by falling out everyone from Diving Stations and ordering sandwiches to be made for all hands. The galley stove was shut down to preserve the batteries so the men had to make do with water. Richard and O'Connell studied the chart intently in an attempt to establish their position. The gunners up top seemed to have ceased firing, so the boat and its external environment seemed eerily quiet. Richard wondered if the reason for the absence of gunfire was that Turkish patrol boats were now hunting them. In the absence of any other weapons to sink submarines, the Turks had begun to employ long sweeps fitted with explosives. It would mean that *E9* and her men would be in peril if they remained on the bottom until nightfall. At least the compass had stopped swinging and had settled on a south-easterly heading.

He had an idea. He opened the lower hatch of the conning tower and climbed up the ladder to the glass scuttles. Removing the covers, he compared the darkness of the water each side. He couldn't be absolutely sure, but he sensed that it was lighter to starboard and then a couple of fish approached the glass on this side to study him. He felt like a goldfish in a bowl and replaced the metal covers before returning to the chart table to discuss it with O'Connell and Steele.

'I'm not sure of this, Pilot, but I think we're lying at the eastern side of the harbour. If that's the case, then we may be lying on this island, beneath Leander Tower. Number One, this is a gamble, but I want you to take the boat gently off the bottom and take her south-westerly. We'll try a course of 190 to start. But keep her heavy. I don't want to go anywhere near the surface. If necessary we'll just bump along the bottom. Of course, if I'm wrong, then we'll merely drive ourselves further aground. I might need my rosary beads and a change of underwear for this evolution.'

Steele ordered the men back to Diving Stations and briefed the two coxswains on the captain's plan. When all hands were ready, he ordered the main ballast tanks to be blown.

'Blow One, Two, Three, Four, Five and Six main ballast.'

Compressed air noisily began to force water out of the ballast tanks. The men felt the boat rock gently, first one way and then the other, before shuddering slightly, telling them that they were off the bottom. The depth gauged remained stuck at 120 feet, but they thought they could feel the boat rising.

'Full ahead. Stop the blow. Hydroplanes hard down,' Steele ordered. The bows thumped the bottom again, but the boat was moving.

'Half ahead. Ease the 'planes and steer 190.'

The helmsman struggled to hold the ordered course due to a westerly current, but the depth gauge began to move. An audible sigh of relief could be heard through the submarine. When the depth gauge showed eighty-five feet, Richard called over to Steele.

'Keep her at that. Find your trim. I'll not risk a fix, so we'll have to hope we're on course for the harbour entrance.'

Thirty minutes later, at soon after four o'clock, he judged it safe to bring the submarine up to PD. *E9* was indeed well clear of the harbour and, after taking a fix, he handed over the watch to O'Connell with instructions to head south-west. He turned to Steele.

'I'm not happy about that first torpedo, Number One. There must have been something wrong with the gyro. Indeed, I wonder if it was the same torpedo that nearly did for us and not a Turkish Brennan. I want all the gyros checked on each of the remaining torpedoes and the bow tubes reloaded. In the meantime, we'll head for our signalling billet and shout about our success. I want the world to know that Constantinople is no longer impregnable.'

He was surprised that Steele's reaction seemed muted. Steele appeared distracted and not at all his usual zealous self.

'Is there something wrong, Number One?'

'No, sir, but may I crave a favour, sir? Before confirming your instructions to inspect each torpedo, overhaul the gyros, reload the bow tubes and make at once for the signalling billet, would you mind walking through the boat with me?'

'Very well, First Lieutenant. Let's go,' Richard responded tersely.

The two officers walked through the boat and he guiltily recognised his First Lieutenant's point. Nearly all the off-watch men were asleep, almost at their diving stations. Those that remained on duty had blank, tired faces without any trace of elation for the achievement of which they had just been a part. They responded to his questions and words of encouragement politely, but without enthusiasm.

'I'm sorry, sir. If you order it, the men will gladly jump to whatever you have in mind, but is it safe? You can see they're exhausted and, to be quite frank, sir, so are you. I'm sorry, sir, but I would not be doing my duty to you if I held my counsel.'

Richard was shocked by Steele's frankness, but admired his moral courage. He recognised that Steele was right and that it could not have been easy for him to imply that the men were being driven too hard. For the first time, he warmed to Steele and he felt ashamed for his earlier unfair treatment of him.

'Very well, Number One. You were quite right to bring me up and I do value your opinion. I shall get my head down. Take the boat further offshore and when you deem it prudent, surface and allow the hands to bathe for an hour. They've done well. You can tell them that.'

He was sure his eyes were deceiving him, but Steele seemed to have just grown even taller with the praise, but he would still not let matters lie.

'If I may make so bold, sir, I think the men would take it better if you were the one to tell them how well they've done.'

'You might be right again. I'll tell them when we surface. Call me beforehand.'

*

The following night, *E9* made contact by wireless with HMS *Jed.* The wireless range was only thirty miles so *Jed* had been positioned in the Gulf of Xeros to act as a relay for messages. The submarines in the Sea of Marmara regularly returned to the Gallipoli Peninsula to transmit and receive signals. On this latest exchange, Richard received intelligence that two brigades of Turkish troops with guns and ammunition were being moved up by train from Smyrna to Panderma on the southern coast, and from Syria via Constantinople to the north. The presence of submarines in the Marmara was causing the Turks to avoid sea crossings, or at least to shorten them.

Richard first mused as to how such intelligence had been gained and then on the C-in-C's news about the troop trains. Panderma was nearer and he could either shell the railhead or attack any troop ships leaving the harbour. Then he reconsidered Steele's idea to destroy the viaduct on the Baghdad railway line. The idea began to appeal to him. If Steele could bring it off, then it would send a powerful message to the Turks that their entire coastline was vulnerable and cause them to waste resources on defending its key points. This would have a greater strategic advantage than sinking a couple of transports. They could come later. His mind made up, he instructed O'Connell to lay off a course for San Stefano Point and sat down with Steele to discuss operations for the following night.

*

Through the periscope Richard could clearly see the white cliffs to the north, reflecting the half-moonlight, as the submarine penetrated the narrow Gulf of Ismid. Earlier in the day, he and Steele had studied all the available maps and charts of the Turkish railway system, and Steele had suggested that Ismid might make a better target than San Stefano Point. Here the main railway line from Scutari to Baghdad followed the coastline for twenty-seven miles along the Gulf and the water was deep enough for the submarine to approach within four hundred yards of the beach. At its widest point the Gulf was only five miles wide, narrowing to a mile, and at its head lay the port of Ismid.

It was a still night and no ships were in sight, so Richard surfaced the submarine, trimmed down to reduce her exposure and continuing to be propelled by the electric motors to reduce her noise. Again he had the feeling of being a Peeping Tom. Ashore he could hear the noises of farm animals and music. Both O'Connell and Steele joined him on the bridge.

'What do you think?' he asked of them. He whispered, even though there was little prospect of being heard ashore, but it was that quiet an evening.

'It looks a good place to put me ashore, sir, but I can't see the railway line or viaduct,' Steele replied. 'It's a shame I don't know how to milk a goat, though. I could bring us back some fresh milk.'

'How about some fresh eggs instead, First Lieutenant?' O'Connell asked.

'Pilot you're always thinking of your stomach.'

'Quiet, you two,' Richard hissed. He thought he had heard something.

Sure enough they all heard a hoot from the direction of Scutari and then the roar of an engine. They strained their eyes in the direction of the approaching sound and before long saw the white light of the locomotive. It rattled past them quickly and then all they could see were the red tail-lights of the guard's van. Suddenly, the tone of the noise changed to a clanging of wheels on an iron structure. Steele counted the seconds.

'It took twenty-three seconds to cross, sir. I'd say that's our viaduct or bridge. It must be about a quarter of a mile long,' Steele announced.

'I think you're right, Number One, but we'll check in the morning. I want to see whether the cliffs are too steep for you to climb. For now we'll head out to deeper water and sit on the layer for the night, but I want to be about our business at 04.00.'

*

The daylight reconnaissance had been of value. Steele was given the periscope to make sketches of the iron trellis bridge and its surroundings. Richard selected a small cove to its east to land him. The cliffs had the advantage that they afforded a screen from any sentries, but it would be hard work for Steele to climb them, weighed down by his pack of equipment. He just hoped he was fit enough for the task.

Two hours after midnight, Steele shook hands with his brother officers and then slipped his long frame into the warm seawater. He was completely naked and his fair skin had been covered in grease to reduce his visibility ashore. The stokers had made him up a small raft from oil drums, on which he was able to float his pack containing his demolition kit, comprising sixteen pounds of gun cotton, a fuse pistol, his clothes and footwear, a flashlight, a bayonet, a revolver and a whistle. Pushing the raft before him, he headed for the beach.

'Do you think he'll make it, sir?' O'Connell asked.

'I don't know. At best he's probably a five per cent chance. The Turks will know the viaduct is vulnerable and should have it well guarded. All I know is that if anybody has a chance of success, it's our First Lieutenant. You go below. I'll see this out on the bridge.'

Once the Navigator had gone below, Richard was left to his own thoughts. Not for the first time he wondered if he had done the wrong thing. Steele was only twenty-three, the son of an earl and a brilliant cricketer. If the war lasted, he would no doubt rise to his own command. If he survived this war, he would have a bright future. Did he have the right to sacrifice such a promising young man on a fool's errand? The responsibility of command began to weigh heavily on him.

*

Steele swam the quarter-mile ashore without undue effort. After dragging the raft onto the shingle, he dressed and commenced his stiff climb of the cliff. Despite the moonlight, he often stumbled in the dark, but soon found his way to the cliff top and the farmyard from which they had heard the animal noises two nights before. He rested behind a chicken shed. The chickens immediately set about squawking, but there was no other commotion. He was thankful he could not hear dogs barking.

Having caught his breath, he set off for the railway line and found it within two hundred yards of the farmyard. Creeping silently, he followed it for about four or five hundred yards in the direction of the viaduct. Suddenly, he heard voices ahead. Just three hundred yards short of the viaduct, two sentries were lying beside the track chatting and smoking. Taking cover in some bushes the other side of the track, he observed the sentries for a few minutes. They seemed comfortably settled and he recognised that he must either turn back or attempt a detour round them. His eyes were well accustomed to the darkness and, with the aid of the moonlight, he noticed that the track was laid on an escarpment. He assumed that if he could quietly slide down this, then there might be a way through the bushes around the sentries. It was a risk he would have to take.

He unslung his pack from his shoulder and, resting it in his lap, slid down the slope of the escarpment on his buttocks. The bushes below turned out to be thorny and it was a painful task to thread his way through them and, moreover, it ate up valuable time. Half way to the viaduct he hauled himself back up to the slope to the track. Cautiously, he raised his head above the rail to look out for sentries. He could no longer see the two he had by-passed, but he now saw ahead, on the curve of the track two hundred yards away, the glow of a fire. Some form of engine or tender was parked there and in the flickering firelight he could see vague shapes of men working on the track, just as it reached the viaduct. It was impossible for him to go that way. He was now potentially trapped between two groups of Turks.

He examined his options. The sensible thing to do would be to retrace his steps. He could still blow up a section of the track. It might only take six hours or so to replace, but it would show the Turks that it could be down. On the other hand, it had been his idea to mount this raid and Miller had been reluctant to allow him the chance. His captain might now be displaying more confidence in him, but Steele still felt he had to prove himself. If necessary he would die in the attempt. There might just be a way to claw victory from the jaws of defeat, even if he had to be mad to attempt it.

He knew it would take too long to continue to follow the escarpment through the thorns and bushes. He was going to gamble on the element of surprise and that the fire would have ruined the night sight of the Turks. Stealthily, he heaved himself up on to the track and, after drawing his revolver from his pack, began a crouched walk-cum-run towards the viaduct.

He made good progress, but just fifty yards short of the working party, he was spotted. Somebody shouted a warning, but he ignored it and now began sprinting towards the men. None seemed armed with anything more lethal than picks and shovels, but armed troops must now have been alerted to come running. Some of the men were clearly alarmed by his headlong approach and cowered in the shelter of the tender. The others stood still, stupefied.

Only five yards short of them, he spotted his objective. The ground dropped steeply on both sides of the track to the sea shore below. He leaped to his left and in his peripheral vision saw three soldiers running towards him, with rifles slung over their shoulders. Madly, and without thought, he scrambled and tumbled down the slope, falling in a heap. In his fall he lost grip of his revolver, but it hung by its lanyard from his wrist. He ran to the nearest pillar supporting the bridge, a pillar of brickwork on which sat one of the heavy iron girders. With his bayonet he began digging into the shingle to form a hole for the explosive charge. Up above, the soldiers began shooting at him, but he was safely screened from their fire by the upper works of the bridge.

He placed the whole of the gun cotton charge in the hole and stamped it into place and packed it with shingle. Without hesitation, he fired his fuse pistol and took to his heels towards the sea. He hung the whistle and revolver from his neck and stuffed the flashlight into his shirt before plunging into the water. He didn't bother to discard his clothing as at any minute he expected shots from pursuers, but none came. He swam on his back out to sea, listening out for an explosion, but he could only hear rifle shots.

After swimming about 400 yards, he was back in the Gulf, but about three-quarters of a mile from the cove where he knew Miller would be awaiting his return. After his earlier exertions, he knew that even he, excellent swimmer as he was, could not make that distance. He headed back to the shore and rested a little while on the beach to recover his strength. He discarded his shirt and shoes and, reluctantly, the flashlight and revolver. He knew he would need the whistle to signal *E9*. Just as he was stepping back into the water, he heard a low rumble, followed by the scream of twisted metal. The charge had gone off and, with huge relief, he realised that he had succeeded in his mission.

To conserve his strength, he swam on his back, south along the coast. Above him, the stars shone brightly, but he could see the sky beginning to lighten. Every so often he blew his whistle to attract the attention of the lookout on board the submarine, but there was no answering call. It was not long before he recognised that he was tiring too quickly. The adrenalin that had pumped through his veins and sustained him from the start of his mad rush along the railway track had now subsided and he could feel the lactic acid building in his tired muscles. Again he rested, blew his whistle and listened for a response. This time he could hear the sound of rifle fire. His fatigued brain worked out that it could only be coming from the cliff tops from the Turks firing on the submarine. *E9* must be close.

He turned onto his front and looked for his boat. An early morning mist was beginning to build on the sea, but through it he could see three small rowing boats coming in his direction. He couldn't accept it and almost sobbed with frustration. With everything else going on, why were the Turks seeking him out? But he wasn't going to be taken prisoner, to rot in a Musselman gaol. Straining every muscle and sinew in his body, he struck out for the shore. Immediately on hitting the beach, he hid behind some rocks and looked back out to sea. Tired and frightened as he was, he burst out laughing. There was *E9* patiently awaiting his return. In the mist and his tiredness, he had mistaken her bow, gun and fin for three rowing boats. His fatigue evaporated and he whooped for joy before hailing the boat at the top of his voice. Somebody heard his shout and waved to him to swim over. He dived into the water whilst somebody manoeuvred the submarine to pick him up just forty yards offshore. It was five o'clock and the sun was just beginning to rise above the mountains to the east.

Chapter 27

Richard was amazed by Steele's achievement. It must have required enormous stamina, not just to have climbed the cliff carrying a heavy load, but to sprint past the working party and then to swim over a mile almost fully clothed. Even more remarkably, this had been done after being cooped up in the submarine for nearly three weeks. He felt guilty at the credit he would no doubt share for the exploit that was all of Steele's making, and resolved on the return to Mudros, to recommend Steele for a bar to his DSC.

The return was now weighing heavily on his mind. The Turks knew he had to return through the Strait sometime and would be waiting for him. The CO of *E7* had advised that extra mine fields had already been laid, but the gauntlet had to be run, nonetheless. He regarded the return to Mudros in two minds. First and foremost, it meant he could return to England and marry Lizzy. Nothing was going to stop him this time. Less sweetly, it would bring to an end his time in command of a submarine. If he were lucky, he might, in time, be given another command, but it would be of a surface ship. He knew he would miss the tight-knit community of a submarine and the professionalism of the men. They were dirty, unkempt and downright coarse at times, but they were the best sailors in the world and he was proud to be a part of their fraternity.

He quickly cast such sentiment to one side. Quite possibly the next time they contacted *Jed*, he would receive the recall signal. He still had five torpedoes left and there was unfinished business. Admiral de Roebuck had not ordered an attack on Panderma, but clearly had it in mind when he had sent the intelligence of the troop movements by rail. The task appealed to Richard's view on how the war should be conducted. Any attack would be in plain view of the townspeople and the psychological effect would be powerful. The Turks would be expecting a submarine to interfere with the troop convoy and be at a high state of preparedness, but he considered his men up to the challenge. Within two minutes, *E9* was on course for Peramo Bay.

*

The steamer lay about 500 yards off and Richard estimated he was 150 degrees on her port side, but although the red Turkish ensign was clearly visible, he could not read her name on the transom. It didn't matter. She was low in the water and obviously heavily laden. Her deck was piled high with rolls of barbed wire and packing cases. He had just decided she would be a legitimate target when one of the crew spotted his periscope and, waving wildly, ran up the ladder to the bridge. Suddenly, a dense cloud of smoke erupted from the steamer's funnel and Richard noted her propeller churn up more water astern, just as she turned sharply to port. He was annoyed as he had still to flood the bow tubes and open the bow caps. The range was opening already and by the time he was ready to fire, she would be a more difficult target to hit. He didn't want to waste one of his precious torpedoes and, since it was pointless to remain concealed, he ordered the submarine to surface, so that he might pursue his quarry at full speed on the diesel engines.

After a few minutes of the chase, it became evident that the steamer would reach the harbour before *E9* could catch her. It didn't matter, he thought. The crew might escape, but the cargo could not. The steamer began to sound several short blasts on her siren to warn the inhabitants of the port of the danger. Through his binoculars he could see several people fleeing the sea front and an equal quantity rushing towards it to witness the spectacle. Inside the breakwater, at one of the piers, was a large liner towards which an officer was leading a column of troops. Another column was forming at the rail head, but Richard could see no sign of any artillery.

The unfortunate steamer was in such a rush to reach the safety of the port that her master did not bother to enter the harbour, but hurriedly berthed alongside the southern breakwater. The crew immediately abandoned ship and began running down the breakwater. It indicated to Richard that she must be carrying munitions. He dived the submarine and ordered the bow tubes to be readied for firing. At a range of 600 yards he ordered one torpedo to be fired. It did not take long for it to strike home. The steamer blew up in smoke and flames and seconds later an almighty explosion blew away the entire end of the breakwater. Pieces of masonry and the remains of the steamer rose sixty feet into the air, before raining down on the harbour and surrounding water. Richard now turned his attention to the liner alongside the pier inside the harbour.

The officer he had previously sighted was beside himself with rage. He was trying to form a squad to open fire on the submarine's periscope but, despite being struck with the flat of the officer's sword, the soldiers were fleeing back towards the town and others were rapidly disembarking from the ship.

Richard was distracted by a dust cloud in the town and spotted a troop of cavalry rushing to the defence of the port, but they were unlikely to be a threat to *E9*, so he ignored them. He lined up the shot for his second bow torpedo and fired. Even before the torpedo had run its course, he ordered the submarine to the surface for a gun action. He regretted the absence of other ships in the harbour. It meant that he was probably too late to head off the convoy of troops from Smyrna, but he could still wreak havoc on the railway head and create panic in the town. He was in a reckless mood. This might well be his last action before the return through the Strait.

As O'Connell and Dodds opened the conning tower's upper hatch, the second torpedo hit the liner and the whole ship's company could hear the explosion. Meanwhile, from the control room, Richard manoeuvred the submarine to enter the harbour astern.

'Slow ahead port, slow astern starboard. Stop engines. Steady. Slow astern both. Steer 123. First Lieutenant, you have the submarine. Leave O'Connell to focus on the shoot.'

The first round from the gun was fired and Richard could see the ammunition party was beginning the task of passing shells up to the casing. He decided to join O'Connell on the bridge. The gunlayer and his assistant now had the range and bearing of the rail head, and were pouring their fire into the station and stationery trains. O'Connell grinned at him.

'This is an occasion for job satisfaction, sir.' He drew Richard's attention to the liner. It had not been completely destroyed, but lay on the bottom with her buff superstructure still visible. There was no sign of the troops who only minutes before had been on the pier, but Richard could see that the cavalry were forming up on another pier and spreading out to send a volley of rifle fire at *E9*. Worse, he could see a field gun being unlimbered. Even a six-pound shell through the casing would prevent them from diving.

‘Check, check, check,’ he shouted. ‘Cease firing and clear the casing.’ Already bullets had begun to zip amongst the stanchions of the bridge. ‘Get below,’ he ordered O’Connell. ‘Diving Stations,’ he roared down the voice pipe and sounded the Klaxons. ‘Half ahead, steer 310.’

He ducked as a bullet knocked off his cap, and saw Dodds hit just after securing the gun. The man crawled towards the forward hatch and stopped. Immediately, Richard flung himself down the outside of the fin and onto the casing, leaving O’Connell to secure the bridge for diving. Dodds was still breathing, but unconscious from a bullet wound through the back. Richard heaved him towards the still-open hatch and pushed him down it head first into the outstretched arms of somebody below. He started to climb back to the bridge and spotted that O’Connell had still not gone below. He looked at the wreckage of the steamer and damaged mole, and simultaneously, he heard the sound of an artillery shell hitting the submarine somewhere. Something hit him painfully in the head. He was blinded by blood and in his dazed state he lost consciousness and fell into the water.

*

Steele could not believe what a forlorn figure the CO looked, floating lifeless on his back, just outside the breakwater. By some quirk of the current, his cap floated only feet from his body. The Turkish horse artillery field gun continued to fire on *E9*’s raised periscope, but could not find the range. The shells fell harmlessly short, macabrely straddling the floating corpse. The atmosphere inside the submarine was incredibly sombre. When O’Connell, after falling down the conning tower and landing in a heap in the control room, had gasped the news of Miller’s death, neither Steele nor the ship’s company had been quite able to comprehend the fact. The captain had always been there for them and it was unimaginable that he would not be there to guide them to even greater success.

For a moment, a ray of hope struck Steele. Through the periscope he observed the captain’s right arm rise up and down as if he was waving. Then Steele realised it was just a movement caused by the ripple of the water.

‘What are you going to do now, Number One?’ O’Connell asked in a hushed tone.

‘Are you sure he was dead, Pontius?’ Steele asked hopefully.

‘Not much doubt, I’m afraid. The shell nearly took his head off. Blood everywhere.’

Steele could hear the tragic news being relayed down the submarine in whispers. It suddenly dawned on him that he was now in command, but there was no time for reflection or hesitation. He knew what he must do. He barked out a rapid set of orders to take the submarine back to the harbour.

‘What are you doing, Number One?’ O’Connell asked incredulously.

‘I’m going back to get the skipper,’ Steele stated resolutely.

Somebody murmured, ‘Bloody right, too,’ and a cheer was heard forward.

‘But he’s dead. There’s nothing you can do for him now.’

‘We don’t know that for sure. Even if he is, I’m not leaving him here to the Musselmen. The man’s a hero and doesn’t deserve that. Pilot, you take the trim. Up periscope. Bearing that.’

‘Green seven-two,’ the periscope assistant called. ‘141 degrees, sir.’

‘Slow ahead both. Steer 145. Down.’ Steele went over to the chart table and scribbled a few lines in the log. Meanwhile, the Coxswain reported *E9* as being on the ordered course. When he had finished writing in the log Steele made an announcement.

‘May I crave your attention, gentlemen,’ he called out loudly. ‘In a few minutes I intend surfacing. I shall need four strong volunteers to be on the casing with a couple of boathooks. I’m going back for the captain.’ He was interrupted by cheering throughout the boat.

‘After surfacing, I’m going to put the boat alongside what remains of the southern breakwater. That will offer us shelter from the field gun in the harbour. I will dive into the water and bring the captain back. From that moment, the Navigating Officer will be in command until I return. Should I fail to return, or in the event of my incapacitation, he has written orders to leave me and the captain, to take the submarine to Marmara Island and either to scuttle her or take his orders from the CO of *E7*, should he make the rendezvous.’

‘You can’t do this, Number One,’ O’Connell interrupted.

‘Hush, Pilot. Hear me out.’ He began stripping. ‘I’ve never met a finer navigator, but do you really think we would make it back through the Narrows without Miller? I’m not the one to take his place. If he is truly dead, then we are in a rather unfortunate position. But what if he's alive? That is why I'm going back.' He turned to the Coxswain.

'I wonder, Coxswain, if I might prevail upon you to take charge of the casing party once we've surfaced.'

'It would be me pleasure, sir,' Haines replied.

Five minutes later, *E9* surfaced on the outer side of the breakwater. The Turkish gunners valiantly tried to hit the submarine, but their shells either hit the already damaged mole or overshot. Steele delayed only to shake hands with O'Connell. Both wished each other luck and seconds later Steele dived into the sea, towing a length of rope behind him. To his surprise, the shelling stopped and no rifle fire was directed his way. He wondered if the Turks had honour, after all. The distance to the captain's corpse was only some fifty yards and he covered it comfortably. Carefully, he tied a loop of the rope around the body and waved to the casing party to begin the task of hauling it in. As an afterthought, he collected the floating cap and was again struck by the absence of shelling. He looked into the harbour and searched out the pier on which the field gun was established. To his surprise, he noted the gunners were standing at attention and the officer in command was saluting. He almost wept at the tribute and, with the captain's cap, waved to the gunners before resuming his swim back to his submarine.

The men on the casing gently hauled their former CO's body up onto the casing and Steele followed up the jumping ladder they had rigged for his benefit. Contrary to O'Connell's report of Miller's injury, his head seemed to be intact and far from being half-blown away, but the eyes were caked in blood. One of the sailors tenderly wiped away some of the blood with fresh water. Miller's death mask appeared to be peaceful. It was almost as if he had just fallen asleep. Unsure what he should do next, Steele placed the cap on his late captain's chest. The new gold braid on its peak still shone brightly, despite the dunking in the sea. He could feel tears welling up in his eyes and he fought to control his emotions in front of the men.

'Coxswain, please take the captain down below and lay him out in the fore-ends. We're going to take him back to Mudros for a proper burial.' He began to climb back up to the bridge.

'Aye, sir,' Haines replied quietly. 'You just leave him to me. I'll look after him.'

As a formality, Haines checked for a pulse in the carotid artery. Suddenly, he became animated. 'Look lively, you lot. Get the skipper down below, and gently. He's alive!'

Steele jumped back to the casing and checked for himself.

'You feel it, sir?' Haines asked, almost beseechingly. 'It's faint, but it's there.'

'My Lord, Coxswain, you're absolutely right. Get him below and into some warm clothes. From now on, Coxswain, your sole responsibility is to watch over the captain. You have no other duties. Understood?'

'Aye aye, sir. Gladly.'

Chapter 28

'There bain't be no prospect of you goin' to a dance for a while, sir. Not looking like thart.' Coxswain Haines washed the wound again with great tenderness before applying a clean dressing. Richard was barely conscious, but he was alive. The whole of the left side of his face was swollen. To add to the scar he had sustained escaping from *D2*, a livid, jagged gash further marred his looks, from the temple to the cheek bone.

Richard muttered something incomprehensible as Haines laid his head back on a pillow of spare clothing.

'How is he faring, 'swain,' Steele asked. Richard was lying in a bunk in the Petty Officers' Mess, aft of the control room, as Haines had reckoned it would offer fewer distractions than the wardroom.

'I reckon 'e'll come through, sir. His pulse seems steady enough an' 'e's young. Mind, his face'll soon turn black and blue once the bruising comes through. 'e won't be no pretty sight for a while, I reckons.'

'But what of the shrapnel? Is there any lodged in his skull? And what of the eye?'

'I'm no expert, sir. Jus' done my basic first aid training like you 'as, sir, but I reckons there bain't be no shrapnel there, sir. Too early to say about the eye, though.' In the absence of any medical staff, first aid was the province of the First Lieutenant and Coxswain.

'Very well. Keep him comfortable as best you can. I shall be in the control room.'

'D'ye not need me, sir?'

'No, thank you, 'swain. We need the captain fit and well for the return through the Narrows. It's more important that you tend to him. For the rest of the day I intend exercising the ship's company in one of the captain's schemes and tonight we will make contact with the *Jed*, report the captain's injury and take our orders. We're due the recall any day.'

The day after the raid on Panderma, HMS *E9* was lying off Marmara Island, her usual spot for rest and recreation during her patrols. The men were well rested, all had had the chance to bathe and the batteries were fully charged. Steele thought it a good opportunity to experiment with a drill he and Richard had cooked up to ease the problem of resupply of torpedoes.

By now *E9* was down to her last three torpedoes, two in the beam tubes and one in the stern tube. Firstly, the torpedo operators withdrew one of the beam torpedoes and set it not to run on firing. It had already been adjusted so that it did not automatically sink at the end of its firing run. The torpedo was then fired harmlessly into the sea and it floated to the surface as planned. Steele manoeuvred the submarine alongside the floating torpedo and the casing party hoisted it inboard using the derrick. Meanwhile, the torpedo loading rails were rigged over the loading hatch. The torpedo was lowered down the rails, as if alongside the depot ship, and stowed in the fore-ends, ready for cleaning and preparation for loading into one of the empty bow tubes. The evolution took nearly an hour. Steele was not happy.

'TI this isn't going to work. We need to think of another idea.'

The TI, a Glaswegian, seemed to agree. 'Aye, I ken the problem. It's no' the time it teks, but the time yon loading rails is rigged.'

'Exactly. We can't risk having the hatched fouled for such a length of time. If the Turks had had an aeroplane up today, we would have been caught with our trousers down. I wondered about using the stern tube. What say you?'

'Weel, it mebbe possible, but it'd need the boat trimmed down aft, right enough. We kid gi'it a go. We'll jus' need a wee bit o' time t' prepare the tube fish feerst, sir.'

'No problem, TI. I'll give you until after lunch and we'll try it this afternoon. I'll need six volunteers to join me in the water.'

He went below to the POs' mess. He was delighted to see that Richard had regained consciousness. Haines was taking his nursing duties seriously and would only allow a short visit. He had neatly bandaged his patient's head such that only the good eye was showing.

'Hallo, sir. I am mighty relieved to see you back in the world of the living. How are you feeling?'

'As if I've been ten rounds with Jack Johnson. I'm afraid I won't be fit for duty for a while. How are you coping?'

'We're managing, sir.' He briefed Richard on the morning's evolutions and his plans for the afternoon and evening, but it soon became apparent that Richard's attention was wandering.

‘You mustn’t overtire the captain, sir.’ Haines intervened. ‘I told yer to stick to a short visit.’

Steele gestured to Haines to join him in the control room. ‘How is he bearing up, Coxswain?’

‘I don’t rightly know, sir. His ’ead’s sore, like you’d expect, but he won’t take no grub, sir. Says it makes ’im feel sick.’

‘Very well. I’ll look in on him again tonight. Keep up the good work, ’swain.’

The torpedomen had had little time for lunch. Steele had insisted that they could not eject the stern torpedo until the previously recovered one was dried, cleaned, prepared for firing and loaded in the starboard bow tube. The men had then had to withdraw the stern torpedo, adjust it so that it would not run on launch and reload it in its home. This had taken several hours. In the meantime, Steele trimmed the boat down by the stern so that the stern torpedo cap was underwater. When the TI confirmed he and his team were ready, they fired the torpedo from its tube. Steele and the other swimmers then entered the water and secured the floating torpedo with steadying lines. They turned the torpedo through 180 degrees, so that its nose now faced the submarine, and guided it towards the open outer tube cap. With some gentle rocking and pushing they were able to guide the tin fish until its head slotted correctly in the tube. It was now time to test the TI’s brainwave.

Steele called up to the casing, ‘Start the pump.’

The order was relayed to the torpedo operator in the after ends. He started the pump to begin draining the torpedo tube. The suction was enough to draw the torpedo smartly into the tube. The outer bow cap was shut, the tube drained and it was a relatively simple matter to open the inner door and withdraw the torpedo nose-first. With the aid of a winch and trolley the torpedo was then transported the entire length of the boat, to the fore-ends. Whilst it would still take some time to prepare the fish for the bow tube, the recovery operation had taken only a few minutes and at little risk to the submarine. Steele looked forward to debriefing the CO on the evolution.

*

That evening Steele returned to PD off the Gallipoli peninsular with great caution. The Turks were now wise to two elements of routine for submarines in the Sea of Marmora. Firstly, submarines had to return to this area to make wireless contact with the communications relay ship. Secondly, they knew that a submarine would be due to exit the sea on the homeward passage. Steele thought it likely the Turks might be lying in wait for him. Even after a careful sweep of the surrounding area through the periscope, he delayed surfacing until after it was very dark. He also closed up extra lookouts. Each time the submarine transmitted, long blue sparks and flashes were emitted from the bridge aerial, potentially giving away the submarine's position to any sharp-eyed lookout. Accordingly, the news that the W/T office had received all incoming messages and transmitted their own came with great relief. As usual, he 'bottomed' the boat overnight on the dense, saline water barrier.

He joined O'Connell in the wardroom. O'Connell had the responsibility of decoding the signals. 'Anything of significance, Pontius?' Steele asked.

'I've still several to go through, but these two will interest you.'

Steele leafed through the note book containing the signal decrypts. The first item of interest was the recall signal. *E14* had signalled her safe arrival through the Strait and *E9* was free to return when her CO deemed it prudent. Steele thought that they should make a start the following night, to give the captain more time to recover from his wound, but it was not his decision to make.

The second signal he read with huge satisfaction. It commented on their earlier foray into the harbour of Constantinople. It was reported that they had sunk a troop ship and the rogue torpedo had exploded against the Customs House Quay. More importantly, panic had ensued amidst fears that the entire Allied fleet had arrived and there were rumours that the Sultan and his ministers had moved to the Asiatic side of the city. Four troop ships had disembarked their troops and all sailings had been cancelled. All the E-boats were now encouraged to follow up on this success. He left O'Connell to finish the decryption of the remaining signals and walked aft to see the captain.

*

Dawn was already breaking as *E9* approached the entrance to the Strait for the beginning of their journey home. Richard had ignored his First Lieutenant's advice and decided to commence the return on the same night of the receipt of the recall signal. One of the later signals to be received had reported that the *Heirreddin Barbarossa* was at anchor off

Nagara Point. The battleship was the sister ship of the *Turgut Reiss*, the ship *E9* had sunk on her first penetration of the Strait in May. Richard assessed the men to be sufficiently rested, the batteries were topped up and he didn't want to allow an opportunity to sink another battleship to slip him by. His one concession, drawn more by Coxswain Haines than Steele, was that he would spend much of the passage resting in the wardroom and only come to the control room for key moments. In fact, it had not been difficult for Richard to make the concession. He still felt very weak and moving his head was not only painful, but made him dizzy. Moreover, he thought it would be valuable experience for his second-in-command to take on more of the responsibility for the tricky navigation.

Richard witnessed Steele dive the submarine and took the periscope once the boat was settled at twenty feet. Even though his good eye, the right eye, was not bandaged, he still found it difficult to focus on the outside world. The strain made his head hurt further. Before handing over to Steele he was pleased to note that the sea surface was ruffled by a fresh breeze. This would reduce the potential for an obvious periscope feather. He also observed that the men were not only cheerful at the prospect of a return to Mudros, but very confident about their prospects for overcoming the coming perils. Again he felt a pang of regret that he might command such men for only a couple more days. With the help of the outside stoker, he staggered over to his bunk and listened to the quiet exchange of orders and acknowledgements as the submarine entered the Strait. The calmness of the exchanges and the peaceful atmosphere combined to send him off to sleep.

After what seemed only a few minutes later, he was woken by a gentle shake from O'Connell.

'Excuse me, sir. I'm sorry to wake you, but we're off Chardak Liman to port. The First Lieutenant wants your permission to dive to ninety feet to pass under the first set of minefields.'

'So soon? What time is it, Pilot?' Richard was confused.

'09.15, sir. We're a few minutes ahead of schedule.'

Richard found it hard to credit that he had been asleep for over five hours, but he felt better for it. 'Very well, but give me a hand to the control room. And bring the camp chair with you.'

Steele took the submarine underneath the nets and minefield without incident and brought her back to PD. Richard tried to concentrate on the situation, but often found himself dozing. In his moments of lucidity he considered Steele's performance. He was handling the submarine with tremendous confidence and competence. The men, too, seemed very assured without displaying overconfidence. Indeed, he felt a pang of jealousy. He knew he was offering little by way of contribution to the smooth running of the submarine and wondered if he was now superfluous. Was that how command worked? You honed the crew's skills to a point where they no longer needed you. Perhaps it was time for him to hand over his command, after all. Steele interrupted his moment of self-pity.

'There are some steamers and dhows lying off Lampsaki, sir. Do you fancy a shot at them, sir?'

Richard could not even be bothered to look through the periscope for himself. His head hurt too much.

'I think not, Number One. I don't want to waste any fish. Let's save the effort for warships or troop ships. Take a look instead at Karakova.'

The port of Lampsaki was on the Asiatic side of the Strait, whereas Karakova was an anchorage on the Gallipoli peninsular. On finding nothing there either, *E9* zig-zagged down the Strait, searching the bays and anchorages on either side. Already the atmosphere was fuggy, but the men didn't seem to mind. As far as they were concerned, the hunt was on and they fully intended to quarter their quarry to the death. As the boat approached the Moussa Bank on the southern coast, they at last had a scent of their prey. O'Connell was on the periscope to give Steele a break.

'Bearing that. Large liner, range 4000 yards.' Everyone's ears pricked up at the report. This time Richard forced himself up to take a look for himself. After plotting successive bearings on the chart, the control room team concluded that the ship was stationary and probably at anchor. Steele approached to within 500 yards of her and confirmed that she was empty. He ordered both bow tubes to be flooded, but refrained from opening the bow shutters and caps. Richard was tempted to allow Steele to complete the attack. It would be good experience for him to gain his first kill. It was an easy shot, but he only had three torpedoes left and wanted to keep them in hand, in case he came across the *Barbarossa*. He explained his reasoning to Steele and was sorry to see the obvious disappointment in his eyes.

Slowly, the submarine navigated the Strait and crossed to the northern shore to avoid the shoals off Nagara Point. Richard felt much better. The prospect of an attack on the liner had shaken off his lethargy and he was now keyed up for the possibility of further action. This time he relieved Steele on the periscope himself, leaving O'Connell to focus on the tricky navigation. Almost immediately, the hairs on the back of his neck stood up. Whilst the Point obscured his view of the anchorage on the other side, he could see the tell-tale plumes of smoke disappearing over the horizon. He recognised the phenomenon. Something large was shelling the troops on the beaches. It had to be the *Barbarossa*.

'Open One and Two tubes' bow caps and shutters.' He did not have to explain any more. The men knew he must have a 'heavy' in his sights.

'Group up. Half ahead. Port ten. Steer that.'

'170 degrees,' the periscope assistant called. The submarine had now rounded the Point and Richard could see the battleship at anchor in the middle of a gunnery shoot. A number of other vessels were milling about her, including two destroyers.

'Sorry, Number One, to have spoiled your chances of sinking a troop ship, but this one's mine. Down.'

He went over to the chart. They had plenty of water beneath him. They would need it once the counter-attack started. The target was lying almost broadside to him, anchored forward and aft to keep her in position in the strong southerly current. He calculated that on his present heading he should be able to fire both bow tubes and then, by a sharp turn to starboard, he could, if necessary, fire their last torpedo from the port beam tube. It would leave them defenceless, but he couldn't afford to miss on possibly his last ever attack. If only he could be sure the precious 'mouldies' wouldn't let him down this time, but would run true. His mind made up, he ordered the port beam tube to be flooded.

'Slow ahead both. Up. Bearing that. Come left. Steer 164.' Nobody spoke except to acknowledge his orders.

'Standby … Fire One.' He saw the torpedo leave the submarine and run true. He watched the second hand on his stop watch pass fifteen seconds and then ordered the second torpedo to be fired. Again he silently thanked the Holy Mary, the Mother of Jesus, that this torpedo was also running true. He could see the two parallel wakes quite clearly and only bad luck or one of the destroyers crossing the line could now save the battleship. There was no need to fire the beam torpedo and nor was he going to witness the fish running home.

'Down. Starboard fifteen. Full ahead. Fifty feet.' He knew the hunters were about to become the hunted.

Chapter 29

Oddly, it was Mother Nature that afforded the ship's company of HMS *E9* more bother than the destroyers. Both torpedoes had struck and the explosions and implosions of collapsing bulkheads were clearly audible to the men but, whilst they could hear the high-pitched whine of destroyer screws astern and above, the submarine appeared to have gained too much surprise and enough of a head start to be in serious danger from above. Their problems began at the nets and mine fields strung between Kilid Bahr and Chanak.

They knew the Narrows to be the most treacherous part of the passage in or out of the Strait and after attacking the *Barbarossa*, the searchlight operators on both sides would be fully alerted. *E9*'s officers had, accordingly, timed their run for after nightfall. The boat was at ninety feet, passing beneath the minefield, when the bows were suddenly jerked up and the boat began to rise. Steele immediately flooded the forward trim tank whilst the hydroplanes operators tried to force the bows down. They had just arrested the bow-down angle when the stern suddenly rose sharply. It was like riding an unbroken horse, but at least Richard and Steele knew the reason this time. Steele ordered the internal ballast tanks to be flooded as he had seen done in similar circumstances in the harbour of Constantinople.

With the extra eight tons of water, they were able to stabilise the angle of the boat at a steady depth of seventy feet, the depth of the layer. However, they could do little about the ship's ahead. Again the boat swung in all directions before spinning to starboard in the eddies of the current. Ominously, the men heard a loud scraping sound on the port side and then the hull listed sharply in the same direction. Richard could not believe that they had run aground on the European shore. The depth gauge showed seventy-five feet. The ship's head began to swing to port and the helmsman struggled to maintain his ordered course. The log speed dropped to a knot.

'I think we must have caught some wreckage, sir. It can't be a net or we would be stuck,' Steele observed. The boat still leaned to port.

‘I agree, Number One. We’d better return to PD for a look.’

Steele pumped out the internal ballast tank, but it made no difference. The boat’s depth barely changed. Moreover, the fore-planes operator was struggling to bring up the boat’s bows.

‘It’s not the trim, sir. Something seems to be holding us down,’ Steele reported. The outside stoker lent the second coxswain a hand at turning the brass wheel that operated the fore-planes and gradually the boat started to rise.

At twenty feet, Richard raised the periscope gingerly. There was no sound of moving vessels above, but that did not discount a patrol vessel drifting on the surface for this very occasion. Mercifully, he could see no vessels in the vicinity, but the sight of something else turned his blood cold. Snagged on the port hydroplane was the steel mooring wire of a mine. Worse still, floating on the surface and being dragged forward by the momentum of the submarine was the dark, round shape of a moored mine. Were its evil-looking horns to make contact with the hull of the submarine, they would detonate the mine and completely destroy her. The mine was bobbing about in the current and creating a wash that should be easily visible from shore to betray their position. He had to react quickly.

‘Keep thirty feet. Down periscope,’ he ordered calmly. There was no point in alarming the ship’s company. ‘Port five, steer 220. We’re through the first mine field, Pilot. A bit to port of track,’ he called nonchalantly, but his brain was working feverishly. He presumed that the sinker of the mine was being dragged beneath the hull. They were approaching the second mine field and needed to go deeper to pass under it. From memory he estimated that the mine was floating at an angle of thirty degrees astern of the fore-plane. If they dived at too steep an angle, it could bring the mine down onto the conning tower or casing with deadly effect. He contemplated surfacing to clear it, but that would be under the vigilant eyes of the gunners ashore. Even a near miss might detonate the mine and eighty pounds of high explosive in close proximity to the casing would be enough to rip the submarine apart. Moreover, the turbulence from surfacing would probably drag the mine into contact with the hull. They were stuck between Scylla and Charybdis, but doing nothing was not an option.

He could see Steele looking at him searchingly and made his decision. If it was the wrong one, then they would know nothing more of it.

'Right, First Lieutenant. Time to take her back down, but we'll do it gently. Ten down, keep ninety feet. Flood the auxiliary.'

As the bows dropped, he imagined the mine above moving closer to the conning tower and held his breath. It crossed his mind that perhaps God was punishing him for all the men he had been responsible for killing. How many men would have died in the *Hela*, the two Turkish battleships, the Turkish transport and the countless steamers he had sunk in the past fourteen months? Thousands perhaps? Certainly hundreds. Twice he had postponed his wedding to Lizzy and just as he held hope of completing his nuptials at the third attempt, he and his men might be about to die. Could this be *Mutti*'s prayers being answered. He knew she was only accepting his engagement to Lizzy under protest. But then, he thought, why would God punish men like Steele for his sins? No, God was just. He would not do such a thing. Suddenly, he knew he must survive. He smiled across at Steele.

'I'm not going to come to PD for a fix this time, Number One. We'll trust to the Navigator's dead reckoning. Is that all right with you, Pilot?'

'Why certainly, sir,' O'Connell beamed. 'We're all feelin' a bit lucky tonight. I suggest we come to starboard onto a new course of 245.'

'Very well. Make it so. Call me when you think we're through. I think I'll take a little nap in the camp chair.'

He could see his two officers exchange puzzled looks, but he didn't care. He knew he was acting strangely, but so might they were they to know what was floating just a few feet above them. He slumped in the chair. He felt tired, but although he feigned sleep, his mind was too alert to the sounds exterior to the submarine to allow him to relax.

Soon everyone was tortured by the sounds of wires scraping along the hull. They had all experienced it many times now and remained visibly sanguine about their futures. There was nothing they could do about it for now. All the time Richard, however, could not rid himself of the thought that the snagged mine was also being dragged through the mine field. Were one of the lead-covered glass tubes of the horns to smash against a mooring wire, then it would be enough to detonate the mine.

He must have fallen asleep, after all, because soon after one o'clock, O'Connell shook his shoulder gently.

'I think we're through, sir.'

Richard checked the estimated position on the chart. Everything seemed quiet. The men were still at Diving Stations, but seemed relaxed and content. No doubt they were thinking of the hero's return. Some of the longer serving hands might even have dreams of being relieved to return home. It was an odd experience. When he had fallen asleep he had known that he might never wake up. Now everything seemed oddly normal. Only he knew that the men were not out of the woods yet.

Two hours later, he recognised that they must now be only five miles from Cape Helles and the exit from the Strait. They were already safe from enemy guns and patrols. Even so, he hesitated about returning to PD. He was nervous of disturbing the equilibrium *E9* and her passengers had developed, but it had to be done sometime and the shallower depth would put them into the layer of outflowing water to speed their passage.

It was still dark when he raised the periscope, but the sky was brightening to the east. The mine was still there, contentedly slewing to one side and the next in the surface current. He recognised that any sharp alterations of course in either direction were out of the question. Now he had to give thought as to how to rid himself of his lethal passenger. On the starboard bow he could see the light of Seddul Bahr and abeam, the forward trenches of the Allied troops. If he disengaged the submarine from the mine now it would be a hazard to other shipping and difficult to find. He resolved to stick with their unwanted companion for a little longer.

Thirty minutes later several vessels could be heard on the surface and this time everyone on board knew them to be friendly. The mood of the boat lightened. On his next look, Richard could see the drifters and patrol vessels ahead. To starboard, the white cliffs of Cape Helles were washed with red as the early morning sunrise reflected off them. The decisive moment had arrived.

'Take a look, Number One.' Richard handed over the periscope to Steele. Steele had almost completed his all-round look when he caught sight of the mine forward.

'Heavens,' he gasped. 'We're towing a deuced great mine, sir.'

'I know, and this is how we're going to rid ourselves of it.'

Steele listened carefully and impassively to Richard before sending for the signalman and instructing him to bring the biggest ensign he could find. A cry of, *'Stand by to surface'* was passed through the submarine. Richard and the signalman opened the conning tower lower lid and readied themselves for the surfacing drill.

On Richard's nod, Steele ordered, 'Blow five and six main ballast. Stop both. Full astern both.'

The way came off the boat and the bows dipped as the stern rose. The water expelled from the after ballast tanks pushed the mine forward of the hydroplane and, as it cleared the submarine, it disappeared, dragged beneath the surface by the sinker suspended beneath the submarine. Richard allowed the submarine to continue astern until he was sure he was well clear of the mine and then altered course for a destroyer he had just spotted coming round Cape Helles. He helped the signalman rig the white ensign and then ordered him to exchange recognition signals with the destroyer. It was the *Grampus*, *E9*'s escort back to the depot ship. They signalled that they had just cleared a mine and, a few minutes later, the destroyer dropped a Dan buoy to mark its position so that the minesweepers could sweep it later. *Grampus* then came up on *E9*'s starboard quarter and as she overhauled the submarine, Richard could see that the sailors were manning the side. The destroyer's men shouted out three cheers and waved their caps to the increasing numbers on *E9*'s bridge. The cheering was taken up by soldiers and sailors on the beach. Richard could not understand the reasons for the fuss, but felt emotional, nonetheless. All that mattered was that he and his men were home at last.

Chapter 30

Christmas 1915

'Turn over, Dick. You're snoring.'

'What?' Richard replied drowsily.

'Turn onto your side. You're snoring.'

'Oh, sorry.' Richard duly turned over, taking some of Elizabeth's share of the bed clothes and causing a draft between them.

Elizabeth massaged her now-free right arm. It had been numbed by Richard's weight as they had cuddled up together after another evening of love making. Once the circulation was restored, she grabbed back some of the blankets and turned to look at her husband of less than a fortnight. She patted him tenderly and then, propping herself up on her right side, she gazed down at his sleeping form in the light of the fire. He was sleeping peacefully, but there was nothing angelic about his looks. An ugly, long and curved, jagged scar dominated the left side of his head, from the brow, past the eye socket, to his cheekbone. She kissed it gently. It still stood proud of his face and, no doubt, might have healed better had *E9*'s complement included a medical assistant capable of some neat stitching. Richard still seemed quite conscious of it, but she loved him no less for it.

She lay down again and snuggled up close to his back and buttocks. She felt she could not have been happier and reached her left arm over to embrace him. As she did so, the wedding band on her left hand glinted in the fire light. For perhaps the thousandth time she regarded it with pride. Dick had returned from the Mediterranean a hero at the end of the previous month and been gazetted for a DSC to accompany his VC. There had been no time to write to warn her, but Uncle William, now her father-in-law, had seen the signal announcing his return and telephoned her at the shipyard. On the eighteenth they had been married in London by special licence. The short notice had necessitated a quieter affair than her mother-in-law would have liked, but that had suited Elizabeth. Dick had been disappointed that so many of his friends could not be there. Of his brothers, only Paul had been able to attend. John was still at sea in the Mediterranean and Peter on diplomatic service in the Netherlands. It had come as a welcome shock for Dick to learn that Paul was alive, despite being shot down over Belgium. He had been equally pleased to discover that Charles had recovered from his wounds and been awarded the DSC for his bravery on the beaches of Gallipoli. They had looked a gruesome trio in the wedding photograph. Paul bore the scars of his burns to the side of his face and Charles was disfigured through missing an ear and a part of his cheekbone. Then there was Dick with that fearsome scar. She chided herself for her levity. Many a family would be mourning the loss of loved ones and others would have kin in far worse shape than her brother and cousins.

However, whilst the wedding breakfast in the Savoy might have been considered a quiet affair, the reception in Cumberland Terrace, the Millers' London residence, only a few days before the wedding, had been a positively grand affair. Dick had been invested with his VC at Buckingham Palace on the same day as Uncle William had received his CB. Even the First Sea Lord had attended the party. Elizabeth had never seen so much gold in one room.

She had been surprised to learn that Uncle William was on such friendly terms with the King, and all stemming from a cruise they had shared in the Mediterranean. She had been invited to the investiture and presented to the King and Queen afterwards. It had been the most daunting event in her whole life, but the Queen had conversed with her quite normally and taken a great interest in their wedding plans. Indeed, it was Her Majesty who had let slip the honeymoon destination.

The memories of the excitement of the past two weeks stimulated Elizabeth beyond sleep. She rose from the bed and put on her robe, shawl and slippers. Richard continued to sleep undisturbed. She blushed with the memory of his exertions just a couple of hours before. After adding two more logs to the fire, she rifled his valise to find the leather case containing his VC and sat with it in front of the fire. Dick didn't seem to place much value on the medal, a trait she had noted he shared with his father with regard to his own VC. Whereas Dick's VC was hidden away in his valise with his other medals, he regarded with more importance the two framed photographs on his dressing table. One showed him wearing his long chauffeur's coat on the casing of his beloved submarine. The other was one taken of him sharing a joke with Lieutenant Steele in the wardroom of HMS *Adamant* the day he had handed over command of HMS *E9* to his successor. Elizabeth wondered if she would ever meet Steele. She felt as if she almost knew him. Barely a day went by without Dick regaling her with tales of Steele's quirky mannerisms or tales of his heroism and ingenuity. At times she even felt jealous of his obvious admiration for him and the bond that they shared, but which she never could.

She opened the box and examined the VC. It looked quite nondescript; just a piece of blue ribbon and a metal cross. Elizabeth knew that the medals were reputed to have been forged from the scrap of one of the Russian guns captured at Sevastopol, but she wondered if that was true. The medal she held in her hand could have been made from ordinary iron. What drove men to risk their lives for something so insignificant? She could not imagine herself or any of her suffragette friends doing so. They had fought for, but so far failed to obtain, something more tangible in the cause of female suffrage. That was the answer, of course. Dick hadn't fought for this piece of metal and that was why he placed so little store by it. He had fought not even out of duty to his country, but for the lives of his men and the honour of his friends and colleagues in the submarine service. He was not alone in that and she admired men for that. Perhaps they were not all pigs, after all.

She replaced the medal where she had found it and returned to the bedside. She leant down to kiss Richard once more and her long hair brushed his face. He stirred and turned onto his other side, exposing the injury-free side of his face. Her heart swelled with love and pride that she had attracted such a man. She wondered what Christabel would make of her now, head over heels in love with a man, and willing to subordinate herself completely to him. Would she think she had betrayed her sex by doing so? She could hear Christabel saying that she had abandoned the Cause by her actions, but she would be wrong. This war was opening up opportunities for women. In her yard alone, one quarter of the workforce was now female and they were beginning to take on the skilled work. Once the war was over, the struggle would go on, but men were not an enemy. Many of her own men were beginning to treat their female workers with respect and learning to accept that fairness and equality were not unreasonable demands. She was confident that after the war attitudes would change.

She felt tempted to creep downstairs to the kitchen. A glass of milk might help her sleep, but she knew it would be cold and dark. Her home in Crosby had been electrified, but this shooting lodge in the midst of Norfolk was still a stranger to gas lighting, even. When Dick had consulted her on the honeymoon plans, she had stated that she wanted to go somewhere quiet and off the beaten track. She had imagined the Lake District. Then Dick had received news of his next appointment and decided that he could not afford to be too far from Harwich or London. She remembered the day Dick had proposed to her in Barrow. She had joked that *E9* was her rival for his affection. Now, once again, Dick was excited by the news he was to have a command, only this time she would have several rivals. When their honeymoon finished the following week, Dick was to take command of another blessed E-boat. Soon thereafter, he was to sail her into the Baltic and take up his appointment as the senior officer of the small submarine force based there. Elizabeth shivered at the thought of the Russian winter and slipped back into bed beside her husband. For now at least, she was his only love and she might as well take advantage of it. She nuzzled up to his prone body and began to caress him intimately. If she couldn't sleep, then there were other ways to occupy the time.

Author's Note

Ian Fleming wrote, 'Everything I write has a precedent in history.' This is most certainly true in the case of, *The Custom of the Trade*. The plot and several of the characters are very much based on real events and people. However, as is the privilege of a writer, I have amalgamated real people into fictional characters, played with the timing of actual events and altered historical facts to suit my story.

The first successful escape from a sunken submarine did not take place until later in 1912, and from a German submarine. The D-class submarines were not actually fitted with internal watertight bulkheads so the escape I have described would not have been possible. I hope my readers will forgive such artistic licence. Richard Miller's heroic actions were inspired by those of Max Horton, Edward Boyle and Martin Nasmith. For a more accurate, but still gripping account of the submariners' war in the Sea of Marmara I recommend the book, *Dardanelles Patrol* by Peter Shankland and Anthony Hunter, sadly now out of print. I hope my story will inspire many readers to learn a little more about a very successful campaign, but largely forgotten because of the failure of the amphibious operation.

Happily, Richard has survived and we hope to meet him again in the Baltic. In the meantime, we will soon learn more of his brother Peter's contribution to naval intelligence in the First World War.

Acknowledgements

Many people have, both knowingly and unknowingly, helped me along the journey to have this book published. It started with my parents who scrimped and saved to give me my education. Rodney Jones and the late Mr Mottershaw (never to be known by his Christian name), my History masters at school, inspired in me a love for the subject. My good friend, John Drummond, not only suffered the boredom of a running commentary on the progress of my writing, but offered much technical advice on submarine operations. Local crime writer, Roger A Price, provided much encouragement and advice on the murky world of publishing. Dr Hilary Johnson and her professional readers offered invaluable advice in turning my early drafts of the novel into its present form. Sheila Turner helped with some proof-reading. I am indebted, too, to Endeavour Press who have given me my first break in writing and treated me most professionally and courteously. Finally, but by no means least, I am grateful to my wife, Hilary, for both putting up with me whilst I wrote this novel, and for freeing me up from the business in order to find the time to write it. I owe you all my thanks.

Printed in Poland
by Amazon Fulfillment
Poland Sp. z o.o., Wrocław